BISHOP

A FRAT CHRONICLES NOVEL

BT URRUELA

ONE

My name is McKenzie Bishop, and this is the last day I'll ever spend in the Army.

I'm not sure what to make of that yet. I know I'm excited to grow a beard, smoke a joint, and do whatever the fuck I want to do, whenever the fuck I want to do it. But I'm scared too. Scared of leaving the only thing that ever made any sense to me in this life. Leaving my family. I'm scared of never again making the kind of friends I made over the course of my six-year career.

And what the hell do I do now anyway?

I don't know a thing about existing with civilians anymore. I don't know banking, or teaching, or any other discernible skill other than killing, protecting, and defending. That was my life for nearly four years. Another two were spent recovering from a horrific injury I never thought could happen to me, regardless of the number of deployments I had under my belt. Regardless of the bloodshed I had witnessed, the friends who had perished in ways you don't even wish upon your worst of enemies. Still, I never thought I could get injured. I felt invincible, for a time; more so with each successive deployment.

"Do you know what you want to do after this?" the counselor sitting across the desk from me asks dubiously as if he's been reading my mind and senses my self-doubt.

I blink a few times to bring myself back to the present. My thoughts often wander to horrible things, sometimes nice things, sometimes dirty things. They flit from one to the other in an everlasting loop, much like Malcolm McDowell in *A Clockwork Orange,* strapped down and being subjected to things I can't look away from or run from, nor understand most of the time. God only knows where I'm headed from here, but I certainly don't owe this man any explanation. Unfortunately, the Sergeant First Class rank pinned on his uniform means I can't respond how I'd like to: "What's it fuckin' matter to ya?"

No, the three stripes on my uniform collar means he gets to play this stupid little game. A few more years and I would've been at his level, and I would've had an infantry platoon of my own had I not been hurt. But a few more years is something I didn't have left in me to give. Not sitting behind a fucking desk at least. And that's certainly where they would've put me had I reenlisted.

I shrug. "I'm not sure, Sarge."

"You have to have more for me than that," he replies, tilting his head with a look of slight frustration, as if my future somehow impacts his own.

Truth is I don't have any answers for him. I'm drawing blanks. And I can't be bothered with the dog and pony show that is ACAP, or Army Career and Alumni Program—a week-long course that's more likely to cause death by boredom than it is to be a helpful transition tool. This meeting with the counselor is the last step for me and the anxiousness of finally being rid of it causes me to fidget restlessly in the seat. I'm trying to pass along to him that I'd like him to *shut the fuck up* and sign off already.

"Sorry, I just don't have a clear answer for you. I anticipated spending my career in uniform. Now that that's changed, I'm not sure of anything. There's a lot to figure out. A lot to figure out and talk through with my girlfriend."

"Well, you're twenty-five ... plenty young to do whatever your heart desires. You've got the GI Bill. Disability checks. The world is your oyster, as they say." He smiles, a used car salesman's smile; too wide to be real, and he's got just enough monotone in his voice to let me know he's done this dance far too many times before. He doesn't care for my answer. He just needs to fill these thirty minutes.

I'm led to wonder what this man knows about the horrors of war; how each dreadful second plays on a loop in your head. He doesn't get how anticipating the future with anything but trepidation from here on out, after seeing the things I've seen, is nearly impossible. I'm at a crossroads in my life; one I never anticipated. It's not so easy for me to figure out what's next, not when I had planned on staying in the Army for at least twenty years before retiring as a Sergeant Major in charge of an infantry battalion, like my father, and his father before him. A rocket-propelled grenade at the end of my last deployment, and the shrapnel that followed, had other ideas. I could no longer serve as an infantryman; therefore, in my eyes, I could no longer be a soldier. I could never see myself like this man, sitting behind a desk, while others wearing the same uniform were fighting and dying in theirs.

I was born to fight. When I lost that ability, I lost a piece of my identity right along with it. A big fucking piece.

"Yeah, I guess we'll see what happens with it," I say through a forced smile, pushing back the desire to tell him how pointless all this is. "Probably just start with gen. ed. courses and figure it out from there."

The counselor tilts his head again, a judgmental furrow in his brows. "Anything spark your interest at least?" he asks.

For fuck's sake.

I ponder this for a moment, my gaze fixed on the cluttered desk before me, my mind lost in thoughts of future days without a uniform coating me, protecting me, empowering me. Without it, I feel naked ... and lost. I feel restless.

Shrugging, I shift my focus back to the counselor. "Nothin' I can really think of. I've always enjoyed acting. Did a few plays back in high school and took some acting classes here in D.C.. Really enjoyed them. It's somethin' I could see myself doin' long-term."

The counselor shakes his head, his lips curled down in a scrutinizing fashion as he grabs a stack of papers from the desktop. "No," he says, still eyeing the papers as he leafs through them. "You've got some great scores all around here," he continues, eventually finding the paper he was looking for and setting it down in front of me. He looks over the top of his glasses in that fatherly way that always grinds my fucking gears. I have a father, and a shitty one at that. I don't need another one. Nor do I need this man's worry or self-serving pity.

He taps the sheet of paper with his index finger, grabbing my attention. I realize it contains the results of an occupational strength test I had to take last week. "There are a lot of options here," he continues. "Doctor, lawyer, intelligence ... I mean, an actor ..." He sits back in his chair and crosses his arms, his face scrunched in displeasure. "How many people do you think want to be an actor? How many roles do they have for—" He stops himself, his focus shifting from my prosthetic eye, surrounded by thick scarring that does well to attract unwanted attention, to the papers in front of him. He clears his throat before looking back up at me, avoiding my prosthetic this time. "I mean, how many people are out there trying to make it? What are the chances?"

I keep my features relaxed, though on the inside I'm envisioning a swift slap across this man's cheek. And not a regular slap. An eye-opening bitch slap.

In a steady tone, I say, "Sergeant Kemp, with all due respect, this is the last day I'm ever gonna wear this uniform. It's a good day, to an extent, but it's a sad day, too. I don't really care to get into a discussion about my future with someone I've just met, let alone someone who's never been in this position before. I've been livin' with myself for twenty-five years now. If I don't got a clue what's ahead, I can promise you that you don't either." I push the test results aside and point to the paper the counselor set them down on top of. "Now you are the last signature I need on my checklist to finish out-processing and get my ass out of here. I would *really* appreciate if you could do that for me and let me be on my way." I find myself leaning forward in my chair now, attempting to say more with my eyes than I am with my words.

The counselor studies me for a moment, creases forming in his forehead as if he is trying hard to figure me out. I lean back in the chair, cross one leg over the other, and smile.

"Okay," he agrees, taking the checklist into his hands, his eyes still lingering on mine. "I just don't want to see you get lost out there." He sighs, grabbing a pen and signing the last empty spot on the form, much to my relief.

I grin. "I can promise you this, Sergeant. There's no way I'll be any more lost out there than I was in here," I respond, referring to Walter Reed Medical Center and all the time I've spent rehabbing here. I point to the map of Iraq and Afghanistan he has tacked to the wall beside us, places I know he's never seen by the lack of a combat patch on his right arm or Combat Action

Badge on his chest. "And definitely no more lost than I was out there. Not even close."

He shrugs, resignation taking up his features, as he hands over the completed checklist. "You've got your own out-processing paperwork, correct?" He drums the pen against the stack of papers in front of me from which he pulled the test results, and I nod, standing from my chair and snatching the paper from him.

"Good to go, Sarge. Got everything I need."

The counselor stands too, and just as I'm about to depart, he puts out his hand. I take it with my own, and he pulls me in.

"Make us proud," he says softly; his coffee breath is noxious. He motions his head toward my right shoulder where the American flag patch sits, just above my 1st Ranger Bat. combat patch. "Make *that* proud."

He lets go, passing me a self-assured nod as he squats back into his office chair with a heavy grunt, a chair where he's likely spent his entire career.

"I'll try, Sergeant. I'll certainly try." I nod, a cocksure smirk on my face as I make my way out of the office.

Packing up the last of my things into boxes, I busy myself as I wait for my girlfriend of nine months, Chelsea, to come by my room. For weeks now, I've tried to talk with her about the future, *our* future; whether I'd stay here for her and start at a community college for a couple years, or whether she goes with me to whatever college I end up choosing along the east coast, many of which have yet to respond to my application. She continually puts it off, though, often changing the subject, which unnerves me. I believe she loves me, I truly do, and though I have a hard time understanding what love even means at this point, I think I love her too. Yeah, she can be a pill sometimes, and we don't have very much in common, but she was around for some of the harder moments I've experienced over the course of my recovery. She put forth more of an effort than any other woman I've dated before; even if she doesn't often try very hard to understand the complexities of my war-weathered mind.

Over the screech of shipping tape, as I seal up my box of medals and Army memorabilia, the last things I must pack, I hear a soft knock at the door. Before answering, I grab the empty bottle of Jameson from my nightstand, creeping with it toward the kitchenette in quiet steps and with a guilty heart, and then I set the bottle gently into the trash as to not alert her. After covering the bottle with some loose bits of trash, I walk excitedly toward the door. Swinging it open, I see Chelsea standing on the other side, a slight smile on her face and a hand on her curvaceous hip, a tight dress clinging to her young body. High heels sharpen the lines of her toned thighs. The usual resting bitch face is ever present, but the curve of her thin lips in a slight smile lets me know she's in a decent mood. And perhaps a little horny.

"Hey, babe." I look her up and down for a moment, an eyebrow raised. "You look fuckin' incredible," I say, embracing her and peppering her neck with kisses. "You're late, by the way," I add, letting go of her and sidestepping so she can enter. I shut the door behind her as my eyes trail the sharp curve of her insatiable ass, one shaped by good genes and endless hours of yoga.

"Yeah, yeah." She rolls her eyes and waves me off with a petite hand, the Oompa Loompa orange staining her cuticles and that distinct chemically smell lets me know she spray-tanned today.

"I've got most of it packed up already," I say, nudging her with my hip.

She looks over the sealed boxes scattered throughout the small barracks room as she steadies herself, saying, "I didn't realize you had so much shit." She glances toward me.

"That's because it would all end up in the closet every time you visited." I laugh, and so does she, that cute little squeak of a laugh I've grown to adore; a laugh she selfishly delivers in slivered doses.

I look her up and down again, the thought process belonging to my dick now. There's no humor in how much I need her. Quirking an eyebrow, I ask, "Did we have plans today I didn't know about, or is this just a wonderful surprise for my last day in the Army?"

"The latter," she says, taking a seat on the edge of my bed and leaning back on her hands, pushing her tits out as she does and smiling a wicked smile. She crosses one tanned leg slowly over the other, and my eyes trace her leg from heel to thigh.

"Lucky fuckin' me," I mutter, biting my lip and shaking my head.

"Oh no. It won't be *Lucky* who's fucking you today, Sergeant Bishop."

"*Fuck*, babe." I let out a quiet gasp, my dick hilting in my shorts. "You are so *fuckin'* sexy."

I dive onto her, throwing her back against the bed and pinning her arms to her sides, looking into her chestnut eyes with flecks of gold before pressing my lips to hers. They are soft, plump, and they bring my dick to the limitation of my gym shorts, throbbing against the soft fabric. I trail kisses down her cheek, across her neck, and to her ear.

"I need you so fuckin' bad," I whisper, taking her earlobe lightly between my teeth and nibbling.

She lets out a heavy breath. Bringing her body flush against mine, she whispers in a demanding tone, "Then take me."

I moan, pulling my head back and looking deep into her

eyes. "You always know how to get me hot and hard." I kiss her collarbone as I reach my hand behind her, carefully unzipping her dress. Pulling it off, I admire the red tint to her face now, the hunger in her eyes. I'm hungry, too.

Insatiably.

And more than anything, I need to feel that perfect fit. I'm desperate for it. Regardless of the bumps in the road that have come between us, the sex has *always* been great. The angry sex, oftentimes, the best of the lot. She's not angry now, no, but the lingering effects of a fight we had a few days ago is still there, and my dick knows it. It hurts now, nearly begging me to let him play.

I admire her Calvin Klein underwear and bra set, my favorite, and I let out a quiet gasp, my dick really aching now, meeting the spot just before pleasure meets complete pain.

"The black Calvins?" I ask, a smirk on my face.

"Just for you," she whispers, stripping them off and tossing them to the floor. She then pulls at my shirt with desperate hands.

Tugging my shirt off, I toss it down with her underwear and bra, quickly followed by my shorts, and lower myself back onto her, turned on by the feel of our bare skin touching, hers young and flawless, mine, scarred and rough. Beauty and the broken beast.

I tease her nipples with my tongue, trailing hot kisses down her clenching stomach, and she writhes beneath me with a gasp. She trembles as my breath meets her clit ... then my tongue, and she presses her hips up, guiding me around her core. Her body seizes as I run my tongue in circles around her sensitive bud. Her legs tighten around my neck, her hands grabbing fistfuls of hair.

Her hands fall to my shoulders, grasping desperately, her

nails digging in, and she begs, "Please fuck me. Fuck me now, Bishop. I *need* you inside me."

The request sends a jolt from my stomach down to my rock-hard cock. How I love it when she says that. I take one last slow lick and then inch my way back up her body, leaving open-mouthed kisses in my wake. Blindly, I reach into my nightstand, my lips meeting hers, as I grab for a condom. Once my dick is wrapped, she clenches her legs around my waist, pulling me in so that the tip of my cock meets her entrance. Our heavy breathing coincides as I guide myself inside her, slowly, just the head at first.

Throwing her head back, she gasps loudly as I enter her fully, grabbing at her nipples and tugging them. She whimpers and then moans.

I pull my dick out and then push it back in, slowly repeating the process, teasing the both of us.

"Fuck, baby. Give it to me. Give it to me now!" she demands, pushing her body into mine, her muscles tightening around me.

Picking up the pace in satisfying thrusts that send charges of energy up and down my limbs, my heart thumps in my chest; my skin is flush with desire. She grows wetter with each exhilarating plunge, and the feel of it has me harder than I ever thought possible—so hard, it feels like my dick might just explode. And after a few more moments of ecstasy, it kind of does. I arch my back, a fistful of her hair in one hand and her supple ass cheek in the other, as I come. Her hand covers her mouth, her eyes closed as she moans into her palm.

As I pull out, I release a pleasurable sigh, and she opens her eyes slowly, letting her hand fall flat to her side, her face flushed and breathing ragged.

I lean down and kiss her. "I love you," I whisper against her lips. "You feel incredible, woman." I shake my head.

After one more kiss, I stand, making my way to the kitchenette, where I toss the condom into the trash. Heading for the fridge, butt-naked, I turn back to see Chelsea hurriedly putting her dress back on, a new nervousness on her face *much* different than the pleasure she previously showed. She's yet to even catch her breath.

My eyes analyzing her as I grab a bottle of water, I scrunch my brows and ask, "Is everything alright?"

She doesn't answer right away, instead, turning her back toward me. She motions behind her and whispers, "Can you zip me up, please?"

I take a swig of water and set the bottle on the counter. Swallowing hard, I approach her and zip the dress up slowly.

"What's up?" I ask, my heart starting to pound for reasons other than the incredible orgasm.

She faces me, biting her bottom lip, her eyes trained on the tiled floor. "Ugh, I hate this," she mutters.

"Hate what, Chelsea?"

"This," she responds, louder now. She motions between us.

Suddenly, my nakedness terrifies me. I feel completely vulnerable, unwanted, rejected. Grabbing my shorts and slipping them on, I say, "You need to tell me what the fuck you're talking about and you need to tell me quickly. 'I hate this' isn't somethin' a boyfriend wants to hear after fuckin' his girl."

"I can't do this anymore," she says, shaking her head as if she's disappointed in herself for saying the words. There's something else in her features too, though, faint, but noticeable.

Relief.

"This?" I ask.

"Us."

I look toward the bed, the sheets strewn about, and I scoff, shaking my head in complete disbelief. "Then what the fuck was that?" I say, my brows scrunching tightly together. "Was I just mercy fucked? *Really*?"

A tear rolls down her cheek, and I instinctively want to catch it with my finger, but I fight the urge.

"I d-don't know," she stutters, more tears falling now. She crosses her arms, hugging herself ... shaking. "I love you, Kenzie. I really do. It's really, *really* hard bringing myself to this point."

The 'Kenzie' part really stings. She's the only one I've allowed to call me by any variation of my first name since I was a kid.

"So why *are* you at this point then, if you love me so damn much?" I question, a sharp heat trailing up my neck, the temperature in the room seeming to abruptly rise.

"How many times have I asked you to quit drinking?" she asks, her eyes on mine now, a new strength in her tone. "*How many?*"

"It's not as easy as just clicking my fuckin' heels. I can't just turn this shit off, you know."

"Have you even tried? I mean *really* tried?"

"More than you give me credit for."

"Oh really." She motions her head toward the trashcan with her lips in a tight line, a smug, knowing look on her face.

I don't have to look to know what she's implying. "That's fucked," I growl. Hesitating, I take a deep, calming breath before moving closer to her, grasping her elbows. "Chelsea, I've tried. I've done counseling. I'm takin' my pills."

"How long did you do the counseling for? One month? One and a half, at best. You half-assed it. And you know that. What about AA? What about the pamphlets I got you?"

I drop my hands to my side, stepping back and letting out a huff. "Listen, I've told you already. I don't like that kumbaya bullshit. That just isn't me."

"And that's exactly why you and I can't be 'us' anymore," she says in a matter-of-fact tone.

"You have got to be fuckin' kidding me." I lower myself to the bed, dropping my head into my hands and grabbing fistfuls of hair. "I just can't even believe this, Chelsea. I can't believe you mercy fucked me. *Really*? Is that love to you?"

"I've gotta go," she says, stepping into her heels as I rest my hands on my knees, looking up at her and fighting back the tears that are trying to break free.

"Just like that then?" I ask. "You fuck me, dump me, and then leave? Nine months and this is how you end it?"

"I did what I could," she says, her voice cutting out, the tears returning. She steps to the door and turns, her hand resting on the handle. "This has been coming for a long time now, Kenzie. I'm sorry. I really am," she says. And with those last heart-wrenching words echoing off the barren white walls, she's gone, leaving me in a state of complete shock.

My heart pounds, my carotids pumping thickly, my thoughts an avalanche. I drop my head in my hands again when the tears come. They coat my cheeks and tumble from my chin, down to the floor. As I choke them back with a stiff throat-clearing, I wipe an arm across my face and allow my focus to drift toward the refrigerator across the room and the demons inside.

A thirst possesses me.

After three shorts steps, a bottle of Jameson is in my hands. The thirst is quenched.

The pain subsides ... for now.

TWO

Cruising the quiet country roads of Western Pennsylvania in my recently purchased Wrangler, I do my best to fight the persistent thoughts of Chelsea from only three weeks ago. Her words still resonate in my mind. Her presence lingers like a ghost. I've done my fair share of crying, and blaming, and obsessing. But I'm past that for now ... or so I'd like to think. The armor only holds for so long. I know that better than anyone.

As I drive, the cold wind rustling the thick beard a medical retirement has allowed me to grow, I hope it's not a mistake to attend a school where I know no one. I worry that I may have acted impulsively after Chelsea dumped me. The anxiety of such a decision being made on a whim is now suffocating, through hindsight.

In the beginning, when my medical discharge was finalizing, the idea of going somewhere new, somewhere where I was an unknown, seemed like a damn good idea. The only good one, really. I wanted to start a new chapter in my life—to find my new normal. So, with that in mind, I applied to schools as far north as Binghamton and as far south as Clemson, and everywhere in between, trailing the Appalachians and all its beautiful glory. Now, as I drive up on Main Street, in the little town of Crescent Falls—home to Buchanan State—a constricting wave of nervousness charges up from my gut to my throat. I'm so used to pushing past these bouts of numbing anxiety that it's been hard to accept that maybe they've gotten worse, maybe they've gotten harder to ignore.

Do I really have the strength to do this on my own?

But then I also know I'm ready for a fresh start. Of that, I'm certain.

Out of all the colleges and campuses I researched, this place had everything I was looking for, beyond the needed distance from both D.C. and Florida. After spending three years in D.C., I needed beautiful woods, rolling hills, and the kind of tranquility you can only find this far from the hectic nature of the city. The persistent horn-honking, the 'hold no doors, say no thank yous' mentality of its high-strung population, and the bumper-to-bumper traffic, regardless of the time of day, all lead to a healthy distaste for that way of life. No way was I going back there, or anywhere like it, and no way was I going back home; not after the childhood I had. I have no family, and no friends outside of the fellow soldiers I met along the way, who have scattered like cockroaches to new duty stations and new responsibilities since my injury. Most have forgotten about good ol' Sergeant Bishop by now.

I scoff, shaking my head as I eye myself in the rearview, annoyed that I've let this new chapter be soiled so soon. Forcing the doubts and anxiety back, I think about what's to come—the excitement of a new life. The possibilities. The potential. I can be whoever the fuck I want to be.

I locate my new apartment complex just past the main road, bordering the college buildings and dormitories that make up the core of the university campus. I take a moment to admire the beautiful snow-tipped Crescent Mountains. Their serrated peaks serve as a backdrop for the small town.

Having set everything up online ahead of time, it takes only a few minutes in the leasing office to sign all the paperwork and grab my keys. I drive around the winding complex roads, looking for Building E, while taking in what will be home for at least the next six months. Every building looks the same—brick foundation leading to a dreary pale blue siding, and inadequately small windows—like some suburbia nightmare, and the parking lot is a testament to social class discrepancies; cars that look to be running on hope and prayer alone share the lot with Beemers and F-250s lifted so high it makes me wonder if Shaq might have one just like it. I guess I'm adding to that discrepancy with my lifted Wrangler and slightly ostentatious tires, but hell, I earned it. It's the vehicle I always wanted, and after becoming bomb feed, I handed over every dime I made during my last deployment to get it. I refuse to feel bad about it.

Finally spotting Building E and pulling into a parking space, I chuckle aloud as I notice the trash bins, even before the start of the semester, are filled to the brim with empty Busch boxes and an equal amount of fast food refuse. Hopping out of the Wrangler, I snatch my large duffle bag—the one that's been with me since basic—from the back seat, and I shoulder it, closing the door behind me. The boxes, I'll grab later.

I take a deep breath, willing myself to feel better about all this as I head toward the front door, trying to focus on the natural beauty that surrounds me, the invigoration of a fresh start, and not the numbing bite of the fierce wind. And not the anxiety that sits at the base of my throat.

I've managed to find a veteran roommate online, so I'm not as nervous about signing up to live with a stranger as I might otherwise be. Having been in the Army, I've met my fair share of people. I've liked quite a few of them, loved a handful, and hated damn near most. I'm not holding my breath here, but I'd rather take my chances with a veteran than a civilian any day.

Entering the building, I look around for apartment E-6, eventually spotting it down the hall, and I make my way toward it. Opening the door, I pop my head in, finding a mostly barren living room—no TV—and cheap, particle board furniture that I'd expect to find in a barracks room or hospital, not a 'fully-furnished' apartment.

I guess this is what 'fully-furnished' means in a college town.

Stepping inside, I shut the door behind me, noticing one of the two rooms has the door closed and an eruption of lights and sounds spill through the cracks. A man's voice yells out in frustration, followed by the sounds of plastic hitting wood, and the familiar pings and dings of a video game in play.

Fuckin' gamers.

I shake my head as I make my way toward the open door across from the gamer's room, and I flip on a light. The small room is sparse, just a twin bed, dresser, and desk. Tossing my bag onto the flimsy bed frame and paper-thin mattress, I open it and begin unpacking, still taking in my surroundings. There's a twenty-inch television on a dresser that looks like it was made in the 90s, a large hump protruding from the back and rabbit ears sitting unsteadily on top.

Nodding toward the set as if it were alive and breathing, I say, "I think you and me are gonna be fast friends."

The anxiety inside me beckons as I stuff clothes into the dresser drawers, my thoughts interspersed with Chelsea, this new, strange, yet oddly familiar environment, and the choking realization that I am no longer a soldier. And I never will be again.

I'm a civilian now. And I'm doing this all on my own.

THREE

I t's quiet.

Cemetery quiet with that same kind of odd, morbid feeling surrounding me. That sweep of prickly cold that comes when death envelops you.

After two previous deployments, I know what a deafening silence like this can mean in a war zone, especially when it comes on the heels of a two-day firefight with little support or visible way out.

I wonder how the hell we even got in this mess to begin with, my ragged breathing the only thing taking my mind off the awful quiet around us as my men await my directives.

It was supposed to be a simple overnight mission for us. The five of us were to be dropped off at the shack we've now been hunkered down in for two and a half days, to provide sniper over-watch on the main road in preparation for a special delegation convoy, and then we were to be picked up the next morning. What we hadn't anticipated was the enemy knowing the plan from the start, likely a gift from one of the many spies who wear the Iraqi Police uniform and pretend to be our allies. They took out our two support squads who were encircling the neighbor-hood in Humvees—Lord knows how those men are doing, how my friends are doing—leaving us alone to fight our way out. In all the firefights and mayhem I have endured in combat up to this point, nothing could've prepared me for the carnage we've seen and caused these past few days.

After fixing communications a day ago, we were able to schedule a rescue chopper from headquarters and received very specific instructions on landing location and time, both of which add an element of danger to this already fucked up situation. But with the break in fighting, this may be our only opportunity for escape. They will bring back the fight—that's a certainty. It's just a matter of when.

"Alright." I take a deep, steadying breath. "Let's move." Waving them on, I lead my men outside of the shack and we aim our rifles out toward the road and buildings around us. The barrel of my rifle trembles with a combination of battle fatigue and fear.

For three hours now, there has been only silence as the remaining combatants limped off, their ranks decimated, morale likely broken, but they are no doubt taking the opportunity to obtain more ammunition and fresh bodies. Dozens upon dozens of their buddies now lay dead or dying in the street. It's hard to decipher the difference between blood and sand anymore. Some of the bodies are from the initial round of fighting that first day and their flesh has been mostly picked clean by birds. I note that a few dogs must've joined in as many of the jagged bite marks are far too large to have been from beaks.

A stiff shudder trails down my spine.

I don't want to feel like it bothers me to see them in this state. I want to believe they're insurgents and they were trying to kill us, so our actions were warranted, their deaths necessary. And *realistically, they were. It was their lives or ours. But I'm also tormented by one frequent thought: should we even be here in the first place? And what's so different between them and me? If I had grown up here, with the childhood I had, would I have found my way to terrorism too? I don't see how I wouldn't have.*

I quickly swallow against the choking weight of remorse and glance back toward my second in command, Sergeant Tommy Callahan, positioned in the back with a machine gun aimed to our rear.

"You ready?"

He nods, but his eyes are wide, his chest heaving with each breath.

Not counting the agonizing moans of dying men, the streets are empty and quiet, the silence deafening. The absence of gunfire after so long is both calming and unnerving.

I nod, my focus shifting back out to the quiet road, my hands gripping the rifle with white-knuckled intensity.

There's a dog bark in the distance and a whistle of the wind as it stirs up the dusty road, but nothing else. The town was abandoned by most residents long before the battle, as they're always warned ahead of time. Others, I imagine, hid themselves away sometime thereafter, leaving this place feeling like a ghost town. It's terribly unsettling.

I glance back once more, this time, meeting eyes with every man on my team. "Watch your asses and that of the man in front of you. Let's get the fuck out of here in one piece, huh?" I say, motioning toward the road.

My men nod, but their faces say it all. They're scared, and they want out of here. The desperation is ever-present in their sunken eyes, but they'd never say a word. We don't discuss things like fear out here. Just like we try our damnedest to not think about remorse or empathy. And that's why they wouldn't know that I'm scared too, so scared I can feel it in my marrow.

"Jensen, Barker... Just like we talked about. You press forward first, Sanchez and I will cover you," I say, my eyes trailing to Tommy—one of my oldest military friends. "Callahan, you watch the rear."

"Roger that," Tommy responds, winking and clicking his teeth as he turns his head back toward the road.

I motion Sanchez forward and he meets me at my side, his rifle aimed down one end of the road, and mine down the other, my muzzle just past the side of the shack.

"Go. We got you," I call over my shoulder.

Jensen and Barker abruptly sprint across the road, kicking up dust with their boots and reaching the other side without incident. They raise their barrels, scanning either end of the road like Sanchez and I are doing, and enabling us to lower our weapons and cross the road after them.

I take a deep breath, looking toward Sanchez. He passes me an assured nod and I count off, "One, two, three," before we take off toward the other side simultaneously. We reach the others without issue, and I breathe out a sigh of relief, wiping the dirty beads of sweat from my forehead.

Motioning behind us, I order, "Sanchez, you get the rear. Jensen, Barker, keep overwatch." I cup a hand to my mouth and, in a half-yell, call out, "Callahan ... Callahan!"

He turns, finally hearing me, and I wave him forward.

After a few deep breaths, Callahan lowers his machine gun and takes off. He's nearly halfway to us when I hear it—the piercing sound of a sniper round echoing down the empty road. My heart lurches in my chest as I see Callahan's face go pale, blood spurting from the side of his neck. His weapon tumbles to the ground with a clatter before he falls over on top of it.

"Nooooo!" I yell, charging forward, but I'm stopped by Jensen and Barker before I can make it very far. They hold tightly, inching me back toward them.

"Sarge, it's not safe," Jensen pleads, a ragged hoarseness to his voice.

"Fuck safety. We aren't leavin' him there to die!" I yell back. "Y'all cover me. I don't care if you see somethin' or not, you spray bullets down that fuckin' road, so I can get him out."

"Roger that, Sarge," Jensen says as he begins squeezing his trigger in indiscriminate bursts down the road as ordered. Barker does the same as I creep my way out onto the open road, my rifle up and ready to fire, but my eyes locked on Tommy.

Once I reach him, I yell, "Callahan ... Callahan..." prodding him with a stiff hand.

There's no response. I can only hear the gargle of blood in his throat as he struggles to breathe.

"Tommy!" I yell, my entire body shaking. Slinging my weapon over my shoulder and squatting down, I grab him by his protective vest and walk backward in slow, meticulous steps, pulling him along with me. He's much bulkier than I am, so the process takes longer than I'd like, considering I'm completely exposed, but I would do anything for this man. I will do anything for him.

As the sweat runs into my eyes, stinging them with relentless fury, the explosion of friendly gunfire erupts from behind me. I hear Barker yell at the top of his lungs, "Sarge, watch out! Rooftop. Three o'clock!"

There's more eardrum battering gunfire as I look to my right while still dragging Callahan. I spot an insurgent with a rocket-propelled grenade launcher sitting on his shoulder, his head no more as he goes tumbling over the side of the building, hitting the dirt road below with a bone-cracking thud.

"Nice shot!" I yell, just as Sanchez comes to my side to help, grabbing Callahan and pulling along with me to pick up the pace.

"Look out!" Barker screams.

By the time I'm able to look up, all I see is a fireball streaking its way toward us, trumping the evening sun in its burning intensity. And then, pitch-black takes hold. I see nothing. I hear only a steady, piercing ring between my ears and the faint, desperate cries of my men. I taste the distinct iron of my own blood as it fills my mouth. I feel what must be my teeth in small oblong pieces like Tic Tacs against my tongue.

I gasp, rising from my sweat-soaked sheets in a panic, throwing a pillow I had clenched in my hands across the room. I don't initially know where I am, my heart thumping in my chest like a bass drum. The pillow hits the desk and topples a mess of empty beer bottles to the ground with a clatter. The sound snaps me to the present, away from the awful dream, and I take a thick swallow, shaking my head as I breathe a sigh of sweet relief.

Two WEEKS I've spent in this prison disguised as an apartment. My roommate never leaves his room; he just plays video games all day long. The few times I have run into him, we've gotten into some military chitchat, which tends to happen when you bring veterans together. Come to find out, much to my dismay, the guy was dishonorably discharged for two DUIs. He was a shitbag in the Army, and now I have to share an apartment with him for a semester. It's almost a blessing he's addicted to video games since he's still the only person I know here. I'd much rather pass the time with Jerry Seinfeld or Doug Heffernan than some idiot with no deployments under his belt who couldn't hack it in the Army.

It does get lonely, though. Yeah, there are about fifty people in each one of my classes, but I'm always the oldest, often the quietest, and how does one strike up a conversation in that kind of environment anyway? You sit down, a professor teaches (if you're lucky. More often than not, it's a teacher's aide not much older than me), time runs out, and you make your way home. That's about it. Between the lectures, my scars, and my social anxiety, it hasn't been an ideal environment for any type of human bonding.

My laptop sits just beside the TV on the dresser where I left it, trying to keep it away from me. The screen pulls at my attention anyway. I should've just closed it. I should've been stronger.

The rush page for BSU fraternities sits on the screen, as it has been for the past few days while I mull over my options.

I'd always wanted to be in a fraternity before joining the military—the brotherhood aspect always appealed just as the military did—and after watching all seven seasons of *It's Always Sunny* in a span of two days, I'm drawn ever closer to the possibility of rushing. As old as I am, I can't help but envision them laughing as I approach the house, wondering what such an old man is doing at a frat party. They'd probably bring attention to my eye right off the bat. And what the hell do they even know about the real world? What it feels like to have your whole life turned upside down in a matter of seconds? What true pain really is?

I scowl at the computer screen. "Fuck that," I grunt, directing my anger toward the laptop. My words are strong, but my thoughts are in revolt. No matter how much denial I'm in, I know I'm fighting a battle I just can't win. I refuse to live like I have these past two weeks, suffocating under the weight of regret and loneliness. I refuse to wallow in the pain of losing the only thing that ever meant anything to me in this life. I refuse to sit here pining over a woman I probably never loved to begin with.

I have to rush. I knew it from the moment I first pulled the website up. No matter how much I deny it to myself, the brotherhood of a fraternity—hopefully a suitable replacement for Army camaraderie—is too strong of a desire to fight. I just don't think I can do this on my own.

FOUR

They set aside three days for Rush Week and I managed to burn through the first two with anxiety and indecision. As the last day winds down, and five o'clock comes around, I find the self-doubt creeping back in, telling me I don't need these guys. Telling me I'll make friends some other way, but I know that's a lie. And as strong as the pull of anxiety is, I've always combated challenges head-on. I did it when I signed up for the Army, all those years ago, to escape a life I despised; the feelings then, much like they are now, a deep-rooted anxiousness that takes hold when I'm in the uncomfortable position of meeting new people. I did it again when the RPG sent rock, metal, and dirt into my face and chest, leading to a medically induced coma, and killing Sanchez and Callahan, changing life as I knew it in a way I never thought possible. The weight of losing them still sits heavy on my soul.

I didn't let the prosthetic eye keep me down, though, nor the scars etched across my cheek and the one running wide and straight from my collarbone on the right side to the middle of my pec. Not the persistent, crippling nightmares, nor the things I could've done differently. Not the survivor's guilt and the dead men whose places I'm desperate to trade.

I've always kept pushing forward, and that's what I intend on doing today. It's why I've willed myself to this road, parked along frat row, observing the houses that line it. Greek symbols sit above each house's doorway.

My palms sweat as I climb out of the vehicle, one slow, hesitant step after another. I shut the door and take a deep breath, scanning the houses for the first one I'm set to visit; perhaps the only one I'll visit. Delta Iota Kappa was the only fraternity to email me back. They said they have other veterans in their ranks too, which was a nice surprise, so they're the only one on the docket for now. I can visit any of the other houses I'd like to, but if I don't need to, I won't.

The Delta Iota Kappa house is situated at the top of the road, which is a steep hill leading down to Main Street. As I cross, I focus my nervous brain on the keg they must have there —it's a frat party, after all—and I figure, after a few beers, my nerves should be well numbed. How stupid of me to not have killed a few beforehand to begin with.

The three-story house is expansive like the others, but unlike the others, it's run down, a sore sight on the otherwise picturesque road. I chuckle, spotting beer cans littering the front yard and the wraparound porch out front. Through the parking lot, there's a sign with an arrow pointing toward an open side door that reads, "Rushes enter here."

I take a deep breath, letting it out slowly as I inch my way toward the open door, rap music soundtracking my arrival from the inside. Just as I reach the door, a guy steps out with a broad, toothy smile. He's tall and muscular, with a mop of disheveled blond hair on his head—messed up in a purposeful way—and piercing blue eyes. Sporting a pair of skinny jeans and the DIK letters in red scrawled across his fitted black tee, he looks like he belongs in the fraternity recruitment catalog.

Putting out a hand, he asks, "How's it going, man? Are you here for rush?"

I take his hand and give it a quick, but firm, shake. "Yeah. The name's McKenzie. But everyone calls me Bishop or just Bish. I emailed one of you guys last night."

"Oh shit, the veteran, right?"

"Yeah, did I talk to you?"

"No, that would've been our Social Chair, Brady. I'm the President of DIK. The name's Trevor. Did Brady tell you we've got some other veterans in the fraternity? Including two of our officers."

"Yeah, he mentioned that."

"We've got the most out of any fraternity on campus. A few ROTC guys, as well. None of the military guys are here tonight, but you'll get a chance to meet them soon. Come on in and make yourself at home," he says, gesturing toward the door for me to enter. "Drinks are in the back by the bar. We're all just hanging out for a few minutes, getting to know each other before we start interviews. Let me know if you need anything."

"Alright. Sounds good. Thanks."

"I'll see you in there." He smiles again—a practiced, superficial smile—before heading around to the front of the house.

I make my way inside and descend a small set of dusty stairs down into the basement. There are people scattered throughout the sizable room, some on a sectional around a big screen TV to my right, others standing near the bar at the opposite end. None of them seem to notice my approach. The music blaring from the speakers set into the ceiling at each corner of the room makes a welcome distraction. Heading toward the bar, I spot three particularly young guys leaning with their backs against the filthy wood top, no letters across their chest, unlike most of the others in the room. They're each clutching a can of soda, which I assume means they're underage. No surprise there, as I reckon not one of them could grow a decent beard.

I nod toward them as I make my approach, but my focus quickly shifts to the cooler atop the bar. A neon Bud Light sign on the wall casts a red glow over it.

"What the fuck?" I exclaim upon reaching the cooler and examining it further. I look toward the first wallflower; a young, rail-thin kid, paper white—the Irish type who freckle tans in the sun without SPF 1000. He's got messy red hair, a wild look in his eye, and he's the only one even attempting a beard, which is patchy at best. His bohemian-ish threads and Bob Marley t-shirt let me know he's probably my guy to see about scoring some herbage.

"There's only soda in here. No beer?" I ask.

The ginger shrugs, looking over to the others, who pass shrugs of their own.

"I was surprised myself," the one furthest down the bar says. He's fit, with dark hair and an innocence to his features that is offset only by a thick scar running along his cheek, and a thicker one trailing down his neck, which intrigues me. I make note of this, so I can ask him about it later, when there's a tap on my shoulder.

"Hey, you're the veteran, right? McKenzie?" a voice asks from behind me, a hint of New York to it.

I turn to see a pretty boy type leaning against the bar, flashing his envy-inducing smile and flipping a mop of pin straight dirty blonde hair out of his eyes. He's wearing a black polo with the collar popped, which I force my eyes not to roll at, and he wears an offensive pair of red shorts I wouldn't be caught dead in, but I must admit, the guy somehow pulls them off.

I shake his hand and say, "Yeah, but call me Bishop."

"Right on. I'm Brady. I was the one you were emailing

yesterday." He runs his fingers through his hair, motioning his head toward the cooler. "Sorry about the selection. The university has a strict 'no alcohol' policy during Rush Week."

"I was wonderin' about that. It said 'rush party' on your website. I'm thinkin' frat party … shit has to be fun."

He smirks, nodding his head as if he can understand the confusion. "Not much fun to be had during Rush Week. That comes after you get a bid." He stops himself, putting a hand up. "*If* you get a bid, that is. Not that I think you'll have any problem with that. But we'll have to vote on it tomorrow." He motions to the three guys behind me and continues, "Have you met these guys yet? They're rushing too."

"No, not properly."

"Let me see if I can remember this correctly," Brady says, pointing to the ginger first. "Charlie, right?"

The ginger nods and shakes my hand. "Yeah, but everybody calls me Mac."

"Yeah, that's right." Brady points to the one in the middle, a tall, gangly fucker with long black hair and a brooding expression on his face. He doesn't look as if he even wants to be in his own skin, let alone at a fraternity house. "Sorry, bro. What was your name again?" he asks.

The tall man tries to hide his annoyance but to no avail. "Jamie," he mutters, his voice barely loud enough to overcome the music.

Finally, Brady points to the young guy with the scar on his face and says, "This is Carter. He's a legacy, so he'll be getting a bid no matter what."

"Carter. How's it goin'?" I ask.

He shrugs and replies, "Can't complain."

"You guys get to know each other a little while we wait on the others, and then we'll get this shit going," Brady says, turning and making his way to the door where Trevor waits.

Carter motions to my prosthetic eye, a slight smile and look of relief on his face. "Can't help but notice I'm not the only one with the face stamp."

"Yeah, that's always a sight for sore eyes." I chuckle, motioning to my prosthetic. "Or should I say, sore *eye*."

"No shit, that's a fake?" Mac asks, leaning in to get a better look.

"A prosthetic, yeah."

"Can barely tell," Mac says, straightening as he shakes his head in disbelief.

"Yeah, I'm pretty lucky."

"That happen in the war?" Carter asks. "If you don't min—"

"Nah. No worries. I'm used to talkin' about it," I say, cutting him off. "It happened over in Baghdad. RPG attack. Shrapnel went through my cheek and into my eye socket. Caught some in my chest as well. Punctured lung. Some other shit."

"Fuck," Carter mutters, shaking his head. "I'm sorry to hear that."

"It is what it is. Occupational hazard." I shrug, passing them a smirk.

"What's an RPG?" Mac interjects.

"Don't you play *Call of Duty*?" Jamie asks, a scrutinizing tone to his voice. "It stands for rocket-propelled grenade."

Mac shrugs. "I got better things to do than shoot fake people with a bunch of twelve-year-olds," he snaps.

"Yeah, rocket-propelled grenade. Only the real kind." I laugh, making an explosion gesture with my hands.

"Crazy shit," Carter says, his eyes wide.

"You ever kill anyone?" Jamie stares at me intently, his words lingering in the air.

There's always some asshat who has to ask that stupid fuckin' question.

"A few, but I don't really like talkin' about it."

"My bad," Jamie says, though with no sincerity in his voice.

"No worries. It was my job. I'm not bothered by it. Like I said, I just don't like talkin' about it … out of respect for the dead." I shift my focus to Carter, hoping to change the subject. I motion to the scars etched on his cheek and neck. "What about you? How'd you get those bad boys?"

Carter's finger trails the length of the scar on his cheek slowly; it's thick and a few shades off from his light complexion. "Car wreck for me. Nothing too exciting."

"Shit must've been bad," I say, my eyes tracing the scars, appreciating the commonality between us.

"Yeah, it was. Really bad. I was young, though. Don't remember much of it."

I can tell by the way he says it, and the touch of sadness shrouding his features, that he remembers more than he'd like to … and more than he's probably willing to admit to himself. How easily I can remember that age—eighteen, nineteen years old with the whole world in front of you, but also sitting squarely on your shoulders. When you've been through a trauma, the weight increases tenfold. The pressure to be 'okay' or 'normal' becomes unbearable. And the realization that you never will be even worse.

Suddenly, the music cuts off and it draws our attention toward the sectional in front of the big screen TV. Brady positions a stool in front of the TV as Trevor motions us over. Another guy I have yet to meet sets up a video camera on a tripod in front of the stool, and the remaining brothers take up the couches behind the camera.

"Alright, guys," Trevor says as we approach. "We're going to go ahead and start interviews now, and hopefully the other guys will show up soon. We'll go alphabetical, so Bishop." His eyes fall on me. "You're first."

I give a quick two-finger salute to the other rushes as they head toward the stairs before I make my way to the stool. Taking a seat, I let out a heavy breath as I feel a wave of heat trail down my back when I realize all eyes are on me.

Trevor chuckles, placing a hand on my shoulder. "Don't sweat it, man. Super easy stuff. This is just a way for us to get to know you better." He gives me a few pats for good measure before swinging his hand over to the camera and turning it on. He takes a seat in a chair across from me and pulls a piece of paper from his pocket. Unfolding it, he clears his throat and looks back up at me.

"So, Bishop, these'll just be standard questions. Cool?"

"Fire away." I nod, and Trevor directs his attention to the sheet of paper again.

"Okay, we are interviewing rush candidate, McKenzie Bishop. Goes by Bishop. So, Bishop, where are you from?"

"I was born and raised in LaBelle, Florida, but I've been all over since eighteen, when I joined the Army."

"What did you do in the Army and how long were you in for?"

"I was Infantry and served a little over six years."

"Okay, and what are you majoring in?"

I chuckle, shrugging. "No fuckin' clue. Just gen. ed. courses for right now and, I guess, I'll figure things out as I go."

Trevor laughs, waving me off. "No worries, man. We've got a lot of undecideds in the fraternity. So, why BSU?" He puts his hand up and motions around the room. "Why the beautiful town of Crescent Falls, Pennsylvania?" he adds in a sarcastic tone. "There are certainly better options out there."

"I don't really get along with many people back in Florida. Didn't really wanna wind up back there. I did my rehab in D.C., so I wanted to be reasonably close if I ever need to get more work done. BSU was one of the first schools to accept me and I liked the area. It really is beautiful. I'm sure if you've lived here a while, it could get old, but I don't know, it's my kind of shit. So, here I am. That's about the gist of it."

"I'm from New York originally, Long Island, so I know what you mean. It's a whole different world here, but one of the best decisions I've ever made, honestly," Trevor says, clearing his throat. "You said rehab? What do you mean by that?" His eyes flit to my prosthetic for the briefest of moments.

"I lost my eye and broke a few bones in my cheek on my last deployment. Caught some shrapnel in my chest too. I went through a couple years of therapy and surgeries to get everything unfucked."

"*Shit.* I saw the scars. Figured something like that happened but couldn't tell the eye was fake."

"My uncle has a fake eye," a rotund young man says from the couch to the right of me. I glance at him, unsure of what to say.

Congrats?

Trevor shoots the kid a glare then looks back at me. "That's Chunk. He's a first-year brother and knows better than to just speak out of turn during interviews. Don't ya, Chunk?" Trevor flashes him a wicked smile.

"You guys know I hate that name," Chunk responds, crossing his sausage arms defiantly.

"Blame your Big Bro, buddy. He's the one who picked it for you."

"Well, I should've been able to pick my own Big Brother instead of ending up with the dickhead I got."

Trevor looks back at me, ignoring Chunk, whose brows pinch together as he mutters something inaudible under his breath.

Trevor continues, "Well, we all really appreciate your service and sacrifice, man. Like I said earlier, we've got a lot of vets and ROTC guys in the fraternity, and we respect all you guys for what you've done."

"I appreciate it," I say, tilting my head and giving him a mischievous smirk. "The ROTC guys still have to earn that appreciation, though. They haven't done a damn thing yet."

Trevor laughs, nodding with understanding, but I notice one of the guys behind him fidgets uncomfortably on the couch, a look of disapproval on his face.

Must be ROTC. Fuckstick.

"Yeah, true. I didn't think of that," Trevor says. "So, what do you think or what do you already know about the pledging process? You're obviously a bit older. Do you think the process will get to you?"

"Honestly, I don't know shit about fraternities, other than what I've seen in the movies. If it's anything like that, I have no clue what to think, or if I'll be able to go through with it. I'm big on respect. And to be disrespected in some of the ways I've seen in movies, I know I won't be able to deal. I'm willing to earn my way—cut my teeth, so to speak—and do the things the other pledges are made to do, but that can be done without bein' disrespected, I think."

Trevor nods as if he anticipated such an answer. "It's nothing like the movies. I can promise you that, man. Like anything else, Hollywood over-exaggerates shit."

I chuckle. "Trust me, I get it. I've seen that sorry pile of shit they call a war movie, *The Hurt Locker*."

Trevor laughs, nodding again. "Exactly. So, it's not anything crazy out there. Pledges will have to put in the time, do some shit they might not normally do, you know, earn their stripes, but you aren't going to be hazed, or fucked with, or anything like that. Nothing even close to what I'm sure you've experienced already in basic training. Besides, we're under probation right now after some pledges complained about hazing last semester.

We've been under a microscope since. All eyes are on us, so in that way you've lucked out."

"Couldn't agree more about earning your stripes. It's necessary for an organization like this, and I'm willin' to put in the effort. Just don't wanna be disrespected in the process."

"Absolutely not." Trevor smiles. "Shit, well, Bishop ..." He looks around to the others seated behind him with an approving nod as he folds the paper back up, his eyes returning to mine. "I don't think I really need to ask anything else. You're pretty much a shoo-in for pledging. We all really appreciate you coming by our house. I think you'd be a great fit. Are you visiting any other fraternities today? Or have you already?"

"No, not yet. But if you say I'm a shoo-in, I don't really wanna fuck with visiting anywhere else. I like that y'all are the *Animal House* around here. The others looked too stuffy for my tastes."

Trevor laughs. "*Animal House* is spot-on. We DIKs don't fuck around. We do it right, and once you get your bid, you'll see. Epic parties, hot fucking girls, and more alcohol than you'll know what to do with."

I nod approvingly. "I can get down with that."

"Plus, fuck the other fraternities, man. They're a bunch of bitches." The others chuckle from behind him. "You definitely chose the right place."

"Right on. Well, I'm ready to do my part."

Trevor shuts off the camera and stands. "Alright, man. Well, if you could send Jamie in next, that'd be great. Stick around for a bit, though. We'll meet with you guys again after interviews."

"Sounds good," I say, standing and shaking Trevor's hand before I make my way to the stairs.

"Hey, Bishop," Trevor calls out, and I stop in my tracks, looking back toward him. He has a shit-eating grin on his face. "What are your thoughts on Jamie anyway?"

I scratch at my chin with my pointer finger while creases form in my brow as I pretend to think it over. After a brief moment, I shrug, swiping my finger across my throat. "Fuckin' weirdo."

A chorus of laughter follows me up the stairs and out the door.

I LIGHT a cigarette and take a puff, leaning my back against the side of the house. Mac and Carter stand around me, as does a new guy who showed up while I was interviewing. His name is Jeremy, and he's got jet-black hair beneath a dirty trucker hat, turned backwards. His gauged ears and eyebrow piercing are a unique juxtaposition to his country vibe and backwoods twang. He's built like he's played sports his whole life, chiseled and lean. His eyes are piercing and stoic, but he's got a wide grin that seems ever-present, a warm spirit that emanates from him.

"What are the rings for?" Carter asks, motioning toward the thick carbon fiber ring on my thumb and the skull rings on my middle finger and pointer.

I look down at them and shrug. "You ever been in a fight with rings on your fingers?"

Carter passes me a skeptical look. "No, I haven't. I take it you have? Is that really why you wear them?"

"It's not why I started, but after getting this one for Christmas from an ex in high school" —I lift my hand and point to the skull ring on my middle finger— "and then beatin' the shit out of the dude I caught her fuckin' a few months later, I was stuck with 'em. Fucked that dude's world up. Fucked up a few more since then, too."

"No shit," Carter says, getting a better look at the ring before I lower my hand. "Looks like it would do some damage."

I nod.

"You been in a lot of fights?" he asks.

"I've had my fair share over the years. You?"

"Not too many fist fights, but I wrestled for most of my life."

"You were a wrestler?" Jeremy asks.

Carter nods.

"I wrestled too. Down home in Allentown."

"Where's that?"

"About two hours southeast of here. Middle of goddamn nowhere, that's what it is," Jeremy responds, chuckling as he pulls a tin of dip from his back pocket and opens it, digging a wad out and stuffing it into his bottom lip.

"Oh, you're real fucking country, huh?" Mac asks with a crooked smile.

"As country as they come, brother." Jeremy laughs, stowing the tin back in his pocket and crossing his arms as he leans against the house beside me. "Cow tippin', trail muddin', squirrel huntin' redneck. You name it, I probably done it."

"Nice." Mac nods with approval. "So how is it around here anyway? I'm from outside of Boston, so this is like fucking Mars to me. Anything fun to do around here?"

Jeremy laughs. "Drink, drink, and drink some more. Smoke the green if that's your thing. Fuck like a rabbit in heat if *that's* your thing. There're about three bars downtown, but the parties are where it's at here in Crescent Falls. That's what I'm doin' at DIK. Ain't gettin' into no parties without them letters across your chest, boys, and I was bored out of my skull last year. Ain't doin' that shit again."

"Sophomore?" I ask.

Jeremy nods and asks, "What about y'all?"

"Freshman," Carter and Mac respond in unison.

"With military college credits, I'm a sophomore too," I say.

"Did y'all attend any other rush events this week? Any other frats?" Jeremy asks.

I shake my head. "Not me."

"I came by here yesterday, and visited Beta Chi the day before," Mac responds. "But they were some fucking assholes. Not my type at all. I swear, if I hadn't known, I would've thought I was walking into a fucking squash convention ... or a Klan rally. But I met some cool guys here yesterday, and I heard this was the most welcoming fraternity, so this is where I'm sticking if I get a bid. Plus, I heard their weed game is strong." His eyebrows dance. "So hopefully my ginger ass gets in."

"I'm legacy, so I haven't bothered with any other fraternities. My dad would probably call for my head," Carter says with a shrug. "What about you, Jeremy?"

"Only DIK. I stopped by here for the first time on Monday and met some cool dudes. Figured I'd give 'em a chance." Jeremy motions toward me. "You meet Sarge yet, by the way? Y'all would hit it off. Funny ass motherfucker."

"So I've heard. Do you know what he did in the military?"

"Not really, but I heard some fucked up stories about him from some of the other guys. He was a sniper or somethin'. Ranger, too. All I know for certain is that the guy's a fuckin' trip. He cracked my shit up. Makes his own moonshine and talks about militias and government conspiracies and shit. Always bitin' down on a half-burnt cigar."

"Interesting," I say, thoughts of all the pretend veterans I've met over the years passing through my brain.

"Yeah, he's a fuckin' trip. I'm telling' ya." Jeremy says as the opening door grabs our attention.

Jamie comes outside and motions toward Mac. "You're next," he says, and Mac scurries inside, the door closing behind him.

"How was it?" I ask.

Jamie shrugs, letting out a light scoff. "You should know. You were in there, too," he responds, annoyance thick in his tone.

"Well, fuck me. You're a fiery little spit fuck, aren't you?" I say, grinning as I light another cigarette. I chain smoke when I'm bored or anxious, of which I'm currently both.

"Sorry," he mutters. "I just hate shit like that. Felt like I was being interrogated or something."

"To be honest, you don't seem like the fraternity type to me," I say.

He shrugs. "I'm trying to be more social this year. My freshman year fucking sucked. But this ..." His eyes trail to the closed basement door. "I don't know." He glances at me. "Did they ask you how many women you've slept with?"

"Nah."

"If you've ever done any drugs?"

I shake my head.

"If you've ever been arrested?"

"No, but I think I got some leniency comin' out of the Army. They seemed to like that."

"That's some bullshit. I mean, not you serving. Just how invasive they were with me."

"Comes with the territory," Carter says, shrugging. "They want to know they're bringing in somebody who can contribute to the fraternity. Someone who will be a good brother. My dad told me all about this shit. It's not going to be a fun couple of months. I mean, we'll have access to a lot of killer parties, alcohol, stuff like that, but a lot of bullshit gets mixed in with it."

"What kind of bullshit?" I ask, and then I grin, adding, "And I've had access to alcohol for a good five years now. Seven if you count my late teens spent at Fort Bragg."

Carter chuckles, shaking his head. "Eh, I'm not really supposed to talk about the process. The brothers asked me to keep everything I know secret, but it's nothing too crazy. Just bonding type shit. Some annoying shit they call 'pledge challenges' too."

"Okay, okay. I guess I'll play along."

"Trust me. It won't be too bad. And it'll be well worth it in the end. My dad is still friends with most of his fraternity brothers."

"I'll just have to take your word for it, I guess."

———

AFTER AN HOUR OR SO, and half a pack of cigarettes, I breathe a sigh of relief as Carter comes through the door and waves the rest of us inside. Once we enter, Trevor motions for us to join him and the others by the seating area. We oblige, and he clears his throat, that broad politician's smile taking up his features again. I can see him so clearly in my mind, ten years from now, in a tailored suit and an American flag pin on his lapel, a gorgeous wife on his arm and adoring constituents calling out their praises, flashing that synthetic smile with evil intent stirring inside. This man was made for politics.

"Alright, guys. We all want to thank you for taking the time to come out here and go through this BS," Trevor says. "I know the interviews aren't too fun, but they're necessary. All the brothers who couldn't be here today need the chance to get to know you as well, before we vote. Once we have our meeting tomorrow and take a vote, we'll be handing out bids. Prepare for Friday evening. We'll be by your dorm or apartment to pick you up if you've received a bid. Other than that, you guys have a good night, and thanks again for coming by."

FIVE

Lying in bed and flipping through the channels after my Friday classes, I suddenly hear a loud knock on the door that stirs me. I toss the blanket aside and climb out of bed with a heavy sigh when another knock echoes throughout the apartment. Walking quickly toward the door, I open it but find no one on the other side, only a post-it note on the floor.

Bending over, I pick it up and read the scribbled words.

Get dressed and come outside.
Five minutes.
DIK.

I smile, crumpling up the post-it note as I rush back to my room. I quickly throw on a pair of pants and a hoodie, my leather jacket over that, and slip my feet into a pair of Chucks. Grabbing my smokes and wallet, I exit the apartment in a hurry. Once outside of the building, a black SUV comes barreling toward me, braking at the last second—tires screeching—with the passenger side facing me. The door opens and an older guy with a military crewcut climbs out, an empty sandbag in one hand and a smoldering cigar in the other. Tattoos line his muscular, tanned arms. He's shorter than I am, but about twice as wide in the shoulders, his envy-inducing biceps pushing the limits of his too-tight t-shirt sleeves.

How the fuck is he only wearing a t-shirt in this weather?!

Behind him comes Brady and Trevor. The three of them line up in front of me, and Trevor passes me a nervous look.

"So, you promise not to kill us if Sarge here throws that bag over your head?" he asks, motioning to the sandbag in the tatted guy's thick hand. "It's just tradition."

"I did it three years ago when I pledged too," Sarge says. "And I was twenty-six, a year older. You know how tradition goes. You were in the Army, too."

I nod, grinning, when I say, "I know it well. So, what are y'all waitin' for?" I motion toward my head.

Sarge smiles and slips the bag over my head gently, and then they guide me toward the SUV, carefully seating me in the back, on the floor.

"Watch your toes," Sarge says, nudging me in a bit and closing the hatch behind me. After a few moments, I hear him ask, "You alright back there?"

I turn to look at the back seat where he sits but can't make out much of anything. I only know it's him by the orange glow of his cigar.

"Not too bad. Though, not too comfortable either." I chuckle. "You really did this shit?" I ask as the vehicle starts moving.

"Yeah. I didn't really give a fuck. I was down for anything at that point. Just wanted to be a part of something. Probably the same reason you're here now. Needed that taste of brotherhood again."

"How long were you in for?"

"I did a little over six years. Got sick of deploying, so I got out and came here. I'm from Pittsburgh originally, so I figured I'd go somewhere close to home seeing as I had been gone for so long."

"MOS?" I ask, the first of my veteran confirmation questions. These are questions veterans ask each other to verify service. They're basic questions any true servicemember could answer, but it trips fakes up expeditiously.

"Eleven Bravo. Ended up going through sniper and Ranger school after OSUT."

One Station Unit Training. In order to describe OSUT, I'll use the words of my drill sergeant when we graduated basic training and moved on to AIT (Advanced Individual Training) school to learn our new jobs: *"Congratulations, motherfuckers. Nothing fucking changes. Now, get on your faces and give me fifty!"*

Test question passed.

"Nice. I was a Ranger too. Been overseas?"

"Yeah, I was with Three-Seven-Five in Kandahar back in '01, and again for the Iraq invasion in '03. And my last one was with the Two-Seven-Five in Helmand."

Test two. Pass.

These aren't numbers just pulled out of one's ass, and any Ranger could decipher them upon hearing.

"Fuck, those were some nasty places. Wild fuckin' West type shit."

"Yeah, you're telling me. It's why I ended up getting out. Just too much fighting." Sarge hesitates. "The guys told me about your eye. Where'd that happen?"

"End of a tour with 1st Ranger Bat. out of Baghdad. Fuckin' saw that shit coming too. We had just been talking about it a few days before it happened. Too many close calls. Too many idiot fuckin' chiefs. Too many insurgents with hate in their hearts and a taste for blood."

Sarge nods. "You remember much of it?" he asks as the vehicle stops, gravel crunching beneath the tires.

"Just blood. The taste of it. My teeth broken to pieces, spitting them out as best I could. This terrible sting that took up the spot where my teeth used to be. I couldn't see anything. My ears were fucked. Ringin' like a bitch. It was all just kind of a blur at that point. Docs put me in a coma for two weeks once we were rescued and I made it to the main combat hospital in Balad. I woke up in Germany, not rememberin' what the fuck happened."

"Fuck, man. Well, glad you're still here with us, fighting the good fight."

"You too, brother. You too."

Trevor clears his throat. "Sorry, guys. Don't mean to interrupt, but it's time to start," he says, reluctance in his tone.

"No worries. We'll talk more later, Bishop."

"Definitely."

I feel a rush of cold air as the hatch opens, and then someone grabs my arm.

"Alright, bud, we can take this shit off now," Trevor says, pulling the sandbag off my head and tossing it aside as he helps me out of the vehicle.

"Thanks. That shit was hard to breathe through," I say as my feet meet the gravel road. Barren trees surround us, along with dense pines dotted here and there, as do about fifty guys with the Delta Iota Kappa letters on their chest, shivering hands in their pockets, and a stillness in the air around us.

Trevor points toward the edge of the road, where I notice Carter, Mac, and Jeremy stand side by side, their arms linked together.

"Head on over there, man, and link up with Jeremy."

I nod and crack a smile as I approach Jeremy.

"Good to see you here, brother," I say, linking my arm with his.

"Yeah, you too," he replies. "Now, I reckon the real fun begins." He lets out a chuckle that's quickly snuffed out by Trevor's projected voice.

"Alright, pledges," he says, pacing in front of us. "First, congratulations on receiving bids for the Spring 2011 class of Delta Iota Kappa-Rho Chapter. We have nearly seventy years of existence at BSU, and over one hundred years of existence for the fraternity as a whole. Many great men have come before you, have stood where you're standing, committing themselves to this chapter and the fraternity. This is a sacred place for DIK-Rho. This is where you start the journey. And this is where you will hopefully end it in two months, as a new DIK brother." He pauses for a moment, stopping in his tracks and looking as if he's gathering his thoughts.

"This will not be an easy process," he finally continues. "You will be tired. You will be annoyed. You will be pushed to your limits. *Trust* in the process. Support each other. Understand that this process is in place so that we are certain this fraternity consists of the best men BSU has to offer. Being that it's the spring semester, there are much fewer of you than there would be in the fall. That means you'll have to lift a heavier load. You'll have to put more in. Are you ready for the challenge?"

There are a few quiet "Yeahs" and nods between us, but Trevor isn't satisfied.

"Let's try that again. Say it like you fucking mean it. I want to hear a 'Fuck yeah' from every swinging dick in line. Pledges, are you ready for this challenge?"

"Fuck yeah!" we yell at the top of our lungs, our voices echoing throughout the woods. I can't help but feel foolish at hearing my own voice echo. I'm taken back to when I was freshly nineteen, standing in formation for the first time, and allowing another man to ridicule and shame me. It feels even more emasculating now that I really am a man and my Army days are behind me.

"That's better." He looks back at the large group of brothers behind him. "VP, you ready to lead this thing?"

"Fucking right," an African-American guy—six-foot-ridiculous and muscles exploding from his tank top—responds. He runs a hand over his head as he approaches our line. Somehow, even as cold as it is, sweat beads speckle his bald head. In a loud, confident voice, he continues, "What up, pledges. The name's Damian, and I'm the Vice President of DIK-Rho. I'll be your point of contact for all things pledge-related. Your pledge class president will be your first in line. I am your second." He points to Trevor. "Prez here is off-fucking-limits. Understood?"

There's a brief hesitation before we respond in unison, "Fuck yeah!"

"Good. Now, follow me."

Damian saunters past our line and motions for a group of brothers at the wood line to make room. They spread out, and he passes between them. We follow behind him down a dirt path leading into the woods, toward a thick patch of pines that look as if they were strategically planted in a spacious circle long ago. Through the pines, I can see the flicker of flames from torches stuck into the ground, mimicking the pines' circular pattern. Damian passes between the trees and we follow in after him. In the middle of the circle stand three men, cloaked in velvet robes, side by side. I feel like I'm in the middle of a fucking ritual sacrifice here, and we're the unlucky virgins.

I recognize Brady holding a skull at the far left of the line. The one in the middle wields a dagger, and the last one holds a book.

"Are we gonna die here today?" Mac jokes as we stop abruptly with Damian.

"Hey Red," Damian snaps, narrowing his eyes at Mac. "This is tradition. Respect it."

"Yeah, yeah, sorry, man," Mac stammers.

Damian motions toward the three robed brothers. "Line up and link up in front of them," he says.

We do as we're told, facing the three robed officers, about three feet away from them. The brother on the far-right steps forward. He holds out the book in his hands to show it to us.

"The bond of brotherhood is sacred," he begins, his voice touched with a rasp and naturally quiet. "You are standing where thousands have stood before you, taking the oath that has echoed throughout these woods for seventy years," he continues, his piercing blue eyes scanning us as the hood casts a shadow over his movie star features. "I'm Zane, the secretary of DIK-Rho, and one of my responsibilities is ensuring you not only repeat our sacred bond after me, but that you understand what it means and represents. The bond you are asked to assume contains three promises. A promise to maintain our principles, a promise to the brothers within this fraternity, and a promise to yourself. Listen carefully as I read this bond, and together repeat it after me: I promise to be guided by the Delta Iota Kappa principles, loyalty, charity, and honor in my fraternal relationships throughout my lifetime."

There is a momentary silence between us.

"Am I talking to myself here, pledges? I said, '*repeat after me*,'" he shouts, or what I imagine is a shout for him. Let's just say, Drill Sergeant school certainly wouldn't be beating down his door.

"I promise to be guided by the Delta Iota Kappa principles, loyalty, charity, and honor in my fraternal relationships throughout my lifetime," we repeat, stumbling a bit in the middle.

"I am a DIK!" Zane says.

"I am a DIK!" we repeat.

"I promise to share mutual respect and understanding for the uniqueness of each brother, depend on them as they depend on me, and support the welfare and wellbeing of every brother. I am a DIK!"

We repeat him, Mac stumbling again over the words, which garners a nasty stare from Brady. I just want to laugh.

"I promise to respect the bond, using my individual abilities to contribute as a responsible frater within the bond, guided by the principles our fraternity is based upon. I am a DIK for life!"

I can't help but feel silly as we repeat him again, but I maintain my bearing. I understand that I'm a unique exception to all this. For most of these brothers, this is the only discipline they've ever encountered. For me, it's a sad realization that perhaps I'm taking backward steps here.

"Good," Zane says. "You don't need to repeat this next part, but listen closely, as it is the very foundation of our fraternity. The first sentence of the bond you have just recited is a promise to maintain the principles of DIK. Our Declaration of Principles states: We believe that the essential elements of true brotherhood are loyalty, charity, and honor. Loyalty that is enduring and steadfast, the beat of fraternal heart. Charity that is spontaneous to see virtues in a brother and slow to rebuke his faults, the strength of fraternal bone. Honor that is conviction without conceit, pride without ego, preparedness, not overreaction, the might of fraternal mind. These are the triple obligations of the fraternal bond. These are the principles that you will carry with you and represent for the rest of your lives as members of Delta Iota Kappa." Zane tucks the book in the crook of his armpit.

"You will have our bond and Declaration of Principles memorized by next Friday," Zane continues. "And if you carry with you these principles, and you commit to this bond, your name will go into this book, and you will enter a brotherhood for life."

Zane takes a step back in line and looks over toward the one with the dagger. "We have a task for them to complete tonight. Don't we, Brother Tim?"

"Oh, uh, yeah, yeah, we do," the middle guy with the dagger stammers as he digs into his pocket with his free hand. A thick, black beard juts down his chin, ending just before the Black Sabbath logo on the t-shirt beneath his robe. He steps forward, finally locating the paper, and he clears his throat.

"Alright fuckers, here's the deal." He holds the dagger in the air and continues, "This dagger represents strength in unity, bravery, and protection. Together we are powerful, our unique —ah, fuck." He takes a look to the sky in thought, scratching at his beard with the tip of the dagger. "Uh, fuck me. I got it—our unique attributes perfectly cohesive. Work together to obtain everything on this list." He holds the paper out toward me. "Bishop, you're the new pledge class president, as chosen by the brothers of Delta Iota Kappa. Take the list and see to it that you and your pledge brothers complete it tonight."

He waves the folded paper at me until I unlink from Jeremy and take it. Opening it up, I have a second to glance over it before Damian clears his throat, drawing my attention.

"Don't look at it yet," he snaps, motioning toward the paper. "Put it away and link back up."

I bite my tongue, folding the list up and pocketing it, as he nods toward Tim, who then falls back in line.

As I link back up with Jeremy, Brady takes a step toward us, raising the skull in his hand.

"The skull represents the secrecy you are obligated to uphold throughout your days as a Delta Iota brother or face a penalty of death," he says. "The inner workings of our fraternity, from chapter level to Nationals, is reliant upon unwavering trust and secrecy. You will share nothing you experience during pledging with anyone outside of the fraternity. You will share nothing that is discussed with brothers after. Understood? Give me a 'fuck yeah.'"

"Fuck yeah!"

Brady takes a step back in line and Damian motions for us to follow him.

"Alright, let's get you to the vehicles, bagged, and back to the house. And then the real fun begins," he says, laughing maniacally, heading toward the road as we trail behind him.

We're all hooded again and put in our respective vehicles like luggage. I link my fingers together over my knees and lean my head against the back of the seat as the hatch closes. My mind is littered with apprehension, wondering if I even fully realize what I've gotten myself into.

"Well, what do you think?" I hear Sarge ask from the back seat.

"Weird shit, man."

Sarge laughs loudly. "Yeah, you can thank the frat forefathers for that. There's a lot of ridiculous shit they put in the book back in the day that we're still doing today for some reason. Just have to play along."

"Sounds like *another* book I know," I say through a laugh. "Shit, I feel like I'm in basic training all over again."

"A little bit, but nothing like what we went through. This shit's a cakewalk, considering." In a softer tone, he continues, "And to let you in on a little secret, once you're done with the scavenger hunt bullshit, you'll be coming back to a rager. First party of the year. That has to be worth getting this shit done fast." He pauses, adding, "Nah, it *is* worth it."

"*Sarge*," Trevor scolds. "What the hell, man?"

"Ah, come on, pretty boy. The dude fought for our fucking country and he's old as dirt. He's owed a little insider info."

"Yeah, alright, but Bishop, just make sure you keep that to yourself. Part of this whole thing is not knowing what's ahead. I know you've done a lot of stuff like this already in your life, so you know how important the element of surprise is when it comes to these things."

"Of course. Don't worry about me. I get it. And I do appreciate the info, Sarge, but who you callin' old? What are you, like fifty?"

Sarge laughs. "Twenty-nine, motherfucker. Old enough to be your father."

"Sarge, uh, you're thirty, dude," Trevor says, chuckling.

"Not for another month, jackass," Sarge says, shooting Trevor a sideways glance.

"Well, you look like you're fucking eighty, so who knows." Trevor laughs. "Oh shit, you can take that stupid bag off your head, by the way. We're almost to the house."

I pull the sandbag off and toss it aside. Wiping the sweat from my forehead, I ask, "How many more times are we gonna be sandbagged like that? Felt like I was a fuckin' captured insurgent."

"Only one more time, on the last day of Hell Week," Trevor replies.

"*Hell Week*? What are you guys, the fuckin' Marines?"

"Fuck no," Sarge says, shaking his head adamantly. "*Never* the Marines."

"Not quite." Trevor laughs. "Not even close. But we have our own version of Hell Week. That time will come, though." The vehicle comes to a stop and the hatch starts to open. "For now, you've got some shit to find." Trevor grins, opening his door and exiting, as the rest of those in the vehicle follow suit. He meets me near the back of the SUV as I stretch my back with a stiff pop and then dig my cigarettes out of my pocket. The other pledges congregate in the parking lot a bit away from us, as dozens of the brothers from the initiation now exit their own vehicles and file through the basement door.

Likely prepping for the party. Lucky bastards. I could really use a fuckin' drink.

"Once you guys get everything on the list, head back here," Trevor says. "There's no time limit, other than it must be done by morning. And obviously, you've got some motivation to finish early." He leans in. "But remember to keep that between us. And have fun, man." He slaps hands with me, heading toward the basement door. As he passes the other pledges, he juts a thumb back toward me. "You guys get with your Prez and he'll get you situated," he orders, disappearing through the doorway.

My pledge brothers shuffle toward me, as I light a cigarette and then pull the list from my pocket, replacing it with the cigarette pack. They surround me as I hold the paper out for everyone to see under the dim streetlight and take a strong pull on my smoke.

Through a smoky exhale, I say, "Alright, looks like we got our work cut out for us. I'm not readin' all this shit out loud but look over it and let's figure out where to start."

Pledge Scavenger Hunt
Obtain one of each of the following:

- *Car tire*
- *Traffic cone*
- *Bra*
- *Bowl filled with weed or a joint*
- *A McDonald's employee badge*
- *Homeless Hank's dirty underwear*
- *Another fraternity's letter*

Record one of you doing the following:

- *Steal food from a restaurant*
- *Kiss a stranger*
- *Sing karaoke*
- *Drink a beer with Homeless Hank*

Take a selfie of the following:

- *With a topless stripper*
- *From the top of Archie's Tower*
- *With a mulleted man*

"Well, fuck. Where do we even begin?" Mac asks as I hand the list over to him.

"We start with a cab," I respond, pulling out my phone and going to work on the screen. "Can you guys find a traffic cone in the time it takes for me to grab my Wrangler?"

"Yeah, shouldn't be an issue." Carter nods. "Could probably locate a car tire too."

"And I've got the joint covered." Mac laughs, his eyebrows dancing as he points to his pocket. "I've got a Crown Royal bag full of them."

"Well, fuck," I say, motioning to his pocket. "Let me have one."

He frowns, letting out a heavy breath and reluctantly pulling the bag out. He opens it, digs in, and pulls out a sad looking joint.

"I'll get you back, Red," I say, snatching it from him and smiling, and then slipping it behind my ear.

"Yeah, yeah," he says, sulking. "Just know you're taking a man's medicine right now."

"Oh, fuck you." I laugh.

"I have glaucoma!" he reasons in a sincere tone, and then he abruptly cracks up.

I shake my head, waving Mac off as the cab pulls up beside us. "Alright, I'll see you guys in a few. One of y'all give me your number, so I can text you when I get back."

Jeremy rattles off his number, and I punch it into my phone before I climb into the cab and it departs.

After making my way back to my apartment and getting my Wrangler, I return to the frat house, smoking part of the joint along the way. As I pull up to the Delta Iota parking lot, I see my fellow pledges in a circle around a traffic cone with a ragged old car tire slipped over it. Mac spins a white lace bra on one finger and grips a lit joint with the other.

"Where'd y'all find that?" I ask, hopping out of the Jeep and motioning toward the bra as I approach.

"We ran into one of my exes," Jeremy responds with a quick wink.

"Must not have been a bad breakup, eh?"

"Nah, it was a fuckin' mess, man, but what can I say? I'm a smooth talker," Jeremy responds, flashing his ghost white set of perfectly aligned teeth. It makes me wonder how a man who dips as much as he does can carry such an effervescent smile.

"Good work!" I take the bra from Mac and inspect it, guessing it's a D-cup, maybe even larger, though I have no clue really. "You sure it wasn't a mistake lettin' her go?" I ask, raising an eyebrow and tossing the bra at Jeremy's face.

Mid-catch, he replies, "Way more to a lady than her tits, my friend."

I laugh. "Way to make me feel like an asshole."

Jeremy shrugs. "I've been doin' that to guys my whole damn life by just bein' me, my friend." He flashes a smile.

"Well, let's get a move on. I wanna get this shit done as soon as fuckin' possible," I say.

"Where to first?" Mac asks, climbing into the Jeep after me. The others are close behind.

"Liquor store," I respond. "No fuckin' way I'm doin' this without a drink."

AFTER GRABBING A FIFTH OF JAMESON, we cruise down the main strip, which is alive with activity as the Friday night festivities pick up. I've traded seats with Mac, who now drives us as I nurse the bottle.

"Let me get a draw on that," Jeremy says from the back seat with gimme fingers.

I pass it back and he snatches it from me quickly, tipping the bottle back and letting out a pleased sigh as he hands it over to Carter.

"Thank ya kindly," Jeremy says, swiping an arm across his lips. "So, what's first?"

I think for a moment. "Walgreens."

"What the hell we getting at Walgreens?" Mac asks.

"A six-pack and hair clippers. And then y'all need to tell me who the hell Homeless Hank is and where I can find him."

"Well, that's easy," Jeremy says. "He sets up right outside of Walgreens most days. It's the only place they let him be."

"Well, that works out."

Arriving at the Walgreens parking lot a few moments later, Mac parks the car and I spot who must be Homeless Hank, seated against the building, just beside the entrance. He's got a stringy gray beard, raggedy clothing with holes throughout, and dirt smudged on his face.

"That our guy?" I ask as Mac switches off the engine.

"That'd be him," Jeremy responds.

"Perfect. You guys let him know what we're doin' here, and I'll grab what we need from the store."

"Oh, Hank knows what we're up to. He's been around these parts forever. And this isn't his first scavenger hunt," Carter responds.

"Alright, well, start gettin' your money together then, boys. I'll be right back." I exit the vehicle and enter the Walgreens as the others empty the Jeep behind me.

A short while later, I leave the store with two large, over-stuffed bags in my hands.

"What the hell did you get?" Mac asks, eyeing them.

"Enough shit to make me feel okay about all this," I respond, my eyes shifting down toward Hank. I set the bags down and put out my hand toward him. "Hank, is it?"

Hank examines my hand for a moment before taking it and giving it a weak shake.

"That'd be me," he responds in a gruff voice.

I look back at the others behind me. "Got the money?" I ask.

"Yeah," Jeremy says, digging in his pocket and pulling out a wad of cash. "What's it for?"

I take it, inspect it with scrutiny, and then look back at them, shaking my head. "What the fuck is this? Twenty bucks?"

"Twenty-four," Mac corrects me.

"That's all you fuckers got?"

Mac shrugs. "We're college students."

I chuckle as I pull my wallet out and add two twenties to the pile. Returning my wallet, I look back toward Hank.

"I've been told you know why we're here?" I ask, not so much a question as it is a statement.

Hank nods.

I hand over the wad of cash, and after momentarily eyeing my hand with confusion, Hank snatches the bills from me and stuffs them into his pocket.

"I don't like any of this. It feels exploitative as fuck, but if we have to do it, I wanna make it worth your while," I say, rifling through one of the bags and pulling out a package of underwear, some t-shirts, and a bag of socks. "I'd like to trade you all of these for your underpants. The ones you're wearin' right now. Would that be okay?"

Hank looks surprised and then nods.

"There's a bathroom inside. You can change in there once we're done here. Does that work?"

Hank nods again, grabbing the clothes from me and setting them to the side.

I pull a six-pack out of the other bag and set it down on the concrete in front of him, saying, "I'd like to share a beer with you as well, and I'll let you keep the rest for yourself. I hope Sierra Nevada is okay. I can't drink the watered-down shit most everyone seems to enjoy in this country."

Hank cackles. "Beer is beer," he reasons as I open a bottle and hand it over to him. I then slide my back down the side of the building, seating myself next to him and opening a beer of my own. I tilt it in Hank's direction.

"Cheers," I say, and he clinks his bottle against mine before we both tilt them back.

Lowering his bottle, Hank eyes the beer label and looks over at me with bewildered eyes as he smacks his lips. "Fuck, that's good!" he says, taking another big gulp.

"I know. A lot better than Bud, I'll tell you that much," I say, laughing. "I just have one more request, or two more, I guess, and then we'll leave you be. For your efforts" —I grab the bag that held the clothes and hand it over— "There are a few cans of SpaghettiOs and soup in here. There's soap, toothpaste, and a toothbrush in there, as well."

Hank takes the bag with his free hand, peeks inside for a moment, and then sets the bag on top of the clothes.

"What do you need?" Hank asks. "A picture, right? What else?"

I hesitate, pulling clippers and double-A batteries from the bag that was holding the six-pack. I remove both from their packaging and set them in my lap, tossing the trash to the side. My pledge brothers look at me with brows scrunched in confusion. I take a long pull from my beer, setting the bottle on the ground beside me and letting out a sigh of contentment.

"If it'd be alright with you, I'd like to shave your head. Into a mullet first, and then after we get a picture, I can shave the rest. Would that be okay?"

Hank nods. "Shit yeah, I could use a haircut. Do we gotta shave it all the way after though? It's cold as my ex-wife's heart out here."

I laugh. "You alright keepin' the mullet?"

"Yeah, who the hell am I tryin' to impress?" he reasons.

"True. Well, much obliged, my friend. We appreciate you puttin' up with this shit."

"Don't even mention it. Other people ain't been so nice about it," he responds, taking a drink of his beer. He lets out a pleased sigh, adding, "Well, let's get 'er done, yeah?"

"Let's do it."

Once I shave Hank's hair into a mullet and take the selfie we need, I send him inside with his new clothes in hand. He brings the toothbrush, toothpaste, and soap with him.

"Mac," I say, as I pick up the loose hair and trash from the ground to toss in the garbage can. A smirk builds on my face. "Can you go in after him?"

"Sure, but why?"

After disposing of the hair and trash, I grab the empty bag from the ground and hand it over to him. I shake it vigorously for him to take.

He inspects it for a moment without moving, and then his

face goes white—even whiter than his already ghost-like complexion—as he realizes what I want him to do with the bag.

"Fucking hell, guys. Why does this fall on me?" he asks, a bit of a whine to his tone.

"You're the youngest one here, no?" I ask, an eyebrow quirked.

Mac huffs.

"Twenty here," Jeremy says, raising a hand. "Twenty-one in six months."

"I'm nineteen," Carter adds, his head rolling over toward Mac who just pouts.

I look at Mac, too, and though I already know his answer, with a smile I ask, "Well, how about you, Red?

"Eighteen, whatever. I'll do it, fuckers," he says. Snatching the bag from me, he adds, "If I catch something, though, I'm spreading it to you ass-cancers."

"Can't catch something you already have," Carter jests as Mac makes his way inside, holding up a middle finger with his free hand as the automatic doors close behind him.

A few moments later, with bagged dirty underwear pinched between two fingers and as far from his body as his arm will allow, Mac makes his way outside. A much-cleaner looking Hank comes out a few moments after him. Mac tosses the tied bag at my feet and crosses his arms with a frown on his face that just gets a laugh out of the rest of us.

Hank plops down where he sat before, picking his beer back up and lifting it toward me. "Well, thanks, fellas."

"Thank you, Hank. I'll see you around, huh?" I say, motioning for Mac to unlock my Jeep as I retrieve the bag from the ground.

"You know where to find me," Hank says with a wink, and I pass him a two-finger salute, making my way toward the Jeep with the others.

As we climb inside and shut the doors behind us, Mac says, "Smart thinking, killing two birds with one stone."

"Fuckin' brilliance," Jeremy adds.

"Work smarter, not harder, gentlemen. The Army taught me that," I say, smiling, then I fling the bagged underwear toward Mac in the driver's seat.

"Fuck, man!" Mac screeches, batting the bag away like a cat attacking a stringed toy. "This is some messed up shit." His voice cracks as he backs away from the bag even more. "I get driving duties *and* dirty underwear duty? That's not fucking cool!"

"Life's not fair, my friend," I joke. "I was eighteen in the Army once, remember. Shit rolls downhill. That's just how it is. *But*" —I pick the bag back up as Mac cowers away from it— "you make a good point." I throw the bag back toward Carter. "Since he's driving, Carter, you're next in line for underwear duty."

Carter tosses the bag behind the back seat and shrugs. "I promise not to cry like Mac did."

"I'm not crying. There's just something in both my eyes." Mac wipes his eyes, then laughs, pulling the Wrangler out of the parking spot. "Where to next, Prez?" he asks me.

"McDonald's," I respond, garnering questioning glances from my pledge brothers, but I simply point toward the golden arches a short distance down the road.

Pulling up the road and into the lot, Mac parks the Jeep, and then I glance back at the others. "Alright, guys, this is gonna be more of the same. I wanna knock multiple items out at once. It's gonna be pretty fucked up though, unless we can do it right," I say, lighting up a cigarette and taking a drag, cracking my window just a bit. "I don't wanna go ruining any McDonald's employee's night, and definitely don't want to get caught up with the cops over a fuckin' hamburger."

"So, what is it we're actually doing?" Carter asks.

"Mac, you're gonna record." I look out the windshield and through the plate glass windows that cover the front of the McDonald's. "I'll distract the one on the left there. Gonna offer her twenty bucks for her name tag. Carter, you and Jeremy will be waitin' in line, like normal customers. When I clear my throat, I want you two to start pretend fightin'. Make it as realistic as possible, though. I want them freaking the fuck out. During the commotion, I'll sneak in and grab one of those burgers from the warming tray. Then we get our asses on out."

"Sounds easy enough," Carter says, his tone dipped in sarcasm.

"You got any better ideas?" I ask, and he shrugs.

"I got nothing," he responds. "Better than dining and dashing like I was thinking. But why do we need to distract them? Can't we just take it?"

"I'd rather not be seen doin' it if I'm able to. No way to do that if those employees are standin' right there."

Carter nods. "Alright, then. Let's do it."

I lead them out of the Jeep, tossing my cigarette into the ashtray beside the door before making my way inside.

After chatting with one of the employees for a moment, I watch Jeremy and Carter come through the doors and get in line from the corner of my eye. I turn back fully for a brief moment and see Mac follow in after them, walking right to an empty table and taking a seat. He pulls the phone out of his pocket when I turn back toward the employee.

"So, twenty bucks will do it?"

She nods her head. "No sweat off my back. Only costs me five to replace." She removes the tag from her uniform top and hands it over.

I swap her with the twenty and pocket the name tag.

"Much obliged," I say, clearing my throat loudly. "Thanks, Alesha."

"No problem, darlin'." She smiles, and I smile back before my eyes flit over to my buddies in line. Alesha looks too.

Carter eyes the menu board, pretending to figure out what he wants to order when Jeremy groans, "Fuckin' hell, boy. Could you take any fuckin' longer to make up your goddamn mind? Are you havin' reading problems up there or somethin'? I'm fuckin' starving!"

Carter looks back, fighting a smile from forming. "Screw you, redneck," he snarls. "Go fuck your sister or something."

"That's old damn news, kid. I'm too busy fuckin' yours these days," Jeremy grunts.

Carter's jaw drops, and he responds with a stiff push, shouting, "My sister would never touch an inbred like you!" His lips quiver, the laughter desperate to escape. "She's got standards, you hillbilly."

Jeremy shoves Carter back against the counter. "If, by standards, you mean my sweaty balls in her eager fuckin' mouth, then yeah, I guess she's got them in spades."

"Can y'all please settle down?" Alesha asks, letting out a heavy sigh.

It's too late.

Carter charges forward, tackling Jeremy to the ground, and begins punching him in the side. They look like real punches, and hell, maybe they are.

"Eat my dick, Deliverance! I will *fuck your soul*!" Carter yells, and the two employees meet them on the other side of the counter, trying their best to break it up with interjecting hands. A few other employees from the back crane their necks to catch the action as I glance back toward Mac. He's getting the whole thing on video while laughing his ass off.

I turn and slink through the opening in the counter, the

cook's eyes moving toward me as I grab a Big Mac from the food warmer. He shrugs, and I shrug too as I nonchalantly walk with it back to the other side. Mac is upright now, camera held high, and I abruptly toss the Big Mac toward him. Surprised by the throw, Mac stumbles a bit as he barely catches the box. Once he recovers, he runs toward the exit with it, carrying the phone in his other hand as he records his escape.

As he reaches the door, he looks back and holds the Big Mac box high above his head as if it's a title belt, all eyes on him now as he yells, "Attica, man! Attica, man!" There's a touch of crazy in his eyes, his hair splayed out in all directions, as he runs out the door, and it garners uproarious laughter from my gut.

Jeremy and Carter cease fighting, and they burst out in laughter too, separating from each other but remaining on the floor.

"Y'all got problems," one of the employees says, waving them off and making her way back around the counter with a huff.

Alesha follows her co-worker, muttering, "Damn frat boys."

I help the two of them up off the ground and lead them out the door, both of them still fighting fits of laughter.

"I said, *sneak* the burger out," I bark toward Mac when I spot him on the hood of my Jeep. He's halfway through the burger already. "And get your ass off my Wrangler."

"Sorry," he mutters, sliding on his rear until his feet meet the ground. "But that shit was hilarious. I couldn't help myself."

I motion toward the other two and then point toward Mac. "Isn't it quite the contradictory sight to see little Mac eatin' a Big Mac?" I chuckle.

Following a laugh of his own, Carter asks, "There were like three other employees back there who probably saw you take the burger anyway. And they had cameras. Was the fake fight even necessary?"

We climb into the vehicle, and I settle into the passenger seat as Mac starts the engine, and then I glance back at Carter and Jeremy with a mischievous smirk on my face. "Honestly ... I just wanted to see if y'all would do it."

"Worth every last beautiful second," Mac responds, chuckling as he pulls the Jeep away from the lot. "I didn't think your voice could even register above a whisper, Carter. What was it again? 'I will fuck your soul'?" Mac bursts out laughing. "Where the hell did *that* come from?"

Carter shrugs. "Have to stay in character," he responds as Mac navigates the Jeep back toward Main Street.

"Does that mean you're game for karaoke?" I ask.

Carter shakes his head adamantly. "Oh hell no. I'm no singer."

"I got this one, gents," Jeremy says. "I have the voice of a fuckin' angel."

"I figure we knock out the serenading to a stranger and karaoke in one shot. Sound good?" I ask, and Jeremy nods.

"Sounds damn good to me, man. Karaoke spot's just up here on your right." Jeremy points to a hole-in-the-wall bar off Main Street, with a 'Karaoke' sign flickering in bright neon red.

Jeremy wasn't lying about his voice. Not even close. He sings "Save a Horse (Ride a Cowboy)," which just so happens to be one of my most reviled songs. It's what I call 'bullshit country,' the kind made for money and not passion. But Jeremy's voice is velvety and alive, and before long, everyone in the place feels what I'm feeling—captivated. He serenades a girl Carter knows from back home and surprises us all when he caps off the performance with a quick dip of the beautiful stranger, his lips against hers, welcome and waiting.

One-upping me, Jeremy is able to knock out three tasks in one go. As we exit the karaoke spot and congregate on the sidewalk, I praise him. "That was some good shit, man. We're knocking them off like crazy. Let's keep it goin'." I take the list out of my pocket and flatten the crinkled paper out, examining it. "Alright, so we've got two more before the big one."

"And what's the big one?" Mac asks.

"Stealing another fraternity's letter," Carter and I respond in unison.

"That's not going to be easy, and if we get caught, be ready to either run or brawl," Carter adds.

"Yeah, that's what I was thinkin'," I say. "And I'm not much for running." I crack a smile, but Mac's features take up a new nervousness. "We've got two selfies to knock out before that. With a stripper and climbing Archie's Tower. Whatever the fuck that is."

"It's this radio tower at the north end of campus." Carter points off in the distance, but it's too dark to see anything. As he lowers his hand, seeming to realize how ineffective pointing is in the dark, he adds, "It's tall as hell."

"Who here can do heights?" I ask.

Uneasy looks cross their youthful faces.

"Not a fucking chance." Mac lets out a nervous chuckle.

"I ain't so good with 'em either," Jeremy says. "'Besides, I'd say I carried my own weight tonight already."

"That you did," I agree.

Carter shakes his head stiffly without a word.

"Didn't you jump out of airplanes or something in the Army?" Mac questions.

I let out a heavy sigh before relenting. "Yeah, but I at least had a fuckin' parachute," I say, laughing. "No worries. I'll take care of it. But it's gonna take some time to get up there, so I think it's best if we split up for these next two. Carter, you come with me to the tower, so you can let someone know if I fall to my death. I really don't want to end my existence on this earth as bear shit. Mac, Jeremy, you guys go get a selfie with a stripper. Tough job you got there." I smirk.

"Harder than ya think," Jeremy says, grinning. "Crescent Falls strippers are fuckin' succubae, man. And we're fresh out of cash."

I chuckle as I gesture toward Mac for the keys with gimme fingers. "Improvise." I laugh, winking. "And remember to protect the boys. Stilettos are fuckin' deadly."

"You alright to drive?" Mac asks, handing over the keys.

I snatch them from his hand, rolling my eyes. "It's my fuckin' car, bitch. And I wasn't born yesterday. Two shots and a drink are like child's play in my world."

Mac shrugs, taking a step back and putting his hands up. "Alright, alright," he says.

"Just get your selfie done and we'll meet up after, alright?" I ask with no intent on waiting for responses. I head toward the Jeep and Carter follows suit. "Text me when y'all are finished," I add over my shoulder, climbing into the vehicle, Carter close behind.

After a few minutes on the road, I turn to Carter and ask, "So how tall we talkin' here?"

"A hundred feet. Maybe more."

"Fuck me runnin'. All this shit better be worth it, goddammit."

"What are you even doing rushing a fraternity anyway? You know there's going to be a lot of bullshit you have to go through. They're not going to fuck with you too much or anything, at least I don't think so, but you're going to have to do some really stupid shit."

I shrug. "You spend enough time alone with the kind of thoughts I got, and a little bullshit starts lookin' quite alright."

"I can only imagine." Carter's focus shifts to the dash, wrinkles of uncertainty taking up his forehead. I wonder just how much this kid holds on to. By the looks of it, he's got the whole damn world on his shoulders sometimes. "It's up here on the right," Carter says, pointing toward a clearing in the pines. He ducks his head a little to get a better view of the tower through the windshield.

I take the turn and slow the vehicle, also dipping my head to try and get a glance at it but to no avail. After a few moments, I finally spot the steel gargantuan jutting into the pitch-black sky, so far up that I can't see the top through the clouds. I let out a heavy breath as I slow the vehicle to a stop, and then I glance over at Carter as if there's a leg sprouting from his forehead.

"People really do this fuckin' shit?"

"Yeah, they have for decades, my man. My dad did it with his pledge brothers. And his father, my grandfather, did it before him. It's something of a DIK tradition."

"I keep hearin' about these fuckin' traditions tonight, man," I say, shaking my head as I swing my door open. "At some point, logic has to win out."

"It's just a part of the process, Bishop."

"Do you wanna do it?" I ask rhetorically with an eyebrow quirked.

Carter's face goes white. He gives his head a quick shake. "Nah, I'd rather not."

"Alright, so just let me bitch then. I didn't say I'm not gonna do it. I'm just sayin', somebody, at some point, has to scratch their head and say, 'Hey, maybe this isn't the smartest move here, havin' eighteen, nineteen-year-old kids climbing fuckin' radio towers.'" I chuckle, heading out into the icy air. The smell of pine and frosty dew surrounds me. It's so cold I can see my breath.

"I guess it's a good thing we've got a veteran to do it for us then, huh?" Carter jokes, hopping out of the Jeep as well, shutting the door behind him. His gaze shifts toward the clouds that surround the tip of the tower like a bonnet. "Fuck," he mutters.

As I grab a pair of combat gloves from my center console and slip them on, I ask, "Yeah, 'fuck' is about right." I shake my head, taking a few deep breaths as my eyes trail slowly up and down the frosted metal monstrosity. "Why do they call it Archie's Tower anyway?"

Stepping up to the base, I put my hands against the thick steel—cold even through the gloves—before looking back at Carter, who hasn't answered me yet.

"Well?"

"This kid named Archie Dugan, back in the sixties or seventies, or something like that ..." Carter's voice trails off, his eyes traveling from the base of the tower to the very top again before looking back over at me. "He ended up falling from the top of that thing, trying to take a polaroid. Died from it."

"You have got be fuckin' kidding me." I shake my head, heaving myself up onto the first rung, my heart pitter-pattering in my chest, I look down at him with unease.

"It's only a tall tale. Nobody knows if it's actually true or not," Carter assures me.

I pass him a nervous smile. "Well, if I fall, I'm headin' straight for your fuckin' head. Don't say I didn't warn you." I laugh before starting my reckless ascent.

Halfway up, I think my heart might just burst from my chest. I don't bother to look down, as I know it'll likely make me sick and freeze me right where I'm at. I've never been good with heights; airborne training was the worst, but that's exactly why I did it. I get off on those things that terrify me the most. Unfortunately, in this instance, I find that, without a safety harness or parachute, my fear is taking much of the satisfaction I'd usually get from a situation such as this. The air is also frigid, my face numbing by the second, my muscles trembling in an attempt to warm them.

Breathing slow, steady breaths, I continue up one rung after another, until I'm nearly at the top, the frigid air around me sending shivers down my spine. There's a churn in my gut as I imagine slipping on one of the last few steps I have left and falling mercilessly toward the frozen, unforgiving ground.

I shake away the thoughts and push on, one slow, steady step at a time as I sing 'The Crimson' by Atreyu loudly to busy my mind. Eventually, I'm at the top and amongst the clouds. Taking a deep breath, I pull myself tightly into the steel beam, locking it into the crook of my elbow, no space between me and the metal. I pull my phone out of my pocket with my free hand, and as I hold it up to take the selfie, I can see the speckled lights of downtown Crescent Falls off in the distance behind me on the screen. A smattering of twinkling stars is set behind it.

"Are you alright up there?" Carter calls out, his voice distant, echoing, nearly inaudible.

I lift a half-assed middle finger on the hand belonging to the arm that grips the beam and snap the selfie, shoving the phone back into my pocket quickly and then grabbing the beam more securely with both hands. For the first time, I look down, and I'm hit with cold sweats instantly. My stomach is set to tumble dry. My heart drums like a Neil Peart solo.

"Havin' the time of my fuckin' life!" I yell down through clenched teeth, dizziness forcing me to bring my eyes back to the horizon. I shut them, taking steady breaths.

What in the ever-lovin' fuck am I doin' up here?

I slowly start my descent, which is far worse than coming up the tower, as I must blindly search for the rungs with my feet.

The last thought that crosses my mind, as my foot slips, is how fucking stupid I must be to be in this position. I don't have long to ruminate over it, though, as the weight of my lower body jerks me down with great force. The breath lurches from my lungs as I squeeze the steel beam with everything I have, envisioning my hands slipping off the frosted metal. As I try and position my dangling feet on the next rung down, I feel the strength in my arms giving way. My mind runs through options and outcomes, my heart racing with every hair-raising second.

Complete and utter *panic* sets in.

SIX

"**F**uck! Bishop, you okay?" Carter calls out.

I take a deep breath, my feet finally meeting the rungs and settling, my arms still wrapped tight around the beam.

"I think I may have just shit myself," I yell back to him, waiting for my heart to stop thrashing in my chest before I continue my descent.

"I thought you were falling, man. Shit. I thought that was it. I was down here ready to catch you, though."

I inch my way down, slower this time, and I reply, "You know that would've just killed you too, right?"

"What?" he yells out in response.

"Hold on a damn second! I'm trying not to die here," I grumble, continuing slowly for a few moments before I eventually come within non-lethal falling range. A few more feet and I'll be back on solid ground.

"If you tried to catch me fallin', you would've died too. That's what I was trying to say," I repeat, hopping off the last rung and breathing out a heavy sigh, never being so happy to feel the ground beneath my feet.

Carter shrugs. "Well, good thing you didn't fall then."

"Yeah, good thing," I say, chuckling and then letting out a heavy breath as my heartbeat steadies.

"HOLY FUCKING BALL SACK, that's crazy, dude," Mac says, eyeing the selfie I took not twenty minutes ago from the top of Archie's Tower. Even after making the trip back to the frat house, a surge of adrenaline still courses through my veins.

Mac and Jeremy had their own story, of course, and they'd told me and Carter all about it the moment we met up as I was still trying to snuff out the steady waves of anxiety the tower climb had brought on. The party rages inside already, the beats from the subs pouring through the side door sound much like my heart when I clung to the top of that tower.

Mac's selfie, by all accounts, is no selfie at all, as just a speck of the topless stripper can be seen at the very top corner of the dark photo.

"I'd say a hell of a lot better than your 'selfie,'" I jest, throwing up air quotes as I lean my back against the Wrangler with a wide grin. "You know you're gonna get an earful for that." I slip a hand into my pocket and dig out my pack of cigarettes.

I pull a cig from the pack and slip it between my lips as Jeremy reasons, "We were out of options." He shrugs. "Them ladies weren't messin' around. Smelled us comin' from a mile away."

"Obviously," I tease, nodding toward Mac's phone as he pockets it. "I would've laughed if you left the flash on or somethin' and she caught y'all."

Jeremy laughs as a look of shame falls on Mac's face.

"Tell me she did. Please, tell me she did." I put my hands together in mock-prayer.

"She chased our asses out of there with her fuckin' high-heel," Jeremy grunts, laughing loudly. "And we're fuckin' blinded still by fuckhead's flash."

"No fuckin' way! That's amazing!" I howl.

"You bet your ass it happened," Jeremy responds, two hands to his gut as he doubles over. "She nearly caught the little fucker too." He points toward Mac who flashes him a look of detest.

I rest a hand on Mac's shoulder and say, "I'm glad you survived to tell the story, my friend."

He scoffs, his eyes wide. "You're telling me. I was scared for my life. It wasn't only the stripper, it was the bouncers, too. And those WWE wrestling, quarterback-sacking bastards could've eaten me whole if they caught me."

Jeremy laughs harder now. "Y'all, I can't even paint this picture for you. It had to be seen in person, and goddamn, I'm sure glad I was able to see it with my own eyes." He points toward Mac. "This motherfucker turned ghost white. Fuckin' hightailed it out of there like his ass was on fire."

"Not like you helped any, you fucking scrotum." Mac narrows his eyes at Jeremy. "Fucker bounced before I even took the picture."

"I couldn't fuckin' see, man!"

Our laughter fills the night air now, loud and boisterous, broken up after a few moments by a high-pitched whistle. We look back and find Damian coming up the road with a six-pack in one hand, and his thumb and pointer retreating from his pouted lips.

"What the fuck you guys doing out here?" he barks. "Don't you got shit to do?"

"We've only got one more thing left to do," I respond, taking a drag of my cigarette as Damian closes the distance between us and analyzes me.

"Well, that was fast. Let me guess which one you got left ...

Archie's Tower?" he asks, more like a statement, followed by a hearty chuckle.

"Nope, Bish did that already," Mac says, a look of unearned pride on his face.

Damian's laughter stops abruptly. His eyes dart to mine and he passes me a doubtful look. "Fuck you. No, he didn't," he says, looking at me but seemingly speaking to Mac.

"He sure as shit did," Mac responds, motioning to my pocket. "Show him, dude."

"Yeah, show me," Damian agrees, a smug look taking up his features.

I pull out my phone, locating my photo album first, and then the tower selfie, before handing the phone off to Damian.

He takes it, looking closer for a moment, his eyes going wide. "No fucking way," he mutters, looking closer. He stares intently and then turns and motions for us to follow him as he announces, "Trevor isn't gonna fucking believe this shit."

He opens the side door, and dance music and lights come pouring out from inside. We follow in after him as he maneuvers his way through the crowd to the couches in the middle. Each of our heads is on a swivel. There are probably a couple hundred people in the basement at the moment, scattered throughout the large room in co-ed clusters. Women outnumber the men three to one, and all the other men have letters on their chest but us.

"Yo, pledges," Damian says, whistling again with his fingers to his lips, and then motioning for us to hurry up with the same hand.

As we approach, Trevor and Brady stand from the couch, both gawking at my phone with sunken, drunk eyes. Their focus eventually flits back up to me with pinched brows.

"You really fucking did it?" Trevor asks.

I nod slowly. "Uhhhh, yeah?" I look from one to the other. "Weren't we supposed to?"

Brady drunkenly sways a bit as he shakes his head. "Duuu-ude," he says, dragging it out like he's fucking Cheech. "Nobody's done that in, like, twenty years or something."

"Twenty-one," Trevor corrects him. "Stuart Middleton back in '89."

I can't believe my fucking ears. Trevor must read my agitation because he puts a hand on my shoulder and smiles like he's about to try and sell me something. Unless it's an explanation, I'm not fucking buying.

"You are a man amongst men, Bishop," he schmoozes. I don't like his hand on me, nor any man's hand for that matter, but I ignore the urge to brush it off. I know he isn't trying to belittle, but to soften the blow of the inevitable answer to the question I'm about to ask.

"So why's it on the list if we're not supposed to do it?"

Trevor shrugs, a timid smile peeking out. He removes his hand and exhales hard. "It's always been on the list. It just hasn't always been done. Most just make up some excuse as to why they don't have the picture—accidentally deleted it, phone broke on the way, too many cops patrolling—that kind of bullshit. Some will just fess up and admit they didn't have the stones to do it."

"So, you guys never did it?"

The looks on their faces answer for them. "No way, man," Trevor says. "Stuart Middleton was the last."

Brady shakes his head stiffly, plopping back down on the couch and snagging his beer from the ground.

"Sarge didn't do it either?" I ask.

Trevor shakes his head. "His grandma died right when we were doing bids. He wasn't around for the scavenger hunt. No doubt he would have though. He was pissed he had to miss it, despite the reasoning."

"Well, fuck me," I say, glancing back toward the bar. "I think I'm due a fuckin' beer, don't you?"

Trevor nods, his eyes wide as he pats me on the back. "Hell yeah, you are. All you guys are free to party. Minors ..." He glances over my shoulder at my pledge brothers. "Don't be fucking stupid. Drink sensibly, and if you get caught by the cops after you leave this motherfucker, you didn't leave *this* mother-fucker. Got it?"

They all must nod because his facial features change from questioning back to their state of—what is it ... admiration? Infatuation? I can't tell what it is in Trevor's eyes, but something about it feels off, saccharine to sugar. Generic to name brand.

"Don't worry about the other fraternity's letter." He chuck-les, shaking his head in disbelief. "You earned that shit."

Mac takes a step forward with his phone outstretched. "Pretty good videos on here, too," he says, winking as Trevor snatches it from him.

I turn, setting a hand on Carter and Jeremy's shoulders and rotating them so that they're facing the bar before nudging them forward.

"Yo, fuckers, wait for me," Mac calls out from behind us.

As he catches up to us, I say, "Well, gentlemen, let's get good and fucked up, huh?"

AFTER PLENTY of beers and conversation between the four of us, the others have left me to the couch to veg out with my last beer of the night before I take my old ass home, while they spend the night trying to pick up girls and likely striking out.

Except for Jeremy. That pretty motherfucker can probably pull some ass.

Three girls—one of which I've noticed glancing at me more than a few times over the past few minutes—who have been loitering by the TV, begin their approach, and the hottest one (the one who has been peeping at me) catches my attention and smiles, motioning toward the couch.

"Mind if we sit?" she asks.

Words, damn you! Words! Ignore the lump in your throat. Ignore the fact that she's possibly the hottest woman you've ever seen.

Fuck!

"Y-Yeah, of course." I quickly slide down, bringing my beer with me and splashing a little bit on my lap. My face feels like it's been scorched by a blowtorch. I try not to look at her. Maybe if I don't see her, she can't see me.

Yeah, that's it.

I sip from the red solo cup nervously as the three of them squeeze in next to me. I close my eyes, breathing in deep as a sudden wave of anxiety pours over me. I realize I'm out of my element here, nowhere near drunk enough, and with no one close enough to come in and share the burden of any possible social interactions.

Then again, a seat may be her only objective.

Of course, it is, you idiot! What, do you think you're special? Did you see her eyes? That body? Girls like her don't fuck with rough-looking dudes like you.

"Tired?" Her voice startles me.

Turning and getting a closer look, I see she can't be over eighteen. Her eyes are bloodshot and baggy, and her face slack, as if she's had a few too many already, though it does little to take away from her undeniable beauty. Her sleek, jet-black hair falls straight as a wire to her petite shoulders, bangs meeting a set of dazzling emerald eyes. Her skin is flawless, tanned. She looks Middle Eastern ... maybe Islander.

She crosses one tight-jeaned leg over the other, her Converse hovering near my own leg as she quirks an eyebrow.

"Gettin' there," I say with a polite smile.

Genius. Pure. Fucking. Genius.

"You're the Army guy, right?" she asks, and the fact that she knows even that is surprising.

"How'd you know?"

"There's a lot of talk about you around here."

"Within the fraternity?" I briefly scan the area around us for no one in particular.

She nods. "And the school," she responds.

"What do you mean, the school?"

"Buchanan State. The school you go to, smart guy." She laughs and bats a playful hand against my arm.

"Sorry, I guess I'm just confused why anyone at this school would be talkin' about me. Let alone, a lot of them."

"It's not bad stuff," she says, inching closer and trying to take a drink from her empty cup. She eyes the cup, confused, and then looks back toward me. "Just stuff."

"What kind of stuff?"

"Badass stuff," she says, a smile tugging at the corner of her lips.

"Well, I'm no badass."

"You got blown up, right? And like, fought bad guys overseas and shit?"

"Yeah." I nod, wishing I had left earlier, not because I don't enjoy her company, or feel grateful to even converse with a girl this beautiful, but because I *always* fuck shit like this up.

"Then okay, you're the badass they're talking about."

I shake my head, letting out an uncomfortable chuckle. "So, what is it they're talkin' about ... besides my time overseas?"

"The guys are just worried about you," she responds, taking the tiny red straw from her drink and chewing on it.

"The Delta Iota guys?"

She nods.

"Why? What's there to be nervous about?"

She leans in. "Do you know how serious these frat guys take this stupid pledging shit?" she asks, the rum on her breath wafting toward me, not unpleasant, just prominent. Subtle hints of spearmint trail it.

"I've got a pretty good idea."

"Yeah, well, think about this thing they love doing—fucking with young impressionable kids—and then having someone like you come along. They know they can't control you like they do the younger guys. But they want you in the frat because you make them look good. They're just worried about you retaliating in some way, messing with their fun."

"I'm not here to fuck with anything, but I've already told them I won't be messed with either." I shrug. "So, we'll see, I guess."

"And they probably *won't* fuck with you. But they'll see how much they can fuck with the other guys until it gets to you."

"I don't really know what to say here."

"I'm not trying to scare you," she says, sitting back and attempting to drink from her cup again before realizing that it's still empty. She pouts.

"Oh, I'm not scared. I just prefer to take things one day at a time and not worry about what might be comin' down the road. I'll give them the benefit of the doubt, for now."

"They like you," she says as if she didn't hear a word I said. Her eyes linger on the military tattoos that comprise a sleeve on my right arm.

"They don't even know me. And how do you know so much anyway?"

"I'm friends with most of the guys. Went to high school with Zach and Brady back in New York. Brady and I fucked for a few months last semester too."

Her candor both shocks me and turns me on a little. My cock stirs from simply the way the word fuck rolls off her tongue.

"You and Brady?" I raise an eyebrow. "How old are you?"

"Twenty."

"Fuck, you look young. I would've guessed not a day over eighteen."

She puts a hand to her chest. "Why, thank you, sir."

"How long have you been hangin' out with these guys for?"

"Too long," she says, laughing. "I was best friends with this guy Eric Danner's little brother, Alex. Alex and I went to school with Brady and Zane. Eric was a DIK brother who graduated last year, so by the time those two got bids, I had already been hanging out here with Eric and Alex for a few years."

"What were you then, like, seventeen?"

"Fifteen, sixteen, something like that. That's how it works out here in the country."

I shake my head. "Crazy."

"What? You didn't party in high school?"

I stifle the laugh that wants to come at the thought of some innocent, well-mannered alternate version of my high school self. You Google 'juvenile delinquency' and I'm the first fucking thing that pops up.

"Well, yeah." I chuckle. "I partied a bit too much back then, but with other high schoolers. Never a frat party. Not judgin' or anything. Hey, do what you do, you know? I'm just surprised your father didn't kill one of these fuckers."

She leans in, an eyebrow quirked, and purrs, "What daddy doesn't know …" before bursting out in laughter.

I laugh too, but only in solidarity. I'm too busy admiring the way her neck moves when she laughs. The way her eyes light up. The hints of promiscuity in her brow arches.

And then the *daddy* rings … the word which brings feelings of upchuck while simultaneously turning me on. I *hate* that word.

And love it.

I guess it all depends on whose mouth it's coming from … and when.

"I could never be a parent." I shake my head, finishing off my beer and setting the solo cup at my feet.

"Don't you worry about me, Army man. I'm a real, live, grown ass woman. I take care of myself just fine."

"I have no doubt about that. No doubt at all. And the name's Bishop." I grin.

"Well, Bishop, I'm Ember, but you can just call me your dirty little whore," she says, pausing for a moment before she bursts out into another adorable fit of laughter, pointing her finger wildly at my face. "I'm sorry, *so* kidding. I just had to see that face."

I touch my cheeks, asking, "What face?" though I know I'm flush. It feels like my skin is burning.

"The one where you look like you've both seen a ghost *and* seen me naked at the same time. Like your brain's trying to determine whether to run away from me or throw me down and fuck me."

"Holy shit," I mutter, trying to understand if I'm hearing this girl correctly, this sweet, innocent-looking girl (though she surely carries a rocker mystique that drives me wild) throwing around F-bombs like she belongs in a Humvee with me back in Iraq.

"What?" she asks defensively.

"I like the way you talk." It didn't sound as stupid in my head as it did coming out of my mouth.

"Well, country boy, I like the way you talk too, but I don't believe I have an accent."

"Neither do I." I laugh. "There's a little New York in yours," I say. "Just a touch. But I meant I like the way you speak freely. Word vomit and such."

She laughs, nodding her head. "That's me."

"Can I ask you a serious question?" I can feel the liquor and beer I've consumed tonight loosening me up a little. *Finally.* There's a comfortable warmth that trails my limbs, a light airiness in my head, a freedom to my words I don't often find when sober and meeting women. Or anyone, for that matter.

"Ask away, Army man."

"Bishop."

"Ask away, Army Bishop."

"No, just Bishop."

"Ask away, Just Bishop." She chuckles.

"Never mind. I think you just answered my question."

She leans forward, grabbing my arm, and she says, "No, I'm sorry. I was just messing with you. Can you please ask?" She pouts, and God does it send a jolt of pleasure to my cock while simultaneously melting my heart. Funny how that works.

I hesitate for a moment and then ask, "Why Brady?"

She looks up in thought, eventually shrugging, and simply responds, "He's hot as fuck."

"Oh Lord," I say, rolling my eyes and shaking my head.

"What? So much judgment in your tone," she scolds. "Like you've never just fucked someone because you found them sexy and they wanted you back."

I shrug, nodding. "Well, yeah ..."

"Well, yeah, so what's the difference, Army man?"

"There is none."

She gasps, pointing her finger at me, the other hand covering her mouth. "You're jealous!"

"No, I'm not."

"Yes, you are."

"No, ma'am."

"Yes, sir. I mean, if you aren't jealous, then you're a misogynist. So, which one is it?"

I narrow my eyes at her. "I'm not jealous of any man. And I'm no misogynist. Not even close."

"It has to be one of them," she argues.

I wave her off, eyeing the watch on my wrist for a brief moment.

She leans forward, exposing more cleavage, and she locks her eyes on mine. "I think you're jealous," she says, flashing a wicked little smile.

She knows what she's doing, and as much as I try and convince myself her seduction isn't working, I know I'm only kidding myself. My pulsating dick tells me so.

"I'm jealous of no man," I repeat, maintaining my composure and turning my focus to a basketball game playing on the big screen TV.

"Do you not find me attractive?" she asks, sitting back against the couch.

I look at her with a wrinkled brow and curled lips. "You're crazy. And I would *have* to be to not find you attractive."

"Oh, really now?"

I soften my features and take a thick swallow. "You know you're gorgeous. Ray Charles could see that."

She licks her lips subtly. "Why won't you kiss me then?" she asks and bats her eyelashes.

"You were with Brady, for one." I scan the area around us, trying to find him through the heaps of people, a drunken disorder starting to sweep its way through them. I don't see Brady anywhere, but wonder if he's noticed who I've been talking to.

When I look back at her, I see she's inched closer, which I didn't think was possible on this crowded couch, her empty cup clenched between her thighs and her manicured nails tapping the rim.

"He doesn't care," she says softly.

"Every man cares. I don't give a shit who they are, or what they say. That's just not a good way to operate. No real man I know would be cool with seein' that. Especially from the new guy. *Especially* from a pledge."

She shrugs, her eyes lingering on the side door to our right. "We don't have to stay here."

"Ember, you're drunk."

"So? Aren't you, too?"

"Not like you are," I respond. "If you still want to kiss me when you're sober ... that's a different story."

"Or, like, we could just kiss right here, right now," she blurts, lifting her palms. "Or somewhere else." She motions toward the back door.

I check my watch again—*one a.m.*

She sighs heavily, and it draws my eyes to hers. She lifts the cup from her lap and scoots away from me a bit, pretending to insert herself in her friends' conversation next to her.

Standing, I catch her attention. I bend down, my mouth meeting her ear, and in a low voice, I say, "Offer stands. If you still wanna kiss me tomorrow, you know where I'll be."

Before she can respond, I trail my mouth to her cheek, kissing it and then pecking her lips, just slightly, but purposefully.

Standing straight, I smile and say, "Later, Ember. Hope to see you tomorrow."

She doesn't say anything in response, the pout still on her face, but her eyes do speak—a subtle glimmer of desire and intrigue.

Nodding, I turn and make my way around the room to find my pledge brothers and let them know the party is over for my old ass. A terrible spin has taken up my brain, and it's time I head home and put my head on the cloud-like Tempurpedic pillow waiting back home to take me to Slumbertown.

SEVEN

W e're linked up in the basement for the fifth night in a row, or is it the sixth? Maybe it's the fourth. I can't even recall. It's not that what's required of us is very difficult. We're usually lined up for a half hour or so before we have study sessions, for both school work and fraternity knowledge, and a few cleaning assignments around the house. It's really the inferiority I feel that fucks with me the most. Tonight, we have another pledge challenge, and after nearly falling to my death on the last one, I'm just a smidge apprehensive about things. But I'm not sure what's been worse —slipping on Archie's Tower or having to clean up after these slobs. I think I'd rather take the tower again. Or just quit. That's always an option.

After all, I've done all this shit before, back when I wore an Army uniform ... and that's the real problem. I've mowed massive lawns, cleaned toilets, and picked up trash in the same uniform I fought and bled in like I was some GI fucking janitor. It didn't make sense to me then, but it didn't matter. I did it out of service to my country; a sense of duty. I was taking orders from men who had served longer and seen a hell of a lot more than me. At that time, I was just a punk kid from backcountry, Florida, desperate for a purpose. If they wanted me to clean, I cleaned. If they wanted me to sweat, I sweat. If they wanted me to bleed, I bled. And I did all three in spades.

Now, it just feels like I'm cleaning the unclean-able for no real purpose. What is cleaned one day is dirty the next, time and time again, and I don't know how it happens so frequently other than it being purposeful. And the study sessions; well, it's hard enough for me to focus on all the boring gen. ed. courses that I hate more and more with every passing second ... tick tock ... of every passing minute ... tick tock ... of every passing day I spend in those classrooms, listening to an unsatisfied over-the-hill professor yammering on about politics more than he does college Algebra. And then I worry that I won't know what the hell I'm doing by test time. And *then* I worry about worrying so much about Algebra in the first place when I know I'll never fucking use this shit again.

Fuck Algebra.

It's not that I don't appreciate the time I've spent with the guys I'm linked up with. Much to my surprise, they're good kids, with good heads on their shoulders. Even at their young age, they're deeper than most. This university is full of the rich and entitled. They mock the professors, talk, or play on their phones from the backs of classrooms, forgetting, or simply not caring that their parents are forking over ten thousand a year for them to learn in those very classrooms. They rev up their engines as they cruise around the quad, over and over again, as if with each lap their dicks grow longer. They mouth off at the bars and clubs downtown, undeterred by superior size, strength, or experience.

In my pledge brothers, I haven't seen a hint of that unrelenting narcissism and deluded ego that seems to run abound here in Crescent Falls. Even Mac, with his manic personality and tendency to whine, has grown on me. I care about these guys and they care about me. And it's about the only thing keeping me linked up and standing on my tired feet in this musty fraternity basement.

"Does anyone know what the hell's going on tonight?" Mac asks, sighing heavily and looking down the line toward me. "How long do we have to just stand here?"

I shrug. "Until they come and get us."

"For Chrissake, Mac. We're all standin' here, just the same as you. We know as much as you do," Jeremy complains.

"I just don't get why they'd have us come this early if they weren't ready for us. And if they're not ready for us, why the fuck do we have to stay linked up like this? It's been what, an hour and a half?"

"It's a part of the process," Carter says.

"But *why*?"

"Mac, your whinin ain't gonna change a goddamn thing," Jeremy scolds, shaking his head.

"Well, fuck me, Jeremy. I'm just curious. You may not mind standing around twiddling your thumbs like a fucking idiot, but I do."

I finally shift my eyes to Mac, and in a patient tone, I say, "Mac, none of us want to be standin' here playing with our dicks right now. We're not supposed to like this shit. We're supposed to conform to it."

Mac lets out an annoyed groan, dropping his head. "I wish we could just have some alcohol or something, at the very least," he says.

Carter laughs, shaking his head slowly. "Careful what you wish for, buddy," he says with a chuckle.

Mac darts his eyes to Carter and asks, "What do you know?"

Carter shrugs. "I know you just need to relax, expect the

unexpected, and anticipate these next two months sucking ass for the most part."

"Is there really a point to all this? And why do we always have to do this shit on Thursday nights? They do know we've got classes tomorrow, right?" Mac groans.

I glance over at Mac, a smirk stretching across my face. "The point, dear Mac, is to separate the weak from the strong. Which are you, buddy?" I lift my eyebrows and shrug. "Think about it."

"Gentlemen ..." Trevor's voice interrupts us as he descends the basement stairs, drawing our attention. Brady and Zane are behind him, each of them carrying a bottle. Upon closer look, I read 'Old Crow' on the label and let out a quiet groan.

"Are you ready for your second pledge challenge, maggots?" Brady asks us, though he avoids eye contact with me.

Did he see me talkin' to Ember?

"Fuck yeah," the others respond loudly, in unison, but I don't. I just stare straight forward, thinking about a cigarette, its sweet, settling smoke filling my lungs.

Trevor puts up his hand, motioning for the other two officers to bring the bottles forward. "Tonight ... is Old Crow Night," he says with a grin. Zane and Brady hold the bottles out toward us.

"What's Old Crow?" Mac asks, examining the bottles with trepidation.

Before Trevor can answer, I respond, "The *worst* shit you'll *ever* drink in your entire fuckin' life."

"Prrretty much!" Trevor laughs. "You guys have to kill both bottles between the four of you before midnight." He motions toward us. "You guys can unlink and take them."

We free our arms, and I shake mine out to get the blood flowing. Mac takes one of the bottles and Jeremy takes the other.

"This bottle's plastic," Mac says, in awe as if he's never seen one like it before, his eyes wide and mouth agape.

"That's what you're focused on right now?" Carter asks, chuckling.

"I'm just saying ... what kind of alcohol comes in a plastic bottle?"

I laugh. "The *worst* fuckin' kind, man."

"And you get to drink it!" Trevor says with a big game show host thumbs up, as the other two take a step back.

"This isn't gonna be fun." I let out a heavy breath as I look to Trevor. "And probably not very safe."

"Nobody's ever died from it," Brady quips, a smug look on his face.

"Is that how we're gaugin' shit tonight? If we don't die, we win?" I joke.

"Just take your time," Trevor says, rolling his eyes at Brady. "You've got seven hours to finish. That's enough time to get drunk, puke, and rally, and then get drunk again."

"And then pass out and die," Carter mutters.

"We swear, if you die, we'll take full responsibility ..." Brady hesitates. "... in letting your parents know you broke in here and stole our liquor, drank it all, and killed yourself." He grins, and I realize it now, looking at his stupid face, how much I'd like to punch it.

"You guys'll be fine," Trevor says. "Tim will be down here in a few minutes to watch you and make sure everyone stays alive since he isn't going to the social with us. No cheating. And if you still have the capacity to walk after this, we'll be down at the Rusty Trombone with Kappa Phi." Trevor pats me on the back. "Have fun, gents. Feel free to pass out here tonight if you can't get home safely."

As Trevor and Brady make their way back up the stairs, Zane stays behind, waiting for them to disappear out the door before he motions for me to join him.

When I approach, he quietly says, "You be the judge when

one of them needs to be cut off. We really aren't trying to get anyone fucked up here. It's just part of the game. Tim isn't going to be watching you too closely, and everyone else will be at the social. Do enough to get drunk, and ..." He gestures his hands as if he's pouring something out. "Just find a way to make that shit disappear."

"I got you. Thanks, Zane."

"No problem," he says, patting my back and following the others up the stairs.

It's the most I've heard him say since the bid ceremony.

"Yo, Bishop, what'd he tell you?" Mac asks as he continues eyeing the unopened liter of gag-inducing whiskey in his hands.

"Nothin'. Just wants to make sure you don't die tonight, Mac."

Mac lowers the bottle, a confused look on his face. "Me, specifically?"

"Yeah."

"He must like me." I break out in laughter, and he looks at me in confusion. "What?"

"It's not that he likes you, he just knows what a liter of whiskey can do to your, uh, body type."

He puts his hands up. "What? *Fit?*"

"No. Emaciated."

Carter laughs loudly, and Jeremy nearly spits up the mouthful of whiskey he's just poured down his gullet, the first Old Crow drank tonight. As he fights back the laughter and swallows, his face tightens, his eyes close. and lips pinch together.

"Argggghhh." He sticks his tongue out, waving at it as spit runs from the tip of his mouth to the floor.

"That bad?" Mac asks, worry taking up his features.

Jeremy nods, his tongue still out, his eyes now open and

desperate. "Any chasers? Somethin'? Anythin'?" he forces out breathlessly.

"There has to be something in the fridge," Carter responds, heading that way to inspect.

"Oh, my fuckin' word, that was the worst fuckin' shit I've ever tasted," Jeremy says, scraping his tongue with his fingers.

"It's gonna be without chasers, I guess. There's nothing in the fridge or behind the bar," Carter says, making his way back over to us.

"You're kiddin' me." Jeremy groans.

Carter shakes his head solemnly.

"Sorry guys. You won't find anything to drink in there." Tim's deep voice pulls our attention to the set of stairs in the far corner that lead to the brothers' rooms, a cooler in his hand, and he's sporting a pink bathrobe.

"Why not?" Mac asks.

Tim walks past us, plopping down on the couch, and sets the cooler next to him. He turns on the TV, pulling a lever on the side of the couch. His combat-booted feet pop up with the leg rest, and I realize he's got nothing on below the belt except his boxers and the boots.

I turn and stifle a laugh. "Comfortable?" I ask as I face him again.

He smiles, his eyebrows dancing as he strokes his long scraggly beard with one hand and grabs a Coors from the cooler with his other. "My legs get hot," he reasons, taking a swig before he starts channel surfing.

"What about the boots?" Mac asks.

Tim lifts one to inspect it. "My feet get cold," he says, settling on a channel and tossing the remote beside him as he lowers his boot back to the footrest. He looks over at us and eyes the bottles in Jeremy and Mac's hands. "No chasers with your Old Crow, boys. You have to do it straight on OC night."

I motion for Jeremy to give me the bottle and he happily hands it over. "Why Old Crow?" I ask, taking a swig and feeling the harsh bite as it trails down my throat. I fight a grimace from taking up my face for no other reason than to show Jeremy up. On the inside, my mouth, throat, and stomach are on *fucking* fire.

"Tradition," Carter responds with a grin.

I laugh, taking another terrible swig and handing it off to Jeremy, who quickly passes it over to Carter.

"I hate tradition," I mutter, pulling the pack of cigarettes from my pocket. "I'm cool with not chasin' that dog piss with anything, but I need to at least smoke," I say to Tim as I motion toward the side door.

Tim glances toward the stairs, and then back at me. "Sure. No cheating though. If I hear the sound of splashing, I'm going to crack some skulls."

"I'm goin', too," Jeremy says, hacking a wad into the bar sink.

"Me three," Mac adds.

Tim looks over from the TV, annoyed. "I don't give a good goddamn who goes to smoke, just no cheating."

"Gotcha," I say, slipping a cigarette between my lips as I snatch the bottle from Mac's hands.

KILLING the last of the second bottle, half of which ended up in the grass adjacent to the parking lot, I toss it onto the couch and raise my hands in the air victoriously, long since drunk as fuck.

"Done, bitches!" I yell, lowering my arms and wobbling from the sudden movement. "Who's goin' downtown with me?" I continue, looking back toward Jeremy seated on the bar top, and then trailing my eyes to Carter and Mac on the couch. Carter is face down on the cushion beside Tim, hands to his stomach and groaning. He's been in this position for a good thirty minutes. Mac is currently passed out on the other side of Tim with a fucking thumb in his mouth and an empty bottle of Old Crow cradled in his arm like a football.

My focus trails back to Jeremy, as he swings his legs back and forth.

"Are they even alive?" Jeremy asks, a slight slur to his words. He otherwise looks okay as he drinks from a beer he stole from Tim, who passed out an hour or so ago after putting down a twelve pack by himself.

Jeremy abruptly lifts his arms. "We fuckin' did it, man!" he yells, hopping off the bar and staggering over toward Mac. He snatches the bottle from Mac's arm and then grabs the one I threw on the couch and sets both bottles on the bar top. He stands back and admires them for a moment, before looking toward me and repeating, quieter this time, but with no less enthusiasm, "We fuckin' did it, man."

"We should get medals," I say, rubbing the new throb that's started in my temples.

"We *should* get medals!" Jeremy agrees excitedly. Shaking his head, he adds, "Damn, right, we should." He hesitates for the briefest of moments before saying, "I'm fuckin' shit-canned, man."

I nod, squeezing my eyelids shut. "You and me both, bud."

"And you're talkin' about going downtown?" Jeremy asks skeptically, forcing me to open my eyes.

"Girls, dude," I reason.

Jeremy looks like he's debating this in his head. He mouths the word 'girls,' scratching a pointer against his temple.

I lean in closer to him. "*Girls*, dude."

He looks at me, his head nodding slowly as he seems to be making sense of what I've just said, and then he yells, "Girls, dude!"

He heads straight for the stairs, but at the last second turns on his heel and points to the three of them on the couch. "Should we check and make sure they're alive first?"

I look back at them, Mac and Tim snoring, Carter groaning, and I smile.

"I cut 'em off hours ago. They're fine." After a brief hesitation, I ask, "Hey Carter, you alive, man?"

Carter groans.

"You sure, buddy?"

He groans again.

"I need words, man."

He turns his head, half opens his eyes, and says, "I'm fine. *Go.*"

"Mac, what about you?" I ask, but there's no response. "Mac?!"

He snorts and abruptly lifts his head, his eyes wide.

"You good, man?" I ask.

"Fucking sleeping," he mumbles, dropping his head back to the couch cushion. "Sleep ... fuck ... waking me up... and shit."

I look back at Jeremy and shrug. "See?"

"Alright, well" —he points to the stairs— "girls, dude!"

Making our way out the door, we start down frat row toward Main Street, probably about as obnoxious as two guys can get, but in our present state, it bothers us little.

A minute or two from the Rusty Trombone, where we intend on meeting the brothers for a post-hazing drink, I notice two guys walking in the opposite direction toward us—staggering is more like it—and they're taking up the entire sidewalk. I wait for them to notice us coming, but they don't. They're in some polos and colorful shorts, a backward snapback barely sitting on their heads, trust fund Rolexes on their wrists, and gold chains around their necks. Frat kids, no doubt. The kind I fucking hate.

Jeremy jumps out of their way and into the street to avoid them, while I turn sideways and try to pass between them.

One of them, a blond, while the other has dark brown hair peeking out from under his cap, glances back and says, "Watch out, *bitch*!"

I turn and wait to determine if he really just said what I think he did.

Jeremy freezes in his tracks and turns too, his mouth slack.

"What did you just say?" I ask, putting a hand to my ear. "I don't think I heard you correctly."

The mouthy blond stops suddenly and glances back with his eyes remaining on mine this time, and repeats, as if I'm deaf and he's sounding it out, "Watch. Out. *Bitch.*"

I turn completely now as he and his friend continue walking away. I follow behind them for nearly a block before the blond bitch looks back again.

"What the fuck do you think you're doing?" he asks, passing me a sneer.

"I'm about to teach you a lesson, boy. The first opportunity I get to beat your fuckin' ass, I'm gonna take it."

"Out on the side of the road, huh? You know how many cops run through here, dumb fuck?"

"Nah, not right here. I'm not that stupid. I won't get arrested for your ass," I say, checking my surroundings.

No cops, no cars, no people. Perfect.

As they continue walking, the drunken swagger still present in their step, I spot a business a block ahead with its front door tucked into a cove—a cove hidden from the sidewalk.

Inching my way closer to him, I say, "But I refuse to let you get away without a lesson learned, either."

Charging forward, I grab fistfuls of the blond kid's shirt and push him into the cove. His friend follows in after us, but not in time to prevent three swift, heavy fists from connecting with his buddy's jaw. Blood spurts from a busted lip and drains from his crooked nose. A look of shock covers his face.

I shoot my eyes toward his friend, who is frozen in his tracks. "You want some, too?" I ask, the blond kid's collar clutched in one of my fists, while the other one rains down on his face a couple more times for good measure, though my eyes are still locked on his friend.

His friend shakes his head, pleading, "C'mon, man. This isn't cool."

"No, what isn't cool is your buddy here thinkin' he can run his cock holster and say whatever the fuck he pleases without consequence." My eyes trail back to the blond kid, who's disorientated and could now pass for a ginger, there's so much blood in his hair. "Today, you learn that your actions come with consequences, *bitch*." I hit him one more time, hard, and he crumples to the ground.

"Hey, Bish. Let's fuckin' go, buddy," Jeremy says, clasping a hand on my shoulder, his eyes darting up and down the road.

I look once more toward the kid, curled up in a ball on the ground, and then back to his friend. Pointing a finger at his friend's face, I growl, "If he doesn't remember this tomorrow, you better goddamn tell him what went on here tonight. You tell him the only thing he's got to blame for his freshly fucked up face is that fuckin' mouth of his. You got it?"

The kid nods, eyes wide.

"Good." I turn slowly and start walking toward the house, more drinks no longer of any interest to me.

Jeremy catches up and I can feel his eyes on me through my peripheral as we walk side by side, but I don't acknowledge him.

"Fuck, man. Wasn't that a bit much?"

I shrug. "Not in my book."

Jeremy hesitates, looking behind us and then back at me.

"All right, but how 'bout we speed things up, huh? Five-Oh do come through here all the time."

I crack a smile, nodding my head before I abruptly take off running.

He chases after me, yelling, "Goddamn you're fast."

Sprinting at full speed, I'm back at the house in a matter of a minute or so, and I take a second to catch my breath as I wait for Jeremy.

Once he arrives, he shakes his head and gasps. "Motherfucker, I ain't in the right shape for this," he says, and I crack up laughing.

He follows me into the basement through the side door, our heavy breathing accompanying us.

"Holy hell, y'all missed a doozy," Jeremy calls out as he kicks the side of the couch.

Mac, Carter, and Tim remain passed out, though Jeremy doesn't seem to notice.

"I'm tellin' y'all, our boy here has some stone fuckin' hands, guys." He throws a few air jabs.

"Jeremy, who you talkin' to, man?" I ask.

He motions toward Mac, Carter, and Tim all cuddled up like newborn puppies, and replies, "*Them*," and then looks at me like I'm stupid.

"Look closer," I tell him.

He approaches the couch, his forehead creased as he analyzes the three of them. After a moment, he leans down toward Mac and yells, "Mac!"

Mac springs to life, his eyes wide as he lets out a yell.

"You shoulda seen our boy here!" Jeremy says, shadowboxing again.

Mac flutters his eyelids as he shakes the cobwebs out.

Carter and Tim rustle in their sleep.

"What the fuck, Jeremy?" Mac whines. "Why you waking

me up, dude?"

"Oh, you were sleepin'?" Jeremy asks with all sincerity.

Mac grumbles under his breath, lying back down.

Jeremy takes a few sidesteps and then leans down toward Carter, yelling, "Carter!"

Carter's eyes shoot open, and Jeremy continues, "You shoulda seen our boy here. Fucked some kid's world up."

Carter rubs at his eyes with his palms and mutters, "Oh yeah?"

"Yeah, you fuckers shoulda seen it."

"Can we hear about it tomorrow, maybe? I'm drunk as fuck … and tired." Carter says, yawning.

"No, you gotta hear it now. Tell 'em, Bish," Jeremy insists, hitting my arm with the back of his hand.

"Yeah, tell us, Bish," Damian's voice carries from behind us. I turn and see him coming down the basement stairs through the side door with a date on his arm, both dressed to the nines, and a mess of equally well-dressed people stagger in behind them.

"It wasn't anything," I say, as Damian approaches.

"Tim, *wake the fuck up!*" he barks.

Tim jolts from his sleep. "W-what's up, D?" he asks groggily.

"How long you been passed out for?"

"Uh, shit, I don't know," he responds, a look of drunken confusion on his face.

Damian looks at me.

"Probably about an hour," I respond for Tim. "We finished the bottles before he did, though. He okayed us." I point toward the bar top, where the empty Old Crow bottles still sit.

Damian eyes the bottles and then turns back toward us.

A few brothers and their dates take up the couches around Mac, Carter, and Tim as they continue the process of waking up, while a group of other pledges with their dates starts to set up the beer pong table. Music now pumps through the speakers. The room, within a matter of seconds, is completely full.

Trevor comes up from behind Damian and puts a hand on his shoulder. There's a drunken glimmer in his eyes. "Did one of you guys fuck up a Beta Chi kid?" he asks, looking us over. He points toward Carter and Mac, who remain half-asleep, their eyes just slits. "Well, obviously, they didn't."

No point in wastin' any time.

"I hit some kid. Not sure about him bein' in Beta Chi though," I admit.

Trevor laughs. "Backwards hat, Ralph Lauren polo, seersucker shorts?"

"Yeah, that'd be him."

Trevor laughs again, and this time, Damian joins in. "You did more than just hit him," Trevor says between laughs.

I shrug. "How'd you know?"

"Dude, there's a whole fucking scene down there right now," Trevor replies, motioning toward the door. "Cops, ambulance, the works."

"Shit," I mutter, wondering if I may have been seen, or if any video cameras could've captured the beating. Suddenly, I'm filled with fear.

"You're all good, man. The kid wasn't even conscious," Trevor says as if reading my mind. "His friend was just blabbering on about some nonsense ... wasted as fuck. The cops were getting annoyed. You could tell."

"You think there are any cameras over there that could've caught me?" I ask.

"No way." Trevor shakes his head. "This is Crescent Falls. The only CCTVs you're going to find around here are by the bank and post office."

"Well, that's a relief."

"How are you still standing after all that Old Crow anyway?

Let alone able to beat some kid's ass?" Damian asks.

"I have an Army liver. A little whiskey don't faze me any."

"A little." Trevor laughs. "You're fucking crazy, man."

"Good on you, Bishop, for real, but you should take those rings off for a bit," Damian says, motioning toward my hand, where the rings sit, bloodied still. "Motherfucker had marks all over his face from 'em."

I pull the rings off, one by one, and stuff them into my pocket. "Thanks, man."

"No sweat," he says, making his way toward the beer pong table.

"You up for some pong? Brady needs a partner," Trevor says, pointing toward the table where a group of people has gathered.

At first, imagining Brady as a partner, my face scrunches with displeasure, but I spot Ember standing next to him, wearing a tight little black dress, spiked Valentino heels, and her hair is up in an adorable ponytail. She takes a drink from a pink flask with the word 'BITCH' scrawled across it in black rhinestones. My mood and mind immediately change.

"Yeah, I'm down," I say, looking back toward Trevor, fighting a smile from forming.

He nods, the look on his face letting me know he's on to me, before he abruptly heads toward the table, and I follow behind him, my sightline traveling back to her.

As I approach, I grab a beer from a cooler in front of the table and stand beside Brady, beginning to fill the cups with him.

"You my partner?" he asks.

I nod.

"You fuck some Beta Chi kid up tonight?"

I nod again.

"Damn, you fucked him up good," he mutters.

"His face looked like the Stay Puft Marshmallow Man's," Ember says with a chuckle, and I glance over at her. Her eyes are on me, her bottom lip between her teeth before she throws the flask back again. She doesn't so much as grimace.

"Nice reference," I say, smiling.

"That's my date, Ember," Brady says, motioning toward her. "Have you guys met?"

The way the knowing smirk pulls at the corner of his lips lets me know he may be on to me.

"We spoke briefly last week," I respond, topping off the last cup and then lifting the beer bottle toward her in cheers before taking a swig.

"So, then you know she's a psychopathic bitch?" he asks and bursts out in laughter.

She immediately sends the point of a Valentino into his shin, and he doubles over with a groan, grabbing at his leg.

"See what I mean?" He laughs again, though there's some pain behind it now.

"I'm a sociopath, you foreskin," she says, leaning back against the wall. "There's a fucking difference." Her disgusted face quickly changes to a smile when she looks back at me.

"No judgment here," I say, shrugging and passing her a smile of my own.

"Doctors get it wrong all the time, Ember," Brady says, giving his shin one last good rub before standing straight again.

"Like they did when they looked at that tiny little chiclet in your pants and wrote 'boy' on your birth certificate? Any medical professional could tell you that thing's a pussy, Brady."

There's a chorus of laughter around us, including my own.

Brady scowls. "Well now, you know better than that. Don't you, bitch?" he says, grabbing a fistful of his dick. The way he says 'bitch' this time is different than before. It's got some bite to it.

"Whoa, dude ..." I take a step forward, but Ember puts a hand up to stop me.

"What are you grabbing there, Little Brady?" she asks, her eyes still locked on his, but hand still up, keeping me in place. "Thigh? Ball sack? Because I sure as hell know all that shit in your hand isn't dick. You'd need fucking tweezers to locate that nasty little thing." She lets out an exasperated sigh. "God, do I know," she groans, and the laughter around us erupts again.

He shoots her a glare as we all continue laughing. This girl impresses me with each word that spills out of her mouth.

"Well, you seem to keep coming back for more, now don't you?" he asks, glancing at me for some reason before he takes his first beer pong shot.

She shrugs, taking another drink from her flask as I take my pong shot. "The doctors said I have a streak of self-loathing behavior too," she says. "Along with the sociopathy."

I fight to break my eyes away from her, but my desire for her is unshakeable.

Brady fumes, but it only seems to excite her more.

"You seem distracted. What was your name again ... Bishop?" Ember asks, just as a ping-pong ball comes bouncing toward my face.

I catch the ball at the last second as Brady interjects, "I mean, what do you expect from the guy with those saggy tits hanging out and shit."

"I have *fantastic* tits," she says, drawing her shoulders back and unnecessarily pushing out her already impressive chest. "The best money can buy," she adds, licking her lips and then flipping him off with a manicured middle finger.

She catches me looking as Brady's taking his shot, and she smiles.

"Why wouldn't I show them off?" she asks, her eyes still on mine. "Bishop, don't you think I have nice tits?"

I shrug. "I'm sure as shit not blind," I say, glancing at her and smirking.

Brady shoots me a glare.

"Don't even think about it, pledge," he says, squaring up his shoulders. "That's mine."

He points to Ember and she rolls her eyes.

"Yeah, you see the fucking 'owned by douche bag' sign on my forehead?" she chides.

Brady looks at her intensely, his jaw clenched. He throws the ping pong ball across the room. "I'm ready to go to bed now, Ember. *Come on.*" He jabs a finger to the floor beside him before he slowly starts to walk away.

"No, I think I'll stay, but thanks for the gracious invitation."

All eyes are on the table. The music is playing, but it might as well not be. The argument is the only thing anyone is listening to, I can tell because I can see the whites of every last damn eye in here. They're all on us.

Brady turns.

"Ember"—he looks to be a few seconds from foaming at the mouth— "you're my social date, I'm the social chair. Get your ass to my room... now!"

"Dude," I say, putting a hand up to calm him down while taking a step forward, keeping my features and tone light. "I don't know what's going on between the two of you. I barely know this young lady right here, but what I do know is it sounds like she's having a good time and doesn't want to go to bed with you, so ..." I shrug. "I mean, dude, leave her alone."

Brady looks over at Trevor and then back at me. He points his finger at me and says, "This isn't the last of it, pledge! Not even close!" He storms off, stomping up the stairs to the first level where the bedrooms are. After a few moments, a slamming door echoes throughout the house.

I look across the table at Trevor and Damian, who both seem to be confused and a little annoyed.

Trevor abruptly lifts his hands and yells, "Party isn't over, bitches!" He slams back a beer before he and Damian, both noticeably fucked up, wander away from the table with beers in hand.

I look over at Ember and mutter, "Well, I guess that's the end of the game."

"Looks like it. I'd play you, but I don't toss balls. I only gargle them."

I hesitate before saying, "Talk normally. Dear God, woman."

She takes a deep breath and replies, "Thanks for sticking up for me," resting her hand against my arm for a moment before drawing it back to her side. Her tone, for the first time tonight, seems genuine.

"I know you could've handled it yourself. I just got sick of hearin' him talk."

"Oh, I totally could've taken care of him myself," she replies, holding herself higher and squinting her eyes like she's Dirty Harry. "I know some shit."

"Some karate shit?"

"Some kung-fu shit."

"Some Muay Thai shit?"

"Some Oolong shit." She karate chops the air.

I laugh. "I think that's a kind of tea. And no matter the fightin' technique, I still got superior strength and knowledge ... seein' as I'm a man and all."

She leans back, curling her lip. "Ha! You *are* a misogynist." It takes me a moment to remember the misogynist topic from our previous conversation. "You *must* be on something," she adds.

"I'm just sayin', it's scientifically proven."

"In what world?"

"Our world. There are some websites I could show you." I pass her a playful grin and a wink.

She laughs, putting a palm to her forehead. "You're an idiot."

"No, I'm drunk."

I smile, and she leans in closer. "You trying to stay here the whole night?" she whispers.

"Why do you ask?"

"I just figured, why not go somewhere a little quieter?"

"I can't have sex with you, Ms. Azar."

She swats my arm. "What makes you think I want to? And how do you know my last name?"

I motion toward no one in particular. "I talked to the guys ... about you."

Fuckin' Old Crow. My brain feels like boiled dog shit.

"And what makes you think I want to have sex with you?" she asks.

"Well, I mean ..." I raise a finger, eyeing it drunkenly. "One, I'm not too bad lookin'." I put up another finger. "Two, you're sooooo fuckin' sexy. Like, holy fuck, you walk into a room and every other girl can just piss off. You're the only one that matters."

She scoffs, waving me off.

"No, I mean it!" I say in my most convincing tone.

"And three?" she asks, and for a moment, I'm confused.

"Huh?"

"You have three fingers up," she says, giggling and pointing to my hand, which comes into focus, and I see I am, in fact, holding three fingers up.

"And three ... I'm so drunk it could be considered rape." I pat her arm, adding, "And I don't want to see you go to jail. You're a good kid. I kind of like you. And you're too pretty for an orange jumpsuit, though, I can only imagine you'd still pull off."

She shakes her head, taking one more drink of her flask before stowing it in her purse. "Well, now you're just pandering."

"I don't pander, young lady. I only speak truth."

Pointing a finger at me, she says, "I really hate you for what I'm about to do," before she digs around in her purse, eventually pulling out a cocktail napkin and a tube of lipstick. Opening the lipstick, she looks at me with a raised brow, as if she finds me humorous. And hell, maybe I am doing something funny. I don't really know. I can't feel my face anymore.

After a few moments, she closes her lipstick and puts it back in her purse. She hands over the cocktail napkin, and I snatch it from her, trying hard to focus my vision as I read.

2198 Chandler Crescent Ave
Kappa Phi House
Thirty Minutes
Ember <3
PS … Not for sex. Cuddles only.

By the time I look back up, she's on her way to the door. I let her go, realizing I should probably stop at the 7-Eleven down the road first, so I can freshen up. My mouth tastes like unwashed asshole. All I can taste is cheap whiskey and ciga-rettes. All I can think about is the way her ass sways in that dress.

Watching her and acknowledging the way she stirs the desire up in me, I become acutely aware of just how hard being good tonight will be. And just how easily my awkward, drunken ass could fuck this up.

EIGHT

fter stumbling into 7-Eleven and buying everything needed to re-hydrate and clean myself up, I wash my face and brush my teeth in their bathroom sink, sprucing myself up as much as I can before I continue on the one-mile trek toward sorority row.

After staggering my way up the street, I walk the block a few times before eventually locating the Kappa Phi house, their letters enormous and positioned on the front lawn in a way impossible to ignore. Impressively, I managed to do so a few times. Walking back and forth in front of the house, I search for Ember through the dark when I hear a *pssst*.

Taking a few steps back, I look up toward the house and grunt, "Huh?"

"*Pssst*, drunk ass, I'm up here!" a voice whisper-yells.

I look up, spotting Ember standing on a deck just outside an open window on the second floor. She's wearing a crimson satin nightgown, and with each gust of wind, I can see her hard nipples indent the fabric. I'm afraid of how sexy I find her right now ... and how much my stomach churns and eyes throb the longer I look up.

"You coming or what?" she asks, and I look around the front of the house again.

I lift my palms to the sky. "How?"

She points to the side of the house and says, "The balcony. Big wooden steps. Bright white. Kind of hard to miss."

"Like those letters?" I chuckle, pointing toward the white and crimson letters, three feet high, perched on the front lawn.

"Huh?"

"Nothing." I wave her off and head toward the stairs.

She wasn't kidding. They're white as fuck.

I make my way up the stairs slowly, gripping the railing as I guide my heavy feet up one slow step at a time. At the top, I feel like how Sir Hillary must have felt all those years ago at the summit of Everest. I put my arms up in celebratory victory for a moment when there's another *psssst* in the darkness.

"What the fuck are you doing, Ricky Bobby?" Ember whispers, and I open my eyes to find her standing toward the front of the balcony with hands on her hips.

"Well, hello," I say entirely too loud. I put a hand to my lips to catch the words already spoken.

She puts a finger to her lips. "Shhhh! Oh my God, Gilbert Godfrey. Keep it down and follow the sounds that are coming out of my mouth." She lets out a light chuckle but is quick to straighten her lips and return to that bossy expression of hers. I can't say it's not hot.

As I approach her, I say, "You know, you're really on point with your references tonight."

"Thank you," she says, rolling her eyes and chuckling again.

I put up an okay sign as she takes me by the shoulder and leads me to the open window.

"I mean, grade A stuff," I add.

She makes me go through the window first, but as I told her before I stuck my leg inside, I feel like I'm going to break something. When I hear a loud crash from within the darkness of her room, it's not a matter of *if* I'll break something anymore, but *what* I might have already broken.

Oh my God, what if I broke a family heirloom? Or china? Or, like, a nacho platter. A really nice nacho platter.

"I'm sorry," I say, looking back at her with a pained expression. "I swear I didn't mean to break your nacho platter."

"Holy shit, Bishop, how much of that Old Crow did you drink tonight? Get your drunk ass inside!" she orders, shoving me. I stumble in through the window fully and then dive onto her bed. There's a loud snap, but the bed maintains its position.

But for how long ...

I slow roll across and then off the bed, catching myself on the floor with my hands and knees before standing up straight. What feels like the smoothest, stealthiest combat roll I've ever taken must've been the literal opposite if I'm to believe the expression on her face.

She puts up a finger, directed first at my face, and then at the bed. "Get your butt in bed! *Now.* Get under the covers! And *be quiet*, you dork."

I look to the bed where she's pointing and ask, "Can I take my pants off?"

"Take off whatever you want. I'm going to brush my teeth. Just please, *please* keep it down. I can get in a lot of trouble for having a guy in my room."

"Oooooh, okay, okay ... quiet as a church mouse." I put a finger to my lips as I slowly creep toward her bed.

She laughs quietly, shaking her head as she exits the room.

While she's away, I strip my jeans and shirt off, and then I put my shirt back on before I eventually settle on removing it again. Crawling under the covers, I realize I have no idea what side I'm supposed to be on. Is she a lefty or a righty? By the door or by the wall? Should I be looking sexy-like, on an elbow or something a la George Costanza? Wait, should I even have boxers on? I'm not going to hook up with her, but to just like feel the tip of my cock against her wouldn't be crossing the line, would it?

She arrives just in time, as my mind needed a break from the drunken carnival ride. Climbing under the covers, she turns, switches off the light, and pulls the comforter to her chin. I wonder for a moment if she wants me to cuddle with her or not. She didn't say anything to me. She just got in bed and rolled over.

Maybe that means I should leave her alone.

Then again, it could just be a test. Like, 'Is this guy man enough to make the first move?'

But now that I think of it, am I man enough to make the first move?

What first move is there to even make? I don't want to fuck. I just want to kiss a little bit.

I mean, I do want to fuck ... just not now.

It's just ... I'm drunk.

But, oh my God, what I'd do to her tight little ass.

"Bishop!" Ember shoots up and looks back toward me with a curled lip. "Are you going to cuddle me or what?"

"Oh shit, well, yeah," I say as she turns back over on her side. "I wasn't sure if you wanted me to."

As I pull her into me, her skin warm and soft against my own, she says, "What do you think it is you're doing over here at this hour? And didn't I mention cuddles on the note?" She abruptly sits up again and turns toward me, her hand running from my collar bone to my nipple. "Wait, your nipples are pierced?"

I feign a shocked expression and grab at my chest. "Oh, my God, are they?"

She quirks an eyebrow for a brief moment before she laughs

and smacks a hand against my chest. "Oh, shut up!" Her eyes fall back to my nipples and her smile fades. When her eyes meet mine again, she clears her throat and says, "Well, that's hot," before she turns and pushes her body back into mine.

"I can't have sex," I say. "It'd be like rape because I'm so drunk. And I don't want you makin' some list."

She turns just her head this time, smiling as she whispers, "Goodnight, you handsome drunk."

"Hey, Ember?" I blurt as she's about to turn away from me.

"Yeah?"

"Can I ask you a question?"

"Sure."

"Why didn't you ever come see me the day after that last party?"

She hesitates for a moment, taking a deep breath, and then she replies, "I wasn't sure if you'd remember me. Thought you might've been drunk. Or maybe I made an ass of myself or something. I don't know. I was pretty drunk myself. Wasted, if I'm being totally honest."

"How could I *not* remember you? Holey jeans, quarter moon earrings, Chuck Taylors on your feet ... and a smile that could take a man's breath away."

"Just as cheesy as the first time you said it," she says, sticking her tongue out at me.

"Good night, gorgeous. You are ... You're one of a kind, you know. Young. *Very* young. But one of a kind. I just want you to know, I appreciate you. And you ... you deserve to be appreciated."

"I appreciate you, too, Army man," she responds, smiling, and kissing me, and then resting her head against the pillow. Nuzzling her body into me, she gives my arms—wrapped around her—a good squeeze. And with her warm body against mine, we both drift to sleep.

NINE

"Bishop. Bishop. Wake up!"

I wake up in a panic—for a moment, still captured in my nightmare, reeling from its vivid entrapment. It takes a few more moments for me to shake the fog off.

"Bishop!" Ember repeats, hurriedly putting on her clothes.

"Sorry, what?" My head is dense, thoughts cloudy. It takes me some time to wake up in the morning, feeling like I'm coming out of a damn coma just about, and when I'm woken up in the wrong way—say, like Ember here, shrieking my name—well, it's like a goddamn heart attack.

"You have to get out of here. Like, now. Our house mom is going to be here any minute, and I'll get in big trouble if she catches you here."

"Oh, yeah, sorry." I sit up, stretching. "My head is killin' me." I slowly lumber out of bed and begin dressing.

"Um, Bishop," she says, her voice calm for the first time this morning.

"Yeah?"

She looks nervous, a little pity in her features, and she points to the bed. "Your eye."

I glance over and see my prosthetic eye on the pillow, staring back at the both of us. A sharp feeling of self-conscious-ness digs out my insides. I can feel it at the bottom of my throat like hot coals, but I keep the look off my face.

Facing her, I shrug. "Would you look at that. I must have been movin' a lot last night."

I retrieve my eye from the bed and turn away from her as I put it back in the socket where it belongs.

"You were. Kicking, arms flailing. Talking in your sleep. You were having a nightmare, I think. Does that happen a lot?" she asks.

"The eye fallin' out or the nightmares?" I chuckle.

She shrugs. "Both."

"Yeah, the nightmares come often. I don't usually sleep with the eye in, but when I do, it can fall out sometimes, yeah."

"Where do you usually keep it at night?"

"Weren't you just in a panic about me bein' here?"

She nods, smiling as the rising sun hits her from the bay window, painting her in rich oranges and yellows.

"It goes in a disinfecting solution," I say, taking a few steps toward her. I wrap my arms around her, pulling her in and kissing her. The taste of her lips, their movement perfect with my own, makes me want to keep doing this all day. I reluctantly disconnect from her lips and smile. "I had a great time last night."

"Ditto." She grins and pecks me, adding, "And next time you stay over, you can just bring your solution with you."

"Next time, huh?"

She nods, this adorable little nod where her bottom lip slips between her teeth, and she bats her eyes just a bit.

"I can't wait." I give her one last kiss for good measure, and then make my way out the bay window and onto the deck. There's light movement around the front of the house—one girl smoking, a few with backpacks leaving for class—so I slink down the stairs to avoid detection. Once I'm on the street, heading back toward frat row, I glance back. Ember stands at the open window, watching me as I walk away. She waves, and I wave back and then I continue on. When I turn the corner, onto frat row, I'm overcome with a sense of disappointment because, at this moment, there's nothing I'd rather do than sneak back over and cuddle her until noon.

Who needs classes?

I HEAD BACK HOME LONG ENOUGH to get cleaned up and brush my teeth, and then I'm back on the road toward Cradle Café, a quaint little coffee shop on Main Street where I'm meeting the guys before our classes. I've been meaning to start, at least once a week, but it took some convincing to get them to agree to an earlier wake-up. I'm not too happy about it myself.

I'm pleased to see all three of them standing out front, waiting on me, as I park my Jeep and hop out.

Jeremy says, "You look like dog shit," as I approach.

Laughing, I shrug and slap hands with him, and then the others. "I don't know about you boys, but I felt like fuckin' death when I woke up."

As we pile into the crowded restaurant and Carter checks us in, I notice a new pep in Mac's step and a faint look of contentment on his face. He's got that unmistakable look that says, 'I just got laid.'

"So, how'd *your* night go, Mac?" I ask as the host seats us.

"You know, a little of this, a little of that." He smiles from ear to ear.

"You got some ass, didn't you, you little shit?"

"I don't kiss and tell," Mac says, shaking his head. "But yeah,

I totally got my dick wet *and* met the girl of my dreams. Same night, what up?" He raises the roof and I laugh.

"That Spanish chick you were dancing with?"

"She's Mexican," he responds. "And fuck yeah. Future baby momma, right there. I'm for real."

"I'm tellin' y'all, my boy Red here was gettin' *down*," Jeremy says, laughing. "That girl was just twerkin' on him, big ol' booty all over his dick, and he's back there like a kid on Christmas fuckin' mornin' with his hands on her butt cheeks."

The four of us share a boisterous, and most likely bothersome, laugh.

"You should've seen her ass out of the dress," Mac says, his eyebrows wriggling.

Jeremy shrugs. "Shit, I ain't mad at ya. I like my women with some curves too."

Mac takes a big sniff. "I can still smell her pussy juice in my beard."

"Jesus, dude, that's foul. Did you not bathe today? And what beard are you talkin' about?" I ask, giving him the stink eye as I analyze the pubes on his face. "Because I've seen teens grow better shit than that."

"No way." Mac rubs his fingers through his ginger face pubes. "This thing is beautiful. And hell no, I don't want to wash her off me. You guys don't understand. I met the love of my life last night. This is an important day. And I need to savor it."

I point to his face. "I still don't see how that correlates with you collecting her juice in your fuckin' beard, man."

"You're a dirty fuck, Mac," Carter says, shaking his head. He then motions toward me. "What about you, Bishop? I noticed you and Ember disappeared around the same time."

"We didn't fuck, I can tell you that. Shit, I didn't want to, as jacked up as I was. My dick wouldn't have worked."

"She's so fuckin' fine. Dear Lord, man," Jeremy says, and Mac nods in agreement.

"You have to watch yourself with her, though," Carter says. "Her thing with Brady has been on and off for a while now. Not really dating or anything like that, but fuck buddies,"

"He's a big kid, you know? Nobody's got a claim to her, or anybody else. The guy doesn't really even like me anyway, so fuck it." I shrug, my eyes shifting to the approaching waitress.

She pours us coffee and takes our order. After giving her my own, I dump heaps of sugar into my cup, stir it, and then take the sweet nectar down in big gulps.

"She *is* hot, though," Carter admits. "Looks like Mila Kunis if she were a rocker chick."

"Fuck yeah, she does," I agree, taking another big drink of the much-needed coffee.

"So, what's up with this next pledge event?" Mac asks. "Damien tell you anything yet?"

"Nothin' about the next challenge. I know tonight we've got the Chapter Advisor visit," I respond.

Jeremy points toward Carter with a judgmental look on his face. "He knows!"

"You know I can't say anything," Carter reminds us. "And I don't know every detail either. I just know stories my dad told me, and I put two and two together."

"Alright, so, put two and two together for us and figure out what fuck-fuck game we're playin' next," Jeremy says, chuckling.

Carter hesitates and then says, "We know Big Bro and Big Sis nights are coming up. If I had to guess, one of them is probably going to be next, but seriously, I have no certainty on anything."

"Do you know what we gotta do for them nights?" Jeremy asks.

Carter shakes his head. "Nope."

The waitress returns and places our food down in front of us, topping our coffees off after, and the three of them are digging in already like vultures to a carcass.

"Do millennials not know table manners?" I ask, shaking my head.

Mac winks, his mouth full of food as he smacks his lips a few times.

I scoff. "It's a miracle you get laid, Red. It *truly* is."

"Do any of y'all know this advisor guy?" I ask as the four of us wait in the van parked outside a trailer, in a park on the outskirts of town. The evening sun hangs low, frosting the van's windows as the temperature plummets. Trevor and Damian wait at the front door of the trailer, knocking periodically.

"No idea," Jeremy responds.

Mac shakes his head and then breathes against the window, fingering 'Suck me' on the condensation left behind.

A smile tugs at Carter's lips.

"What do you know?" I ask.

"He's a fucking lunatic," Carter responds bluntly. "Or so I've heard. I've never met him, but everyone knows about him here. He's kind of a legend."

"How old is he?" I ask.

"Pushing fifty, I think. Maybe forty-something. Who knows? He's been the Chapter Advisor for DIK-Rho for a long time now. I know that. Maybe fifteen, twenty years."

"And he's crazy?" Mac asks.

Carter nods stiffly. "Batshit crazy."

Trevor and Damian turn and make their way back, disap-pointment on their faces. Just as they're about to reach the van, the trailer door swings open from behind them. Standing on the other side, a stocky man with a thick, disheveled mohawk holds a cigarette in one hand and a Busch in the other. He's shirtless with a burgundy robe on, and the bags under his squinty eyes tell me he hasn't been awake for long. That, or he's just smoked some weed.

Damian waves us out of the vehicle as Trevor makes his introduction.

As we pile out, the man looks us over one by one, flicking his cigarette butt out toward the road, and then taking a long swig of his beer.

"Line up, pledges," Damian says, and we do as we're told.

The advisor takes a step out of his trailer, his eyes scanning our row back and forth, then he clears his throat. The cold begins to turn his bare stomach red, but he doesn't seem to mind.

"Welcome to my humble abode. I'm yer host fer today's festivities, JD McGinnis. The JD stands fer Jack Daniels on account a' I drink it so damn much." He grunts, draining the last of the beer can, and then crumpling it up. He tosses it to the ground and lights another cigarette.

"Does JD really stand for Jack Daniels?" Mac asks.

JD shakes his head, letting the smoke exit his mouth in little circles. "Nah, my given name was Jameson Decker, but ain't nobody allowed to call me that."

"Well, if you liked Jameson, that'd really work out well, huh?" I say, cracking a smile, and he shoots me a glare.

"Jameson?!" he barks. "I don't drink that distilled horse piss!"

"It's actually pretty good," I argue.

"No, no, no ... it'll be JD to y'all, or Señor Advisor. Or Marky Mark."

"Oh, were you an early nineties pop sensation?" I ask, smirking.

He shakes his head, taking a long draw from his cigarette, and looks at me through the smoke. Abruptly, he jumps up and does a full body twist. Landing unsteadily, he starts to grind his hips. "No ... but I got his moves. *Ow!*" He grabs his crotch with one hand and runs his other hand along the side of his head like he's Fonzie. He then turns on his heel and motions for us to follow. "C'mon inside, boys. We've got some Jack to drink and some Principles to recite."

Entering the trailer, I find weed is most definitely to blame for his fucked up eyes as the smell clings to the air.

After making each of us stand side by side to recite the Declaration of Principles—only Mac fucking it up, of course—he squeezes the four of us together on a musty couch across from him as he lounges in a recliner with his sandaled feet propped up. Trevor and Damian sit on the edge of his bed at the rear of the trailer, and well, isn't that just cute.

The interior of his glorious single-wide looks like a museum for the fraternity. The official seal, color, and letters are everywhere, from the throw rug by the front door, to the lamp beside his recliner, to the wallpaper that lines the walls.

JD tilts his head, nodding toward me. "You the vet, I reckon?"

"That'd be me. Bishop." I put my hand out and he leans forward, shaking it firmly, and then passes me a quick salute.

"88 Mike myself. Served in Desert Storm 'fore I came here. Yer in a long line of Army brethren here in DIK."

"Happy to be a part of it."

"And we're happy to have ya." His eyes trail the four of us. "All y'all. Welcome to my home, and to this night in the process. By the end of this night, y'all will've killed this bottle a' Jack with me and told me all about DIK history. Tell me like I still got shit stains in my drawers." He snaps his fingers toward Trevor and Damian. "One of y'all grab us some shot glasses. Top cabinet next to the fridge."

The two of them argue in whispers before Damian huffs his way toward the kitchen.

"Delta Iota Kappa is a way of life, gentlemen. It's a brother-hood," JD continues. "It's a family. We have each other's backs —" He's interrupted by Damian setting four shot glasses onto the coffee table. "Y'all are on the cusp of greatness. Ya gotta finish strong. Work together. And the whole world is at yer disposal."

I fight the urge to scan his small trailer, judgment burgeoning.

He fills each of the shot glasses, and I wonder if he's forgotten one for himself, but then he holds the bottle up in a cheers. "Grab yer shots, boys."

We retrieve them from the table and meet the bottle in the air.

"I'm an asshole. I'm an asshole. I'm an asshole till I die. But I'd rather be an asshole, than a goddamned Beta Chi," he chants, tossing the bottle back.

We look to each other with confusion, but shrug and down our shots after him. I fight the urge to vomit mine back up as I slam the shot glass back down on the coffee table.

Nope, *haven't missed Jack one bit.*

"Let me tell y'all a story, boys ... an important one," JD says, leaning back in his recliner with the bottle, after filling our shot glasses back up. He waves toward them with his free hand. "Take yer time with those. We got plenty more waitin' on ya." He lets out a heavy breath and then continues, "I was stationed in Korea, back in '89. On leave one time, I went down to the Philippines. Beautiful place, if ya ever catch yerselves around the area, but *goddamn*, is it hot. Hotter than the devil's taint. I'm talkin' sweatin' like a whore in church, gentlemen. So, in the Philippines, they got these special kinda bars. Nice places. Cheap beer. Topless bitches. Great place fer us military folk."

He motions to me, and I nod along, though I have no idea what he's talking about.

"Let me tell y'all, if you'd a' told me this story without me seein' it fer myself, I'd a' told ya to shove it where the sun don't shine. But God as my witness, these women put goddamn bananas in their pussies." He pauses for dramatic effect. "Bananas in their pussies, gentlemen, and they walked around with these bananas shoved up inside 'em. They went from table to table, and if ya put yer hand out—"

"Oh no," Mac groans.

"Oh yeah. Ya bet yer ginger ass. Ya put yer hand out, and she'd let that banana slide out just a little, and then she'd cut a piece off fer ya usin' her snatch like a goddamn cigar cutter."

"Oh no," Mac repeats, shuddering, and shaking his head with his hands to his mouth.

"Oh yeah, Carrot Top. If ya decided to put yer hand out, ya had to eat that piece of banana, no question."

"Wait, so, like, you *had* to eat it? I mean, what, do they hold a gun to your head?" Mac asks.

JD leans in a little and responds, "Goddamnit, Richie Cunningham, it's called tradition. Yer civilian ass just couldn't understand." He looks toward me. "Right, Bishop?"

I shrug. "I mean, I'm not puttin' my fuckin' hand out. Christ no. But I can see the honor in eating the motherfucker if you have the stones to."

"Damn straight!" JD hollers. "It tasted like soured milk."

Mac puts a hand to his mouth and groans.

"I can tell by y'all's faces yer wonderin' what the moral to the story is."

I nod. "Absolutely, yes!" I reply with a grin.

"The lesson learned here, my friends, is that when yer offered fruit from a woman's puss, ya don't eat it, or else ya may find yerself in a Filipino medical clinic fer gonorrhea of the mouth the next morning."

There's a still silence between us as we mull over what he's just said before Jeremy cracks up laughing.

JD waves us off with a laugh of his own. "I'm just fuckin' with y'all. But I sure as shit ate that banana. I don't think I'd put my hand back out though. Not that I don't enjoy some overripe puss," he says, matter-of-factly. "Ya gotta enjoy the stinky stuff sometimes too. They need lovin' just like the sweet ones do."

"I don't know if that's true." I laugh. "Seems unsanitary."

"Let me tell ya, some of the best pussy I ever had smelled like Homeless Hank's rotten asshole."

"Hey, JD. Can we get some of that?" Damian asks.

JD side-eyes him. "None a' this." He cradles the bottle. "It's fer me and the pledges. Y'all can grab Busch from the fridge." He motions his head toward the kitchen.

"How nice of you," Damian mutters as he crosses the room.

"I don't like them two very much," JD says, motioning toward Trevor and Damian, and not being discreet about it in the slightest. "I've spent many a year here in Crescent Falls, gentlemen. I've seen hundreds of boys come through here and become men. The DIK way a' life is a good one. It's a proud one. It's an honorable one. And goddamn, is there pussy aplenty!" He slaps his knee, cackling before he refills our shot glasses.

"You ever wonder how many STDs pass through this motherfucker?" I ask, chuckling.

"More than ya know. I've had a few close calls myself. Lotta run-ins with the tainted pussy."

I shake my head, a disgusted knot in my throat. "Is there a line where maybe too much has been said?" I ask.

He shrugs, tossing back the bottle before settling it back in his lap. "I don't believe there is. Ask me in about an hour when I get real filthy."

"Oh, I can hardly wait."

———

"Now LISTEN, fellas. I ain't talkin' about regular ol' butt play here. I'm talkin' straight fist in the ass. *Elbow deep.*" JD grunts, the bottle, near empty, wobbling in his hands. "She had these rubber gloves in her nightstand. Big tube a' Astroglide too. Took two fists most nights."

I shake my head slowly, my eyes wide. I shouldn't be shocked anymore by the shit that comes out of his mouth, but I am. "That's fuckin' disgusting, dude," I say.

"Ya don't know the half of it. When ya got two whole arms up inside a chick's asshole, ticklin' her small intestines, ya pull back out and that asshole's all puckered up like some alien fuckin' pod, man. All angry like. Y'all must a' seen some of them videos."

"Unfortunately," I respond, shaking my head. "For the briefest of fuckin' moments thanks to a dickhead in my squad. I'm not a fan like you. That shit grosses me out."

"Oh, I get off on it, man. Seein' that gapin' butthole after I've worked the fuck out of it. *Shit.*"

"I feel like we've talked about ass stuff just *so much* tonight." I laugh, feeling a heavy buzz after five or six shots.

"Welcome to my world," JD says. Whatever that means.

"Did we pass the test?" Carter asks, and JD one-eyes the bottle.

He nods. "In about one more shot, y'all are good. Mac, ya need to study more. Everybody else, y'all are good in the history department."

"Will do," Mac says, his drunken eyes trained on the floor as he picks at his fingernail. "Sorry."

"It's all good, Rick Astley." He points his finger at us. "Y'all are a team. The three of ya need to help him out."

"Roger that," I respond, nodding my head. "I should've kept up with it."

"Well ..." JD nods toward the bottle, a drunken gleam in his eyes. He pours the last four shots and holds the bottle up. "This is the last of it. I ain't got nothin' else for y'all. See ya again in about two weeks. Prepare yer livers and yer come control, gentlemen. It's gonna be an epic fuckin' night!"

Come control?

TEN

The basement is empty of everyone but the four of us, linked up against the wall and impatiently waiting for something to happen, just as we've been doing for the past hour. Thursdays have become my new most detested day. You're off the hook, Monday. *For now.*

"This fucking blows," Mac whines.

I nod. "It's more like basic training than I ever thought it would be."

"What makes you say that?" Carter asks.

I think it over for a moment, trying my best to ignore the pain radiating throughout my knees and ankles. My joints are wobbly and worn from years of ruck marching with ninety pounds on my back and the unforgiving nature of the ground after one too many Airborne experiences. As a result, I feel it every second I'm left standing here on concrete that provides absolutely no relief.

I look to Carter, replying, "Just the hurry up and wait bull-shit. Not tellin' us when shit goes down, or what to expect. Just one big mind fuck."

"You're telling me," Mac groans.

"They're bound to come down soon," Carter says, and as the words exit his mouth, the basement door swings open.

Trevor comes first, followed by Tim, Brady, and Zane in their robes with paddles in their hands, and Damian and Sarge behind them. Sarge has a paddle in his hand as well.

They line up before us and Trevor takes a step forward.

"Pledges, welcome to Big Brother night. Tonight, you will further deepen your bond within the fraternity as you accept a bid into a DIK family. Each family represents a legacy that has existed since the start of DIK-Rho in 1922. These families share a special bond throughout a DIK brother's lifetime. The family means commitment. Commitment to yourselves, your family, and the fraternity as a whole."

Trevor motions toward Sarge. "Sarge, can you take a step forward with your paddle, please?"

Sarge does as he's asked, a grin on his face as I read the paddle:

DIK
Spring 2011
Big Bro
Sarge
Little Bro
Bishop
Warrior Family

I pass him an approving nod as Trevor continues, "Brother Sarge, are you prepared to recite the Big Brother Oath?"

"Roger that," Sarge says, nodding toward Trevor. His eyes trail back to me and he continues, "I, Blake 'Sarge' Maddox, understand that my duties as a Big Brother are to serve as a mentor and friend to my Little Brother through the pledging process, and for the rest of my life as a Delta Iota Kappa fraternity member. I will share with him the knowledge and standards of our fraternity. I will guide and assist him through his personal development and during his lifelong pursuit of excellence in keeping with the standards of Delta Iota Kappa. I will instill in him personal responsibility through the integrity of my actions as a true Big Brother and a DIK Gentleman of Excellence."

Trevor looks to me as I fight back the laugh that's aching to bust free.

"McKenzie Bishop, do you accept Sarge as your Big Brother, and promise to be open-minded, loyal, and giving in your fraternal family interactions, to always give your best effort in not only being a brother to your fraternity, but by committing to the Warrior Family within DIK-Rho?"

"What if I say 'no' here?" I ask.

Damian doesn't like it very much, but Sarge chuckles.

Sarge shakes his head. "You don't got a choice, buddy."

"So, do I say, 'I do' or somethin' like I'm marryin' your ass?"

Sarge laughs again.

"Just respond with 'yes,'" Trevor interjects.

"Yes, Sarge," I respond, looking at him with googly eyes and holding back the laughter in my chest. "I do."

"Welcome to the Warrior Family," Sarge says, giving me a bro hug.

"What does that even mean?"

"I'll tell you about it after," Sarge responds with a mischievous smirk.

"After *what*?" I ask, and he slaps the paddle into his free hand a few times.

"No fuckin' way," I say. "That's some homoerotic shit, man."

"It's tradition," Sarge corrects me, his eyebrows dancing.

"Bend over and pull down your panties. I get a hit and you get a hit."

I narrow my eyes at him. "Wait, so I get to hit you, too?"

"That's the *only* way it works in a fraternity. A hit for a hit."

I think on this for a moment, shrug, and then bend over, exposing my bare ass. "Well, alright. Let's do this shit."

"He's got about fifty pounds on you," Damian says with a chuckle. "This ought to be rich."

I shoot Damian a sideways glance as I say, "Sarge, do your worst, man, so I can pull my fuckin' pants up."

"Now that ain't some shit you hear one vet say to another every day," Jeremy says, laughing.

I spot Sarge backing up a few paces through my peripheral, and I turn forward in response, letting out a heavy breath. I focus on a distant point through my mind's eye, doing my best to shed the anticipation. There's a stillness in the room for a few moments until I hear Sarge's heavy boots meeting the concrete floor in quick steps.

I take a deep breath.

Whack! The slapping sound echoes throughout the basement as the wood meets my bare ass. On the inside, I'm dying, the pain radiating from my ass cheeks and down my thighs in burning trails, but I don't let it show. I keep my face even keel. I pull up my pants and stand straight.

Turning back around, I nod slowly and pass Sarge a grin. "Meh. Not *too* bad, old man." I point to his chiseled biceps. "Though I guess those are just for show, huh?"

Sarge shakes his head as everyone else looks on, baffled.

"Jesus Christ, dude," Trevor says, his eyes wide.

"I should've expected as much," Sarge quips as he hands over the paddle reluctantly. He turns, unbuckling his jeans. Then he bends over and slips his ass out.

I don't give him a running start as he did for me, but I don't have to; I played baseball for years when I was younger. With that in mind, I rear the paddle back and slowly return it to within a centimeter of his ass to get the aim down. After doing this a few times, I bring the paddle down as hard as I can, and it cracks against his bottom with a loud smack.

He crumples to the floor, catching himself on his knuckles as he grunts in pain. Then he stands up straight, steadying himself, as he turns back around with a grin, rubbing a stiff hand against his ass with a grimace.

"Probably the worst one I've had," he says with a shake of his head as he buttons his jeans back up.

"Appreciate it," I reply, smiling wickedly.

"Alright, Bishop. Link back up with your pledge brothers. We've got three more to get through before the real fun starts."

I link back up and watch as Mac and Tim exchange hits— Mac nearly crying from his—then Zane and Carter, and finally, Brady and Jeremy.

As the four of us are linked back up—the three others shifting uncomfortably where they stand, grimaces on their faces—Trevor and Damian head to the bar for a moment, digging in the refrigerator and coming back with four bottles of liquor. Trevor hands Patron off to Brady and Jim Beam to Tim, as Damian gives Zane a bottle of Jack Daniels and Sarge what looks like moonshine in a large mason jar. I take a thick swallow, my saliva becoming thick as I eye the jar in his hands.

"Pledges ... Big Brothers ..." Trevor announces. "Now, comes the easy part of the night. Family bonding. Each Big Brother has chosen a bottle of liquor that he will share with his Little Brother, and you will both have it finished within the next three hours. You'll spend that time getting to know each other better. Pledges, unlink, and let's have some fun."

AFTER SARGE and I are about halfway through the jar, I can feel my head ablaze, my body numb, and my heart pounding. We sit in rockers on the front porch which overlooks frat row. Drunk frat boys and sorority girls pass by in clusters every now and then on the sidewalk below.

"I mean, just think about it," Sarge says, gripping the jar in one hand and a cigar in the other.

"I have been," I say, chuckling. "The past three hours you've been talking about it. I still don't see how it's possible."

He leans in. "How could it not be? We know the government has abilities and technologies outside of our knowledge. We can agree on that part of it, right?"

I nod.

"So, who's to say they don't have the ability to see into the future? To know what's coming. Through intelligence, or some machine or something ... or some motherfucker with ESP."

I look at him skeptically. "Now, you're stretching."

"The government has an agenda. That's all I'm saying. I think they know about crimes before they happen sometimes, through intelligence probably, and they let that shit happen anyway to drive that agenda."

I shrug. "It's sound in theory, I guess. I just feel like somebody would've talked about it by now. It would've gotten out."

"See, I'm the type who believes there is nothing outside of our government's moral boundary, including murder. And that kind of shit would be so 'need to know' the amount of people who'd be able to talk would be minimal."

"We definitely need to change the subject." I laugh, pointing to the sky. "They're probably listening."

He grins, obviously picking up my facetious tone. "And what would you like to talk about, young one?"

Passing the jar off to Sarge and lighting up a cigarette, I ask,

"Did you get everything you expected out of this fraternity experience?"

He thinks on this for a moment. "It wasn't what I anticipated getting into it, but I've gotten everything out of it that I could."

"Are you sick of it at this point? I know you don't hang around the house much. And at ceremonies, you look about as impressed as I am by all this stupid shit."

"It gave me a good distraction for a while until the newness of it all wore off. When it's all said and done, my expectations were too high. I missed the Army. I was having a hell of a time transitioning, and so I was trying to find a substitute brotherhood. Problem is, a fraternity isn't the Army, and it never could be." He lets out a deep sigh, biting down onto his cigar as his eyes trace the night sky.

"Do I really show my cards that bad?" he eventually asks, a smirk building on his face.

Shaking my head, I respond, "Nah. I mean, you hold an officer position. You show up when they need you to. Seems like a lot of brothers around here really look up to you, including myself. Nothin' more you can really ask of someone. It's just, you don't seem like you're as frat-tastic as the rest of these guys."

He laughs, nodding his head as he removes his cigar from his lips and replaces it with the mason jar. He takes a swig, swallows hard, and then he says, "Yeah, I'm certainly not. Some of this shit has gotten quite old. *I've* gotten quite old."

"When did it all start gettin' old for you?"

"When I realized all these guys like to do is get fucked up, do drugs, fuck chicks, and sleep all day." He shrugs. "That, and like I said, I realized I was old as dirt playing a young man's game. It felt time to move on about a year after I pledged and true colors started to show. That's when people started finding out about me too. Took away some of my aura, I think. Some of that badass Army mystique I carried around for a year."

"What did people start findin' out?" I ask.

He chuckles, shrugging, as he replies frankly, "That I'm gay."

I rear my head back as he returns the cigar to his lips and hands the 'shine back over to me.

"Shut the fuck up," I say, blindly grabbing the jar and taking a swig. Though, my doubtful eyes never leave his, a tight scrunch in my brow.

"No bullshit," he replies.

I study his expression.

Genuine.

"There's no fuckin' way you're gay. Not a chance," I argue, shaking my head.

"Believe it, Bishop. It's the truth. I've been out for a handful of years now."

"C'mon, man. I can't tell if you're fuckin' with me here or not."

"I'm not." Sarge grins, dabbing the cigar out and reaching into his pocket. He pulls out his phone as he takes the jar from me.

Scrolling through his phone, he eventually says, "Aha," and faces the phone screen toward me. He takes a drink of the 'shine with his other hand, a wide smile against the brim of the glass.

On the screen is a photo of Sarge, a few years younger, wearing an Army t-shirt, and walking in what can only be a Gay Pride parade, a small rainbow flag in his hand. He locks the screen and stuffs the phone back into his pocket, chuckling as my jaw belongs to the floor now.

"Does everyone here know?" I eventually ask, disbelief still written on my features.

"The people that need to, yeah. And they know I have a

boyfriend in Pittsburgh—Jonah—who I love. That's the main reason I'm not around so much anymore. They respect and understand that for the most part. There are some good guys in DIK, seriously; there's just a lot of shit in the ranks, too. Just like any other organization, I guess."

"How'd you deal with bein' gay in the Army?"

"I didn't," he says, chuckling, but there's some pain masked behind it. "I didn't talk about it, didn't feel it, didn't acknowledge it. Not until I got out. I was a shell of a man for most of my life. When I joined the Army, it was my everything, my identity. It's all I knew and cared about. It took meeting Jonah about five years ago to find myself. My love for him allowed me to see myself for who I really was, and not just the rough exterior I surrounded myself with before him."

"Wow, that's really awesome, man."

"*He's* awesome," Sarge says, smiling. "I'm just lucky."

"Were you ever straight?" I ask, and he laughs. I immediately feel stupid for asking such a senseless question.

"I pretended to be for a while. I was married once. For a spell. But straight? Me?" He laughs. "Nah."

"No shit. You were married?"

"That's right. Married my high school sweetheart. I was trying to do what was expected of me, I guess. I was married to her for two years before it all fell apart. Like I said, I had this barrier up no one could breach. I didn't feel. I just existed. And war became my mistress."

"And you knew while you were married that you were gay?"

"Bishop, I knew since I was a kid. I was just following the pattern. Until the pattern just didn't make sense to me anymore."

"Do your Army friends know now?"

"Most of them. Some, I just can't tell. Probably should, but likely never will."

"I can't even imagine havin' to tell everyone. To even *need* to tell everyone. It shouldn't matter." I hesitate for a moment, pulling out another cigarette. "What about your parents?"

"My parents are both gone now, but my mom was the first person I ever told. She supported me, no matter what. Helped me a lot through my divorce. It was a really difficult time. My dad never knew and probably never would've wanted to know. He was a farmer with that old-school mentality. But he loved me. He was just the 'what you don't know, doesn't hurt' kind of person."

I lift the nearly empty jar of moonshine and pass him a smirk. "Now, I don't have to worry about you makin' moves on me, seein' as I'm drunk, do I?" I take a chug as he laughs.

"You wish. I like my guys skinny and a little on the feminine side."

"So, what's so different between that and a woman?"

He grins, swiping the jar from me. "I don't need to give you an anatomy lesson, do I?"

"No, no. I mean, like if they're feminine and kind of girly-lookin', isn't that about the same as datin' a woman?"

"Well, let me ask you this. Would you fuck a feminine-looking gay guy?"

I shake my head firmly. "Nope. Nothin' against it. I just like the pussy."

"Okay, so it's not the same. And I like the dick."

"Got it."

"I like dude's buttholes. Man pussy."

I laugh loudly. "I'm pickin' up what you're puttin' down. Good to go."

"Does it bother you?"

"Only when I think about it."

He laughs, shaking his head. "I feel the same way about pussy."

"I don't know how. Pussy is delicious, man."

"*Some* pussy is delicious," he corrects me. "Remember, I played straight for a few years and she wasn't always flowers and spring meadows down there."

"Yeah, that's true," I agree, grimacing. "But you fuck what people shit out of."

He passes me a doubtful look. "You're telling me you've never fucked an asshole?"

"Well, yeah. Of course, but ..."

He chuckles. "Of course, nothing. It's the same thing. Dude ass. Woman ass. It's all the same. There aren't different brands. It's called good personal hygiene, Bishop."

"I've had some bad experiences."

"Haven't we all. You have to enema. It's a must," he says.

"I think we've talked enough about assholes tonight, actually."

"You did say you wanted to change the subject." He grins wide.

I laugh and then look over toward the parking lot, hearing faint noises. "I wonder how the other guys are farin'."

Louder now, a cackle comes from out of the darkness, and then obnoxious howling. Mac abruptly scurries across the parking lot on all fours. Tim follows behind him, laughing, with a beer in one hand and his phone in the other, recording.

"Mac! What the fuck are you doin'?" I yell, standing. Sarge stands too, and we lean over the railing. Mac is down by the street now with a leg hiked up as if he's pissing on a hydrant.

Sarge laughs. "This motherfucker," he says, shaking his head.

"Dude is a fuckin' lightweight. Then again, he can't weigh more than like ninety pounds."

"He looks like a bulimic Carrot Top," Sarge quips, and I burst out in laughter.

"Like Ellen's red-headed cousin ... who happens to be bulimic. And addicted to cocaine," I add as Mac crawls back toward the porch.

Tim pockets his cellphone and heads our way.

"Wolfpack Family!" Mac yells, followed by an annoyingly high-pitched howl.

"That red-headed fuck is drunk," Tim bellows, his eyes bloodshot and the beer can unsteady in his hand.

"And what about you?" Sarge asks, pointing to Tim's crotch where a large wet spot sits. "Did you piss yourself, Tim?"

Tim looks down slowly, inspects his piss-coated sweatpants, and then his eyes trail back to us. He shrugs. "Would you look at that."

Mac, standing now, makes his way toward us in zig-zagging, uncoordinated steps. "I'm a fucking wolf, man!" he yells, howling again. "Wolfpack, baby!"

"Mac, shut the fuck up," I say, chuckling as I shake my head at him. "Where's everybody else?"

"I'm a wolf," Mac repeats, trying his best to look at me, but his eyes are distant.

I put two hands on his shoulders, forcing his eyes onto mine. "You drank too much, buddy. What's everyone else up to?"

Mac sighs, his bourbon breath turning my stomach. "Downstairs. Zane went to bed and Jeremy is passed out. Brady's hooking up with a chick."

"What about Carter?"

"He's in the basement. Drinking. Drunk."

"By himself?"

Mac nods.

I look back toward Sarge, and he motions to the door. "Go ahead, man. I'm just a short cab ride away from some more moonshine," he says, passing me a wink.

I shift my eyes back toward Mac and pat him on the shoulder. "Get some rest, Red."

Mac nods, his eyelids fluttering. "I'm crashing on the couch tonight," he mutters.

I pat him one more time before dropping my hands to my sides. "Y'all are gonna catch somethin' from those couches one of these days." I laugh as I slap hands with Sarge. "Have a good night, brother. And thank you."

"No problem," he says, pulling me in for a bro hug.

Before I let go of his hand, I say, "*Really*, I mean it. Thanks for trustin' me enough to open up."

He nods. "That's what family's for. Welcome to the Warrior Family, brother," he says.

"Wait, what's that even mean?" I ask. "You were supposed to tell me earlier, but then we got drunk."

"Since 1922, any brother within the Warrior Family has served in the military."

I nod approvingly. "Fuck yeah! I love that. Alright, man. Well, have a good night," I say, making my way around the house to the side door. I can hear Mac's heavy footfalls behind me. Heading through the door, I see Carter on the couch cradling a beer in his lap and Jeremy passed out next to him.

Mac beelines toward the bar.

"How you feelin', man?" I ask, taking a seat beside Carter.

He takes a deep breath, belches, and responds, "Fucked. Up."

I laugh, motioning toward Jeremy, who is angled awkwardly on the couch next to him, his mouth wide open and a puddle of drool on the cushion. "Fared better than him. And let's not even talk about Mac," I say, my focus shifting toward Mac as he clunks around in the refrigerator.

He hiccups, his head wobbly as he looks over at me. "I feel like dog shit."

"Yeah, I'm not faring too good myself. Gonna cab my ass home here in a few. Just wanted to check on you."

He waves me off. "I'm good. I'm good. Going to crash here tonight."

"Alright, man."

"You know, Bishop," he says, raising a finger in the air. "I'm really glad you're doing this with us. I'm glad you're our president."

"I'm glad too, man. I probably wouldn't still be here if it weren't for y'all."

"I don't think I would be either," he says. He swallows thickly and then adds, "You know, I used to have a real brother. A sister, too." His focus shifts to the TV, though it's not on.

I'm caught off-guard, gulping. Hesitating, I study his darkening features before asking, "The car wreck?"

He nods, his face reddening, his focus still lost. "My mom was driving," he mutters. "You might have heard about it." His eyes eventually come back to mine. "It was all over the news. There was a documentary on it, too." He says this with a spiteful tone.

"How long ago was it?"

"Back in 2005. I was fourteen. My mom was acting really weird, like she was drunk or something. But they found nothing in her system, or that's what my dad always told me. I never brought myself to watch the documentary or read any of the articles. I want to keep my memory of her as it used to be. Before all the chaos."

He picks at the beer label on his bottle, a wrinkle of exasperation etched on his forehead. "I can't tell you how hard it was to ignore all that. It was a fucking circus. Everyone trying to figure out who to blame. But they really didn't care. They just loved the ratings it got." He hesitates, taking a deep breath and gulping.

"My mom killed five people that day," he continues, and his words ice my veins, a shiver sweeping down my spine. He shakes his head, and I can see the sharp curves of his cheekbones as he clenches his jaw, the thick scar on his cheek tightening, his solemn eyes on the frayed beer bottle label he picks at.

"You don't have to talk about it if you don't want to, Carter. I appreciate you sharin' what you have."

He waves me off. "No, I want to. I don't ever talk about it, and I get pissed at myself sometimes for pretending like it never happened. For pretending like they never existed." He shakes his head firmly, his expression reading inner turmoil. "My grandma, my sister, my brother. And then the two in the Explorer. All gone. I was sleeping. It's the only reason I survived, you know that? It's like how drunks are always the only ones to survive a bad wreck. It's why I can't tell you what happened that day."

"Oh fuck," I mutter, remembering now exactly what he's talking about. It *had* been all over the news for weeks. Months, even. I may have even watched the documentary at one point though I can't recall much of it. Just the details he now lays on me—a wrong way crash, the mystery surrounding the mother and her behavior that day, and another bit of information from the documentary passes through my thoughts ... a message she had left for her husband just before the crash.

"You remember it?" he asks.

I nod. *"What's Wrong with Mommy?"* I ask, and he nods his head slowly, his eyes glistening over.

"That'd be it. You watched it?"

"I think I did, but I can't recall anything from it, other than what you've just shared. Sorry, man."

"Do you remember the message?"

I nod, my lips pinching together and brow furrowing as I find it hard to see him hurting as he is. He's so young, and the whole world sits right in front of him, wide open and ready for the taking. Yet he suffers just as I do, for reasons much different than my own. I chose to join the Army. I chose to put myself in harm's way. He was just a kid led astray down an unfair road.

"The police leaked the voicemail my mom left my dad just before the crash and the documentary crew and news people got their dirty little hands on it." Tears well in his eyes. I want to console him somehow, but I don't know how.

There's a silence between us for a moment. I set my hand on his shoulder and I squeeze, which seems to allow a few more tears to fall.

"They just kept digging and digging. Of course, they'd find something. Of course, they would. And what did it do anyway? What did my dad's affair have to do with fucking anything? It changed nothing!" he growls, dropping his head into his hands.

I move my hand to the nape of his neck, wanting to say something but left completely speechless.

"Ugh," he groans, sitting up straight again. "Sorry, man. Not trying to be a bitch." He lifts the beer bottle and shakes his head. "Fucking alcohol."

Giving him another good squeeze, I say, "Hey man, don't apologize for shit. Not a goddamn thing. We've all got our crosses to bear. It's tough to share some of that shit, so I appreciate you makin' the effort. And honestly, I knew from the moment I met you that there was somethin' different. A deeper connection. Some commonality, you know? We've both suffered. I mean, *really* suffered. More than most of these fuckers at this school. We're survivors, man. Remember that. And don't beat yourself up too much about this stuff. I know it's hard, but this wasn't your fault. It wasn't."

Carter takes a deep breath, a bit of resolution taking up his features. "How did you get past all the shit you've been through?" he asks.

I shake my head, responding, "Honestly, I don't think that shit ever goes away, man. I sure the fuck haven't gotten over the things I've been through. I've snuffed them out enough to exist in the present as best I can, but the experiences and thoughts, and all the shitty emotions that come along with them will always be up there ..." I motion to my head. "Swirlin' around, and just fuckin' waitin' to turn any normal day to shit."

"Do you take anything to maybe help with it?"

"I've been on a few things over the years, but I could never stick it out. It's nice to feel level-headed and all, but not when the tradeoff is losin' all passion and personality. I felt like a zombie. And don't even get me started on Zoloft. I could fuck for hours on that shit and still not come."

"Doesn't sound so bad to me."

"Yeah, maybe not if my own hand couldn't even cut it. A man needs to clean the pipes."

He laughs, nodding his head in agreement. "Yeah, that sucks."

"I don't know if pills are the answer anyhow. I mean, what do they really do? Block out the shit you've been through? Block out the negative memories and emotions? You can block them out for a spell, but that doesn't mean they aren't still there. Don't mean they won't come back and bite you down the road. I don't know, I've just always liked facin' that shit head-on. Grab that pint of liquor and ice cream, throw on a comedy, and just fuckin' embrace the shit. Sometimes you just have to accept the crappy days for what they are and hope tomorrow brings you better."

"How often is tomorrow better?" he asks, and I hesitate briefly, thinking on his question.

Finally, I say, "Not as often as I'd like. It's hard most days. I have to remind myself often how much worse it could be. How much worse it's been."

He nods. "Yeah, I think that's why I started keeping it to myself back in the day. I always got the feeling people thought I was digging for sympathy, and that's the *last* thing I want. I hate that look of pity people give me."

"Yes! I get that same damn look when people ask about my eye. Like, 'fuck you, take your pity elsewhere.' I've got buddies who look nothin' like they used to, thanks to the unrelenting fuckin' brutality of fire when it meets skin. Guys that'll shit in bags for the rest of their lives. I can't feel sorry for myself, so I refuse to let others feel sorry for me." I hesitate for a moment before adding, "It's a tough battle to fight on your own, though. So just know you can talk to me whenever, and I'll never view it as a ploy for sympathy. Not ever. That's not how friendship works. And what you've been through ..." I shake my head. "That's some heavy shit. You deserve to unburden yourself sometimes."

"I appreciate that, Bish. And same goes for you."

Realizing I haven't heard a peep from Mac since my conversation with Carter started, I crane my head toward the bar and eye it curiously.

"What the hell happened with Mac? Did he sneak out of here while we were talkin' and I didn't notice?"

Carter looks over too and shakes his head. "I don't think so. He was being stupid loud. We would've heard him."

"Yeah, he said he was stayin' the night here too," I say, standing and making my way over to the bar.

As I approach, the first thing I notice is the mini-fridge door wide open, and then Mac's hand covered in a pile of toppled beer bottles. He's on the floor in front of the mini-fridge, his hand still inside. He lets out a light snore.

I laugh loudly, motioning for Carter. "Dude, you have to see this."

Carter approaches my side and cracks up upon seeing Mac in his current state.

"Fuckin' lightweight." I laugh, making my way around the bar and crouching down next to him.

"Hey Mac, get up, dude." I nudge his back and he stirs but doesn't wake. "Mac!" I repeat, louder now, and he raises his head slowly, looking at his hand first, buried in cold beer bottles at the bottom of the fridge, and then over at me through the slits of his eyelids.

"My hand's cold," he mutters, laying his head back to the floor as he shivers.

"That makes sense, considering your current predicament," I respond, laughing. "Get up, dude. It's time to get you reacquainted with the semen couch."

ELEVEN

In the week since our last pledge challenge—Big Brother Night—I've learned more about the fraternity and its hundred-year history than I have in any of my college courses. Being an undecided major means I get to knock out all the prerequisites I've yet to take, so my list of courses is like a recipe for fucking boredom and failure. And with having to learn so much fraternity bullshit and continuing our cleaning duties around the house, I've looked forward to the opportunity to get out of the house, see my dudes, and maybe drink a little ... or a lot. Who the fuck knows when it comes to DIK pledging.

We've been waiting in the basement now—the four of us—for nearly fifty minutes, but at least we weren't made to link up tonight. Instead, we were greeted down here by Brady, in all his hungover glory, who told us to relax until the night began.

Carter has looked nervous all evening, and though I've asked him and been denied a few times already, I feel the urge to ask him again what tonight will entail. I *know* he knows. I can see it in his eyes. And it doesn't look good.

He seems to notice what's about to come as he puts a finger up and digs into his pocket, his eyes on the other two as they fuck around near the bar. They've already checked the refrigerator three times for beer that isn't there, and now they're convinced there's some liquor hiding somewhere in the utility closet.

"Hey," Carter whispers, motioning to his jeans. He pulls a pint of Captain Morgan from his back pocket. "You're going to want to have some. *Trust me.* Just don't let the guys see. I don't have enough for all of us."

"Tell me what's goin' on, man," I plead, reaching for the bottle. He covertly places it in my hand, looking toward the others again as they continue digging through the closet. "And where the hell did you get this?"

"I just got a fake ID in the mail," he responds, his eyes still watching the closet closely.

I take a long swig, and then another for good measure before passing it back over, then he takes one himself. He grimaces as he swallows it down.

"I'll tell you when we get closer to it," he says, his face scrunching in displeasure. "You just want to drink as much as you can right now."

"You're freakin' me the fuck out, Carter. And you could've goddamn told me sooner, so I could've brought my own liquor."

"I know. They just really fucked with me hard about talking. They freaked *me* out.'

"Well, fuck ... pass that shit back over before the guys get done fuckin' around."

He hands it over and I take another big gulp before giving it back. He pockets it just as Mac exits the closet and groans, Jeremy just behind him.

"Fuck!" Jeremy says, shrugging with his palms in the air. "Ain't no liquor anywhere. This is some bullshit." He approaches us and points toward Carter. "Carter, what the shit is goin' down, man? You been weird all fuckin' day."

"No idea," Carter responds, shrugging. "We just have to wait and see."

"Is there gonna be any more of that gay shit?" Mac asks, pretending to swat a paddle.

Carter laughs. "I'd expect a lot more of that," he says. "That's just fraternity life for you."

"Blame the forefathers, right?" I ask.

Carter nods. "Exactly."

"I can totally see them in their pantaloons, spanking each other with paddles," I quip.

"I don't think they wore pantaloons in the Twenties." Carter laughs.

"Fuck off. Don't ruin my joke."

As the words leave my lips, the basement door opens, drawing our attention. Only Brady and Trevor come down, which surprises me, as I heard way more people clodhopping about upstairs. They're both dressed in suits, hair purposefully disheveled.

They scale the steps as Trevor says, "Alright, pledges. It's time to start your third challenge. You'll follow us out to the van, and we'll be taking you to a separate location."

"What about the alcohol?" Brady says, nodding his head toward us.

"Oh yeah," Trevor responds, snapping his fingers. "You all remembered not to drink anything today, right? Tonight's challenge is going to require you to be one-hundred percent sober."

We all nod our heads.

"Alright, let's go then."

We follow Trevor and Brady to the van and hop inside, eventually making our way down frat row toward Main Street. Just as we reach it, Damian makes a sharp right turn, pulling into a lot at the back of some building, amongst the trash dumpsters and discarded pallets.

"What the fuck," I mutter, taking in our surroundings, as Trevor turns back toward us.

"You guys follow Brady inside through the back. I'm going around front. I'll see you in a few minutes," he says, finishing in a singsong tone, a grin on his face as he opens the door and hops out.

Brady follows suit, motioning for us to follow him as he heads toward the back door. He holds the door open for us as we empty the van and approach. As we pass through the doorway, he says, "Let this be the only time I hold the door open for you bitches."

It's the 'bitches' that earns him a sneer as I follow Jeremy inside, Carter just a few steps behind me. Brady's expression doesn't change, though; the cocky smirk remains.

What I would give to beat that look off him.

"Line up in front of that door," Brady says, pointing toward the only door in front of us, as white as the painted cinderblock wall surrounding it. There are a few mop buckets, some mops and brooms, and a pile of boxes scattered around the narrow back room. Music plays from just past the door, so loud I can make out the song, though I can't decipher the lyrics.

SexyBack.

Brady follows us in, shutting the door behind him and cockily striding over to us as we wait beside the wall.

"You motherfuckers got no idea what's coming tonight," Brady says, laughing. "I hope you're ready for this shit."

The music softens a little and an announcer's voice replaces it, too muffled to understand. Brady laughs again, shaking his head. Mac gulps and I can feel the tension Carter carries in the air. I'm about to beat the secret out of him to be quite frank.

"No. *Fucking.* Clue," Brady continues, still pacing with his hands on his hips. As he studies us in a superior manner with that contemptuous grin on his face, the door abruptly opens.

Trevor comes through, an excited look in his eyes and a wide smile on his face. With him, comes flashing dance lights and music that deafens. There's a wraparound bar, and it looks to be filled, but beyond that, I can't see much. Trevor places his hand on Jeremy's shoulders and motions his head toward the club.

"You're up first, pretty boy," Trevor says, guiding Jeremy toward the entrance with an arm around his neck.

Jeremy grins. "Let's get 'er done," he responds as they disappear into the club, the door shutting behind them, snuffing out the strobe lights. There's high-pitched whooping on the other side, and I look to Carter with a quirked eyebrow.

"That sounds like a lot of girls," I mutter, and Carter just nods, a nervousness in his features.

"What'd you say, Bishop?" Brady barks.

"I said, 'It sounds like a lot of chicks in there.'"

"Yeah, it does," Mac agrees, wide-eyed and nervously scratching at his patchy beard.

"Oh, there *definitely* are," Brady says, a giddiness to his tone I don't like much.

After a nerve-racking minute of silence between us, my focus darts toward the door as it opens again, and Trevor comes through, the smile even wider now. "It's your turn, Red. Bishop, you're on deck," he says, gesturing for Mac to come through the door.

Mac hesitates, taking a gulp as he looks back toward us with fear in his eyes. "What's happening?" he asks Carter, who, in turn, just laughs nervously.

"Come on, Mac," Trevor says, nudging Mac through the door.

The song cuts out and an announcer says something over the PA system before a new song begins—*Pony*—and the door closes behind them.

I gasp, eyes going wide, mouth slack. "We're fuckin' strip-ping, aren't we? *Aren't we?*" I shout, the red flags finally visible.

Carter nods, letting out a bit of nervous laughter.

"Butt fucking naked," Brady laughs.

"Fuck me," I groan, putting a hand out toward Carter. "Give me the fuckin' bottle." I snap at his back pocket, but he doesn't go for it right away, instead looking toward Brady as if he's been caught stealing.

"What bottle?" Brady asks.

"My bottle. I made Carter hold it for me." My eyes remain on Carter and I gesture for him to hurry up and hand it over. "And now I want it back."

He hesitates, looking at Brady and then at me again before he finally digs it out and hands it over.

"You weren't supposed to drink alcohol today," Brady snaps, a lip curled back.

"No offense, Brady, but I'm a grown-ass man, and if I have to strip for a bar full of people, I'm doin' it with some liquor in my fuckin' system. And a lot of it." I unscrew the top and toss the bottle back, killing about a quarter of it. I take an extra-long drink since I know Brady is watching me intently. Once I finish, I hand it over to Carter. "Want some?"

Carter looks at Brady and then me, and then the bottle, before he reluctantly takes it from me and throws it back.

"You fucks!" Brady growls. "You're so fucked for this, pledges. Get ready for some serious fucking punishment."

Carter saves just a little bit for me, handing the bottle over and then shrugging as Brady still glares at him.

Brady scoffs as I kill the remaining rum. Just as I toss the empty bottle to the floor, the door swings open for a third time. The whooping and cheering on the other side have risen a few decibels as the song fades out. Trevor eyes the bottle on the ground and then up toward us, laughing.

"Smart motherfuckers," Trevor says, grinning as beads of sweat take up his brow line now. His eyes fall on me. "You ready, boss?"

I shrug, my heart pounding in my chest, but my face reading Sunday morning. "Let's do it," I say, walking toward him, enjoying Brady's defeat.

Trevor puts a hand on my back, leading me into the packed club. He laughs as the announcer shouts into the mic, working up an already worked up crowd. The spacious bar is filled top to bottom with frat brothers and their dates, dressed up and all their eyes on me. Mac is in the process of getting his clothes back on at a table by the bar, he looks to be cursing under his breath, which brings me a smile, and Jeremy whoops it up for me from beside Mac, clapping his hands wildly.

I flip him off.

Leaning in, Trevor says, "Just down to your boxers, man. Until the song stops. For them *right there*." He points toward the dance floor where the crowd disperses, and an opening awaits. At the back of the dance floor, seated in chairs that line the wall, four girls clap and cheer for my approach.

My heart fucking *pounds*.

"Everybody give it up for Biiishop!" the announcer shouts over the PA system as Trevor pats me on the back one last time before he scurries off toward some brothers beside the dance floor. The unmistakable beats of Sugarhill Gang's "Apache (Jump On It)" overwhelm the sound system. I take a deep, steadying breath. My head starts bobbing instinctively as I get closer to them. My thoughts pass to *Fresh Prince of Bel-Air* ... Will and Carlton ... and I smile, letting the thoughts comfort me, while moving my head a little more with the music. As I approach the seated girls and scan their line, there, at the very end, is Ember, looking on with intrigue and gleeful anticipation.

I swallow thickly, ignoring the anxiety that creeps into my

mind, and, instead, I focus on the rum and how light it's made my feet feel—how loose it's made my hips. As the liquor warms my skin, the inhibitions I normally possess snuffed out like a trapped rat, I move my body. It's not some *Magic Mike* shit, but I can hold my own.

As the chorus hits for the first time, I find myself in front of the row of chairs and pretty much slow fucking the air in coordinated movements. Some of the girls get into it, dancing right along as I strip my t-shirt off. One of them looks a little nervous, her eyes flitting from me to the bar to the crowd and then back, her bottom lip between her teeth as if she's punishing herself for looking at my naked torso, and it's her I focus on ... well, her *and* Ember. I know Ember's watching. And maybe I'm saving her for last for a reason. Maybe, I want to toy with her.

I pull my belt off next, immediately wishing I had spent *much* more time at the gym than I have been, as I'm half-naked now, in a room full of people, and sucking in doesn't seem to be doing the trick. Then again, I've always been harder on myself than I should be.

The crazy thing is, eventually, I don't feel any of them behind me. It's as if they disappeared; my focus locked on the four seated before me. There's an electric ball of energy in my chest, right at the base of my throat, and I wear a smile from ear to ear that lets me know I'm doing something I never thought I would ... and loving every minute of it, if I'm being honest with myself. The jolt of pleasure you get when you push yourself outside of your comfort zone is unlike any other.

I flip the belt toward Ember down the line, and she catches it, a wide smile stretching across her face. She folds the belt in half and whips it lightly against her other hand as she quirks an eyebrow.

Unbuttoning my jeans, I continue down the line toward her.

I thrust my hips with each step, the nerves completely numb

now, and the excitement her smile brings me leading the way. She laughs wildly, batting me away playfully and whipping the belt toward my ass, and it encourages me to fuck with her more. I grab each of her wrists, pinning them to the wall above her head. The belt crashes to the floor as I thrust along to the music. She looks, at first, surprised, and then intrigued. I do one full body air grind with her hands still above her head, the fading music overtaken by her deliriously adorable laughter. It's contagious and gets a bellyful from me as well. I let her arms go and take her hand when the music completely dies, and the DJ takes to the mic.

"Thanks for bein' a good sport," I say into her ear as I wrap her up in my arms.

She smiles as I let her go, and says, "Thanks for the show!"

Trevor approaches and sets his hand on my shoulder as he laughs. "Hell of an effort, man," he says. "Now, put your clothes back on and get over there with your pledge bros. It's Carter's turn." He then makes his way toward the back door as I collect my clothes and bring them with me to the guys near the bar.

"Nice work, old man," Jeremy jokes as I slip my jeans and shirt back on.

"I'm sad I missed you fuckers," I respond as the announcer takes over the mic again.

"Everybody put your hands together for your last pledge of the night ... Carterrr!"

As the announcer starts up "Work It" by Missy Elliot, Carter reluctantly walks toward the dance floor alongside Trevor.

"God, I hope they're recording this shit. I have to see yours, Mac," I say as Trevor finishes his pep talk with Carter before he's fed to the wolves.

Jeremy bursts out laughing, simultaneously patting Mac on

the back. "It was ... the best thing ... I ever fuckin' saw," Jeremy says between laughs.

"Fuck you," Mac says, crossing his arms and pouting. "I don't fucking dance."

"Shhh." I put a finger to my lips and motion toward the dance floor with my other hand. "I have to see this shit."

After Carter's shameful attempt at stripping for the girls, with moves I haven't seen since middle school, the three of us laugh our asses off and bust his balls from across the room. Trevor approaches Carter from behind, patting him on the back, and saying something to him with a disappointed shake of his head. Trevor then motions us over. As we approach, Damian comes up beside him with a mic in his hand and passes it over.

Trevor grabs the mic, taps it a few times, and then says, "Alright, pledges, congratulations on passing Big Sis night. Big round of applause, please." As he puts his hand up to present us, the brothers and their dates clap and whistle loudly. Trevor waits for the noise to die down and then continues, "You are now to make sure your Big Sis, A, doesn't spend a dime tonight and, B, parties her ass off. No exceptions." Trevor motions to the four ladies we danced for and adds, "Ladies, meet your Little Brothers. Big Brothers, introduce them." Trevor motions toward the chairs lined up in front of the dance floor as our new Big Sisters empty them. "If any ladies want a front row seat for a dance from Damian, now's your chance."

As if he had thrown seed for pigeons at the park, a cluster of women race for the chairs, falling over each other as they fight over them. Four of them finally power their asses onto the chairs and the others walk away, heads hung.

It's then that Trevor backs the group of us—pledges, Big Brothers, and Big Sisters—toward the bar, handing the mic back off to the DJ.

"Ladieees," the DJ calls out as Ember wiggles her way

between the group of Big Brothers and Sisters who are cluttered between us as introductions are being made with the other pledges. I've yet to see Sarge. "It's time to get you a little piece of Damiannn," the DJ yells, spinning Usher's "Yeah" as the ladies respond with a chorus of high-pitched squeals.

Ember approaches me, a dangerous little smile on her face, as Damian strides to the center of the dance floor, his jacket, button-down, and tie now scattered across the ground, only a wife beater and suspenders still covering his chiseled torso. All the ladies scream for him, but not Ember. She still looks at me, digging blindly in her purse, and then pulling out a folded-up piece of notebook paper. She hands it over.

"What's this?" I ask, half-yelling as I combat the heavy beats.

"From Sarge," she says, still holding it out for me.

I take it and unfold it, reading over Sarge's doctor scrawl.

BISHOP,

Surprise! Sorry I couldn't be there. It's Jonah's birthday on Sunday, and we're celebrating in Pittsburgh over the weekend. I got us this really nice dinner cruise and promised not to bring up any conspiracy theories (you have no idea how big of a present that really is haha).

I hope you have fun! I've heard around the house that you're into this Ember girl and I know you don't get much time outside of pledging, so enjoy this time with her. A hundred in drinks on me. Enjoy!

Big Bro

PS … You aren't allowed to bone your Big Sister.

PSS … But I mean, shit happens.

I look back at Ember, smiling as I fold the note back up and pocket it.

"Where's this hundred dollars?" I ask, squinting, and she pats her purse.

She motions toward the bar. "Drink?"

"*Please.* That was fuckin' intense."

"Oh, I can only imagine. You did good though!"

"You say that as if you're surprised." I grin, leaning against the bar and trying to look as James Dean-esque as I can.

"I mean, you're white. Odds are not in your favor."

I crack up so hard it catches me off guard, and I put a hand to my mouth. "You aren't kiddin'," I say, dropping my hand and impulsively searching for the barkeep. I *really* need a drink. With the amount of people packed into such a small area, my heart has been racing since I entered, for reasons other than my first striptease. I know I'm not in any danger, I don't see myself in a war zone or anything like that, but it's like a part of my subconscious isn't quite in the know.

Ember turns, sets her palms to the edge of the bar and leans forward in a way that makes me think she's trying to show off her tits, or test me. My unavoidable glances are subtle, accordingly.

"I consider myself quite the bad bitch," she says, shaking her head. "But you will *never* catch me doing something like that. I'd die of a panic attack before I ever made it on the dance floor." She laughs as she pulls a twenty from her purse—presumably Sarge's money—and sets it on the bar top. She then orders two Fireballs from the bartender.

"Well, I don't think you can die from a panic attack. So, there's that."

"Yeah, but I can only assume that I would get completely and utterly shit-canned beforehand. The panic attack would lead to me fainting. The alcohol would lead to me vomiting, and then I'm choking on my own vomit. Ipso facto, the panic attack would've killed me."

"Maybe ... or you could say the alcohol killed you. Or the vomit."

"You could." She shrugs. "One of those chicken and egg scenarios, I guess?"

"I guess." I chuckle, and then take a glance around the room. "I'm sure somebody here would've saved you though. After you fainted and choked on your own vomit."

She looks at me with complete seriousness, and she asks, "But would I really want them to? I just choked on my own vomit, in front of a hundred people, after a panic attack. My reputation's just gone. Seriously, that fucker's extinct."

"You know, maybe you could just move ... or something. I don't know. Death seems like an extreme step."

"Pussy," she mutters, and then finally breaks into a fit a laughter. "You're ridiculous."

"And you're not?"

"Not as much as you, buddy."

"This a tit for tat game or something?" I ask.

"This is gonna be a long night, isn't it?" She smiles as the bartender trades the twenty in her hand for the two shots in his own.

She lifts her shot glass and clinks it against mine, her eyes study me.

"I think that's part of the rules," I respond, smiling before I throw back the shot as she does the same. We set the glasses back down on the bar top with a loud clink and I let out a manly grunt to combat the throat burn. Her face remains steady.

She quirks an eyebrow. "As I was saying ... pussy."

"Hey now. I've beaten dudes' asses for less."

"Don't threaten me with a good time!"

"You sure you can handle it?" I ask, wiping a forearm across my lips.

"Don't test my abilities," She responds, and then her hand abruptly dives into her purse. She digs around a bit and the pulls out that pink flask of hers. She spins the top off and offers it up. "Woodford?"

I nod, grabbing the flask, though my stomach turns at the thought. Taking a swig, I fight the disgust from my face and hand the flask back to her. She takes a shot of her own, and then she studies me as she screws the lid back on.

"Ember, aren't you upset you're missing the show?" I ask, motioning toward Damian who is now down to a g-string and has his ass in one of the girl's faces. Brady and Trevor have joined him in semi-nudity on the dance floor, grinding for the giddy girls in chairs before them.

Ember glances over, but her eyes quickly flit back to me. She shrugs. "Not my cup of tea," she says, taking another swig from the flask.

"What's your cup of tea then?" I ask, and her eyes run the length of my body.

"I'm looking at it," she responds with a grin.

"Shut up."

"I'm serious."

"What is it about me that attracts you? Because I know it's not my looks. The scar and fake eye take away that possibility."

She sets a hand to my face, her eyes lingering on mine as she says, "I find you stunning, scars and all. And in my honest opinion, it makes it sexier knowing that happened fighting for our country. And besides that, I love who you are as a person. You're down to earth. And real. More so than any guy I've met here. Or ever."

I nod, not even fighting the smile that stretches across my face. "I could say the same about you."

"Well, I beat you to it," she says, that sexy little grin tugging at her lips. "So, I win."

"Why do I get the feelin' you *always* win?"

"You do seem to be a reasonably smart man," she responds, smirking.

"I like to think so. But I, too, am used to winnin'. So, we may encounter some problems down the road."

She hesitates, lifting the flask to her lips, but not taking a drink. Instead, she asks, "Are you willing to find out?" with a tilt of her head.

I nod as she takes a small swig and passes the flask back over. I take a drink, swallow against the burn, and say, "I'm one-hundred percent willin' to find out. I'm even willin' to be wrong on occasion ... a *few* occasions."

"Only a few, huh?" She eyes me, a smile building on her face as she nods, digging back into her purse. She trades the flask for another twenty and smacks it on the bar top.

"Two more, Andre!" she calls out over her shoulder.

"Do you know *everybody* in this town? And why are we even drinkin' from the flask if we've got Sarge's money?"

Her face twists in judgement. "Do you know how expensive Woodford is here? Fuck no," she says, poking her tongue out. "And I told you, I've been coming here since I was sixteen, remember? I kind of do know everybody." She takes a step forward and runs a hand down my lapel. "So, how drunk do you plan on getting tonight?"

"That's a good question. Do we have plans for later?"

"Hmm ... I had a few things in mind. They'll require you not to get wasted and cry rape again though. Or get preoccupied with some invisible nacho platter." She laughs.

I grimace at the r-word. "Was I really sayin' that shit?" I ask as Andre delivers our shots.

"You absolutely were. And I wasn't even planning on giving you the goods."

"So, what's changed?"

She grabs the shot glasses and passes one off to me. As she holds hers up, she says, "I like you, Bishop. And I hope you like me too."

"You know I do."

"To getting to know each other better then," she says, and clinks her shot glass against mine, before killing it.

"To the best Big Sis a guy could ask for," I add, downing my own shot and returning it to the bar top. "No shit."

"What do you say we take this flask back to your place? Maybe you could make me dinner and we could watch a movie." Her eyebrows wriggle.

"You aren't in the party mood tonight?"

"I'm *always* in the party mood. I'm just not in the people-ing mood tonight."

"Well, I think it sounds like a great idea then. I've got no food at the apartment though, so how about we order a pizza?"

"Make it pepperoni and mushrooms and you got yourself a deal." She puts a hand out, waiting for me to shake it.

"Mushrooms, huh? A woman after my own heart." I shake her hand, but just before she lets go, I pull her in and kiss her. She acts surprised at first, but then leans into to me, grabbing my waist. I've missed the feel of her satin-soft lips, the taste of the whiskey and hint of spearmint on her breath, the touch of her body against mine. I crave it all and kiss her with a fervor and passion I don't recall feeling much of in my life before this. Not outside of combat that is.

It's electric.

As we part, she smiles, her eyes opening to slits, and she mutters, "Well, that was something."

"Yes, it was. I fuckin' love your lips."

"They certainly love yours *right* back."

"I've always put a lot of weight on kissin'. A good kisser is hard to find, you know? And worth its weight in gold."

"You got that right." She slides a hand from my waist to the nape of my neck, her other hand settling on my chest as she kisses me again. She has to stand on her tiptoes to reach me, and I find it ridiculously endearing.

"Let's get the fuck out of here," I whisper as I pull away from her, our breath intermingling.

"Now, you're speaking my language." She grabs me by the sleeve and pulls me toward the door. As I follow behind her, I look around the room for my guys, but they're scattered all over the place. When I give up and trail my eyes back forward, I catch Brady starring daggers at me from across the room. I crack a smile as Ember reaches the front door and throws it open.

"Quit dragging your heels," she says with a laugh, slapping a hand against my chest.

"I was lookin' for the guys so I could let 'em know I was leavin', but—"

"Eh, they're grownups. They'll be fine." She throws a hand up, snapping for a cab coming down Main Street.

We make out the entire cab ride to my apartment, and it probably would've been awkward if the shots hadn't started making my inhibitions waver. As we stumble out, I throw the cab driver a ten and shut the door behind us. Leading her inside, it's hard not to ache for her when I eye her supple ass. It's hard not to notice the thin line of her thong beneath the fabric of her tight black dress. I can feel a tingle of pleasure at the base of my balls, an ache rooted in my loins.

Once inside the apartment, I smack her ass and motion toward my room. "I'll meet you in there. Gonna grab some beers."

"Yes sir," she says, saluting, before turning on her heel and sauntering toward my room.

I shake my head, watching her as she goes, and knowing that tonight, I will be inside her, experiencing her, feeding this *insatiable* appetite for her body.

Grabbing two beers from the fridge, I make my way to my room, noticing she's made herself quite at home. She's kicked her heels off and sprawled out on the small twin-size bed, the remote in her hand and *Saved by the Bell* on the TV.

"I love Nick at Night," she says, taking the beer from me and scooting over so I can lay with her.

"What the hell do you know about Bayside High?"

She gasps, offended. "How dare you! I grew up on this stuff. Nick at Nite has always been my shit. *Family Matters*, *Saved by the Bell*, *Fresh Prince* ... all of it."

"Okay, okay. You have to admit not many twenty-year-olds can say the same thing though."

She pretends to poof her hair out. "I am quite unique, if you haven't figured that out yet."

"I'm beginning to. So, quiz time, can you sing the intro to *Fresh Prince?*"

Abruptly, she sits up and starts rattling it off, flailing her hands about as if she's an MC. "... Shooting some b-ball outside of the school, when a couple of guys who were up to no good, started making trouble in my neighborhood," I sing along with her.

When we finish, she busts out in laughter, attempting to steady her beer bottle, but some splashes out anyway. She calms herself, wiping the beer on her dress away with her hand as she says, "Don't doubt me, punk."

Sitting up, cross-legged as she is, I tilt my beer. "Noted. You are just full of all kinds of surprises, huh?"

She clinks her bottle against mine and then we both take a drink.

"What's your all-time favorite show? And if it has the name Kardashian in it, I am bootin' you from this tiny ass bed."

She shakes her head and sticks her tongue out in a pretend gag. "No freaking way. I hate the Kardashians. I'm into stuff like *Parks and Rec* and *The Walking Dead*. Loved *Sons of Anarchy*, too. And of course, the classics. *Friends, It's Always Sunny, Arrested Development, The Office*."

"Dear Lord, marry me now, woman."

She snickers. "Good answer?"

"The best answer!"

"What about you?" she asks.

"Well, all the ones you mentioned, for sure. *The Walking Dead* kind of wore me out after a while, so did *SOA*, but that's just me. I gravitate toward comedies. I've seen all the dramas ... *Breaking Bad, Shameless* ... and they're all good shows, but after a while, the drama just gets to be too much. A lot of that has to do with my rehab. For a long time, I was in and out of surgeries, stayin' in a barracks where I knew no one, so TV shows and movies became my escape. The funnier they were, the better I felt."

She nods. "That definitely makes sense." She runs her fingertips against my scar, slowly. "Does it bother you to talk about it?"

"No, it really doesn't. It's been about three years now, and with it being on my face, I've gotten a lot of questions over that time."

"You're probably sick of talking about it though."

"With strangers, yeah. But with people I'm trying to get to know, I don't mind. It's a part of who I am. What would you like to know?"

"Do you remember much of it?"

"I remember everything leadin' up to it." I take a gulp, the images swirling my mind as they do when I think about it, the hot sun overhead, the death surrounding us, the sounds of gunfire, the smell of burning flesh, distinct and pungent. "I remember my buddy gettin' shot and I ran out to get him, tried to drag him out, and then we were hit. And it just went black. I woke up in a hospital in Germany with no clue as to how I got there or the events that transpired after the explosion. Everything I know I learned from reports."

"Did your buddy die?"

I nod. "Two of them," I mutter.

"I'm sorry," she says, resting a hand on top of mine and squeezing it.

"It's okay." I force a smile, motioning to her purse resting beside us. "Can I get that flask though?" I chuckle nervously.

She smirks, taking it out and handing it over.

"I like your style, by the way," I say, motioning toward her with the flask before I take a heavy swig.

"What do you mean?"

"The pink flask, the heels with the spikes on 'em, the Chucks, this little badass persona you carry around."

"It's no persona," she corrects me, snatching the flask from my hand. "It's just me." She takes a drink.

"Well, I dig it."

"I dig you and your badass Army persona."

"No persona, my dear. I bleed Army. I was born and bred for it."

"What did you do over there?" she asks.

"Infantry."

"Is that like the frontline guys?"

I nod. "Yeah, we did a lot of raids, counter IED patrols, shit like that."

"Were you ever scared?"

"Shitless." I hesitate, letting the three deployments wash over me. "It was terrible at the beginning of my first one. I thought every day goin' outside the wire was gonna be my last. But when it's not, over a period of time, when you survive your first gunfight and IED blast, you sort of get used to it. It becomes your new normal. So, you worry less. Of course, the fear comes back when you lose that first guy, and then the second, and the third, and every one thereafter. Because it reminds you that you're not immortal. A lot of us veterans, active duty people, we have that feelin' of invincibility, because we've experienced so much. We forget how easy it is to die out there. How valuable life really is."

Her eyes are saucers, her mouth in an O. "Wow ... I've never really known anyone in the military, except Zane. And he only deployed once. I was scared to death when he did."

"What service was he in? I've noticed he doesn't talk very much. Haven't really gotten to know anything about him."

"He was Air Force. I'm not a hundred percent sure what he did. But you're right. I've known him all these years and I still don't really know him. He's always been the quiet type."

"Fuckin' Air Force," I say, scoffing.

"Oh yeah, you guys hate each other, right?"

"It's a healthy, competitive hate. Every Army guy wishes he were in the Air Force, even though we'd never really admit it. And every Air Force guy wishes he were on the frontlines doin' the Lord's work. They'd never admit it either. They've also got it ten times better than us lowlife soldiers. Better bases, more pay, better jobs."

"So why didn't you go Air Force?"

"Well, first off, my grades in high school were fuckin' abysmal. They didn't want my ass. Second, I've always wanted to fight. I wanted to be that guy kickin' down doors and gettin' into firefights and shit."

"Was it everything you thought it would be?"

"It was. It *certainly* was. I loved my time spent overseas. I loved fightin', doin' some good, helpin' people. I guess I just never realized how much it all wears on you. Being in a state of high adrenaline over a year, year and a half period of time, it really gets to a human being. It scars you up real good."

"I love your scars." She brushes a hand against my thick facial scars again.

"Thank you." I smile. "But I meant the internal ones."

"Well, I love those too."

"Lady, if you had even a glimpse of those, you'd be runnin' for the hills."

She scoffs, shaking her head adamantly. "No, sir. We all have a little internal scarring, some have a lot, and considering yours were caused by serving this country, I think you get a pass."

"I don't want a pass. I just want them all to just go away." I force a weak laugh. "Ugh, how did we even get on this subject?"

"You sure it doesn't bother you talking to me about it? Because it doesn't bother me."

"No, I guess I'm still just trying to make sense of it all."

"What do you mean?"

"It's just, I don't know, it's all still so new. I was in the Army fightin' the enemy for years, until one day I got blown up and the fightin' just stopped. And then I was in the hospital fightin' to get better. And that gave me a healthy distraction for a while. Now, I'm just a civilian. Now, what am I fightin' for?"

"Why not look at it as a fresh start?"

"Oh, I certainly have. I do. But with every fresh start comes the fear of failure. The fear of the unknown."

"The unknown can be scary, yeah, but it can be exciting too." She takes both of my hands into hers and squeezes. "You never know what lies ahead."

"More liquor in my future, I think. And some other things."
I grin, setting a hand to her cheek and kissing her.

"Pizza?" she asks against my lips.

"And ..."

"*Saved by the Bell?*" She smiles.

God, that fuckin' smile might end me.

"And ..."

She reaches a hand toward my crotch, grabbing a handful of
dick. "Oh my," she says, arching an eyebrow. "You're going to do
something with that thing, I hope. I mean, that is if you're not
too drunk again."

I take her beer from her, setting it on the nightstand along
with my own. Then I throw her back against the bed, straddling
her as I pin her arms down.

"Not a chance," I say, peppering her neck with kisses, her
soft skin blushing with my touch.

She moans, arching her hips up into me as I work my lips
and tongue up her neck. As my lips meet her ear, I whisper, "As
much as I love this dress, I think we need to get you out of it."

She glances up toward her hands, still pinned to the
mattress. "I may need those back then."

"Aw, come on," I say, releasing her hands and sitting up. "I
thought you had skills."

"Oh, you're about to find out just what kinds of skills I possess,"
she purrs as she sits up and moves her hands behind her back, struggling with the zipper. "Hands-free dress removal is *not* one of them."

She manages to unzip her dress and slips the straps off her
shoulders. I slide it down her body, and as I do, I admire her
flawless skin, a large tattoo of Little Red Riding Hood on her
ribcage. Little Red is perched on a swing amongst a densely
populated forest of dead trees; a wolf peers from the distance. I
trace the tattoo with a finger as I toss her dress to the floor.

"That is fuckin' epic," I say, admiring the smooth line work and rich colors. My finger moves from her ink, down to the see-through satin panties she's wearing, the curves of her pussy lips defined and bringing a wave of desire over me. "These are epic too."

"You like?"

"Fuckin' do I. I'd have to be a lunatic not to."

"I wore them just for you," she says, and I tilt my head.

"Did you now?"

"I sure did."

"So, you were anticipating us hookin' up tonight, huh?"

"If you turned me down again, you would've gotten a heel to the balls."

"Oh, *really* now. Brady not cuttin' it anymore?"

Her mouth gapes, her brows pinched together as she says, "Ugh, your timing is terrible. I'm just about naked in your bed and you bring *him* up?"

As she tries to wiggle her way out from beneath me, I put a hand to her shoulder. "Wait, wait, wait ... rewind. Let's pretend I never said that, okay?"

"Hmmm, I don't know. The mood is waning. I might need a little encouragement." As she leans back on her elbows, she passes me a cocky little shrug, eyeing her pussy.

"I think that can be arranged. You just lay back like a good little girl and let me make you come."

She points a finger at me, narrowing her eyes, and says, "There are no good girls in this room. Now, do something with your mouth besides talking." She grins, laying back.

"Yes ma'am," I say, leaning down and kissing her stomach. Her abs clench against my lips, her body writhing as I move closer to her core.

I don't start on her pussy right off the bat, instead, biting her inner thigh, licking the spot where her panty line meets skin, and then blowing the saliva dry.

She lets out a quiet moan, a hand moving to my head where she grabs a fistful of hair.

"You better fucking stop teasing me, mister."

In response, I lick her pussy lips lightly over the thin fabric. She tightens her grip on the good bit of my hair she has clutched in her hand. She drives her hips into my face. With her other hand, she pulls her panties to the side, exposing the most beautiful pussy, and I have to take a second to admire it, to thank my lucky stars that it's me who gets to see it, and taste it, and touch it. I knew it was going to be good by the way it indented the slick satin of her panties, but hell, this pussy is legendary!

"Dear God, that's a PSP if I've ever seen one," I mutter, giving my head a quick shake.

"PSP?"

"Porn Star Pussy. It belongs on film."

"Well, thank you. But I don't think so. Now, less talky, more licky," she says, and I can't help but laugh. She laughs too but does her best to stifle it.

"Don't mind if I do." I swoop down, sliding my tongue against her hot entrance, collecting up the wetness that has already taken hold, and then I replace her hand with mine, gripping her panty line and pulling it even further to the side. I want to see the whole thing. I want to savor this moment.

She uses her free hand to grab the remainder of my hair— at least it feels like it—and she lets out a loud gasp, pushing my head into her. I continue licking and sucking on her hot little clit. I can't get over the taste of it. So good, I could stay down here for hours cleaning her up, hearing her breathy moans, feeling her thighs quivering against my head. I've always loved eating a girl out. Shit, it's essential. But this is something else. This woman has some magic going on down here, or else sex with Joanne wasn't as good as my memory serves me.

It's then, my tongue mid-stride, I think of Seymour Butts, a curly-haired Jewish man—rail-thin, with a dick T-Rex would envy. I came to know him through a popular porn film among military men. This particular film has been passed from one soldier's external hard drive to another to another in an endless chain. In the video, Mr. Butts teaches men how to make a woman squirt. In all the things I've learned, in all the years of my life, Mr. Seymour Butts is responsible for the *most important*. He has brought hours of pleasure to tens of thousands of military spouses, girlfriends, and post-deployment one-night stands over the years, and as her beautiful pussy sits before me, I can't wait to see if I can get her going.

Still licking her clit, I inch two thick fingers inside her, her pussy clenching around them, which makes me want to fuck her right then and there, but I refrain. I love the tease. I crave it. With the pads of my fingers resting inside her, I start a come-hither motion with them, intensifying the pressure with each movement of my fingers, speeding up as she grinds against me for more.

"Oh my God," she gasps, squirming against the mattress. "Oh, my *fuck*, that feels so good."

I continue with this finger movement as I feel the inside of her pussy swell, readying itself to squirt. Licking her bud harder now, I circle it with my tongue and take it into my mouth, sucking it as she pushes her body up into me, her heels digging into the mattress. I know I'm close. I'm so fucking excited, I don't let up with my tongue or fingers, working them both uniformly until I get it—she lifts her hips completely off the mattress, her pussy digging into my face as she lets out gasps into the palm of her hand. The fingernails on her other hand dig into my shoulder as her cum sprays onto my tongue. I keep the pressure going with my fingers, trying to push her to the brink. As much as she's squirted onto my mattress and into my mouth, I'm guessing she's never done this before.

She slaps her palms against the mattress, looking up with disorientated eyes as she takes in the mess of cum now wetting her ass ... wetting everything. She puts a hand to her mouth. "Oh my God, I'm so sorry. I-I've never done that before."

"*Sorry?*" I ask, shaking my head. "There's nothin' to be sorry for. That was fuckin' sexy."

I push her back down, pulling her soaked panties off and tossing them to the floor with her dress. She follows suit with her bra, and my God, her tits are perfect little handfuls, nipples made for sucking.

"You need to be inside me, *right now*." She breathes heavy, taking me in with seductive eyes.

"You don't have to ask me twice, darlin'." I unbuckle my belt, stripping it off quickly and tossing it to the floor, before I shed my pants and throw them into the quickly accumulating pile of clothing at the base of my bed. My boxer briefs go next, and before they're even at my ankles, my cock is fully erect, a bit of pre-cum at the tip.

Naked now, I settle the head of my dick against her. I work the tip in circles around her entrance, combining my pre-cum with the beautiful mess left behind from her orgasm. A dizzying buzz trails from my cock to my groin with every brush of my head against her clit, and then travels throughout my body. The warmth reverberates, her wetness teasing my head and making it throb with excitement. I love the way she looks at me as I stand over her, the way she bites her bottom lip. Her submissive nature in bed is a stark contrast to her normal self, which makes it that much hotter. A wave of adrenaline washes over me as I enter her slowly.

I settle inside her, the feeling electrifying. Letting out a pleasured sigh, I work my shaft in and out slowly, watching her every movement, admiring the way her hands clinch the bedspread.

"My God," I gasp as I pick up the pace; her wetness surrounds me, warms me, drives me.

"Yes, yes," she breathes, her hands moving to my stomach, her fingernails raking my abs. "Fuck me, Bishop. I want your cum. I want to taste it."

Hooooooly shit.

Any time a woman has said 'I want to taste your cum, or 'come on my face', my dick takes immediate notice. It becomes difficult to control.

I think baseball, curling, a Michael Moore documentary.

Not yet, dude!

Her eyes stare daggers into me, her hands roaming my body. I can feel the come stirring but continue fighting it off. I want her to go again. As I pull completely out of her, she gasps, her legs quivering as I guide her to her side. Bending one leg and keeping the other one straight, her beautiful round ass is completely exposed, feeding my yearning to return.

"You have such a beautiful ass, woman," I say, taking both cheeks in my hands and squeezing them. Spreading them, I lean down and lightly stroke my tongue against her asshole. She squeals and then lets out a moan.

"Holy fuck," she gasps as I circle her tight little hole with my tongue. She reaches back and grabs a fistful of my hair, driving my face into her. Tasting her makes my dick harder than I thought possible and makes the desire to be inside her again too much to bear.

Straightening back up, I grab ahold of her hips and drive my cock inside her. It tightens around me, letting me know she's close. I pick up the pace, driving my hips into her, feeding off every squeal and moan, every breathless gasp, and the way she looks back at me with those needy eyes. I work my fingers against her clit in motion with my hips.

"I'm gonna come!" she shouts, her hands splayed out and grabbing for the pillows. Her body shakes as I drive into her. I can feel a swell at the base of my cock, a tingle that lets me know this orgasm is going to be a good one.

As she screams out, her pussy constricting against me, her toes curling, I feel the buzz rush from the base of my cock through my shaft and back again. I pull out just as the orgasm is about to hit. As I start to jerkoff, she drops to her knees and slaps my hand away lightly, taking my dick from me, and putting it in her mouth; deep throating every inch immediately.

"Fuuuck." The word escapes my mouth without thought, simply driven by utter satisfaction. I throw my head back and groan as the cum releases into her eager mouth.

She slowly pulls back, letting my sensitive cock run along her tongue before she lets him drop. She runs one finger along her bottom lip, and then she sucks the remaining cum off her finger.

I feel as if I could grow hard all over again just at the sight, though I know he'd be very unhappy with me. He'd let me know it by the prickly jolts of pain that resonate from the tip of my dick immediately after orgasm. For this woman though? Bring on the fucking pain.

Catching my breath, I fall to the mattress, my dick slowly ticking downward, and my heart pounding. "Holy *fuck*," I say, shaking my head.

"What?" She smiles, resting a hand against my sweaty stomach.

"That was probably the best fuckin' nut of my life."

"Shut up," she says, rolling her eyes. "You're so gross."

"I'm not gross. I'm a guy."

"Same difference, I guess." She laughs.

"Goddamn, I need a cigarette."

She nods. "I think I need one too."

Lying next to each other in bed, watching *Full House* with stomachs full of pizza, her head rests on my chest and my arm is wrapped around her. She traces her finger in figure eights against my bare skin. I find myself filled with a budding energy, an undeniable connection to her, an overwhelming joy when I'm with her. I feel more alive than I have in a while.

"You're somethin', you know?" I say abruptly, and she tilts her head up toward me, smiling.

"Oh yeah?"

"*Definitely.*"

"You're something, too."

"I just didn't expect to meet someone like you here," I tell her.

"Someone like me?"

"I mean, you're young. Most of the young kids here meet my expectations of today's youth. I didn't anticipate meetin' a twenty-year-old with so much depth."

She laughs. "You're such an old man."

"I know, I know." I smile, shrugging.

"It's okay. I'm an old soul."

"I can tell."

"And you just used the word nut, so your brain is obviously stuck in early twenties anyway."

Laughing, I shrug and reply, "Touché."

"You surprised me as well, you know."

"How so?"

"I don't think you understand how many people were talking about you."

"I really don't. I just don't get it."

"You're the new guy, the one with a killer story. There's like this mysticism that surrounds you here."

I roll my eyes. "That's so ridiculous."

"Maybe, but still, it's there. And so, when I met you, I was so fucking nervous. I think I half-expected you to be an asshole."

I quirk an eyebrow. "Me?"

"I didn't know. Army man. Hurt in combat. Older. I wasn't sure what to expect."

"I don't much like livin' up to stereotypes." I grin, rubbing a hand across her naked back.

"You definitely don't. You are so centered. And down to earth. It's crazy."

I shake my head. "I don't know. I can be a dick sometimes."

"If it's necessary, maybe. But I don't see you being a dick for no reason."

"I try not to be," I say. "I try to maintain perspective. Put myself in other people's shoes."

"Well, I like it." She smiles.

I run my fingers through her hair, admiring her natural beauty and the starry gaze in her eyes.

"Well, I like *you*," I respond, feeling corny but not really giving a fuck.

"I like you too, Bishop." Her focus shifts back to the TV, and we lie there, her and I, until we drift to sleep wrapped up in each other's arms; *Nick at Nite* serving as our lullaby.

TWELVE

"So, where'd you disappear to last night?" Mac asks as I approach him, Carter, and Jeremy in front of the diner, the morning sun making the bit of snow on the ground blinding.

Pocketing my keys, I shrug. "I looked for you fuckers, but Ember wasn't feelin' it. What can I say?"

As I hold the door open for them, Jeremy quips, "Well, ya missed out. It was a fuckin' riot last night, man. We painted the damn town red."

I follow in behind them toward the host, who seats us in what's become our usual spot.

"I'm pretty sure I don't regret a thing." I grin as I take a seat at the table.

"Mac pretty much fucked his girl at the bar," Carter says, rolling his eyes.

"Shit yeah, he did." Jeremy laughs.

Hey," Mac says, faking offense. "There was no penetration."

Jeremy puts a finger up. "No penis penetration, that is," he says, and we all burst out laughing.

"You fingered her at the bar, dude?" I ask, and he shrugs.

"A little bit," he responds, laughing. "Dude, my girl is a filthy little whore. I can't help it."

"Same girl?"

He nods. "You bet your ass. That's my woman, dude. I told you. I'm serious as a heart attack, I'm going to make that woman my wife one day."

"Does anybody think this girl has been tearing Mac's ass up in the bedroom, strap-on style?" Carter asks, chuckling.

"Abso-fuckin'-lutely," I say, shaking my head. "I thought that was just to be assumed."

"Fuck you guys," Mac replies, flipping us off. "And another fuck you for not warning me what was coming last night." He holds the middle finger up a few moments longer just for Carter.

"Hey, they told me not to. I could get kicked out if they find out I did." Carter shrugs. "Besides, you didn't do as bad as I did. Fuck, I knew what was coming and still sucked."

"What were you supposed to do, practice in front of the mirror?" I ask, chuckling.

"No, but I could've drank more," he responds.

Mac scoffs, putting his hands up. "*You fucking drank?* I thought we weren't supposed to."

Carter shrugs. "I wasn't about to strip without some liquor in me."

"You're such a dick!" Mac shakes his head as the waitress approaches with pad and pen in hand. "Why the fuck wouldn't you tell us?"

"I told you, I'm not allowed to," Carter says.

The waitress takes our orders, Mac grumbling away under his breath.

As she departs, Jeremy tilts his head, narrowing his eyes at me. "Correct me if I'm wrong, but you seemed to be a little liquored up yourself out there on the dance floor, Bishop," he says, passing me a knowing glance, his eyes trailing to Carter.

"I don't know what you're talkin' about," I lie, shrugging and taking a sip of my coffee.

"You motherfuckers." Mac shakes his head, his brows pinched together.

"Hey, I didn't have enough to go around," Carter says.

"You could've given us *something*." Mac pouts now, crossing his arms.

I laugh. "Stop your whinin', Mac. It's over with now." I look to Carter and then back to the others. "So, I haven't been given any information from Damian, other than the social coming up on Thursday."

Mac puts his hands up and cheers. "Our first fucking social," he says. "Finally!"

"Y'all got dates already?" I ask, and Mac nods right away.

"You know who the hell I'm bringing," he says. "I'm gonna have my Mexican princess on my arm."

I motion toward Carter. "What about you?"

He shrugs, curling his lips. "Eh, I'm just going with a friend from back home. I haven't had the luck Mac has lately."

"We need to remedy that," I respond, my focus shifting toward Jeremy, who seems distracted. "What about you, bro?"

Jeremy shrugs, taking a long drink of his coffee before responding, "Haven't really thought about it."

"What about that blond you sang to at karaoke on the first night? You got her number, right?" Mac asks.

"Yeah." Jeremy shrugs again. "I might ask her."

"Wait." Mac puts a hand up. "Jeremy, have you gotten your dick wet at all since we started pledging?"

Jeremy shoots him a glare. "I get my own. I just don't go around broadcastin' it like you do, you ginger fuck."

"I'm just saying. You're the prettiest one out of all of us.

Shit, compared to us three, you're fucking Adonis. You should be slaying the pussy," Mac argues.

"How do you know I'm not?" Jeremy asks, cocking his head. "You're a dumbass, Mac," Jeremy responds, shaking his head. "Until you're sleepin' next to me every night, you can't say shit."

"That sounds like an invitation." Carter laughs, and the rest of us join in.

"He couldn't handle this shit," Mac says, rubbing his hands slowly from his chest to his stomach.

Jeremy looks at Mac, arching an eyebrow with a grin plastered on. "Mac, I could be Elton John-gay, I'm talkin' rainbows comin' out my fuckin' asshole, and I still wouldn't stick my dick in you. Shit, I'd probably break your anorexic ass."

"I'm not anorexic!" Mac groans, motioning toward the plate of food in front of him. "It's not cool for you guys to always give me shit about that. It's not my fault."

I rub fists in my eyes dramatically. "Oh, boo fuckin' hoo, Mac. You better grow a sack quick. Y'all can give me shit about my eye. If I do recall, y'all already have a time or two." I motion toward Carter. "For Chrissake, Carter's frat nickname is Scarface."

Carter shakes his head, his lips curling into a frown. "Zane. Fucking asshole," he mutters.

"See?" I point to Carter's face. "This is my first time hearin' about his feelings on the matter."

"Well ... my nickname is Red!" Mac argues. "I'm not even really a ginger."

I shoot my eyes toward his head and laugh. "What the fuck do you call that color, then?"

"Strawberry blond," he responds, and the rest of us burst out laughing.

"Strawberry fuckin' ginger, man." I shake my head. "There's nothin' blond about that mop on your head."

"I hate you fucks," Mac grumbles.

"You love us. Now, finish your food. I need to get to class," I say, motioning toward his plate.

"Well, if you fucks would ever stop talking," Mac responds, grinning, and then shoveling the last of his eggs into his mouth.

THIRTEEN

"So, a real official date, huh?" Ember asks, leaning against the Kappa Phi mailbox, the sorority letters lit behind her. She's wearing a puffy North Face jacket, faux fur lining the hood that's pulled over her head. She flashes a brilliant smile.

"Yes ma'am. If you ever get in the damn Jeep."

She arches an eyebrow. "And here I thought an Army gentleman was taking me out."

I chuckle. "If you only knew how ungentlemanly the Army Infantry really is, my dear," I respond, hopping out and hoofing it to her side but careful to look for any ice patches. I open the door for her and present a hand.

She gives a little curtsy and hops in, a smirk on her lips. It's quite endearing how she has to hike herself up into the lifted Jeep, like she's doing a fucking pull-up.

Closing the door behind her, I make my way back to the driver side and hop back in.

"You comfortable, Madam?" I ask, smirking.

She looks around, seemingly taking in the interior of the

vehicle as I pull away from the house. She gives an approving nod. "This is a sweet ass car! A lot better than mine."

"It's not a car. It's a Jeep," I correct her, and she rolls her eyes. I continue, "What do you drive?"

"A black El Camino."

I shoot my eyes over to her. "That souped up El Camino that's always parked in the lot across from the quad?"

"That's her! Her name's Elvira."

"Well, fuck, I wouldn't call my Jeep better than that beauty. I'd take that ride any day. I love El Caminos. Classics."

"I've always loved them too, but then again, around my house you didn't have an option. My dad was always a huge fan, he had one when he was younger, and he bought Elvira when she looked like complete shit. Interior faded and worn through. The engine was a complete mess. The summer between my freshman and sophomore year of high school, while all my friends were poolside or going to the mall, I helped my dad fix her up. I just wanted to spend some quality time with him. I didn't have any clue she'd be mine one day. Then he surprised me on the last day of summer with the keys. Put a big red bow on it and everything. It was adorable." She hesitates for a moment and then adds, "Where are we going, by the way?"

As I take the highway on-ramp, I reply, "I wanted to get away from the college town vibe, so I booked us a table at this spot out in Slippery Rock. It's called—"

"Gallagher's?!" she cuts me off, waving her hands excitedly.

"Yeah, have you been there?"

"Not yet, but I've been wanting to sooo bad! I saw it on one of my favorite shows a few months ago."

"*Diners, Drive-Ins, and Dives*?!" I'm shocked to learn someone other than me watches one of my favorite shows. "I'm seriously in love with that show, and I saw that episode the other night. It's why I booked us there. Felt like kismet." I smile as she buzzes with excitement, adorably so. "You are too fuckin' cute."

"And you're too fucking sweet. Mr. Romantic over here. I'm sorry for talking shit earlier. I really was just messing with you, you know. I don't do the whole car door opening thing. I just wanted to see if you would." She grins.

"Good, because I was about to tell you there's no way I'm hoppin' my happy ass out when we get there and racin' to your side to get the door for you. I hate those guys." I laugh. "I consider myself a gentleman through and through. I'm a country boy with country values after all, but I put that shit up there with holdin' a lady's purse. It just isn't right to do to a man."

She laughs, patting her metal studded clutch. "I guess you won't be carrying the 'Bad Bitch' for me anytime soon, then?"

I shake my head firmly. "No ma'am. You got two perfectly healthy arms more than capable of toting that thing around. You get in some freak accident and break both your arms, or get bacterial meningitis and lose 'em, well, then you hand that thing right over."

She grins. "You are so fucked up. And how exactly would I hand it over?"

"Wait. Ms. Badass herself is callin' *me* fucked up?"

"You are, talking about missing arms and shit."

"I'm just bein' informative. And you missed the moral to the story."

"I must've." She smirks.

"I'm just lettin' you know there are circumstances where I'll hold your purse for you. That should be a good thing."

She shakes her head. "Glad to know if I ever lose my arms, I have you to carry my purse for me." She hesitates, looking as if she's stifling a laugh. "Will you pull the trigger for me too?

Seeing as I wouldn't be able to blow my own brains out." She bursts out in laughter.

"Damn, woman. Who's fucked up now? Talkin' about shootin' yourself if you had no arms. I know a few guys with no arms, you know."

She shrugs. "And they're probably the bravest mother-fuckers on earth. I'm not so sure I'm in that category. I'm not sure what I'd do if I couldn't finger myself."

A laugh bursts from my lips and my eyes go wide. I look over at her with a grin. "Did you really just fuckin' say that? Only you could turn a conversation about double arm amputees sexual."

She shrugs, a smile tugging at the corner of her lips. "We all have our own weird kinks. Mine is leather bondage and amputee porn."

I just shake my head.

She continues, "Besides, I don't want you carrying my purse. The whole reason we pay so much for purses is so that we can show them off." She cradles her purse tighter to her side as if she's hugging it.

"Where do you get the money for all this nice shit anyhow? I'm not quite in the fashion world, but I know enough to know you've got some high-end items."

"You being judgmental, punk?" She points a finger at me.

I put a hand up defensively, smiling. "No. Not at all. I'm just curious."

"Well, it's not Daddy's money, if that's what you're think-ing. Which is absolutely what you're thinking." She scrutinizes me with her eyes as she puts a finger near my cheek. I try to focus on the road, but it's so close to my face, it's hard to ignore. "I can see it in your face," she adds.

"Not at all. I wouldn't judge you if that *was* how you got

such nice things. I call that a good family. Wish I had that shit growin' up."

"Well, most everything I own that's high end, I paid for it myself. Except the car, I guess, but I put as much blood, sweat, and tears into her as Dad did. It was *our* project. Anyway, you're gonna laugh, but I actually do these YouTube videos—makeup tutorials, product testing, shit like that—and they've kind of blown up over the past year."

"You make money off those things?"

"If you have enough viewers, yeah. Ad dollars."

"That's fuckin' awesome. Go you!"

"Yeah, I had no idea when I started, but it's been nice having that extra cash flow the past year. Not having to rely on my parents and all. Obviously, I've been spoiling myself a little." She pats her bag.

"As we all should sometimes. I've done the same. I did with this Jeep. Sometimes you have to just go out and drop a couple Gs on somethin' you don't really need."

"Or oftentimes," she adds.

I navigate the Jeep onto an off-ramp and take a right toward downtown Slippery Rock.

"Again, no judgment. I treat myself all the time," I assure her.

Hitting the dim lights of the scarcely occupied town square, I pull into a parking spot off the road as a wave of energy builds in my chest. Not a nervousness, but an excitement. A connection between two people hardly found in this life. A buzz of anticipation for the possibility of so much more.

"Are you excited?" I ask as I meet her on the sidewalk, locking my Jeep, and blowing hot breath into my cold hand.

"You bet your ass I am," she says, poking her tongue out at me as I open the front door for her.

"Why, thank you, sir," she says as she passes through.

"No, thank *you*." I smile, following in after her.

As we're led to a table, I pull her chair out for her and wait for her to sit, and then I grab a seat in the one across from her.

"So, we've seen each other three times now. Spent the night together twice. And ..." My voice trails as a mischievous smile spreads across my face.

"And?" she asks sharply, narrowing her eyes at me.

"And I feel like I know nothin' about you."

"Well, why haven't you asked?"

I laugh. "Night one, you were wasted. Night two, I was wasted. Night three, we were, um, preoccupied." I grin and she swats me across the arm with the back of her hand.

"Why don't you ask away then, Geraldo?" she asks, tilting her head.

"Were you even alive when Geraldo was on the air?"

"I didn't have to be to know who he is," she retorts, a smirk fighting to break free. "Were you alive when J. Edgar Hoover was cross-dressing?"

"No, but—"

"No, but you know that he did so ..."

"I mean, no one really has proof of that."

She scoffs, still fighting the smile. "For Chrissakes, Bishop. Lincoln delivering the Emancipation Proclamation then. Or MLK's 'I Have a Dream' speech. Were you alive for those?"

I shake my head, playing along.

"But you know about them, don't you?"

I nod.

She shrugs. "So ..."

"This conversation really got away from us." I smile as the waitress approaches.

Em mouths, "I'm gonna get you," as the waitress asks if we'd like anything to drink. I order my usual double Jameson on the rocks and she orders a straight Coke, I'm assuming because she doesn't want to test her fake ID outside of Crescent Falls, where standards are more lax. It reminds me of how much older I am than her and just about everyone else in Crescent Falls.

After we order some crab cakes to start, the waitress departs, and Ember's brows draw together.

"What?" I tilt my head.

"You're quickly getting on my bad side," she says matter-of-factly.

"Why do I get the feelin' that isn't a hard thing to accomplish?"

She swats at me again but misses this time, and I cheer victoriously.

"Not so fast, Grasshopper. For the student shall never overtake the master." My eyelids close to slits and I throw a few karate chops through the air.

She laughs, shaking her head. "You are such a nerd."

"And you're out on a date with a nerd. What's that make you?"

She snort-laughs, covering her face with both hands. "Either really generous, or goddamn stupid."

I shake my head. "Rude fuck!"

"Hey, you started it," she argues, poking her tongue out at me.

"When did I start it?"

"When you took me out on a date and expected me to behave myself."

"Hey!" I point a finger at her, holding it there as I tilt my head. "I *never* asked you to behave yourself. I just expected you to reserve the aggression for unsuspecting bystanders."

"Oh, we could totally do that."

"You have specific plans?" I ask, wrapping my fingers around the whiskey glass and jostling the ice as she sips on her Coke.

"Well, there's a shit ton of suburban shithole houses around here with unsuspecting kids snuggled comfortably in their beds," she says.

I pull my head back, my forehead wrinkling in confusion. "And you're wantin' to kidnap these kids or ...?" I arch an eyebrow and she bursts out in laughter. Some of our fellow patrons glance over at us.

"No, you idiot. But we could always, like, scratch a stick against their windows, wake them up, and then maybe, like, pretend to be zombies or something."

"I was thinkin' kill a few beers at Lookout Point and hit some golf balls. Or, like, maybe bust up a few mailboxes. I'm not trying to get on some sex predator list."

"Pussy," she mutters, taking a sip of her drink, but smiling wide against the rim.

I shake my head slowly, handling my own glass. "You're pushin' it tonight, woman. I'm not afraid to bend you over my knee right here in front of everybody. God as my witness."

She quirks an eyebrow. "Shoot, what are you waiting for?"

I chuckle, nodding my head in approval. "Now that sounds like a better plan than creeping around some kid's bedroom window."

Shrugging, she says, "It's not that bad of an idea. I mean, mentally scarring some kids for life, that shit would be funny." Her lips turn up in a wicked grin.

"Jesus, woman. Why do I get the feeling you lit your Barbie's heads on fire?"

She scoffs. "*Barbies?* I had action figures growing up, mister. And yes, I would make them slaughter each other, and some, occasionally, at some point or another may have faced the wrath of a flamethrower, aka my Bic and a can of kerosene."

A laugh escapes my lips. "We would've been real good friends back in the day. I was a little fuckin' pyro too."

"Well, yeah, that would've been nice had you not grown up in the roaring twenties." She pokes her tongue out at me.

"I have a toothbrush older than you," I quip.

"And you're on a date with me, you little perv."

"Hey, I'm the older man with the younger woman. I think that makes me smart in society's book. You're the younger woman with the older man. That makes you kind of gross. I'm a senior citizen, for Chrissakes."

Her hands meet her mouth to catch her laughter as the waitress approaches with her pad and pen. Ember spots this and does a little happy dance. After the waitress takes our food order and departs to grab us a fresh round, Ember leans her elbows on the table and sets her chin against her palms.

"You're staring, old man."

I grin. "You're gorgeous, young lady."

She drops her hands to her sides and smiles. "Why thank you."

"So now that I get some alone time with you, tell me about what makes you *you*. I wanna know it all."

"That's such a broad topic," she responds, chuckling.

"How about this ... What was growin' up like?"

"Well, my mom is my best friend in the world. I learned everything I know from her. She took care of me and my brother when my dad died, and never, not once, did she ever feel sorry for herself. She pushed on for us. To give us the life Dad would've wanted for us."

"God, I'm so sorry. When did that happen?"

"When I was twelve. Car wreck. He was coming down a road where he had the right of way and a drunk driver ran a stop sign on a cross street going sixty and hit him. Killed him instantly, or so the EMT says. Mom never did let me see him. She wanted my memories of him to stay untarnished."

I think back to my first deployment, three months in. I had

only been in the Army a little over a year at that point. I was scared shitless. We were coming in from a mission one day, hot, tired, disorientated, and right when we turned onto the road leading to the base, an improvised explosive device detonated underneath the Humvee in front of mine. Up until then, I didn't know what complete destruction was.

I think about dismounting my own Humvee to check on them, and walking up on my squad buddies, Specialist Adam Landon, Private First Class Greyson Matthews, and Sergeant Tony Morrison, left in pieces inside the tattered Humvee. Blood and flesh coated the interior, along with torn bits of uniform and the most awful smell I'd ever experienced. There was also the screaming. I'll never forget the screaming. Private Jackson Perez lay in the backseat, alive, but his life was fleeting. Both legs were severed at the hip. There was too much blood and flesh to see whether he'd lost more than that. He didn't have to. The color in his face drained quickly as his eyes rolled around in his skull.

And, eventually, the screaming stopped.

I wonder if I'd rather not have those memories; if I could remember Landon, Matthews, Morrison, and Perez as I knew them around the smoke pit, bullshitting about women, and home, and freedom.

"Do you wish you had seen him?" I ask, trying to busy my mind, but regretting the question immediately.

She takes a moment to think before she shrugs. "I don't know. I was livid with my mom at the time for not letting me. Absolutely fucking livid. But as I got older, I started to understand. When I read the autopsy report in high school, it made all the sense in the world."

"Fuck, that's terrible."

"But like I said, my mom stepped up. She took on the role of mother and father for my sister and me, and she kicked fucking ass. She's my hero."

"What's her name?" I ask.

"Leaona."

"And what does she do?"

She narrows her eyes at me. "You wouldn't believe me if I told you."

"Try me out."

"She writes romance and erotica books."

"You're shittin' me," I say, a bit of disbelief in my tone.

"I told you, you wouldn't believe me."

"For real, she writes, like, Fabio books?"

She laughs out loud, shaking her head. "Well, it's come a *long* way since those days, but yeah."

"And your sister? What about her?"

"Cassia..." She hesitates, her eyes meeting the ceiling as she thinks it over. "I love that girl, but she's a spoiled little shit. She's the youngest at eighteen, so she got everything her little heart desired. She's awesome, just a bit of a wild child right now. I worry about her graduating and starting college. She'll need a new liver by the time she gets her degree if she's not careful." She laughs.

"I surely can't judge. I've been known as a bit of a wild child myself."

"Why am I not surprised?"

I nod, smirking. "I like to meet expectations."

"So, what about you? Any siblings?" she asks.

The waitress brings our new drinks, temporarily interrupting our conversation. I thank her, turning my attention back toward Ember as she turns and walks away.

Taking a sip first, I lick the stray whiskey from my lips and say, "Only child here. Always wished I had a big brother though. But I've managed to make some really great friends over the years. It's just a shame because they're all over the place these days."

"Yeah, I can relate. Everybody from New York ends up going somewhere else for college. It's just too damn expensive staying in state. So, people end up all over the northeast. I also don't really get along with most girls. I think they find me intimidating."

"I can see why."

"Hey, I'm a sweet girl when people aren't fucking idiots."

"I can see that too, and I'm sure your friends can as well, but you do carry that bad bitch vibe. I think a lot of other women are intimidated by unabashed confidence. I can relate. Most people assume I'm an asshole because I speak my mind."

Nodding, she says, "That's why the majority of my friends are guys; they're easier. And that's why Zane and Brady are the only ones I really know around Crescent Falls from back home. Well, them and my best friend, Holly."

"Is she a Kappa too?"

She nods. "We came here together. She's my lobster, and pretty much my guardian. If it wasn't for her, I may not have made it out of our freshman year alive. I stress quite a bit. She's always been that motherly, nurturing type. Even when we were kids. Really good at calming me down if I get overwhelmed." She hesitates, before correcting herself, "*When* I get overwhelmed."

"It's good to have friends like that. I've always found myself in that role with my past friendships. In high school, I befriended all the kids who got picked on. It hurt me so much to see them treated like shit without the ability, desire, or, I guess, fortitude to fight back. A few of them I tried to give fighting tips to. I told them the truest words that I've ever learned, which are, when you stand up to a bully, that motherfucker will back down. They pick on the weaker ones 'cause they know they won't fight back."

"So, you're a fighter, huh?"

"Eh, I wouldn't say that." I work to keep the grin off my face as the blatant lie slips through my teeth. "But I've been in my fair share. I think every man needs to be in at least one fight. And he certainly needs to take a punch, so he knows his chin isn't made of glass."

"I've been in a fight before. Once."

"I don't doubt that one fuckin' bit. Tell me the story."

"It was my senior year. I was with the same guy all throughout high school until he cheated on me that first semester. I dumped him, and he moved on to that bitch. So anyway, fast forward to the second semester and he's still dating her but hitting me up again. So, what do I do?"

"Revenge fuck?"

She shrugs. "I mean, she knew he was mine when she decided to open her legs for him."

"So, that's what you fought over?"

"Kind of. I sent her a picture of him sleeping naked in my bed with the words 'got ya, bitch' written on it. She lost her shit. Started spreading rumors around the school about me—prostitute, diseased, stinky pussy—whatever, that shit doesn't bother me. Never has. But then she started talking shit about my dad. Everyone from where I grew up knew my dad. He was the mayor for a long time before he got sick of dealing with the bureaucracy of it all, but they always wanted him back and they all still loved him. So, shit spread around quick. She told people my dad had cheated on my mom and molested me. When it got around to me … I lost my shit. The minute Holly told me at lunch, I marched over to where the girl was sitting, snatched her tray, poured her food over her head, and I smacked the shit out of her face with it."

"With the tray?!"

"Yup. And then I threw the thing and just went crazy on her. Started throwing wild fists. I probably only landed a quarter of them, but it was worth it." She laughs. "The vice principal had to pull me off her."

"Damn!" My eyes go wide. "You *are* a bad bitch."

She shrugs, a playful cockiness in her mannerisms. "You don't talk about my family and get away with it. Especially not my dad."

"Nothin' but respect for that. And I wholeheartedly agree. Some fights are worth fightin'. So, did you get suspended for it?"

"Expelled, actually. They wanted to charge me, but my mom spoke with her mom, talked to her about the issues I was having after my dad's death, and luckily, her mom agreed not to press charges if I went through this anger management bullshit. I had to finish out my degree in this summer school program and earned a boxing fracture on both hands. That was fun!" She lets out a laugh. "You should've seen me trying to tie my shoes with casts on both hands."

"Not to mention other things." I laugh.

"*Lots* of things." She rolls her eyes.

"No lie, I had this buddy at Walter Reed—that's the hospital in D.C. soldiers get sent to after gettin' injured. So, this guy was on foot patrol and got hit by a buried improvised explosive device. It took off one of his arms clean, and the other was left danglin'. It ended up gettin' cut off too by the time he made it to D.C. So, this guy, awesome fuckin' dude, he would get piss drunk with me and just talk endlessly, about everything. I loved it because it required little of me. The days I was feelin' like a pile of shit, we'd go out, grab some beers at the bar, and he'd just tell stories."

"Wait, I hate to interrupt, and I hope this doesn't come off as inappropriate, but how did he drink the beer with no arms?"

"A straw." I chuckle, eyeing her with a 'duh' look on my face. "He always had to use a straw."

She hits her forehead with her palm. "Holy shit, I'm an idiot. Sorry, please, continue."

"Well, after a few months of this, I got comfortable enough to start askin' questions. Of course, you don't wanna be disrespectful. The man lost both his arms at twenty-three, for Chrissakes, but obviously, curiosity is a motherfucker." I pause as the waitress brings over our plates.

She sets them down and asks, "Can I get y'all anything else?"

"Just another round, please. Thank you." The waitress nods before departing, and I turn my attention back to Ember. "So, anyway, I had two questions that had been naggin' me from the moment I met him, and I finally felt comfortable enough to ask him." She takes a bite of her food, her eyes on me, when I ask, "You don't have a weak stomach, do you? This might not be the best thing to share while we're eatin'."

She waves me off, chewing her food, before she says, "No way. Iron gut. Continue."

"Well, I always wanted to ask him how he jerked off and how he wiped his ass."

She nods, a slight look of shame on her face. "I was wondering that too."

"Well, first off, he laughed in my fuckin' face about the jerk off question. He goes, 'Bro, I got no fuckin' hands, what the hell am I supposed to jerk it with.' He was awesome about it though. Told me our occupational therapist, Harvey, got him a pocket pussy. It's really the only way. He puts it on the bed and then goes to town."

"When you say puts it on the bed ..."

"He uses his feet."

"That's amazing."

"Yeah, the dude could do just about anything with his feet by the time he left Walter Reed. Harvey, he's still a great friend of mine, spends his life makin' sure these men and women comin' back real fucked up learn to adapt to their new normal. He helped me a shit ton."

"Sounds like an incredible guy."

"He's the *best*. Biggest heart out of anybody I know. And his love and dedication toward the people he serves ... it's incredible."

"It's good to know people like that are taking care of you guys."

I nod, taking a bite and washing it down with some whiskey.

"So, what about wiping his ass?" she asks, and then takes a bite of her own.

Swallowing first, I reply, "This is the craziest fuckin' part. So, this poor guy had to learn to wad up the toilet paper with his foot, sit back on top of his foot like he's stretchin' his quad, and he'd have to kind of grind against the paper. Can you imagine?"

Her face answers for her. She shakes her head slowly with wide eyes, a hand meeting her mouth. "Oh my, that poor man."

"Yeah, I felt terrible for askin' honestly, but then I remembered all the times people asked me about my eye. People are curious by nature, some more than others. I guess, at the end of the day, it's better to ask and learn, than to not and just assume. He took it in stride like everything else in his life. Even with all the difficulties, all the rehab—I mean, he was there for four years before I got there—he still kept a level head and cool demeanor. He spent the majority of his damn twenties at Walter Reed, re-learnin' how to do everything. And even with all that, he was still one of the happiest and kindest people I've ever met."

"You guys are all so freaking brave."

"It's guys like that I look up to. He never stopped fightin'. Always kept a smile on his face. Never complained. If I had lost my arms, or been burned all over, or lost my dick ... fuckin' hell, some guys have to shit in a bag for the rest of their life." I shake my head. "I don't know, those people inspire the fuck out of me. They're the brave ones. They're the ones keepin' the rest of us lucky ones in line."

"You're pretty inspirational yourself, you know?"

Smiling, but feeling awkward, that tight uneasy grip beneath my sternum, I say, "I appreciate that."

"I appreciate you! I appreciate you telling me about yourself and your life. You've lived so much already. It's crazy to even think about. It makes me want to spread my wings a little bit."

I grin. "You gonna join the Army?"

She shakes her head firmly. "Not a fucking chance. I don't like being told what to do."

"Yeah, I didn't much either comin' into it. Fuckin' hated it actually. Luckily, I was young, and the drill sergeants were just scary enough that I kept my fuckin' mouth shut."

"Was basic training hard? I've asked Zane, but he doesn't really say much."

I laugh, giving my head a quick shake. "Zane's basic training and my basic training were *vastly* different. I'm pretty sure the Air Force's is even shorter than ours, but yeah, way less privileges, way more bullshit, plenty more sleepless nights and smoke sessions."

"Smoke sessions? You could smoke cigarettes in basic?"

I chuckle, shaking my head. "*Fuck,* do I wish that's what smoke sessions entailed. No, it means when they punish you for whatever transgression through physical activity. Whether you played a part or not, most often, everyone would feel the pain. They make you do all kinds of labor-intensive exercises over an extended period of time. It's fuckin' miserable. I swear to Christ, when I first got there and went through those first few smoke sessions, I thought my body was gonna collapse in on itself like a dying fuckin' star."

We both laugh.

"So, you hated it then?" she asks.

I shake my head immediately. "Not one bit. Were there times I hated? Absolutely. *Plenty* of 'em. But it made me the man I am today. I was a degenerate punk as a youth. I hated authority—teachers, cops, my parents. Hated school. Hated feelin' so goddamn trapped in that little town. It was suffocating. I've always considered myself a bit of a free spirit. I've always had that desire to travel and explore, to be adventurous. It's one of the reasons I joined the Army. And it gave me what I yearned for."

She shakes her head, a look of understanding in her features. "I *so* feel you there. I had the choice of staying in New York for school. I got accepted to SUNY-Oneonta, and my mom wanted me to stay really bad, but I just felt so trapped there. Claustrophobic. I knew *everybody*. I always felt like there was more out there. One day, I want to go backpacking across Europe for like a month or two. Just get away and video blog every step of the way. I think I could really find peace that way." She pushes her nearly clean plate away from her, her eyes distant as she looks to be lost in thought.

"I think you should. Sooner the better. I don't know if you want a family or not down the road, but from what I've seen with friends, that always snuffs globetrotting out pretty quickly. And then you get to the point where you say, 'Okay, we'll travel once the kids leave the house,' but by the time the last kid's out, you're both so broke from puttin' 'em all through college that you don't have the money to do the traveling you intended. So, then you say, 'Well, we're only fifty. Still young. Still plenty of time. We'll save up money and travel when we retire.' Well, by the time sixty-five rolls around, you're up to your neck in hospital bills for your diabetes and gout, and generally don't enjoy leavin' your couch, let alone the fuckin' country."

She chuckles. "Jesus, you've thought this through."

"My mind's always goin'." I shrug. "There's a gerbil just runnin' his ass off in that wheel between my ears."

"Same here. As for the 'having a family' thing, while I do want to have a family one day, it's about the last thing on my mind right now. I'm in no hurry to have kids, and unless it's absolutely right, I'm in no hurry to meet anyone either. I believe when the time is right, the universe will put everything into motion."

"So, what would I be considered?" I grin. "A placeholder?"

"You? You caught me by surprise to be honest. Completely."

"How so?"

"You've seen the idiots here. They aren't much better back home. My experiences with men have not been good. To put it as bluntly as possible, my relationship lineup is a collection of assholes, liars, and douchebags with one thing in common."

"What's that?"

"They were excellent actors. They portrayed themselves to be the ultimate catch. They did everything right—held the doors, paid for dates, bought nice gifts—but it was all for show. Once they wooed me and won me, the façade started to fade. Before long, you're waking up to a complete stranger with a penchant for verbal thrashings and violence."

"I'm happy to say I don't fall into that category. Actually, violence against women of any kind is on my list of 'Things That Get You Fuckin' Hit.' Right up there with animal abuse."

She nods. "Yeah, that shit makes me sick." She abruptly snaps her fingers. "Oh, I completely forgot, I wanted to ask this earlier, but we got sidetracked. Where is your friend now? The one who lost his arms?"

"Oh, Jude? He's livin' back home now, just outside of LA. He left Walter Reed about a year before I did and started school out there. We still catch up on the phone from time to time. I'm actually really fuckin' proud of him. Last time we talked, he told me he had taken a semester off and pursued stand-up comedy and was actually startin' to get some traction around the scene. Got himself an agent and everything."

"No fucking way. That's so awesome!"

"Yeah, so obviously I'm trying to get out there at some point and catch his act. Pretty fuckin' sweet he has the balls to do that. I've acted plenty in my life, but to stand up there and try to make people laugh ..." I hook a finger in my shirt collar and pretend to let in air. "No fuckin' way. That has to be the hardest thing ever."

She shakes her head. "Nope. I couldn't either. But I definitely have mad respect for those that have the balls to do it," she says. "So, acting, huh? Is that what your major is?" She smirks, leaning in, adding, "It's kind of hilarious you've already been inside of me and I still don't know your major."

"Yeah, isn't that supposed to be, like, the first thing a person asks when they meet another in a college town?" I chuckle. "No, I'm undecided right now. I've thought about actin'. I've thought about it a lot. But I also know the likelihood of makin' it is slim to none. I'd be better off usin' my retirement pension to buy lotto tickets."

"Wait, so you get a monthly pension?"

"Yeah."

"A good one?"

I nod.

"You dumb fucker!" she shouts, eliciting annoyed looks from the surrounding tables, but a smile stretches across her face. "If you make a good pension, why *don't* you chase your dreams?"

"I could ask you the same question." I finish off my whiskey, grinning at her against the rim of my glass. "I assume if you're makin' money on YouTube, you probably have a lot of followers."

"Quite a few, yeah."

"Wait, how many?"

Her eyes fall to the tabletop and her face goes a little red as if she's gone bashful. "It's so lame."

"What is?"

"Talking about this stuff. It's boasting."

"I asked the question, so it doesn't count as boasting," I argue, and she rolls her eyes, letting out a heavy sigh.

"A little over a million and a half. I'm one of only a small percentage who've reached a million."

"Holy fuckin' shit!" I say, eyes wide, and it garners a throat-clearing from a neighboring table. I put a hand up and mutter a 'sorry' before turning my attention back to Ember. "I figured if you were makin' ad money, you had to be doin' good, but *a million and a half*? That's a stupid amount." I chuckle as she sips down the last of her drink. "So, it further supports my argument. You're obviously makin' pretty good money with that many subscribers, and you said you wanted to do video bloggin' in Europe, which, seen by that many people, would be fuckin' huge. So why *wouldn't* you take time off from school now, and go chase your own dreams?"

She has a half frown, half smile on her face as she crosses her arms. Rolling her eyes, she says, "I guess you got me there, shithead."

"Aw ..." I tilt my head, a ridiculous smile on my face. "Have I mentioned how much I love your terms of endearment for me?"

"Have I mentioned I wore my sharp heels tonight?" She quirks an eyebrow as the laughter exits my mouth.

"You ready to get out of here?"

She nods. "Yeah. You ready to burn off dinner?" She bites her bottom lip, a look of seduction on her face, and it takes everything I have not to take her into the bathroom right now and fuck her silly.

"You have no fuckin' clue," I say, shaking my head.

———

WE BARELY MAKE it through my front door before she pounces on me, grabbing at my shaft and kissing my neck. As I shut the door behind us, I realize my roommate is in the kitchen grabbing a bowl of cereal. He looks right at us, his weasel face scrunched in confusion as she sticks a hand down my pants, unaware he's watching. I go to say something, but her hand cupping my shaft has it ticking its way to full form.

"Sorry, dude," I manage to say, as I have an internal battle between mind and my shaft.

Ember shoots her eyes over to him as she yanks her hand out of my pants, and then bursts out in laughter. "Oh my God, I'm so sorry!" she says, turning back toward me with a wide smile still on her face. She mouths an 'oops' and says, "I'm gonna head to your room. I think I've made a fool of myself enough already," she says, blowing me a kiss and turning on her heel toward my room.

"Um, hey man ..." my roommate Matt says in that Milton voice of his. "Can I, uh, talk to you for, uh, just a second?"

I cross the living room to the kitchen counter. "What's up?"

He cranes his head around to look toward my bedroom and then back at me. "Um, the last time she was here, uh, you guys were kind of loud, and uh, you know, the walls are, you know, they're thin, so I hear everything."

I think first about the amount of times I've heard his stupid fuckin' video games all the way in my room with both doors shut.

Motherfucker may drink Mountain Dew all night to stay up for his Call of Duty missions, but some of us have to fuckin' sleep.

"I'll try, man, but I don't think we were really bein' that loud."

"Well, I mean, I kind of, uh, I heard moans and stuff, and she was saying your name quite loudly. You know, if you could just keep it to a minimum."

I nod, my lips pinched together to keep the curse words in. "Okay, we'll try to do that for you, Matt."

He takes a bite of cereal and the glasses slide down his nose. "I, um, I appreciate it," he responds with a mouthful of soggy, half-eaten cereal.

I turn, a wicked smile stretching across my face as I make my way to the room. I shut the door and walk straight toward Ember, who lays on my bed clad only in black Victoria's Secret lingerie, her eyebrow arched seductively. She's taken by surprise when I grab her hand and pull her up to her feet. I then squat just a bit, wrap my hands around each of her thighs, and pull her legs up, indicating for her to wrap them around me. She does, crossing one foot over the over behind my back and locking in as I push her against the wall with a thud. My lips are a breath away from hers.

"He said we were too loud last time," I whisper, smiling. "Now, all I want to do is fuck you till the whole goddamn complex can hear you."

She smiles wide, her eyes beaming as she nods. "You better get started then."

I smirk, and then my lips crash down on hers as I kiss her hungrily.

Walking her back to the bed, I lay her down again, and she says, "If you really want to make me scream, you have to do that trick with your fingers again. My God, it felt so good."

"Oh, I can definitely do that and more, woman."

"You going to make me pay for being a bad little girl?" she asks, tilting her head and pouting.

"Oh God, I'm gonna do more than that. I'm fixin' to make you come more times in one night than you have in your entire life."

Her eyebrows lift, and she says, "That won't be very hard with the duds I've been with. We better shoot for twice as many just to be safe, huh? Now, what the fuck are you waiting for, soldier?" She slips a hand down to her panties and pulls them to the side, exposing that beautiful pussy of hers, glistening now from how wet she is already. She points with her other hand.

"Fuck," I mutter, shaking my head as I look her tan skin over, dropping down and kissing her, nibbling my way down her stomach and meeting her clit with my hot breath.

She gasps as I slide two fingers inside her, come hithering as I lick around her bud in soft strokes. Her body tightens and then quivers in cycles as I continue applying pressure, so anxious to taste her sweet cum.

When her eyes start to roll back in her head and her toes curl, I know I'm close. Picking up the pace, her whimpers grow to moans, which—with fingers moving as fast as a metal guitarist's—turn to screams of pleasure as she begins to squirt.

"Oh. My. *God*," she screams, her words broken up by the force of my fingers inside her and the power of her climax. "*Oh, my fucking God!*" she yells out, louder now, as more cum squirts from her pussy than I've ever seen.

"That's it, baby. Come for me," I say, and she gasps, her skin flush, her body writhing.

Her trembling hands reach out aimlessly. "Stop, please. Oh my God, you're killing me."

I grin, slipping my fingers out of her and giving her clit a peck. As I lift myself off of her, she lets out a heavy, pleasured sigh, and then stands, putting two hands to my chest and pushing me onto the bed.

"It's your turn now," she says, her breathing heavy, an

eyebrow arched. She squats, pulling my belt from the loop of my pants on the floor and standing with it. She folds the belt in half and extends it out in front of her.

"You gonna spank me? I don't know if I like the sound of that." I eye the belt skeptically.

"No, but when I'm done with you here, I want that thing." She points to the Big Bro paddle Sarge gave me, which now hangs on my bedroom wall. "And I want it hard."

"You serious?"

She nods her head in this innocent, yet seductive manner. "But after I'm through with him." She reaches down with her free hand and brushes the tip of my throbbing dick, which is tenting my boxer briefs. Abruptly, she wraps the belt around my wrists with a mischievous little twinkle in her eye. "Now, you keep your hands to yourself or a spanking *will* be in order. Understand?"

"Are you sayin' I can't pull your hair when my dick's in your mouth? Because I kind of love that."

With my hands now bound, she stands straight and points a finger at me. "Don't. Move."

She traces a finger from my pec, down my stomach, to the bulge in my boxer briefs. After teasing the tip of my cock with her finger, she grabs ahold of the waistband and pulls them off, tossing them to the side.

"Mm, such a pretty dick," she purrs, dropping to her knees and wrapping her fingers around me. "Does he want to touch the back of my throat?" she asks, tilting her head.

My heart races, my desire for her relentless. "Fuck yes, he does!"

She smiles, licking just the tip with a soft stroke, but even that sends a surge of energy through me. "You have a nice thick cock," she says, and the word 'cock' leaving her lips is just about the most beautiful sound I've ever heard.

"You're pretty good at gettin' him up in a hurry."

"I guess now it's my duty to keep it that way then," she says, an eyebrow arched with her fingers wrapped tightly around my shaft. She switches her hand with her mouth and takes me deep, down one inch at a time, until her face touches my stomach, the tip meets her throat.

She gags a little, and it turns me on even more.

I throw my head back, gasping as I fight against the tight belt. I want to touch her, to grab a fistful of hair and make her go faster, but I don't. I can't.

She sucks harder, faster, bringing me right to the edge, my toes curling and thighs seizing, before she slows it down. She looks up at me with seductive eyes, my cock going in and out of her mouth, and the sight of it has me so turned on I can barely stand it.

"Please, baby. Please. I'm so close. So *fuckin'* close."

She moans to my words, and the hum against the head of my dick has my legs going numb.

She pulls my cock out of her mouth, and in the most innocent voice, asks, "Does Daddy want me to swallow his cum?"

I nod, my heart racing, my body ablaze. "You better," I growl.

Returning to my pulsating cock, she sucks and strokes it, faster and faster and faster. She knows I'm close, so she picks up the intensity.

"Oh my God. Right there! Right there! *Yes!*"

Just as I climax, she takes my entire dick down, further than I thought it could ever go. Holding it there with her top lip meeting my pubic bone, the cum drains from my cock down her throat.

As she pulls away, taking a step back and observing me, I try and catch my breath. My body is in an all-out buzz.

"Oh my God, woman. That was ... incredible."

"Why, thank you," she says, blushing a little.

"No. I'm not fuckin' kiddin' here. Welcome to the 'Best Blowjob I've Ever Had' club. Members ... one."

"Shut up," she responds, waving me off.

"I'm serious. And that trick you did at the end. Oh, my fuckin' word. I can't even process a thought right now"

"It was hot watching you come." She hesitates, before adding, "How about you put that giant dick inside me now so I can make you come again? What do you think?"

I shake my head. "I think you need to get that sexy ass over here and sit on my dick. That's what I think."

"Any other demands, Sergeant?"

"Yeah, get me that paddle off the wall before you do. It's time for some corporal punishment."

FOURTEEN

Thanks to an uptick in class work for me and a test Ember has today that she's been studying for, I haven't seen her all week. Not since she left Sunday morning, a morning that consisted of perfect amounts of sex, cuddling, and Netflix.

It's hard to make sense of what I'm feeling. Not long ago, my heart was being stomped on by Chelsea. Now she hardly even crosses my mind. Not since Ember has taken up residence. As confident as she is, like me, she shows damage too. She possesses this darkness, this depth, that I connect with on a visceral level. I find myself yearning to talk to her, to get to know more about her, to give in and let my heart take the wheel. But in the same breath, the ever-present anxiety persists and warns me against making any rash decisions. It reminds me about my weary heart and the battering it's taken over my lifetime.

I trace the *Corazon Agotado* ink that arches over the grenade-heart tattoo I had inked on my bicep after my first deployment, smirking and shaking my head. Taking a pull from my cigarette, I think back to that time, sitting in the tattooist's chair at Fort Bragg. I was one month removed from my deployment to Iraq, and five months removed from finding out my high school girlfriend had moved in with another man shortly after I deployed. She didn't even bother telling me. Twenty years old and heartbroken, the tattoo was a reminder that the worst kind of scars are the ones you can't see. The ones we wear on our hearts.

"Earth to Bishop."

I hear the voice, I can make out the words, but I'm completely zoned out.

"Yo, Bish." Mac snaps his fingers in front of my face and it startles me. He takes a step back, putting his hands up. Carter and Jeremy stand behind him.

"Shit, man. Y'alright?" Jeremy asks. He points to my hand. "Your cigarette's about out."

I look down and see that the ash has built up to about half an inch, and the ember has reached the filter. Tossing it into the butt bucket, I rise to my feet, shaking my head.

"Fuck, I was zonin' out hard. Barely slept last night. Y'all got a crazy amount of work in your classes too? Like, more than usual?"

Mac nods. "Yeah. They're getting us prepared for midterms," he says.

"Well, I fuckin' hate it."

"Yeah, and this frat bullshit doesn't help any. Anybody got a clue what's going on tonight?" Mac asks as I light another cigarette.

I shrug. "All Damian told me was that it involves JD."

"Oh Lord," Jeremy says, chuckling. "That motherfucker is a mess."

"Y'all wanna make a bet? Twenty bucks says he talks about ass, or shit, or somethin' involving the asshole within the first ten minutes," I say, pulling out my wallet and grabbing a twenty-dollar bill.

"You're talking to a freshman here, man. Twenty dollars to me is a fortune," Mac responds.

Jeremy grabs his wallet. Nodding, he says, "I'll play that game. I got twenty on him sayin' it by about the twenty-minute mark."

"So, does it work like *The Price is Right*?" Carter asks. "I get everything over thirty minutes?"

"Fuck you." Jeremy laughs, handing over his twenty and pocketing his wallet.

"How about this, I got twenty on the fact that he'll mention anal sex first. Pick a topic. Whatever he brings up first, winner gets the pot," I say.

"Sounds good," Jeremy says. "I'm bettin' on him talkin' about poo." He laughs.

"Alright, I'm game," Carter says. "Mind if I pay you later?"

"Sure," I respond.

"Okay. I've got twenty on him talking about fisting, doesn't matter if it's ass or pussy," Carter says, and I nod with an approving smile.

"Game on, bitches," I say, stacking the twenties, folding them, and stuffing them in my pocket. "This should be interesting."

"Now GENTLEMEN, before we start the pledge challenge tonight, I wanna have a heart to heart with y'all," JD says, sitting in a chair in the middle of the basement, a cold Busch in his hand and a cooler full of them at his feet.

We are on the edges of our fucking seats, in a half-circle in front of him, waiting to see who will win the bet. He's been here only ten minutes so far, and topics have consisted of the difficulties that accompany pissing with a hard-on in the morning and the gas Mr. Chow's General Tso chicken gives him. Carter was really interested in that one. I can only assume he was hoping that the gas conversation would naturally lead to JD sharing with us the consistency, texture, and color of his last bowel movement as well, making Carter our winner. Thankfully, for Jeremy and me, he didn't.

"Do y'all have any clue what tonight's about?" JD asks, leaning in with his elbows on his knees.

"Nobody's told us shit," I respond.

"Well then, let me fill y'all in. Tonight, ya face a challenge. A challenge against each other. A challenge unlike any other. A *cock* challenge. And it involves my favorite thing on God's green earth ... strippers."

We look at each other, confused, before JD continues, "And before we bring the girls in here, and before I explain to y'all just what this challenge entails, I need to let y'all in on a little life lesson. I need all ears, cause in less than ten minutes y'all may find yerself in this predicament and yer gonna wish you'd listened."

Perking up in my chair, I grin, knowing the "life lesson" he's about to lay on us involves a stripper, and I can only deduce he did something to her asshole from what I know about him.

He clears his throat. "I'd just finished basic trainin'. We were at this titty bar outside Fort Leonard Wood with some of the other graduates. We got shit-canned. I'm talkin' 'Y'all might as well leave the bottle' drunk. I went from a broke ass high school kid down in 'Bama, to a goddamn soldier who couldn't touch his bank account fer three months of trainin'. Let me tell ya, fellas, I made it fuckin' rain that night." He abruptly stands and acts it out, tossing imaginary bills with quick swipes of his fingers against his palm.

"And I'm gettin' fuckin' lap dances out the ass. Twenty bucks, she touches my dick outside my jeans. Fifty, she'll give it a good stroke to the tune of "Pour Some Sugar On Me." Classy kinda place. I dished out hundreds that night, fellas. Hundreds. And by the end of the night, when I was so pissed I could hardly see straight, I went in fer one last dance."

He hesitates, taking a deep breath. He looks like he's a doctor about to tell us we have cancer. "Gentlemen, that was one last dance I shouldn't a' taken," he says, taking a seat again and shaking his head somberly.

I want to bust out laughing, at nothing more than how completely odd this motherfucker is, but I don't. I'm too engrossed in the story.

"I'm sittin' there, my dick harder than Chinese Trigonometry, and I pulled another fifty out of my wallet and slipped it in her g-string. She pulls my fun gun out and starts strokin' it." He pauses, taking a deep breath through his nostrils as he eyes us. "Fellas, there's somethin' about the smell of White Diamonds and pussy that just gets me juiced. I could feel the nut collectin' up in my balls like a fuckin' scrum and then it comes shootin' out all over her hand. Now, I ain't proud a' this, but when that nut was exitin' my balls, I ... well ... I managed to get so worked up that I shat a little bit."

"Yes!" Carter cheers, a fist in the air.

Jeremy and I let out disappointed groans.

JD looks at Carter, a tilt to his head and his eyebrow arched. "No, guy. It ain't yes! It's a big fuckin' no, in fact. Capital N. Capital O. When it happened, I could tell it wasn't a whole lot by the wetness against my ass cheeks, so I figured I could play it off long enough to get the fuck out of Dodge." He shakes his head, shame in his features. "I wasn't so lucky, fellas. That shit stunk to high heavens and she freaked the fuck out."

"Dear Lord," Mac mutters, shaking his head.

JD raises the pitch in his voice to sound like a woman, waving his hands frantically, and says, "'Oh my God, Jimmy!

This motherfucker shit himself. Get him the fuck out of here!'"
Returning to his normal pitch, he continues, "And so this big pro
rasslin' cocksucker throws my ass out. And damn it if I didn't
shit myself again when I hit the ground. Now, y'all don't understand. When ya mix as many alcoholic beverages as I did that
night, it turns yer guts into a bag of feral cats. Even after shittin'
myself twice, I had more in me. So, I ran into the bushes and
finished the job."

Mac bursts out laughing. "I'm so fucking confused."

"I'm gettin' to the point, goddammit. If you'd just open your
ears, Kathy Griffin. Now, hold yer tits. I'm tellin' a story here."

"What did you even wipe with?" Carter asks.

JD stink eyes him for a moment and then asks, "What was
yer name again? Lance Bass?"

"Carter."

"Carter, I gotta question for ya. Ya ready?"

Carter nods.

JD continues. "There were certainly leaves on the bushes I
could a' wiped with. A few fast food bags. But Carter ..." He
leans forward, looking him in the eyes. "If I just shit my
goddamn pants twice, why in the hell do I need to wipe?"

Mac cracks up and I just shake my head, a stupid grin on my
face.

JD sits back, clears his throat, and crosses one leg over the
other as he takes a swig of his beer. "Moral to the story is, gentlemen, when those strippers are dancin' on ya tonight, if ya feel
yer gut rumblin', ya need to get the fuck out of here. I don't
wanna see the same thing happen to y'all." His facial features go
serious, a wrinkle in his brow. "One casualty is enough! Never
again, goddammit," he says, putting a fist in the air and then
pounding it down onto his knee.

"So, we're just getting lap dances today?" Mac asks.

"Not just any ol' lap dance, Molly Ringwald," JD responds.

"My name's Mac."

"Goddammit, ya think I don't know that, Conan from Late Night with Conan O'Brien?" JD remains straight-faced, taking his attention off Mac and focusing on all of us. "Y'all are gettin' lap dances while yer wearin' only underwear. Last man standin' wins." He tilts his head. "Well, I guess standin' ain't the right term." He chuckles. "The last one of y'all to get a hard-on wins the prize."

"What's the prize?" I ask, concerned it has something to do with stripper pussy. Or, considering who we're working with, stripper asshole.

JD turns to me and smiles. "The prize? The prize is, ya don't gotta take part in tonight's second challenge with all the losers. Tonight, those of ya who can't keep yer dick down gotta eat a raw onion like an apple. All of it."

"Motherfucker," Mac huffs.

"Yeah, it *is* a motherfucker. Enjoy yer dances, ladies. And for you losers, the DIK Apple awaits." His lips curl into a smile as he turns toward the door. "Bring 'em on in, fellas!" he yells loudly.

Trevor, who has been standing idly by the back door, swings it open and in comes a group of brothers, hooting and hollering as they lead four of the ugliest strippers I've ever seen down the small set of stairs and into the basement. JD motions toward us, a giddy smile on his face. Music begins playing over the speakers.

"Right there, ladies! There's yer prey." He looks back at us, the strippers approaching his side, as well as every officer except for Sarge. "Gents, get down to yer skivvies."

"Where did you find these fine ladies?" I ask as I stand and start undressing, keeping the sarcasm from my tone so I don't catch a stripper heel to the throat.

"Oh, they're the best money can buy off a' Back Page. Well,

I mean, not the very best, I ain't a rich man, but they're decent." His eyes fall on the strippers and he ogles them for a moment. One of them is in a stars and stripes swimsuit, her messy, matted black hair a welcome sight compared to the girl next to her, wearing a rebel flag swimsuit, her head shaved half-bald. The other two wear gold and burgundy, Buchanan State's colors. They look no less disheveled and coked out than the other two. They look like they'd rather be in the utility closet shooting up. But that's neither here nor there. I have the unfortunate task of receiving a dance from one of these women, and I don't know what would be worse, eating a goddamn onion or enduring a longer dance than necessary.

"Bishop, yer Pledge President, so you pick first," JD says.

I raise my hand, asking, "Can we talk first about Mac's tighty-whities?"

All eyes in the room shift to Mac, who wears a pair of Fruit of the Looms. A wave of laughter rolls through the crowd.

"What?" Mac whines, lifting his arms in the air and analyzing himself.

JD takes a few steps toward Mac, an inquisitive look in his eyes. "Goddammit, son. Are ya twelve years old? Are there shit streaks in those things?"

"What's wrong with these?" Mac asks, looking stupefied.

JD gets down on one knee beside Mac as if he's a father coaching his son. "Listen, Seth Green. Everything is wrong with them things. *Everything*. But worst of all, they give the boys no room to breathe. Danglies need room to breathe, son."

"I think they're comfortable," Mac says, looking over toward us as if we're going to save him.

"Mac, you look like you're gettin' ready for fifth grade gym class," I quip, grinning.

JD nods, motioning to Mac's chest. "And what the good

goddamn is wrong with yer body? Ya look like one of them UNICEF poster children."

"I have a high metabolism."

"He looks like a red-headed Cryptkeeper," I say, laughing.

"Like a used tampon," Jeremy adds. "Get it? He's skinny, white, and red at the tip." He chuckles.

"I fucking hate you guys." Mac crosses his arms, pouting.

"Now, y'all leave poor Annie alone." JD stands up and makes his way back to the strippers. "Besides, we got a challenge to tend to. Bishop? What's yer fancy?"

"Well, I'm feelin' patriotic today. Let's say we go with the red, white, and blue."

She smiles at me as I motion toward her, and I see that she hasn't got a full set of teeth. A chill sweeps up my spine.

"Country Boy?" JD looks to Jeremy.

"I gotta go with the rebel flag," Jeremy responds, winking at her as he turns his hat around backwards.

"Justin Timberlake?"

"I guess I'll go with burgundy," Carter says, pointing to her but averting his eyes.

JD points a finger at Mac. "Alright, Eric Stoltz, from the Oscar winnin' drama, and in my opinion, under-appreciated film, *Mask*, that leaves Charlene with yer ginger ass," JD says, putting his hands on the shoulders of the woman in the gold swimsuit and leading her to Mac. "Ladies, assume yer positions. Trevor, ya know what to do."

Trevor nods and heads to the stereo near the bar. He turns it up. The strippers approach us, walking seductively, but goddamn does it turn my stomach. Nauseating smells permeate from them as they get closer, the smell of old McDonalds and stale cigarettes.

Abruptly, the song changes, and Sir Mix-A-Lot takes over, rapping about big butts and turbo 'Vettes. The strippers begin dancing in our laps, jerking and twisting in uncoordinated movements, their asses smashing up against our junk. My lady in the stars and stripes grinds away like she's at an eighth-grade dance, and though I find her to be hideously ugly, I can't help the sensation of pleasure stirring in my groin.

It's only a moment before JD lifts his hands high in the air and yells, "We got our first loser!" He points to Mac, who drops his head in shame as the stripper departs, exposing a solid hard-on pushing the limits of his tighty-whities.

"Sonofabitch!" Mac groans, trying to cover his shaft with his hands.

"Betcha wish ya weren't wearin' tighty-whities now, huh?" JD cracks up, pacing back and forth in front of us as the other brothers crowd around behind him, watching and cheering us on. "Who's gonna be next?" he shouts, clapping his hands together as he eyes each of us, occasionally bending down to get a closer look.

Carter falls next, not long after Mac, and I don't know what will hurt him worse, eating the onion or the ribbing he got from JD for having a "small" dick. I'm not trying to look at anybody's cock, but from what I saw, he isn't much less than average. He and Mac now both hang their heads in shame with onions in their hands.

"Down to our last two! Who's it gonna be?" JD calls out as if he's a color commentator.

I've thought about everything I could over the first few minutes—baseball, ballet, taxes, senior citizen pussy—but I've found myself losing control, the build-up of energy in my sack becoming too much to bear. I can feel my dick start to twitch as she continues twerking, her thick ass driving me to a loss against Jeremy.

I look over at Jeremy and say, "Fuck you, man. I'm winnin' this."

He smirks. Shaking his head, he responds, "Not today, old man. I'm takin' this one home."

JD leans over and eyes Jeremy's crotch. He straightens, surprise on his features, and says, "Not so much as a chubby! What about you, Bishop?" He leans back down and eyes mine, before he bursts out laughing. "Dead in the fuckin' water!"

"Fuck!" I yell, fighting the urge to close my eyes, to enjoy this. "I'm not gonna break! Baseball. Baseball. Baseball. Baseball!"

I'm shit out of luck. It's not two seconds until I feel the tip of my hard cock meet her ass. She stands straight, exposing my hard-on, and JD claps his hands.

"And we got ourselves a winner!" he shouts, lifting Jeremy's arm in the air. He looks down at him and adds, "We gotta see how long this motherfucker can go," as he lowers Jeremy's arm and takes a step back to observe.

"Do we have to?" Jeremy asks, disgust evident on his face.

"Yer goddamn right we do. We got records to maintain here. The record currently sits at three quarters of the way through 'I Luv Dem Strippers'" he says just as "Baby Got Back" ends and 2 Chainz takes over.

"We're gonna be here awhile! I got godlike control," Jeremy says, shrugging. He motions his head toward the rebel flagged stripper and says, "Do your worst."

"Oh, I will, baby," she purrs, licking her lips and cupping each melon-sized breast.

Somehow, Jeremy made it all the way to the Ying Yang Twins rapping about salt shakers, the fifth song to play as we ate our onions before JD finally called it. JD then proceeded to get a dance from each one of the strippers, their hairy pussies bare and in his face. They were doing lines of blow, the five of them, in the utility closet when I left like he was some kind of fucked up trailer park kingpin.

Once home, I get in bed to rest my tired legs after brushing my teeth about twenty times to get the onion taste out of my mouth, but it still lingers. The warmth of the blanket wrapped around me while I watch the leather pants *Friends* episode for the millionth wonderful time quickly gets me so comfortable, I drift to sleep, thoughts of Ember and our social date tomorrow circling my brain.

FIFTEEN

Decked out in my best suit, a black Kiton two-piece I splurged on after my second deployment, I wait on the front porch of the fraternity house, smoking a cigarette. The other frat and pledge brothers walk down the hill with their dates toward the Rusty Trombone as I wait for Ember to show. Being my first social, and with Ember set to be on my arm, I was a little nervous getting ready, making sure everything was perfect, and for the first time since the pledging process started, I'm wearing my Purple Heart eye. It's a prosthetic I had to grow to love, as it brings more attention than the normal ones do. There's no iris or cornea painted on this one, only a pupil with a Purple Heart medal painted on top. When I wear it now, I feel a sense of pride.

If they're gonna stare anyway, I'm gonna let 'em know where I got it from.

Ember is running late, and I'm on my third cigarette. My black leather wrapped flask, the one I received as a gift for being the best man at Tommy Callahan's wedding, is in my hand, and every few moments I sip a little Jameson from it, priming myself for a good night out, and to prepare for the feelings of sweeping anxiety I know the crowded bar will undoubtedly bring.

Before long, a cab pulls up, much to my relief, and the door pops open. Ember exits the vehicle, a crimson flared dress clinging tightly to her torso, a pair of bedazzled Louboutins on her feet. Her beauty mesmerizes, even under the dim streetlight.

She's dressed to the nines ... and *breathtaking*.

As she saunters up the sidewalk toward the porch, she glances at me with a tight smile. I can tell by her expression that something's up.

"Everything okay?" I ask, pocketing my flask as she approaches and gives me a tight hug.

"Yeah," she mutters, her eyes falling to the ground.

I put two fingers beneath her chin and tilt her head up, smiling as her gorgeous eyes meet mine again. "Tell me what's goin' on," I demand in a soft tone.

"It's Brady," she says, letting out a heavy sigh. "That's why I'm late."

A wrinkle of concern crosses my forehead, a twinge of anger buzzes in my chest. "What did he do?"

"Nothing. I just got off the phone with him a few minutes ago. He was just kind of being a dick."

"About what? *Us*?"

"Yeah, he's mad I'm going to the social with you."

"Fuck that! He's got no right to be mad. You aren't together. You've done nothin' wrong."

"I know, I know." She takes my hands in hers. "Let's just go have some fun, okay?" She forces a smile.

"Okay, but I'm gonna say somethin' to him tonight when I see him."

"No, you don't have to do that," she says as we start toward the sidewalk. "He's not going to the social anyway. He's too pissed off."

I stop dead in my tracks, and she stops along with me. "So, where is he?"

Her eyes flit to the fraternity house, and then back to me as she shrugs.

"He's in the house?" I ask.

She nods, and I turn, making my way toward the front door in a hurry.

"Bishop, no! Let's just go, *please*?" She grabs for my arm as I reach the front door. "Please, babe?"

Turning back to her, my hand on the door handle, a determined look in my eyes, I say, "Ember, he needs to know it isn't right what he's doin'. He can't treat you like this. Or make you feel this way."

"It's okay. I've already told him all that."

I open the door but don't enter right away. My eyes remain on hers. "But he hasn't listened. Just stay out here, gorgeous. I'm not gonna do nothin' stupid. I just wanna talk to him."

I go to walk inside, but she clings to my hand. Pulling her into me, I kiss her deeply, passionately, before leaning my head back and smiling. "I promise everything will be okay," I say, kissing her once more, and then I make my way inside and down the hall, the front door closing behind me.

I reach Brady's door, the third one on the right, and knock on it just as I hear the front door opening. Looking toward the noise, I see Ember creeping inside the house.

"Dammit, Ember," I scold just as Brady's door opens. Turning toward him, I see first the scowl on his face, then his shirtless torso, ripped far more than mine with a good twenty extra pounds of muscle.

"Can I help you?" he asks in an annoyed tone.

"Yeah, you can actually." I set a hand high against the door frame, an intimidation tactic, no doubt. "I need you to stop givin' Ember so much shit for hangin' out with me. She's a grown-ass woman," I say just as she approaches.

He shoots her a nasty glare.

Raising my voice, I say, "I need you to not act like she's your possession. I need you to be a man here." His eyes fall back on me, anger lines in his forehead. "Y'all aren't together. She's a single woman. So, leave her the fuck alone. Got it?"

Without waiting for a response, I drop my hand and turn, grabbing Ember's hand, and leading her away.

"I'll keep that in mind," he calls out from behind us.

As we reach the front door, I look back toward him with a smirk, saying, "Be sure you do, kid. Be *very* sure."

Opening the door and waiting for Ember to pass through, I wink at Brady, and then I follow her out.

As we make our way toward the sidewalk, Ember warns, "You want to be careful with him. He's got a temper. It's all the 'roids he takes."

Squeezing her hand, I smile and say, "Ember, I'm not worried about that little bitch. I've been in my fair share of fights. I've handled my own. And I'm not afraid of him, or anybody else."

"I just don't want the drama, you know?"

"I don't either. Trust me. But if it finds me, I'm ready and willin' to take care of it."

I let go of her hand and slip the flask from my back pocket. Handing it over to her, I ask, "Want some?"

She digs into her purse and pulls out her own pink flask with a smile and a wink. "Handled."

"Well, cheers then." I clink mine against hers and lift it to my lips. "To an epic night."

"To your dick inside me later," she adds, taking a drink as I burst out in laughter, a little of the liquor flying out of my mouth.

I wipe an arm across my lips and say, "Goddamn, woman. That was out of left field. Though I don't know why I'm so surprised."

"Too much?" she asks just as we reach Main Street. There are people everywhere, going to and from the five bars that dot this small downtown. The Rusty Trombone sits a block to our right, its Nashville-esque sign framed in rusted metal with the bar name in bright shimmering letters that light the street out front.

"Not even fuckin' close. I love when you talk dirty," I admit, guiding her toward the front of the bar, where a cluster of brothers and their dates stand, smoking cigarettes with drinks in their hands.

"Well, there will definitely be more of that later," she says with a sexy little smirk as we approach the group. The only one of them I've really gotten to know is Tim. I internally chuckle as he sports an ill-fitting suit with a Metallica shirt under the jacket and combat boots on his feet.

"What's up, bro?" I ask, slapping hands with him. "How is it in there?"

"Fucking crowded. I needed a breather. This is exactly why I never do these things.

Overcrowded as fuck. Waiting an hour for a fucking drink. It's not just our social in there either. There's a few going on."

"No shit?"

"No shit."

"Which fraternities?"

"Alpha Zeta and Beta Chi."

"They arranged a social with us and *Beta Chi* in the same fuckin' building?"

"Yup." Tim nods, shrugging. "Brady's bright idea, I guess."

"Well, let's hope it don't turn into a fuckin' fight club in there."

"If it does, you come and get me, alright?" He smirks. "I might be heading back here

otherwise."

Patting him on the back as I start toward the door, I say, "You bet," followed by a

chuckle.

As we enter, almost immediately, Ember lets out a squeal and goes running toward a short blond in a tight red halter dress. They embrace, and then Ember excitedly walks her by the hand over to me.

As they approach, Ember motions toward the cute blonde with a killer smile, and says, "Bishop, this is my best friend in the world, Holly. Holly, this is my friend Bishop."

Shaking her hand, I say, "Awesome to meet you, Holly! I've heard great things."

"Great to meet you too," she responds with a cute little smile. "And I've heard quite a bit about you myself." She bumps hips with Ember, and Ember rolls her eyes.

"Shut up, bitch. Don't give away my secrets. Now, where is this new boy toy of yours?"

Holly motions toward the bar. "He's grabbing a drink. Do you want to meet him over there?"

"Sounds good," Ember responds, grabbing my hand and pulling me along after Holly.

SEVERAL SHOTS DOWN, and too many beers to count, my pledge brothers and I, with our dates, stand in a large circle by the bar. It's been chaos around us all night, with so many people in the building, which has led to a bit of excessive drinking to calm my nerves. Unfortunately, once the drinks add up, the line between comfortable drunk and uncomfortable drunk is just a sliver. I've danced over that line by this point and my head is floating. Drunken conversations cross back and forth between the lot of us, but I'm not particularly engaged in any of them.

Jeremy whistles loudly, garnering the group's attention, and he lifts his glass in the air. "Guys, I ain't tryin' to get sappy, but I'm drunk, so fuck it. It's been a great time gettin' to know y'all. I'm lucky to have such awesome pledge brothers. And to your beautiful dates, thanks for makin' all of us look good tonight, ladies. Cheers!"

"Cheers," we repeat, and just as I'm about to take a drink, it's Mac's face that lets me know something's up.

His mouth goes slack, a wrinkle of concern in his brow, and he points behind me. I turn, and just as I do, I see a beer bottle coming straight for my head. It smashes against me, breaking into dozens of tiny little pieces. I take a step back, grabbing for my face as I make sense of what's just happened. As I wipe the blood from my eyes, I see someone charging for me. It's when he's inches away that I realize it's the same guy I beat the fuck out of a few weeks ago.

He tackles me, the back of my head hitting the bar top as I'm taken to the ground. I see stars. I'm immediately taken back to Army combatives; as drunk as I am, and as much as my head now throbs, it comes instinctually. With one swift move, I've countered his attack and found myself on top of him in a full mount. It's when I start pounding his face with the palms of my hands that I completely black out.

I don't come to again until I feel a deep burn in my eyes. I roll over and grab my face, gasping for much-needed air. As I fight to see something, anything, I feel my arms being grabbed by rough hands and I'm turned over on my stomach without much care.

"What the fuck!" I call out as I feel my hands being cuffed, my vision still blurry.

"Do not resist!" a voice yells as I'm helped to my feet, and I fight to see through the burning haze.

"What the fuck is goin' on?" I plead, as the tears well in my eyes, brought on by the mace that now blinds me. Snot and saliva run freely to the ground.

"Walk," the voice says sternly.

"My eye, man," I say as I'm forced to walk in staggering steps, still blinded. "I've got a prosthetic eye in. It's burnin', man. I need to rinse it out. *Please*."

"Let's get you outside first," he responds, guiding me along. "Watch your step here."

I take small steps forward until I'm outside, the dim streetlight breaching the haze, the cool wind rustling past me and of much relief to my burning eye sockets.

"Can I please just rinse this shit out? I'm not trying to run. I'm not trying to fight. I just wanna wash my eyes out."

"He's bleeding too, Eric. Pretty bad," another voice says. I try and rub my eyes out on my shirt, but it just gets more of the mace in them.

"Fuck!" I shout, batting my eyelids and fighting back against the intensified sting with gritted teeth.

I feel hands take hold of my wrists, removing the handcuffs. I lift my palms to my face, about to wipe my eyes when the officer who cuffed me says, "Hey, hey, hey. Don't rub your eyes. It'll make it worse. Officer Collins, grab me a water bottle. And get one of those EMTs over here."

"Roger that," the other cop responds.

I'm in a daze. My head burns from the open wound, my eyes, little balls of molten lava.

"Here you go," he says, setting a bottle against my hand. "Pour it in each eye. Go ahead and use the whole thing."

I do as I'm told and the feel of the cold water rushing into my burning sockets is one of the best sensations I've ever felt. It's borderline orgasmic. I pop my prosthetic out and rinse it well before returning it to the socket.

"Feel better?" he asks as I pour the rest of the bottle into each eye.

"Much better. I was hopin' to not have to ever go through that again. Haven't been gassed since basic training. It's just as shitty as I recall."

He laughs.

Batting my eyes, a slight burn persists, but I can now see what's going on around me. Though it's cloudy still, I can make out hundreds of people on the street in our vicinity. Some with phones up, recording, others just gawking as hordes of people tend to do when something out of the ordinary happens. Flashing lights from an ambulance, fire truck, and about three cop cars paint Main Street in red and blue.

I am the main attraction.

Scanning the crowd, I spot Mac, Jeremy, and Carter standing back behind some officers, who are keeping people at a distance. Behind them, there are more DIK brothers, Trevor and Damian, and Ember is just to their left. She has pity in her eyes, a wrinkle of concern in her brow ... and something else, something that grips my heart like a vice ... disappointment.

An EMT approaches, his tired eyes studying me. "Pretty good gash you got there. Gonna need stitches," he says, the officer nodding in agreement.

Officer Piscotty, as his name tag reads, is a middle-aged man with a thick Sam Elliott mustache, salt and pepper, and he has the beginnings of a retirement gut. "You gonna need to take him in, I'm guessing?" he asks, and the EMT nods.

"Yeah, do you need to get a statement still?"

Piscotty shakes his head. "You alright to ride in the cruiser to the hospital?" he asks me. "It's gonna be a bit until we can get another ambulance out here."

"I don't mind," I respond. "Do I need to be cuffed back up?"

Officer Piscotty eyes me for a moment, an eyebrow quirked when he asks, "What service were you?"

"Army Infantry. Six years."

"That how you lose your eye?"

"Yeah."

"I was Marine Corps Infantry. Desert Storm," he says, reaching a hand out toward me, and we shake hands briefly. "You gonna run on me? Or try to fight back? Cause I still gotta take you in after you get stitched up."

"I'm not goin' anywhere. I just want this fuckin' burning to stop."

"It'll start to fade here soon. I probably should've just used my taser."

"Yeah." I laugh. "I would've much preferred repeating that experience."

AFTER GETTING my head cleaned up, seventeen stitches put in, and engaging in the usual military chitchat with Officer Piscotty throughout, we're at the police station now, in a stark interview room. My hands are still uncuffed and there's a hot cup of coffee in front of me that tastes like brewed dog shit. The officer sits across from me with paperwork in front of him and a pen in his hand. Pulling a pair of reading glasses from his breast pocket, he perches them on the bridge of his nose and eyes me over the frames.

He clears his throat. "So, tell me what happened ... from the beginning."

"All I remember is standin' at the bar, drinkin' with my

friends, and the next thing I know, this guy is hittin' me over the head with a bottle. The bottle shattered, he tackled me, and I fought back. End of story."

"Not quite. Do you know why he hit you with a bottle?"

"No idea."

"So, it was completely random?" He eyes me skeptically, as if he knows something I don't.

I nod.

"Yes?"

"Yeah."

"Had you ever met the victim before?"

"The *victim*? Is that what we're callin' him? What does that make me then?"

"I didn't mean that how it came out. I just don't think you realize the damage you've done. We just got an update on him from the hospital. Four missing teeth. Broken jaw. Broken orbital. You really messed him up good. He's gonna have a long recovery."

A new nervousness sinks its teeth into me, a choking knot in my throat. "I don't remember that."

"You don't remember what?"

"I don't remember hittin' him that much. I kind of blacked out, I guess."

He breathes out a heavy sigh, scratching at his chin, and his eyes study me. "We've collected video from the establishment. Statements from witnesses. One of those witnesses claims he saw you attack his friend a couple weeks ago, the young man in the hospital now. He said you beat him up pretty good. There are reports that support his claim."

"He says it was me? Well, he's sadly mistaken. I've never met that kid in my life. Not ever. And I haven't fought since before my Army days."

His eyes are locked on mine. He seems to be plenty aware of the bald-faced lie I just presented him with. I don't look away.

"We have nothing on your involvement in the previous incident, but what you did tonight went too far. You're a trained soldier. He's a twenty-year-old kid. I don't care what he thinks, a kid is just what he is. And now he'll be lucky if he's not drinking out of a straw for a while."

"He attacked me," I say firmly.

He nods. "Yes, and that'll be taken into account."

"So, am I arrested?"

"As of now, yes. We'll set bail in the morning. You can make a phone call and have one of your friends or family post it."

I lean forward, my elbows on the table. "Listen, he's a twenty-year-old *man*. An *adult*. He hit me over the head with a bottle. A *weapon*. Cut me open. Then he charged me. I hit my fuckin' head against the bar top. I've got the stitches to prove both. Eyewitnesses too. Instinct kicked in. Did I mean to take it to that level, no. But I was just defending myself. He was underage and under the influence. That has to account for somethin'."

A look of understanding passes over his features as he takes in what I've just said, his head slightly nodding. "Well, nothing's official yet. You spend one night in jail, and that might very well be the only one you do. Alright?"

"Roger that." I sit back in the chair and cross my arms, nausea taking hold as I think about the prospect of legitimate jail time.

"And Bishop." He stands, putting out his hand. "Thank you for what you've done for this country. I mean that."

I stand too and take his hand in my own, shaking it for a moment.

"From one vet to another," he continues.

"Thank you for pavin' the way. And for bein' cool with me tonight."

"Just get some sleep. Everything will be sorted in the morning and then we'll go from there. Alright?"

"Sleep?" I laugh. "Yeah, we'll see about that."

SIXTEEN

After a restless night of toss and turn-riddled sleep, in a cell with seven others—some coming down from drugs and mumbling throughout the night—I'm grateful to take in the fresh morning air and feel the warmth of the early sun against my skin. My bloody, torn suit is bagged and in hand, swinging along at my side. I'm aware of the hundreds of dollars it will take to repair it, but it's of little concern at the moment.

"Appreciate you comin' to get me," I say, glancing over at Sarge as he walks beside me.

He waves me off. "Don't even mention it. I just wish I could've been there last night."

He digs keys out of his pocket and unlocks an M5 in the parking lot. As the headlights blink and horn beeps, I tilt my head toward him.

"Damn, bro."

"You like?" he asks with a smile on his face as he opens the car door.

"What's not to like. She's beautiful," I respond, climbing in after him. It still has that new car smell, the leather and carpet spotless. "Jesus, bro. OCD much?"

He grins. "Like a motherfucker."

As he pulls out of the parking space, I say, "I'm actually glad you weren't there gettin' wrapped up in that shit."

"No, I wouldn't have gotten involved outside of pulling you off of him before you turned his face into a jigsaw puzzle." He chuckles.

"I just fuckin' blacked out, man. Lost it."

He motions to the freshly stitched wound on the side of my head, the spot that still burns. "You had every right to lose it. And that's what friends are for. To step in if need be. Whether you're getting your ass beat too bad, or you're doing the beating. Speaking of which, what the hell were your pledge brothers doing at the time?" he asks as he exits the police station parking lot, navigating the M5 toward Main Street.

I shrug. "No clue. Next thing I knew, I came to and I had mace in my eyes. Come to find out, two officers were just strollin' by when the fight started and these fuck clowns shoutin' 'Fight, fight, fight!' are the only reason they even came inside. Funny how that shit works. I've been in so many fights in my time, ones with far uglier outcomes than last night, and I never got caught. Always got away with it. I beat this kid's ass in basic training, for Christ's sake. I guess, you get away with shit and get away with shit and get away with shit until one day your luck just runs the fuck out."

"You'll be alright, man. He attacked you first."

"I was arrested, bro. Booked. This shit's for real."

"Well, like I said, I got you a great lawyer. He's a dear friend of mine. He served too. You're in good hands, bro."

"And you said he's meetin' us at the diner?"

Sarge nods.

"I really appreciate you settin' that up, Sarge. Seriously. And thanks for the change of clothes."

"Hey, what are brothers for? I got your back. We're going to get you out of this, man. Your luck hasn't run out just yet." He winks and passes me a reassuring nod. Pulling into the diner lot, he parks the car and lets out a heavy breath, adding, "Well, you ready for this?"

"I don't have any other choice." I flash him a tight smile. Exiting the vehicle, with Sarge following suit, I motion toward the door. "He already here?"

"Should be."

Sarge leads me inside, and just to the right, in a red pleather booth, an aged man sits, a tailored sport coat showing off a still impressive physique. As he notices our approach, he stands, smiling and putting out a hand.

"Blake, what's up, my friend." He shakes Sarge's hand, taking him in for a hug before turning to me. "Bishop, Adam Silver, good to see you."

I shake his hand. "I appreciate you meetin' with me."

We take a seat in the booth and I notice the stack of papers in a manila folder at the table.

"You've been busy." I chuckle, pointing toward the stack.

"I love my job. And I love helping veterans like you. When Blake called me last night—late, I might add" —he narrows his eyes at Sarge with a grin— "he told me all about you and what you've given for this country. I'm making this my priority. I want to let you know that."

"I really appreciate that. Truly. So, I take it you've read up on the situation?" I motion toward the folder again, and he nods.

"I have. And I don't think they have a case here. The bottle became a weapon the moment he hit you with it. *He* should be the one with assault charges. *Aggravated* assault at that."

"How sure are you I'll be okay here?"

"Community service, maybe. A fine, perhaps, due to the excessive nature. But no jail time. Nothing like that. I need a little more time as these surveillance videos are handed over to investigators before I can give you a hundred percent, but I'll throw you a ninety-five percent certainty you won't see another night in a cell. Not for this anyway."

"That's good to hear."

As the waitress fills coffee cups for Sarge and me, Adam digs through the pile. He mutters, as if to himself, "You've never had any run-ins with the law either."

"At least I haven't been caught for anything," I respond, smiling.

Adam chuckles. "Yeah, well, that helps us out. I really don't want you to worry. I don't know what Blake told you about me, but I've served my own time as a JAG lawyer, and I work pro bono for veterans now. I've helped a lot of guys get out of some shit. You're gonna be one of them. I'm not promising zero repercussions, but I fully believe we'll be able to make a good deal here."

"And you feel good about no jail time, right?"

"Absolutely. You messed him up really good, no doubt about that. But they're going to see you were just defending yourself here. You're going to be okay."

"Thank you ... so much," I say, and he shakes his head.

"Don't even mention it. A friend of Blake's is a friend of mine. And considering what you've done for this country ... you deserve some goddamn leniency." He passes me a convincing look. "We're going to get this handled. Just give me a week and I'll have an answer for you as to what's coming next. Okay?"

"Should make for an interesting week," I jest, taking a drink of my coffee and hoping that this man really can keep me out of a cell.

I can't help but think the worst.

My anxiety rages.

The bottle calls and I *hate,* now more than ever, that it speaks so clearly to me.

SEVENTEEN

The next morning, at breakfast with my pledge brothers, I have only one goal in mind: finding out what happened when I blacked out, beyond what the police report says, beyond what I already know, and, most importantly, why Ember hasn't texted me back.

As we're seated at our usual table, they have solemn looks on their faces.

"So, who's gonna be the first to let me know what the *fuck* happened the other night?"

With wide eyes, Mac says, "All I know is, that fucker came out of nowhere and busted the bottle over your head before I could even say anything. And then you went all UFC on his ass."

"Yeah, I remember that. I remember wrestling him on the ground and hittin' him a few times, but hell, the shit they said I did to him ... no fuckin' recollection."

"You went fuckin' ham, man," Jeremy says, shaking his head. "Like, remind me never to fuckin' piss ya off." He lets out an uneasy laugh.

I wave him off. "Shut up, bro. I'd never fight y'all."

"Well, that's a goddamn relief, because you're a fuckin' hooligan."

"What did I do?"

Mac laughs, saying, "You were using these crazy ass palm punches." He throws a few hands in the air to demonstrate. "Next thing you know, his face is fucked, like flattened cartoon fucked, and cops are storming in."

"Ah, thank you, Bas Rutten," I say, smiling. "That's where I learned the open palm punches from. I'm surprised I actually pulled it out in a fight though. Never have before." I shrug. "Always wanted to."

"Well, I guess you can say you have now." Mac laughs. "Who's Bas Rutten anyway?" he asks.

Carter answers for me, "He's a UFC fighter. I've seen videos of his. He's an animal. Dude punches with his palms because it takes away the possibility of, like, rolling a wrist or getting a boxing fracture, or whatever."

"Yup." I nod. "And it's a smaller contact point, so there's more force behind it. It's supposed to be effective as fuck."

Carter laughs, shaking his head. "I'd say that's a definitive now. He was down for the count about two seconds in."

"And how long after that did I keep hittin' him?"

Carter laughs. "About another minute until the cops arrived, I guess. Shit, I was as drunk as you were. Felt like I was in a movie, or something."

"Jesus."

"Yeah, it was gnarly, bro," Mac says.

"And why didn't y'all help me? Pull me off him or somethin'?" I ask, and they look around at each other, none of them speaking.

"We tried," Carter responds defensively. "Jeremy and I both did. You were having none of it."

"Well, fuck." My gaze drifts out the plate glass windows, coated in morning dew.

"What did the lawyer say?" Carter asks, pulling my attention back to the conversation.

"He thinks because the kid used a bottle on me and attacked me first, they really don't have a case. The only thing I'm really in trouble for is the excessiveness."

"So, you're going to be alright then?" Carter asks.

"I think so, man. I'm convinced of it after meetin' with the lawyer. Just hopin' for the best and we'll see what comes of it." I take a sip of my coffee and then tilt my head, thoughts of Ember crossing my mind. "So, can anyone tell me why Ember isn't responding to my texts?"

All of their eyes fall on the tabletop. It's then I know for certain I did something foolish.

"Well, speak up, fuckers. I'd really love to know."

Mac clears his throat, looking as if he's searching for the right words. "It was when you started pounding him and after you pushed us off. I guess Ember knows him from back home," he says, pausing, a look of trepidation crossing his face.

"And?" I ask.

Mac takes a thick swallow. "She tried to pull you off too. I'm pretty sure you thought it was us again and you pushed her away kind of hard."

"Well, fuck." I shake my head. "Was it really bad?"

"It wasn't like overkill or anything," Mac responds. "But you shoved her pretty good, dude. And she definitely wasn't happy about it. If I had to guess, that's probably what she's pissed about." He hesitates for a moment, and then adds, "Well, that, and you rearranged her friend's face."

I shrug. "I mean, the asshole did bring a bottle to a fist fight."

"Do you remember him?" Jeremy asks, furrowing his brows. "I mean, from before the other night?"

I nod. "Yeah, I did the moment the fucker attacked me."

"Well..." Jeremy lets the word linger. "I reckon you taught him two lessons now. But I don't think he'll be forgettin' this last one."

EIGHTEEN

"Okay, Bishop. Like I said, great news. The *best* news," Adam says, sitting across from me at the diner, taking a drink of his coffee. I've been an anxiety-ridden mess over the past few days, waiting to hear back from him. When he called me this morning and said he had good news, I raced to meet him.

"Yeah? What's it lookin' like?"

"Well, you won't get off scot-free, but after going over the evidence with the family, and them learning about your past, they agreed not to press any charges if you go through a VA substance abuse program. Their other son is in the Navy, I guess, so they have a lot of respect for you and what you've done. They don't want you serving any time, and they understand their case is flimsy, regardless, but if you make it through this program, you won't have to deal with any of that. No charges. No trial. Just a seven-week program, and you're good to go."

"What does the program entail?"

"Well, if you agree to it, we've got you set up next Thursday to see a" —he rifles through papers in a manila folder before locating one and reading it— "uh, Dr. Carleigh Jacobs."

"And how often would I have to see her?"

"Weekly. You'd have an appointment every Thursday morning. Does that work with your schedule?"

I nod. "Yeah, that's fine. I only have one class on Thursdays, but it's in the afternoon. I'm assuming I can't drink durin' this thing?" I ask, more concerned than I'm trying to project.

"Well, yes and no. Certainly no drugs. You'll be piss tested every week before the appointment. You'll want to give yourself two days before each appointment to get the alcohol out of your system as well, but outside of that, you can drink, no problem." He sighs, his lips pinched together. "Just be careful. I would certainly keep yourself out of similar situations. You do *not* want to get caught up in anything else, or they will throw the book at you."

"No problem. I can keep my nose clean." I hesitate a moment, the idea of substance abuse counseling causing incredible amounts of dread inside me. "And this is the best option, right?"

"Absolutely. Like I said, you'd likely be found not guilty, I'm almost certain of it, but why risk it? This is an easy out. And if you're anything like me, you could use a little help with your transition process. I have love for the bottle too. I get it. Take advantage of the program and the opportunity to end this in the easiest way possible. Does that sound good? I don't want to force your hand here."

I shake my head, waving him off. "No, that sounds good. Tell 'em I'll do it."

He puts his hand out with a smile, and I shake it. "Good man! These seven weeks will fly by and you'll be able to walk away, unscathed. This is a good day, Bishop."

"Yeah ..." My voice trails off, my mind caught up in the what-ifs, but still so thankful to have an out. "A *great* day. Thanks, Adam."

NINETEEN

Walking in the door behind her, the first thing I notice about my new doctor is that this woman of cougar status is sculpted like a twenty-year-old; the curve of her ass in a thigh-length skirt steals my attention and leads me to wonder what she's wearing underneath. I mentally scold myself for the perversion but feel it all the same.

"It's great to meet you, McKenzie," she says, a slight rasp to her voice that reminds me of Scarlett Johannsen. She puts a hand up toward the chair in front of her desk.

As I take a seat and she makes her way around the meticulously kept desk, I scan the office. It's barren, except for a few certificates on the wall—no photographs.

"Bishop, please," I say, repositioning myself in the stiff chair.

As she takes a seat, she quirks an eyebrow. I admire the age and wisdom she carries in the smile lines and faint crow's feet, and how fucking sexy she is despite them. Or maybe because of them. Her midnight black hair cascades down in a long braid against her shoulder, making her look like Pocahontas or Lara Croft. There's a light touch of gray throughout that I admire her for keeping. It adds a touch of wisdom to her features. An elegance I find highly attractive. Her ocean blue eyes are captivating.

"So, you like to be called by your last name?"

I shrug. "It's an Army thing."

"I've treated a lot of military members, Army included, and I can understand that attachment. So, Bishop, let's talk about why you're here."

She grabs a pair of glasses from the desktop, sliding them on and feeding into the librarian fantasies I've already been attempting to stifle.

"I beat a kid up," I respond, shrugging, my eyes shifting to her ring finger. Vacant, but a tan line remains.

She nods, her gaze drifting. "Well, you did a little more than that."

"I reacted to a fucked up situation as best I could."

She puts a hand up, looking at me over the black frames of her thin glasses. "Please, one of my rules is no cursing in this room."

I grin. "My apologies. What are your other rules?" I ask, arching an eyebrow.

She's unaffected, leaning her elbows on the desk, a pen now gripped tightly in her hand. "That you be honest in here."

I hold up two fingers.

"That you are open to the treatment I have to provide over the next seven weeks."

I hold up three fingers.

She ignores my fingers, staring intently at me. "And that, by the last appointment, I see fit to pass you through this program. You must take and pass a breathalyzer and drug test before each visit, as you did this morning."

I nod, holding five fingers up for a brief moment before dropping my hand to my lap with a smirk. "I can agree to these terms ... but Doc, can I ask you a question?"

"Sure."

"Does it work the same for you? The whole honesty thing?"

She narrows her eyes at me, reading my features. "What do you want to know?"

"You have a tan line on your ring finger," I say, and she covers her left hand with her right, her eyes falling to them.

"We aren't here to talk about me, Bishop," she responds.

"I wasn't trying to make you uncomfortable. I was just curious what happened. I figured I'd be sharin' a lot about myself in here. Maybe it would help if I knew a little about you too."

She sighs, but her face shows resignation. "I guess that makes sense," she mutters, rubbing the tan line on her ring finger mindlessly. "I was married for a very long time."

"How long?"

Her eyes meet mine again. They've taken on a solemn look, but they're still so alive, bluer than blue. "Twenty-one years ..." She lets her words linger. I try not to let the surprise show on my face.

"Wow, Doc, if you don't mind me askin' ... how old are you?"

She laughs. "Old enough to be your mother."

"And how old is that?"

"I think it's time I ask the questions," she retorts.

I ignore her. "Have you been divorced long?"

She chuckles, shaking her head. "No more questions. Now, Bishop, I want to hear about that night. In your own words. I've read the reports. I want to hear it from you."

"He hit me with a bottle."

"I saw that. And I know you would've likely won this if you went to trial. Why didn't you? Why did you choose this program?"

I think on this for a moment, my eyes shifting to her near

blank walls. "At the end of the day, maybe I wanted a little help. I knew what the process of a trial would involve, whether I won or not, and I thought counseling might be a better option."

She eyes me, unconsciously chewing on the end of her pen. She points it at me, the tip glistening with saliva that turns me on more than it should.

"You say you wanted the help. What makes you say that?" she asks.

I shrug, shaking my head. "I don't know. Maybe I got a problem with the bottle. Maybe some anger stuff along with that. This transitioning shit isn't easy."

"I don't imagine it would be. Do you think this incident would've happened without the addition of alcohol?"

"If I would've counterattacked someone attacking me with a bottle? Yeah, I would do that sober just as quickly as I did it liquored up."

"Okay, and what about the fight before that? The one that led to him attacking you."

"That's unproven."

"Unproven, but obvious. None of this will reach the police. It won't make it beyond this room. But he attacked you because a friend pinned you as his attacker a few weeks prior. He admitted that he didn't remember, but the friend was adamant about it. Now tell me, did alcohol play a factor in *that* incident? Maybe a little of the anger too?"

I nod. "Yeah, most likely. But here's the thing, Doc. How many times in this life are these assholes gonna get away with bein' assholes until someone like me teaches them a lesson? People like that, they can't get away with bein' a dick their whole lives."

"*Language*," she says, and I put my hands up apologetically. "So, what led to that initial fight?"

"He ran into me. I was about to apologize, and he said,

'Watch out, bitch.'" As I say it, I feel what she must be feeling right now, if her face is any indication; it sounds fucking stupid.

"You needed to teach him a lesson?"

"I felt compelled to, yeah."

"Does it make you feel better to hurt people?"

I hesitate, scratching at my beard. "People who deserve it." I shrug. "Yeah. I fuckin' love it. Maybe I get off on it a little."

She tilts her head. "Language," she says sternly.

I put my hands up in retreat. "Sorry, bad habit obtained from the military."

"I told you, I've treated servicemembers and veterans for a long time. I understand the desire, maybe even the need to curse, but I believe more in one's ability to control themselves and their actions. And that there's a time and place for everything."

Continuing on, mindful of my words this time, I say, "Look, I take full responsibility for what I did to that kid." I throw my hands up in the air. "Both times. But both times, you bet he deserved it. If I had ten chances to do it over again, I'd do it the same way every time. Drunk or sober."

"As bad as you did it?"

My lips pinch tightly together, and I shake my head. "No, probably not." I hesitate, correcting myself. "Okay, *definitely* not."

"Do you have a problem with alcohol?" she asks bluntly, and an awkward silence lingers once the words leave her lips. "Honestly?" she adds, filling the silence.

"I don't drink alone often, so I don't consider myself an alcoholic. But in social situations, yeah, I guess I go too far. But like I said, I would've had the same reaction sober."

She taps her pen against the stack of papers in front of her. "And I see here you are part of a fraternity?"

"Pledging one, yeah. What of it?"

"How old are you?"

I grin. "You didn't answer when I asked you!"

She rolls her eyes and says, "I'm forty-seven."

"I'm twenty-five, and you don't look forty-seven in the slightest."

She chuckles, shaking her head. "We're talking about you here, Bishop. So, tell me, why a fraternity?"

"Do you know how hard it is to transition from the military?"

"I've said it a few times now, I've worked wi—"

"No, no, I know that you've worked with us, but have *you* transitioned from the military yourself?"

Her eyes fall to the desk, and I immediately feel bad.

In a lighter tone, I continue, "I'm just sayin'... it's *really* hard. Harder than I ever thought possible. My first few weeks at BSU were some of the worst of my life. I missed the brotherhood. The camaraderie. And, in all honesty, I've always wanted that fraternity experience. I was in the Army, dreamin' of the chance. That traditional college life."

"And is it everything you thought it would be?" she asks, and her words stun me. I'm taken back to my talk with Sarge about how quickly the fraternity wore on him.

How quickly it's wearing on me.

"Is it?" she asks again, breaking me from my thought storm.

I shake my head. "It could never be the Army. I don't know why I thought it could be."

"You were desperate," she says, but it comes out more of a question.

I nod. "Yeah ... yeah, I was. I hate bein' alone. I like havin' someone. Lots of someones. Even if those someones aren't who I thought they would be." There's a brief silence in the room before I add, "Though, genuinely, my pledge brothers are awesome. I feel lucky I've had the chance to get to know 'em. I guess I just feel like there's somethin' more out there. That maybe I'm regressing a little bit."

"What do you want in this life?" she asks, catching me off-guard.

I hesitate before responding, "I thought I knew. I thought it was military all the way. I had prepared for that through three fuckin'—" I cut myself off, putting a hand up and continuing, "freakin' combat tours."

She waves me off. "Speak freely, if you're speaking honestly," she says.

"Well, I've always wanted to act. The adrenaline and, just, energy I felt during combat, I've only ever felt that type of high either jumpin' out of planes or bein' on stage."

"So, you want to be a stage actor?"

"I want to be in movies. I love the stage, and I'd wanna do that on the side, but guys like Brando, Sinatra, Dean... Hanks, Denzel, Bale... I mean, those guys are my heroes. Actors and movies have been somewhat of a savior in my life, especially throughout my recovery. They've always been that bright spot, that escape, you know? I'd love to be that for someone else."

"Do you plan on majoring in acting?"

I chuckle, shaking my head. "Do you know what kind of response I've gotten every damn time I've told someone I'm thinkin' of goin' that route? It goes all the way back to my parents."

"What was your relationship like with them growing up?"

I put my hands to my throat, pretending to choke it. "Constricting. Overbearing. Anti-everything. They sucked the life out of a room."

"Anti-everything?"

"Anti-black, anti-Jew, anti-homosexual, anti-immigration, anti fuckin' everything."

She nods.

"They raised me on hate. And it wasn't until I hit my teens when I realized how much bullshit they really fed me."

"Do you deal a lot with your past?"

I force a laugh. "The military or the childhood?"

"Both."

"Well, I guess it's the same answer regardless. They're both a force to be reckoned with. A shadow attached to my ass I feel like I can't ever shake. They're a reminder that, as far as I run from this shit, as many years as I remove myself from it, it's still right there, nippin' at my heels."

"Do you think that's why you drink?"

"It's why I party. I'm social when I drink. Antisocial and lonely when I don't. So, what do I do?"

"Figure out why it is you feel antisocial and lonely when you're sober?" she asks, shrugging.

"Easier said than done, Doc."

"If I have to call you Bishop, then you have to call me Doctor Jacobs. No more of this Doc stuff."

"What about a first name?"

She narrows her eyes at me, a smile tugging at her lips. "Carleigh is fine too, though I'd prefer Dr. Jacobs."

"Carleigh. I like it." I nod.

She chuckles. "Okay, Bishop. Let's get back on track. How much do you drink per week?"

My eyes roam to the ceiling. I shrug. "A few times."

"Do you get drunk each time?"

I laugh. "Most of the time. Yeah."

"Why is that funny to you, Bishop?"

"Well, I mean, I don't drive. I don't harm anyone else. I'm just havin' fun."

She jabs a pointer toward the file in front of her. "You *did* cause harm to someone, Bishop."

"He *fuckin'* deserved it."

"*Language*," she says, at a volume just below a shout, her eyes staring daggers through me.

I back down, my lips curling into a grin. "I was speakin' honestly though," I say, and her face reads as anything but amused.

"Is it your thing, to get a rise out of people?" she asks, resignation finally taking up her features.

I immediately feel bad. Leaning back into the chair and crossing one leg over the other, I admit, "It's my thing to challenge people, I think. If I'm really diggin' deep, I think it's an armor I wear. It's something I use to protect myself."

"And why do you feel the need to protect yourself? To push people a little if they try to get close?"

"Because my parents were fuckin' shit," I blurt, putting my hands up. "Freakin' crap."

"You're okay, Bishop. You know what I mean by cursing. When it's directed at me, you're wrong. When it comes naturally through you telling your truths, I can accept it."

"Is that what these next seven weeks will entail, me tellin' my truths?"

"Among other things, yes. When I sign off on this, it'll be because I think you've made some real strides. That you have become more aware of your capabilities having been a decorated Army Infantryman, and what you can do to mitigate these types of situations in the future. You're a weapon, Bishop."

I laugh, waving her off. "No, I'm not."

"*Yes,* you are. I've read your paperwork, both military, and what you did to this kid. You can't just go around breaking jaws. That can't always be the answer."

"In my life thus far, it's been the answer a time or two."

"Was it worth it to knock out this poor kid's teeth?"

"*Poor kid?*" I roll my eyes. "He attacked me with a bottle." I motion toward the stitches still in my head, the hair shaved around it. "A damn weapon. He could've done a lot more damage. I knew a guy in Germany who got attacked with a bottle. He was left with a scar worse than what the RPG left me. That"—I throw up air quotes — "'kid' is really an adult. Twenty years old and drinkin' on a fake ID, if I'm to believe the police report." I motion toward the folder of paperwork between us. "He is, pardon my language, a goddamn adult. Maybe I was drunk. Maybe I was excessive. But he attacked me first. And in the spur of the moment, instinct kicked in."

"Do you think this fraternity may be putting you in situations, as a twenty-five-year-old combat vet who has a taste for alcohol, that maybe you shouldn't be in?"

"Who are you to judge?" I ask

She frowns, her arms crossing.

"Who am I to judge myself?" I say, trying to keep the peace, softening my features and hoping my words didn't hit too hard. "I don't know where I'm headed. I don't know where I should be. I follow my heart. Wherever it takes me, I follow it. What else am I gonna do?"

"Maybe acting is your thing. Maybe it isn't. But I don't think it's healthy for you to be around this drinking culture. Not if it's something you struggle with."

"So, maybe I head to LA and struggle to become an actor. Get addicted to cocaine and sell my body for sex to pay rent." I laugh, but her expression remains unchanged.

"I never said going to Hollywood and trying to become an actor was your thing, but maybe it is. Maybe you find something else you love more, but being in a fraternity, in that sort of environment, it's *not* good for you. I'm certain of that."

I shrug again. "Maybe it is. Maybe it isn't. We'll see."

"Well, you need to keep yourself out of trouble these next few months. You know that at least, right?"

"I do. And I will. I just have another month of this pledging shit. Another month, and I'll figure out where I go from here."

"Another two months you spend in that chair right there, talking shit out with me. Another two months you spend away from the drugs, and away from the bottle," she says matter-of-factly, and I can't help but laugh.

"Seven weeks, Carleigh. And *language*, please." I smirk, giving her a wink.

She lets out a heavy sigh, saying, "I have a feeling this'll be a *long* seven weeks."

A laugh breaks free from my lips. "Oh Doc, you've got no idea."

TWENTY

It's been a hell of a week. Yesterday was my first appointment. I went straight from there to class, and from there, I went to the DIK house for study session and to clean. After that, we had the joy of picking up bits of confetti and separating them into colors, six in all. Considering the basement was filled with the confetti, so much so that the concrete floor could barely be seen, it was around midnight when we finally finished. I slept like shit and then had a long day of classes, so the social tonight is just about the last thing in the world I want to do. Unfortunately, for me, all socials are a requirement for pledges, mostly so we can play 'clean up after the pigs' once the party has died down.

At the social this week, one without another fraternity involved, thanks to a stern talking to Trevor had with Brady, we are all dressed in early 90s fashion—acid wash jeans, parachute pants, and side ponies aplenty. I settled on AC Slater; I'm wearing a curly black wig and a short-sleeve button up with a ludicrous pattern, the sleeves rolled as required.

I can't help but look for Ember, wanting to see her even if

it's just so I can apologize. I've texted more times than I should've, still with no response.

The social is in the DIK basement this week, a byproduct of my previous actions, not that any of us mind. Most of these guys get to stumble up the stairs to their rooms, some to fuck their revolving girl, others jerking off to MILF and BBW porn. The younger brothers have the benefit of an active cab system and close proximity to the dorms and apartments. It's a win-win.

I tilt my head toward Mac, who's dressed as Urkel. "You think she'll show?"

He shrugs. "Give it time, dude."

"Where's your girl?"

"Studying for tests." He frowns. "She's on her period anyway."

"Jerkin' it to internet porn tonight then?" I ask.

"Or working for a blow job."

"Good luck, bro," I say doubtingly.

"I have my ways."

"A forceful hand?"

"Study stress relief." He wriggles his brows and it brings a laugh out of me.

"Hard sell."

"We'll see." He takes a drink of his beer. I motion mine toward the couch where a few of the brothers sit.

"You see who Brady's with?"

Mac chuckles. "Yeah, chick looks almost unconscious."

"For real. And he's still all up on her. What the fuck is he thinkin'?"

"Wait." Mac points, studying them. "Her eyes are open. A little bit."

"Well, she's obviously trashed."

"She *is* grabbing at his dick," he argues, and I see she is, in fact, cupping his testicles at the moment, but she doesn't look to be even aware her hand's there.

Or am I seein' things? If it weren't Brady, would I see things the same way?

"I still don't like it," I mutter.

Mac sets a hand to my shoulder as Carter and Jeremy approach with fresh beers.

"You don't want to find yourself in anymore trouble," Mac reminds me.

"What're y'all talkin' about?" Jeremy asks, and I wave him off.

"Nothin'. Just bullshit." My eyes remain locked on Brady.

"You okay, Bish?" Carter asks, and my eyes trail to his.

"I don't like what I'm seein' over there." I motion my head toward the couch, and they both look.

"I ain't ever seen him with her before," Jeremy says, turning back around and shrugging.

"Neither have I," I agree. "Where'd she come from?"

"Beats me," Jeremy responds. "I didn't see her with him earlier." His eyes fall on me. "Bro, ya need to stay out of trouble."

"That's what I was saying," Mac adds, and I shoot him a glare.

"I understand the predicament I'm in. I experienced it already yesterday, having to spill my damn guts to a stranger. It don't mean I'm gonna let a woman be raped."

"Whoa!" Mac's mouth goes wide, his eyes flitting around the room as he puts two hands up defensively. "Watch the r-word, man. I don't think that's what's going on over there."

"No?" I scrutinize him with my eyes. "What do you call fuckin' an unconscious woman?"

"He's not fucking her," Mac responds.

"*Yet,*" I hiss.

"And she ain't unconscious ... much," Jeremy adds.

I narrow my eyes at him. "Y'all got a lot to learn about the real world and how a real man operates. I'll tell ya that much."

"You've never fucked a drunk chick before?" Mac asks.

"A drunk chick while I was drunk too? Yeah. A drunk chick who can barely keep her eyes open and is borderline unconscious? No, bro. Not a fuckin' chance. I grew up with morals. Obviously, you fuckers didn't."

"I think they're just worried about keeping you out of trouble. Shit's been going around about Brady and his feelings about you," Carter says, playing devil's advocate, much to my dismay.

"I think y'all need to stop worryin' about me and start worryin' about what you're willing to look past," I respond, shaking my head.

A brief awkward silence passes between us as I sip my beer and continue watching Brady and the girl on the couch intently.

"How about we get out of here and smoke a J?" Mac asks, breaking the silence. He pulls his Crown Royal bag of joints from his pocket, his brows wriggling.

"Tempting," I respond, eyeing the joint as he removes it from the velvet bag, desire sweeping over me as I look back over to the couch. "But I am not goin' anywhere until I make sure fuckface behaves himself. And you know I can't be smokin' during this counseling anyhow."

"C'mon, Bishop. We've got one month left," Mac pleads. "One month and we're made men. Can't you just keep out of trouble until then?"

I point to Brady. "*That* motherfucker's the only one who needs to be worried about trouble findin' him tonight. I'll be alright, gentlemen. I have a habit of gettin' out of shit."

"And a habit of runnin' into it a time or two as of late, my friend," Jeremy adds, chuckling. "I've seen the blood to prove it."

I smirk, tilting my head and arching an eyebrow. "And what repercussions came out of those two scenarios? A few therapy sessions?" I shrug. "Fuck it. Bring 'em on. It isn't gonna dictate how I operate. Never will."

"Alright, man. Alright," Mac says. "Well, I'm going out to the porch to smoke, for whoever wants to join me."

As Mac turns to head toward the steps, Jeremy shrugs. "That'd be me, fellas. I'll see y'all in a few." He throws up a peace sign and follows behind Mac.

I look over at Carter with an eyebrow cocked. "Well, you goin' with 'em?"

Carter shakes his head. "Somebody has to watch your ass."

"Nobody has to watch my ass. Especially not some guys about half my age."

His lip curls back. "I'd like to think we're your friends first. And we aren't trying to fuck with you here. Just trying to watch your back."

I put my hands up in retreat. "Alright, alright, I'm just fuckin' with you. Just don't like bein' told what to do."

"Shit, I'm definitely not trying to tell you what to do. Just throwing out suggestions. Take them or leave them."

As he says this, I spot Brady helping the girl to her feet. Her body is slack, her shoulders and head slumped, and he has to stabilize her with his own body as he helps her along in slow steps toward the stairs.

I jab a finger toward them. "See! I fuckin' told you, dude."

I start to follow them, but Carter grabs my shoulder. "Bro, are you sure about this?" There are wrinkles of concern in his forehead, his worried eyes flitting from me, to Brady, and back. "You may not make it through pledging if something were to happen."

I shrug. "So be it. I couldn't give a fuck a about pledging." As I try and turn, he tightens his grip on my shoulder.

"Maybe he's just putting her to bed, man. Maybe they're dating or something."

"I've never seen her here before, man. Jeremy said so too. And he was just gropin' her like they were shootin' a fuckin' porno. If he's not takin' her up there to fuck, I'll give you my Jeep."

"Tempting offer, but seriously, what are you going to do, bust his door down?"

"I'll knock and see what's up."

"And if he doesn't answer?"

I look back and see Brady and the girl are gone now. "Damn it, Carter. He's probably already up there fuckin' her!"

"So, what if he is, Bishop? C'mon, man. Let's go smoke with Mac and Jeremy."

I tug my shoulder away from Carter's hand and shake my head. "Carter, if you don't see a problem here, I don't know how to help you. I can't sit idly by and watch this shit go down. Go outside with the guys. I'll be fine," I say, turning and making my way to the stairs that lead to the brothers' rooms.

I stride up the steps, two by two. Reaching the top, I charge down the hallway toward Brady's door. A few of the rooms' doors are open and music blares from one of them. Once I reach Brady's door and turn, I notice some heads peeking out from down the hall.

"Brady just bring a girl in here?" I ask, pointing toward his door, and one of them nods.

I knock on the door hard.

No response.

I knock again, harder this time, my foot bobbing relentlessly, my heart beating wildly in my chest.

"What do you want?" a faint voice calls out from the other side.

"Brady, it's Bishop," I yell. "I need you to open this fuckin' door."

As I hear grumbling on the other side of the door, I notice more heads peeking out now, and a few of the brothers standing out in the hall. At the end of the hallway, I see Carter standing at the top of the steps, a worried expression on his face.

"Brady?" I repeat.

"Fuck off, man," he responds.

Knocking again, I say, "Brady, you need to open this door right fuckin' now, or I'll *break it the fuck down!*"

"Fuck off!" he repeats, and I scoff, taking a step back and shaking my head. I then heave a boot into the door with a loud thud.

"Bro, what the fuck?" a voice calls out down the hall.

I don't respond.

"What's that pledge doing?" another one asks.

Abruptly, Brady's door opens a crack, and he glares at me from the other side, his face beet red. "Are you fucking deaf, pledge? I said *fuck off.*"

"Oh, I heard you. I just don't give a fuck what comes out of your mouth, other than tellin' me whether that girl is in there or not."

"What girl?"

"You know *exactly* what girl. The one who was pretty much passed out while you were gropin' her."

"Oh, fuck off. Get the fuck away from my room, pledge," he says, trying to shut the door, but I put a shoulder into it, surprising him and muscling the door open.

He looks at me, his face scrunched in both confusion and anger. "Are you fucking kidding me?" he barks, shoving me back against the door, closing it, as my eyes take in the girl, lying there, braless, panties mid-thigh, her eyes completely closed, a little vomit on the mattress beside her lips.

My wide eyes trail from her to him as he has my shirt balled up in each fist, his face just inches from my own. Squatting a little, I charge forward, throwing my palms into his chest and shoving him down hard onto the floor. He lands and the air drains out of him. He takes a deep breath, looking up at me now with wild eyes. There's commotion from the hall behind me.

"No. Are *you* fuckin' kiddin' me, bitch?" I jab a finger toward the girl passed out on his bed. "How old is she, eighteen? Nineteen years old? She's passed the fuck out, dude, and you were gonna fuckin' rape her?"

He looks over at her, and the anger in his face dissipates. "S-she was awake a second ago, dude." He sits up. "Rape? What the fuck are you talking about? Get the fuck out of here."

As he slowly rises to his feet, I respond, "Not without her, scumbag," as I make my way to her side. I pull her panties up and set her legs straight on the bed, careful not to lay her in the throw-up.

"Oh, fuck you, you judgmental prick. Who are you to come into *my* fucking room?"

The door opens behind me, drawing my attention. Trevor pokes his head in. "What's going on in here?" he asks, looking around as he opens the door wider. There are about twenty brothers behind him, eavesdropping. Carter's one of them.

"This motherfucker is trying to rape this chick and I'm gettin' her the fuck out of here," I say as I take a knee near her still body and collect her clothes from the floor. Setting them on the bed, I put two fingers to her neck. There's a steady beat.

"Fuck you!" Brady roars, and his incoming steps draw my attention. He stops just in front of me, the vein in his neck bulging, his muscles flexing, hands clenched in tight fists.

"Brady, calm down," Trevor says, stepping forward and putting a hand out.

I turn back toward the girl and begin putting her clothes on.

"Bishop, what are you doing in his room to begin with?" Trevor asks as I wipe a little vomit away from her cheek with Brady's bedspread.

"Yeah!" Brady adds, jabbing a finger at me.

I roll my eyes, turning my attention back to the girl as I figure out the best way to get her out of here.

"Fuckstick here decided to take a nearly unconscious girl up to his room to fuck her, and I didn't let him. That's what I'm doin' in his fuckin' room."

"She wasn't unconscious, bro. Not when we were hooking up. When she got sick, I just laid her in bed so she could get some sleep. That's what I was doing when he fucking burst in here."

I glance back at him with a sneer, shaking my head. "Give me a fuckin' break. When I got to the room, her underwear was half off. She was literally lyin' on the edge of your bed in the missionary position, you fuck."

"*Bullshit*. This motherfucker has had it out for me since day one. He's just making shit up to try and get me in trouble," Brady says.

"Yeah, I guess I put the throw-up there too, huh? You're a fuckin' idiot. I haven't been the one with a chip on my shoulder. I couldn't give two fucks about you, Brady. All I care about is gettin' this girl home and out of the room of a fuckin' rapist."

Brady charges forward, soccer kicking my stomach.

He hits me square, but I'm able to absorb most of the force with my arm. It stings like fuck, but I take a deep breath and stand, clenching my teeth against the pain. Trevor has two hands on Brady's shoulders now, pulling him back.

I take another deep breath, forcing a grin. "That one you get for free, Brady. But understand this. The next time you put your hands or your feet on me, I will fuckin' *end* you. That's not a threat. Never has been in my life, never will be. It's a fuckin' promise. I will make you feel a whole fuckin' world of pain, boy."

I turn back around, looking for the girl's purse. Spotting it at the end of the bed, I take a seat and go through it, looking for her phone, but keeping Brady in my peripheral.

"Bishop, you really shouldn't be in here," Trevor says as I locate her wallet first.

"About two more seconds and I won't be." I open her wallet, reading her ID. I look back up at Brady with a snarl on my face. "Yeah, eighteen, like I thought, you sick fuck."

Brady scoffs as I toss the wallet back in her purse and pick up her phone. The screen is filled with text and call notifications. Dozens of them. Pulling up her text messages, I see twelve unread from a contact titled, 'Bestie.'

> *Hey April, where did you go? We're ready to leave.*
> *Ape, I'm getting worried. Text meeeeeee.*
> *Seriously, I will call the cops.*
> *What the fuck?! April ... CALL ME NOW!*
> *April?!?! Please!*

"Bishop." Trevor's voice rings throughout the quiet room.

I pull up 'Bestie's' contact information and press call, lifting the phone to my ear.

"What the fuck is he doing?" Brady scoffs, raising his palms into the air. "Trevor, get this stupid fucking pledge out of here."

"April?!" a concerned voice comes over the line. "April, are you okay?"

"Hey, this isn't April, but she's with me at the DIK house. I was trying to get her home."

"The *DIK* house? How the hell did she wind up there?"

"I have no idea, honestly, but she was here, sick and passed out. I went on her phone and found you. Do y'all live together?"

"Yes ... oh my God, I can't even believe this. She was with us at Brass Monkey for a social with Pike. She said she was going out for a smoke, and next thing I know, we're ready to go and she's nowhere to be found."

"Well, she seems to be okay. She's just had way too much to drink. Can I call a cab for her? I'll ride with her to make sure she gets there safely."

"Yes! That would be amazing. Thank you. We're at the Theta Nu house."

"Okay, you there now?"

"Yeah. We have been since she disappeared."

"Alright, no problem. We'll be there soon."

"Thank you."

"Don't mention it." I hang up the phone and toss it into her purse.

"Trevor?" Brady pleads, and Trevor takes a step toward me as I stand from the bed.

"Can we talk outside?" he says, motioning his head toward the door.

I shake my head. "Sorry, man. I have to get her home. Her friends have been worried sick about her for hours." I sneer at Brady before grabbing her purse, and then I lean over her, tapping her cheek lightly to wake her.

"April, can you hear me?"

Her eyelids flutter, mouth agape.

"April, open your eyes, hun. Don't you wanna sleep in your own bed?"

Her eyelids flutter again, opening to slits. She groans and then nods. "Yeah," she grunts.

"Okay, then stand up for me." I grab her arms, the purse annoyingly tumbling along with me, and I pull her to her feet.

"Trevor?" Brady says again, his voice whiny, pathetic.

April's eyes start to close again, and I give her a good shake. "April, we need to walk outside, okay?"

Her eyes open and she looks over at me slowly, a hiccup escaping her mouth. "I'm so tired," she mumbles as Carter pushes his way through the other brothers and comes into the room. He grabs one of her arms and throws it over his shoulder.

"Come on, April. One foot in front of the other," he says, nodding toward me.

I nod back as I look toward the door. "Make a hole!" I bark as the gawking brothers remain motionless in front of the doorway. They quickly scatter like rodents.

"Seriously, Trevor, this is bullshit," Brady says from behind us as we help her through the doorway.

"We'll deal with it tomorrow," Trevor responds.

We don't stay long enough to hear any more of Brady's bullshit. Walking her down the hall, ignoring all the open doors and curious eyes, we lead her out onto the front porch. We steady her onto the couch, and then I retrieve my phone from my pocket to call a cab.

As we wait for it to arrive, Trevor comes outside, thankfully without the presence of Brady. He has a look of exasperation on his face.

"Trevor, honestly, I don't wanna hear it," I say, putting a hand up and shaking my head.

"Alright. I get it. But what about Monday? Can we get together and talk about this?"

"What's there to really talk about?"

"Can you just come by before study session? Just like a half hour early."

"Not if Brady's gonna be there."

Trevor hesitates before he agrees. "Okay, that's fine. Do we have a deal?"

He puts out his hand as the cab pulls into the parking lot.

I refrain from shaking it, but agree, "Deal."

As Carter and I help April to her feet, Trevor says, "We're not the bad guys here, Bishop."

I shake my head, a contemptuous smirk spreading across my face as we lead her to the cab. "I don't even know what the fuck that means," I respond without turning back.

After helping her into the back seat, Carter asks, "You want me to come with you?"

"No worries. It's just right up the street. I'm just gonna take the cab home after. I've had enough bullshit for tonight."

"Okay, man. Have a good night." He slaps hands with me, and as I turn and get in the cab next to her, he adds, "Sorry I doubted you earlier, bro."

Settling in the seat, I shake my head, my hand on the door handle. "Don't worry about it. I get where you were comin' from. You just have to think about other people too. Talk to you tomorrow."

"Tomorrow," he responds, and I close the door behind him.

"A quarter of a mile ride?" the cabbie asks as he backs out onto the road and then pulls away. He lets out a scoff.

"Better than carrying her, my friend."

He nods.

A half a minute later, we're on sorority row and the cabbie pulls up in front of the Theta Nu house, where a few girls stand out front with concerned looks on their faces.

"Oh my God, April. You gave us such a scare," one of the girls says, approaching my opening cab door.

"Wait for me here, please," I say to the cabbie, tossing him a twenty.

"I presume you're Bestie?" I ask as I get out and the girl helps me guide April out of the cab safely.

"Yeah. Jennifer. Thanks so much for bringing her home," she responds as two other girls approach us.

Their presence brings April out of her stupor a little more, and she smiles. "Sistersss," she says, her head wobbling as one of them trades spots with me. The other one switches with Jennifer, and they help April toward the door as Jennifer stays back with me.

"Really, thank you for calling me and bringing her over. Where did you find her?" she asks.

"There's a party at the DIK house tonight. She was there. Passed out."

"Passed out?"

"Yeah."

She quirks an eyebrow, her hands on her hips, and asks, "Why do I get the feeling there's more to the story?"

I chuckle nervously. "Probably because I'm a terrible liar."

"So ..."

"So, I first noticed her at the party with one of the brothers. She didn't look so good. I hadn't ever seen her around the house before, so I didn't think she was with that guy or anything. And then, well, he ended up takin' her to his room."

"Did he *fuck* her?" she asks, a hand meeting her mouth, a look of horror crossing her features.

"No, no ... I didn't let anything like that happen. But you guys need to be more careful with the drinkin'. Some of these guys will take advantage of that shit."

"Honestly, she wasn't really that drunk at the party tonight. And I don't know why the hell she would've went to the DIK house in the first place. We don't ever hang with you guys because of that shit."

"Really?"

"Yeah, the DIK basement is considered the Roofie Room around the Theta Nu house."

My stomach turns.

Who have I acquainted myself with?

"Well, fuck, I didn't know that. Maybe check her phone. See if she's been talkin' to some guy in DIK. Maybe he invited her to the party."

"Do you know the guy she was with?"

I hesitate, caught between doing the right thing and being a rat. "Barely. I'm new here."

"You're in DIK, though?"

"Pledging, yeah."

She frowns. "How old are you?"

I laugh. "Old enough."

"What's his name?" she asks.

I hesitate before responding, "Brady," sure of the fact that it will come back to bite me in the end but knowing that this girl deserves the truth about her friend.

TWENTY-ONE

I stayed away from the DIK house the rest of the weekend. I've been contemplating dropping out of pledging, but then I think about my pledge brothers, both Mac and Carter, telling me how much they relied on me through the process. If I did quit, I'd feel like I was giving up. Not giving up on the fraternity—because fuck them if they think I'll look past some goddamn sexual assault bullshit—but giving up on my guys. It may not matter anyway. As I park the Jeep along frat row, I'm just a few minutes from my meeting with the DIK officers. They may not want me to stay. And if that's the case, well then, they can just swallow my load.

I don't play that game.

Trotting down the steps and into the basement, I chuckle at the sight of them—Zane, Sarge, Tim, and Damian—seated around a long table, Trevor at the head. He motions to the empty seat across the table from him.

"Thanks for coming, Bishop. Have a seat," he says with regretful eyes.

I chuckle again, shaking my head at the nonsense. "I feel like I'm walkin' into a fuckin' tribal council or somethin'," I joke, pulling the chair out and taking a seat. "Was all this really necessary?"

"Unfortunately, yes. A complaint has been filed against you, and we must formally look into every legitimate complaint," Trevor responds.

I grin. "Oh okay, so I'm good to go then, right? I mean, you said '*legitimate* complaint.'"

"Bishop, you tried to beat down an officer's door. You forced your way into his room, unwelcome," Trevor says.

"Not to mention all the Theta Nu girls coming by, giving us shit. They might file a complaint against us, you know. You're gonna ruin our rep running your mouth like that," Damian says with a snarl.

"Am I in the *goddamn* Twilight Zone right now?" I shout, scanning the faces around the table, stopping on Sarge's. "Sarge, c'mon, man. You know I'm in the right here."

He nods. "One-hundred percent. These assholes know how I feel. Still had to be here," Sarge grumbles, crossing his arms and shooting Trevor a look of disgust.

My eyes trail back to Trevor. "Is this how you're choosin' to run your fraternity? Protecting pieces of shit like Brady, who take advantage of drunk young girls?"

"Hey! That's my boy you're talking about," Damian barks, jabbing his thick pointer finger at me.

"Yeah, and your fuckin' boy is a creep." I scoff loudly. "Y'all must have me *sadly* mistaken. If you thought you were gonna get me here and somehow convince me I was wrong, or get me to apologize to that little shitstick, you are wastin' your breath. If this is an organization that promotes the sexual assault of women, I don't think I wanna be a part of it anyhow."

"Please, there's no need to speak like that. We are not that kind of organization. Not one bit," Trevor says.

"Oh yeah? Well, while you all are worried about me

ruinin' your reputation with the sorority girls by tellin' 'em about Ted Bundy up there, you should probably also know that Theta Nu calls this basement the Roofie Room. Hence why your buddy Brady hasn't been able to organize a social with them."

Zane and Tim look toward Trevor and then back at me. "That was from a long time ago," Trevor says.

"Obviously not as long ago as you think," I respond, shrugging. I lean back in the chair and cross my arms. "So, what's it gonna be, gentlemen? You know where I stand. It's right in the same spot I was standin' in before I walked through that basement door. Why waste time here? Y'all do what you need to do."

Trevor clears his throat, looking toward Damian when he says, "After looking at the circumstances and speaking with VP, we've decided to take a vote among the officers, excluding Brady, over whether or not you remain in the pledging process. We just think it's important to get a consensus here, since so many are upset within the fraternity. Damian will give you a call tonight after our meeting to let you know what's been decided. If you remain with us, going forward, we ask that you try and stay away from Brady and his room."

In my head, I'm standing, flipping every motherfucker off in here but Sarge, and walking the fuck out. But I think to my guys and the bond I've formed with them over the past few weeks.

"If Brady keeps his nose clean, I couldn't give two fucks what he does. But I will *never* look past sexual assault. And Trevor" —I lean in for emphasis— "havin' sex with an unconscious woman, or even attempting to, *is* sexual assault. Don't get your definition twisted to protect your boy. It isn't one that can be manipulated at will."

Damian shoots daggers at me with his eyes as I stand from the chair. I look them all over, slowly, contempt in my features.

Eventually, I land on Zane and I keep my eyes on him until he looks at me.

"How long did you serve in the Air Force, Zane?"

He looks startled and confused. "Uh, um, four years."

"And you went to basic training, right?"

He frowns, looking across the table at Damian and then back at me. He lets out a nervous chuckle. "Um, yeah. You kind of have to."

"That's what I figured. But I'm confused. See, I don't know how Air Force basic training works. But in Army basic, one of the first things we learn are the Army Core Values. Loyalty, Duty, Selfless Service, Personal Courage, *Honor, Respect, and Integrity.* Integrity. To do what's right, legally and morally. To adhere to moral principles. Whether others are watchin' or not." I lean both hands on the table, looking Zane dead in the eye. He breaks eye contact. "*Integrity*, Zane. Had you joined the Army, you would've learned a little something about that."

With that, I turn on my heel and make my way toward the basement steps with a deafening silence left in my wake.

Just about the time I reach the apartment, my phone chimes with a text from Sarge.

You're still in. Not sure if that's good news or bad news for you haha.

After parking, I text back, *The jury's still out on that one lol. So, you gonna be a bro and tell me who voted what?* before making my way inside the building.

Heading into the apartment, my phone goes off again.

Haha Fucker. I knew that was coming. You can't say shit, roger? I'll fucking blow your Jeep up. I have the capabilities, you know? hahaha. Yays were me (obviously), Tim, and Zane. The nays were Trevor and Damian.

I'm shocked to read Zane's name as one of the yays. Plopping down on my bed and turning the TV on, I sit back and text,

Wow, Zane is a shocker. I figured after my little rant, he would've been happy to see me go.

Sarge texts, *I think you shook some sense into him. Damian should be calling soon, by the way. Head's up, they want you to come back for study session.*

I laugh, shaking my head, as I type, *Yeah, that's one phone call I'm not gonna take. Would you look at that? It's naptime. Thanks for the info, bro. Talk soon. I'm getting them ZZZZZZZZZs.*

TWENTY-TWO

Carleigh eyes me curiously over the frames of her glasses. I know she's not trying to be sexy, but she is. As she leans back in her chair, a sigh escapes her pursed lips.

"So, you won't talk about any of the fraternity stuff?" she finally asks, and I shake my head.

"I can't. I'm not allowed to. It's part of the code." A smirk crosses my face, my tone facetious.

"Do you hear yourself?"

"Are you bein' judgmental, Doc?" My smirk persists.

"I told you to call me Carleigh, or, preferably, Dr. Jacobs."

"Are you bein' judgmental, Carleigh?" I repeat.

"Well, do you? Because here's what I'm hearing. You're a twenty-five-year-old Army vet who served your country honorably. You started college, then joined a fraternity, you're drinking multiple nights a week, and now you're fighting. To me, it's clear the fraternity has played a part in this transgression, and you're sitting there telling me you can't talk about it. That's a problem for me."

I breathe out a sigh of resignation. "I can't talk about the pledging process and what it entails. As for the partyin', yeah, you bet your ass it's led me to more social drinkin'. But it's either drink out there with friends, or drink alone at a bar by myself or in my room."

"I thought you said you were only a social drinker during our last visit?" She quirks an eyebrow.

I let out a nervous chuckle. "That may have been a slight exaggeration. But I don't drink alone now."

I smile, and she just laughs, shaking her head. "And how many times a week are you drinking with the fraternity again? You probably don't have any time to drink alone."

An abrupt laugh escapes my lips. "What can I say? I hate bein' by myself."

"Why do you hate being alone so much?"

"A number of reasons ..." I let my words linger in the air, each reason passing through my thoughts.

"And they are?" She lifts her pen to take notes, and it irks me as it always does. Yeah, I know she needs to keep record of what we discuss, but I hate knowing that there will be evidence of my thoughts out there for anyone to read. And that's exactly how the VA operates.

"I have tinnitus."

"Okay."

"So, I constantly hear ringin'. Both ears, but it's worse in my right."

"And this is from the explosion?"

I nod. "That one, and all the ones before it. The fire-fights too. I'm really lucky to even have any hearin' left at all. But the tinnitus is no joke either. It started after my first firefight. Got worse with each deployment, but it became unbearable after the RPG. It took me months to tune it out."

"But it's still there?"

"Oh yeah. In silence, especially. It's why I always have a TV or music goin'."

"Or people around you, talking."

"Exactly. And when I'm alone with my thoughts, especially when I'm sober, it's like, this invisible prison. It's suffocating."

"What kinds of thoughts?"

"Who I was in the Army and who I am now ... my childhood ... the battles I've fought, the friends I've made ... and all that I lost since the explosion. A future that seemed much brighter than it does now."

"Are you ever suicidal?"

I shake my head firmly. "No, not at all. I've never been. Yeah, sometimes shit sucks, but I've never been the type to think about suicide. Flood the emotions with liquor, maybe a little marijuana here and there ... yeah, I'm guilty of that. But I could never contemplate ending it all. Can't even fathom it."

"What about your childhood? Does that intrude on your thoughts often?"

I nod, my focus shifting to the sterile walls. "Yeah, it does."

"What kind of thoughts?"

I let out a heavy breath, shaking my head. "My dad was a military man. And he did a whole hell of a lot for this country. He was my hero growin' up. But he wasn't ever much of a dad. His expectations of me were always well above what I could have ever achieved."

"Did he ever hit you?"

"Until I got big enough to defend myself."

"And your mother?"

"We divin' into all the heavy stuff today?" I ask, grinning.

"And your mother?" she repeats.

"No, my mom never hit me. But she pretended my pops didn't either. She turned a blind eye, and I don't know which is worse. I think she was bipolar, though she'd never accept havin' some sort of mental defect. She'd spend days and days in bed, her door locked. She'd only leave to get food, which was few and far between. I don't think she took all my dad's deployments too well. But then she'd have these periods where she was the best mother a kid could ask for."

"I couldn't diagnose her without evaluating her, but yes, those examples do seem to sway toward bipolar." She hesitates, the pen meeting her full lips, her eyes on the ceiling.

Calm yourself, Bishop. Calm yourself.

"Was it hard for you being an only child?" she asks.

"Yeah, it was hard takin' the brunt of everything. Hard not havin' someone there to cope with. We moved so much when my dad would change duty stations that I never really got to connect with anyone growin' up. Not until he retired, and we finally settled in Florida, but by then, I was already a teen. Already fucked up."

"But in the Army, you did connect with others?"

"Yeah, with a lot of people. But then, you know, you lose some guys, and that always sticks with you, and you end up losin' others through distance. There's only a handful I even still communicate with."

"Why is that?"

"Guys don't keep in touch like women do. We don't often visit each other. The friendship kind of fades. Don't get me wrong, if you ever see each other again, it's like a day hasn't passed. But they move on with their lives, and you move on with yours, and it's like two passin' ships in the night."

"How does it make you feel to not have a closer relationship with them?"

"It's hard."

"How so?"

"So, when I got blown up, we were at the end of our tour. We were so close to goin' home. About a month into my recov-

ery, they were all comin' back, havin' their 'welcome home' cele-
brations and enjoyin' two weeks of leave, and then they shipped
off to new duty stations. Meanwhile, I was in inpatient all that
time."

"Is there maybe a little resentment there?"

"Unfortunately, yeah."

"Well, that's understandable. Did anybody visit you after
you got hurt?"

"Yeah, a few friends from my unit, but that's pretty
much it."

"So, you spent a lot of time alone?"

"Oh yeah. For a good two years of recovery. I had a girlfriend the last bit of it, but I definitely kept her at a distance
too."

"How did that relationship end?"

I laugh, shrugging. "Alcohol."

"Did you do something? Hit her?"

"No, no, nothin' like that. I would *never* hit a woman. She
just didn't like how much I drank. She wasn't ready to put the
work in."

"Tell me the truth. Outside of the past two days, have you
been drunk?"

"Is my honesty here gonna negatively affect the outcome of
this program?"

"No, it won't."

"Yeah, I have."

"How much?"

"I had some beers this past weekend. Jameson on the rocks
Tuesday night, just because."

"You didn't go overboard though?"

"Actually, I didn't even get drunk. Maybe a little buzzed.
Just wasn't feelin' the social scene this weekend. I spent a lot of
time hangin' around the apartment."

"When you do drink, is there some commonality in what leads you to it? Some feeling, or memory, or experience?"

I think for a moment; having never really thought about it before, it's hard to pinpoint. "I think the anxiety has a lot to do with it," I finally reply.

She nods. "And what does the anxiety feel like to you?"

"Well, I get a lot of headaches and jaw pain, because when the anxiety is gettin' bad, I clench my jaw without even realizin' it. I notice that my mind runs about a mile a minute. I can't lock on to any one thing for too long. When some of the things my mind conjures up are hard memories from the past, it's like ... bein' a boxer, takin' a right jab, left jab, uppercut, repeat. The thoughts and memories keep comin'. Keep hittin'."

I hesitate, but she doesn't take the pause as an opportunity to speak; instead, she remains focused, waiting for me to continue.

"Um, there's this ball of nervous energy, like one of those plasma balls at the Science Center. It's electric, radiating, choking. I can't sleep. Don't want to eat. The only thing that seems to quell it is a substance of some sort."

"What about medication?" she asks.

"I'm on Zoloft. And that's after trying a hundred other things at Walter Reed. It's the only one that seemed to work even half-assed without turning me into a mindless zombie. Without it, I'm a goddamn mess. I hate myself."

"You hate yourself off of medication, or alcohol?"

I go to speak, but the words don't come right away. I think her question over again. "Fuck, maybe both."

"Where do you think the hate comes from?"

"Well, I'm extremely self-analytical, so I do actually have a theory on that. I think it stems from my parents, and never bein' good enough for them. Mostly my pops. I think it led me to this self-deprecation I struggle with now."

She smiles. "I think that's very astute."

"I think I wanna start askin' *you* some questions."

"That's not why you're here. I didn't beat a kid half to death."

Rolling my eyes, I say, "Oh, c'mon now. Half to death? That's a bit much. And can we come up with a deal at least?"

"What do you mean, a deal?"

"Like, I ask you a question, then you ask me a question. One for one."

"I don't think so."

"Two for one?"

She gives a tight shake of her head.

"*Three for one?*"

She shakes her head again and says, "How about this? Five for one, and no extremely personal questions. That wouldn't be appropriate, nor do I care to become the patient in my own office." She smiles, and I chuckle at her last comment.

"Okay, deal. I think you've definitely already got your five in."

She nods, motioning with her hand for me to go ahead.

"Did you just move into this office?"

She shakes her head. "No, I've been here awhile."

"Why is it so barren? No photos. Keepsakes. Memorabilia."

She grins. "Five for one, remember?"

"Wait, no, that's not fair! It was a two-part question."

"I don't think so," she says, chuckling.

"Goddammit. I'm losin' at my own damn game."

"Yeah, shame you underestimated me, Bishop. Now, back to the real reason you're here. What is it you hate most about yourself?"

"I'll remember this in four more questions, Carleigh." I narrow my eyes at her. "I think the thing I hate most is not bein' able to shake the awful shit. The shit that sticks with you. I've done some counseling, read some self-help books, I've taken the medication and the necessary steps, but I still feel this way. Like I've got nothin', like I'm goin' nowhere. I feel like my identity has been stolen."

"You may not be in the Army anymore, but that doesn't take away what you've done. You're a hero, Bishop."

"I'm no hero," I snap. "I was just doin' my job. I wish I was *still* doin' my job."

"But you're not, and you never will again," she says matter-of-factly. She lifts her palms. "So, what's next? I know it's hard, but you're only stuck in this limbo because you haven't yet started to move forward. You just need to figure out what's next for you. Find a new passion and chase it. Besides acting, is there anything else you're interested in?"

"I'll count that as two questions, by the way, since you're the one who wants to be all technical. What's next? I don't know. I get through these classes somehow and figure out a major. And I have other interests, but nothin' that could be considered career-worthy. I play guitar, a little photography, shit like that. Nothin' that's gonna make me any money."

"Well, technically, that shouldn't be your biggest concern. It doesn't need to be since you have your pension. How are your grades, by the way? Has the fraternity process caused any issues?"

"And that would be questions four and five, Ms. Jacobs. My grades are shit, to be honest. And while the fraternity hasn't helped, if it weren't for their mandatory study sessions, my grades would probably be even worse."

"Why are you having such difficulty?"

"That's a sixth question, Carleigh." I wag my finger at her.

"Just answer it."

"Okay, but I get two." I put my hand out. "Deal?"

She eyes my hand but does nothing. "Answer the question, Bishop." She fights a smile from her face.

"I fuckin' hate classes. I hate the material and just bein' in there. Half the kids in my classes are fuckin' morons who think they're still in high school, and the professor is a dude two years older than me, and not a professor at all, come to find out, but a grad student. Did I mention I hate the material?" I chuckle. "I find myself starin' at the clock on the wall a hundred times over the course of an hour. Lately, I've been taken back to somethin' an old squad leader said to me once, when I was about a year into the Army. He asked me what my plans were when my contract was up. I said I wasn't sure. At that time, bein' an abused private and shit on by everyone, I truly wasn't sure. The freedom of college sounded intriguing. He asked me, 'How did you do in high school? Did you like it?' I said, 'My grades were shit, and I hated goin' to class.' He laughed and said, 'Stay in the Army, son.'"

We both laugh.

I lift my hands. "So, at the end of the day, maybe he's right. Maybe I just wasn't cut out for this school shit."

"Or maybe just not the classroom environment. Have you tried online courses?"

I nod. "While I was at Walter Reed recovering, I took a few, but I don't have enough willpower for that shit." I hesitate a moment before adding, "Hey, that was another question!"

She smiles wickedly. "Go ahead and ask yours, Bishop."

"What happened with your husband?"

Her eyes shoot to her ring finger and she sighs. "I told you no personal questions."

"Do you like me, Carleigh?" I ask, catching her off-guard.

"Huh?"

"Do you like me? Do you think I'm a good dude?"

"Absolutely. In the little time I've gotten to know you, I think you're a 'good dude.' Why?"

"Well, I have this weird trust thing with doctors. Always have. Too many fuckin' assholes at Walter Reed who don't give a shit about their patients. And the VA system ... shit, I won't even get into that. So, with all the experiences I've had, it's hard for me to connect with a doctor. Especially in the mental health field. With somethin' like this, I want there to be a level of trust between us. A connection."

"I want that, too."

"Part of that is me gettin' to know a little about you. I like you too, Carleigh. I think you're a good lady." I chuckle. "And I'd like to get to know more about what makes you tick. If you have a little internal scarring of your own, even better. Then we can relate."

"He cheated on me," she blurts. "Had been for years, I guess."

"Jesus."

"Yeah, twenty-plus years of marriage, and who knows how much of it he was cheating. There were a million red flags ... it's just, when you love someone that much, it's easy to look past those signs. It's easy to look past the verbal abuse. It's funny, being a therapist, helping those in messed up situations and eventually finding yourself in the same."

I smile. "Do you have sessions with yourself?"

"Don't we all?"

"You got me there. I analyze every single move I've ever made more times than I could comfortably admit."

"It's not such a bad thing. It *can* be. But recognizing and acknowledging past mistakes is a very mature and responsible thing to do. We must take accountability, but not dish out unnecessary blame. You made a mistake. You're human. Move forward and learn." Her eyes trail to the clock on the wall and then back to me. "We're just about out of time, but we'll continue this next week? I want to talk more about the school stuff and maybe come up with some goals for the future."

"Sounds like barrels of fun," I say, giving her a thumbs up.

"Get out of my office, you ass."

"Carleigh, *language!*" I smile, standing from the chair. "Thanks for everything. And hey ..." I wait for her eyes to meet mine, and when they do, I continue, "Forgive me for sayin' it, but your ex is a fuckin' moron. Any man who would risk losin' you for some extra shit on the side never deserved you to begin with. Same goes for a man who would talk down to you or talk bad about you. You're a catch, Carleigh."

"Well, thank you. But flattery doesn't get you very far in this office." She grins.

"Good thing I was just speakin' honestly then, huh?" I wink, making my way to the door. Turning back, I add, "Bye, Carleigh."

"Bye, Bishop," she says as she passes me that gorgeous smile, before she shoos me away.

TWENTY-THREE

We're at the beginning of Hell Week, whatever the fuck that means. I'm thankful for getting last Thursday off from pledge challenges at least, but I imagine if they felt the need to give us a break, these next five days will be nothing short of absolute dog shit. They haven't told us anything since giving us a list of things to bring with us in a backpack—a change of clothes, a flashlight, hygiene products, and a brick—leaving us here in the basement to fend for ourselves. Mac has been bitching since Brady left us an hour ago, moving from the couch, to the bar, to the stairwell, and back again. Jeremy sits on the bar top as he has since we were left here, and Carter and I sit on the Semen Couches, fucking around on our phones.

"Fuck!" Mac yells, checking the fridge for the thousandth time. "I can't take this shit much longer."

"Mac, it's the beginning of fucking Hell Week!" Carter shouts louder than I've ever heard him get. "Chill the fuck out."

"I'm just saying, let us do something here other than picking each other's assholes."

"Where have your hands been, Mac?" Jeremy says with a laugh.

"You haven't felt that?" Mac asks, grinning.

"You fuckers need to just calm your tits and play a game on your phone or somethin'. You're workin' yourselves up for no reason," I say, and Jeremy shoots me a glare.

"You talkin' about me?" he asks. "I've been mindin' my own business, thank ya very much."

"Okay, but you're eggin' him on."

Jeremy points to Carter. "So is he," he argues as the opening doors draw our attention toward the stairs.

Trevor strolls down first, Damian following close behind.

Damian motions toward the back wall. "Line up, pledges!" he shouts.

We link up in front of the concrete wall and await further instruction.

Trevor paces in front of us, as he always does, and says, "Damian, do you have the bottle?"

"I do," Damian responds, pulling an empty beer bottle from his back pocket.

"Do you know what to do with it?" Trevor asks, more of a statement than a question.

Damian lifts the bottle, eyeing each of us as he does, before he slams it to the ground. It shatters in pieces, scattering across the concrete floor. He eyes the remnants of the bottle, and then each of us again, in a drawn-out process. He pulls a few glue sticks from his other pocket and tosses them atop the shattered remains of the bottle. "Glue it back together," he says. "You should be able to drink out of it in four hours."

With that, both Damian and Trevor make their way back up the stairs as we unlink and scan the mess of glass across the floor in front of us.

"How the fuck are we supposed to do that?" Mac lifts his

arms and drops them dramatically.

"Well, you got what you asked for Mac. You happy?" I shoot him glare, letting out a frustrated sigh.

"Seriously." Jeremy leans over and picks up one of the glue sticks. "How the fuck are we gonna do this?"

"It's had to have been done before," Carter reasons.

I shake my head. "Like Archie's fuckin' Tower? And who the fuck exactly is gonna be drinkin' out of this thing?"

They all avert their eyes.

"What the fuck did I get myself into?" I groan.

"For real," Mac adds.

"C'mon, Prez. You gotta be our leader here," Jeremy says, shrugging. "How do we do this?"

I let out a whoosh of breath, my hands meeting my hips as I observe the mess of glass shards around us. "We start puttin' it back together, I guess." I sigh. "Let's start collectin' up the pieces."

OUR FINGERS CUT AND BLOODIED, the bottle is finally back together, though drinking out of it isn't likely. Trevor has it in his hands and eyes it over for a moment, inspecting it, and then he passes it over to Damian, who then inspects it himself.

After a moment, he looks at us and then throws the bottle back down on the ground, shattering it to pieces for the second time.

"Not good enough! Do it again!" he yells, turning around and leading Trevor back up the stairs.

"Motherfuckers!" Mac yells once the door has closed behind them, his face bright red.

"Welcome to Hell Week, guys," Carter says with a weary tone and an exasperated look on his face.

TWENTY-FOUR

"Wake the fuck up!" Damian yells, startling me out of my broken sleep. I wipe my eyes which are burning from the light now filling the basement. "I said, wake up! Hell Week, day two, has started. Remember when you're going to and from classes every day this week, we have your class schedules. We know where and when your classes are, and we won't hesitate to boot your ass out of pledging a week before you become a brother if we find you fucking around."

As we stand from the cold floor, the repercussions of sleeping with only a blanket separating me from the concrete make themselves known. I stretch my stiff back with a loud pop as Trevor motions to the four of us.

"Remember, you must carry your bricks with you every-where," he says. "If a brother runs into you and asks to see your brick, you must show it to them. If you're not in class and at the house, you're to be cleaning or studying for midterms. No exceptions. Now, get to cleaning, pledges."

Mac grumbles his way to the utility closet as the rest of us shuffle behind him to grab cleaning supplies, all of us likely wondering the same thing: Why the fuck are we subjecting ourselves to this?

I'VE NEVER in my life been more thankful for classes; though, in each one, fighting to stay awake was a challenge. It felt like I was in basic training all over again. Back then, we got little sleep, as we are now, and we'd physically exert ourselves for hours upon hours. After that, they'd make us sit in an air-conditioned classroom to learn about field dressing wounds and how to properly take apart an M-16. *Really* riveting stuff.

Now that my classes are over, freedom has vanished, and we are two seconds from finding out what fuck-fuck game we get to play tonight.

We're linked up in the basement as Trevor paces. Damian stands to the back with his chiseled arms crossed and a don't-fuck-with-me glare on his face.

My feet are killing me from cleaning for most of the day, and my busy mind is running at a mile a minute.

I want to quit.

I want to punch Damian in the face and run.

But I want to help my boys get through this too.

Fuck!

"Tonight is a very special night," Trevor says, an ominous tone to his words that worries me. "You will be tested on your patience and mental acumen."

Just then, Tim comes forward with three boxes in his hands, stacked on top of each other. As he gets closer, I notice they're puzzles.

Fuck.

Damian grabs one, Trevor grabs the other, and simultaneously, the three of them open the boxes and dump the pieces into one big pile.

"Let's put some puzzles together, huh, pledges?" Damian says with a shit-eating grin on his face and a big thumbs up.

There's a collective groan among the four of us.

TWENTY-FIVE

The thought of a bed and pillows has my head adrift in the world of the half-living. It's not that five hours of sleep isn't enough for the normal person, it's that it's *not enough for me*. Not to mention, my desire to put an old familiar sitcom on and just lay down and chill is insatiable. I can almost see Jerry right here as I mop, red lights from the Kenny Roger's Chicken sign painting his anguished face.

I can see Joey changing into Thanksgiving pants and Ross getting a level-eight tan.

We haven't been able to drink during Hell Week either, which I'm sure would please Carleigh. I've never wanted alcohol so bad in my life. Or a therapy session for that matter. I'd do a body shot off JD's unwashed asshole right about now if it'd get me out of more cleaning and challenges.

The door abruptly opens, and Trevor and Damian enter, descending the stairs. Behind them, Brady comes, and the sight of him makes my fucking blood boil.

"Pledges, welcome to the third night of Hell Week," Trevor says, that plastic smile of his irritating me more with each passing day. He motions toward Damian. "The wheel, good sir."

Damian heads to the utility closet as Trevor makes his way back up the basement steps. He opens the door once more, and through it come brothers with plates in their hands.

Damian exits the utility closet with a large spinning prize wheel in his hands. He sets it on the bar top. Looking closer, I see these prizes are no prizes at all. Each triangle reads something different, something horrible. Bull Testicles, Raw Fish, Maggots, Worms, Sour Milk, Grasshopper, Pig Intestines, Underwear Head.

As my eyes move from the wheel to the brothers approaching us, my mouth drops open, my eyes wide. They carry plates with raw fish, worms, a cup of curdled milk, maggots, dried grasshoppers, a pair of stained underwear, and what I would imagine to be bull testicles and pig intestines, though I can't tell the difference between the two.

"No fucking way," Mac says, his eyes wide and face contorted in a way that makes me think he's just been told he's dying.

"Yes way! Welcome, pledges, to the Wheel of Death. There are two items on this list you will be eating tonight. Chance will dictate which two they will be," Damian says, an evil smirk on his face.

"Pledge president, you're first," Trevor says, motioning toward the wheel.

I let out a sigh, shaking my head as I shuffle toward the bar. "I can't believe I'm fuckin' doin' this." I point toward my pledge brothers. "You're welcome, fuckers."

I step up to the wheel, my eyes shifting to Damian who stands just beside it. I want to smack the smile right off his face, but I'd also like to live to see tomorrow.

Spinning the wheel, the time it takes to stop feels like an eternity. I don't even want to look, closing my eyes instead and waiting.

"Bull testicles!" I hear Damian yell, and my heart sinks.

I open my eyes, and Damian motions behind me. One of the brothers walks forward with a plate of some pinkish, brown meat cut into cubes. Shaking my head, I grab a piece, slimy and warm, and I eye it for a moment. First letting out a deep sigh, I then shrug and toss it into my mouth, swallowing without bothering to chew. I do the same with the remaining pieces and then return to my place in line, linking up with Jeremy as my stomach turns. I don't show the complete disgust I'm feeling on my face. I have a reputation to maintain. But I have never been closer to vomiting in my life; my mouth completely dry, my throat fighting back regurgitation.

Mac is next, and he gets spoiled milk. I've never seen a funnier sight in my life. He ends up finishing half of it and throwing it right back up into the glass.

Jeremy pulls the pig intestines and seems to take it just fine.

Carter gets grasshoppers, and though it isn't pretty, he manages them down alright.

When it comes back around to me, I survey the options that are left and quickly stumble on the underwear.

"Before I fuckin' spin here, I have to ask, are we supposed to eat that dirty-ass underwear?" I motion to the plate with the filthy tighty-whities on it.

"No, no, no," Damian says, waving me off. "That's the cool part. It's the one thing you don't have to eat." By his tone, an idiot would assume he has good news coming. I know better by the evil smirk tugging at his lips. "You just have to wear them on your head," he says.

My eyes go wide. "Are you fuckin' shittin' me?"

"Nope," he responds smugly.

I shake my head. "All I can say is, if I land on that, I'm sorry guys, but I'm out of this bitch."

I spin the wheel, and look this time, knowing that this spin will determine my continuation with this fraternity.

The wheel slows, stutters, and eventually stops on raw fish, and I'm not quite sure whether I'm relieved or disappointed. Taking the raw filet from the plate, I dispose of it quickly, and without much trouble. I eat enough sushi for the texture not to bother me. It's the warmth that brings those familiar feelings of nausea, along with the bull nuts that still sit heavy in my stomach.

I go back to my place in line as Mac walks toward the wheel cautiously, his bottom lip between his teeth and a serious wrinkle in his brow. He moves his hand to the wheel but hesitates a moment before he spins. When the wheel stops, the only person in the room not laughing is Mac.

Underwear Head.

Mac turns toward us, his mouth agape, eyes wide. "This is so fucked!" he whines, throwing his hands in the air.

"This is fucking Hell Week, bitch!" Damian howls. He starts chanting, "Underwear head! Underwear head! Underwear head!" and before long, everyone in the basement is chanting along with him. The brother with the plated underwear holds it out for Mac. Mac eyes it, and then us, his head shaking slowly.

"On with it!" Trevor shouts, motioning toward the dirty undies.

Mac reaches out, but hesitates, his hand trembling just inches from them.

"Put it on, pledge, or we'll put it on for you," Damian threatens with an evil little smirk on his face.

Mac pinches the underwear by the band with two fingers, lifting it from the plate, inspecting it with a curled lip. "This is so completely fucked. Whose underwear even is this?"

All eyes fall on Tim as he lifts his robed hand into the air, flashing the rock on sign. "Ran a mile in that pair two years ago when I was pledging." Tim grins, his eyebrows doing a little wriggle.

Mac gags, dropping the underwear to the ground. "Fuck this, I can't." He crosses his arms and shakes his head.

"You don't and you're out," Trevor says bluntly.

Mac's eyes trail to the underwear wadded up on the floor, and then back at us.

I shrug. "It's now or never, Red."

He squats, lifting the underwear with two fingers again, and shakes his head before he pulls it over his face in one swift movement. The basement goes crazy, brothers cheering and whooping it up as Mac removes the underwear and throws it to the floor. It meets the concrete about the same time as his mess of vomit does. It splatters across the floor and the brothers closest to it jump back, though some still makes it onto their shoes.

The basement gets even louder, the cheering deafening.

"We got a puker!" Trevor yells, and he's met with more raucous shouting.

Mac shuffles toward our line, still hunkered over with hands to his gut.

"Uh-uh. Where you going, Mac? Grab a mop," Trevor says, shaking his head.

Mac turns slowly, a pitiful look on his face as he shuffles toward the utility closet.

Trevor points to the wheel. "Jeremy, you're next."

Once Jeremy effortlessly takes down some maggots, he strides back to the line.

"Jesus, dude. You got an iron gut," I say as he links back up with me.

"Country boy, brother. I grew up eatin' every goddamn part of the pig!" he responds as the brother with the last remaining plate, worms wiggling away on top of it, approaches Carter, holding the plate out for him.

Carter takes a deep breath, letting it out slowly before he takes the mess of worms and tosses them into his mouth. He tries to swallow, but gags. Tries again. Gags again, and then finally takes them down and keeps them there. He holds a tight hand to his stomach as he makes his way back over to us, shaking his head with shame written on his face.

"Pledges, congratulations on successfully completing day three of Hell Week. Get some rest. It's going to be another early morning tomorrow," Trevor says, sending a shiver down my spine as the raw fish and bull testicles form a nauseating slurry in my stomach.

TWENTY-SIX

I've never been more thrilled to see the inside of a VA hospital in my life. We were woken up at six this morning to go on a seven-mile run. Of course, Damian and Trevor led us, their football crafted bodies running us ragged as they barely broke a sweat. As I sit in the air-conditioned office, the hum of the air vent creates a cozy ambience. I can feel my eyes shutting on their own.

"Bishop?"

I shoot my eyelids open, caught off-guard by her voice. Shaking the cobwebs out, I respond, "Yeah, sorry. What did you say?"

She laughs. "Well, you sat down, I asked how you were doing, and your eyes started closing. Have you been having trouble sleeping?"

"You could say that. It's Hell Week in the fraternity."

"Hell Week?" She laughs. "What in the good Lord is that?"

"It's just our last week of the pledging process. A whole lot of horse shit. Not a lot of sleep."

She shakes her head. "Didn't you have enough of those games in the Army?"

"What can I say?" I shrug. "I guess I'm a glutton for punishment."

"So how have you been otherwise, Bishop?" Carleigh asks, her smile warm but her body language apprehensive, as if she's still trying to figure me out.

I sit back in my chair, a wide smile on my face as I give her a shrug. "Livin' the dream, Doc," I reply.

She narrows her eyes at me. "What did I say about calling me that?"

"Sorry, Carleigh. I'm livin' the life most people can only dream of," I say facetiously.

She smirks. "If sarcasm could be measured, I think you'd be pushing red."

"It's my second language," I respond, smirking.

"Why don't you tell me the truth, Bishop? It's getting to you, isn't it? I can see that."

"The disrespect, mainly." I shake my head. "It's been rough."

"So, tell me again, why are you doing this to yourself?" she asks, a bit of pleading in her tone.

"I need to see it through."

"Why?"

"Because ..."

"Because *why*?" she repeats, sternly this time.

"Because that's what I do. When I start somethin', I finish it. Is that so hard to believe, Carleigh?"

"You're so beyond this though."

"And who are you to say that?" I ask, more harshly than intended.

"I'm your therapist, and somebody who has gotten to know a little about you. You have to trust me, Bishop. I'm not your enemy. I'm not the bad guy. I'm your friend. I only want to help you."

"You wanna help me?" I ask, arching an eyebrow.

"Yes," she responds, exasperated.

"Make these thoughts go away. I'll take a magic potion, acupuncture, fuckin' voodoo, I don't care. I just wanna stop feelin' this way."

"What way?"

I take a deep breath, my heart pounding in my chest as the floodgates begin to open. "I wanna stop feelin' so damn alone, even with so many people around me. I wanna stop hatin' myself so much for things I can't fuckin' change. I wanna stop feelin' so goddamn sorry for myself." I hesitate, my eyes on the floor, when I continue, "I wanna know who the fuck I'm supposed to be now."

"Why do you put all this pressure on yourself?"

I shrug, shaking my head. "I don't know. It's just how I've always been. As much as I live in the moment, as much as my Peter Pan Syndrome influences me, I hate not knowin' what's ahead. I hate not knowin' where I belong."

"You still have so much left to give, Bishop," she says, leaning on the desk, her brows furrowed with concern.

I roll my eyes. "Like what?"

"I don't know." She shrugs. "You tell me."

I lean forward. "I was meant to be a soldier, Carleigh. It's what I was born to do. It was taken away from me. Poof. *Gone.* Where do I go from here? What do I do?"

She puts a hand up, as if she's trying to calm me. "Okay, Bishop. I'm not trying to get you worked up."

I hadn't even realized I was getting worked up. I let out a heavy breath and say, "Sorry, Carleigh. I didn't mean to get so tense. I'm just ..." I shake my head, sighing. "I'm lost. And fuckin' tired."

"Well, that's why you're here."

I laugh. "No, I'm here because I beat a kid's face to shit."

She smirks. "I'm a big believer in 'everything happens for a reason.' You're here with me because you need this counseling, Bishop. You do have a problem."

Her words hurt, the truth in them the most painful, but before I can retaliate in anger, I'm overwhelmed by the concern in her features, as genuine as the smile I sometimes get out of her.

"I know I do," I mutter, my head in my hands.

"And how do we fix the problem?"

I chuckle. "Isn't it your job to figure that out?"

She's not amused. "It's both of our jobs, yes, but I want to know what *you* think it will take to resolve this. To feel okay about yourself and where you're headed.

"I couldn't even tell you, Carleigh. I really couldn't. I just don't know who I am anymore. I'm mentally exhausted. Drained. I can barely think, let alone figure out how to fix this catastrophe." I point toward my head, letting out a heavy sigh before adding, "I hope you're happy, by the way."

"What about any of this makes you think I'd be happy?" she asks, rearing her head back and her lips pinching together.

"Me spillin' my guts."

"Well, yes, I am happy you're being open and honest with me. It's necessary if we're to make any progress."

"How many military members have you worked with?" I ask, seemingly catching her off guard with the abrupt shift in conversation.

"A lot. Why?"

"How many would you say you've helped?"

She shrugs. "I don't know, Bishop. Not enough. It could never be enough."

"Do you think you can help me?"

"Will you continue to be honest with me in here? Be open to change? Willing to accept your own fault in this?"

"The first two ... yes. But willin' to accept my fault in this? What do you mean by that?"

"I mean, you have a lot of power, Bishop. You're assertive, dedicated, loyal. You have the ability and the determination to pull yourself out of this. You just have to want to. You have to *need* to. We've both agreed you have a problem here. Now, how do we fix it? Where do we go from here?"

"Other than me needin' a beer immediately after this session?" I grin.

"You probably are, aren't you? I imagine you do after every session."

I shrug. "Maybe. Maybe not."

"Bishop!"

"Carleigh!" I smile.

She scoffs and says, "You're going to be the death of me, you know that?"

I nod, my lips in a tight smile. "I'm not an easy nut to crack, doctor."

"Promise me this one thing," she says, her pointer finger aimed at my face.

I put my hands up in retreat. "Yes, ma'am. Anything."

"Be honest in here. *Always*. We will only find progress through truth."

"You sound like Dr. Phil," I joke.

She narrows her eyes at me. "Do you agree?"

"I agree, Dr. Jacobs. Cross my heart and hope to die."

"I'll stick a needle in *your* eye," she says, heaving a hand toward me as if she's attempting to stab me. "Now, let's talk about those grades."

"Carleigh, I have to be the cleanin' bitch for a hundred dudes. I'll talk about anything and everything you'd like, for as long as you'd like."

"You'll regret saying that." She smiles, wide and efferves-cent, maybe even a little flirtatious.

I've decided, right here, right now, that one day I will bend this sexy minx over her desk and have my way with her. As she talks, it's hard for me to focus on anything else but that round ass of hers perked up and waiting for my rock-hard cock. In my head, she looks back at me with those devastatingly beautiful eyes, her bottom lip between her teeth, her face saying, "Fuck me silly."

TWENTY-SEVEN

W e've made it to Hell Day, the final day of Hell Week.

Our weary, tired bodies stand linked up after being hauled from the frat house in a van to, I presume, the DIK initiation site. The smell of cedar and dirt surrounds us. It's not entirely warm out, but the bag over my head burns me up regardless.

Have we been here fifteen minutes?

Thirty?

An hour?

My mind runs a mile a minute. Each second standing here feels like an eternity.

Carleigh.

Ember.

My deteriorating patience.

"Pledges, unlink and remove your sandbags," Damian says.

We do as we're told, and the relief of the cool wind against my sweat-coated face is amazing. The evening sun filters through the dense woods sporadically, and the only sound around us now is bird songs and cricket chirps. Damian stands with his arms crossed, a smug look on his face. Trevor, Tim, Zane, Brady, and Sarge stand in line behind him. They're all in combat-style gear—cargo pants, web belts with knives attached, Under Armour dri-fit shirts. Sarge even has a keffiyeh around his neck. Outside of the five of them, there are no other brothers around us. But the dirt road that leads here is lined with probably thirty or forty cars as far as the eye can see.

"Welcome back to our sacred ground," Trevor says. "You all have done well over the past two months. You've put in the time. You've learned the traditions and history of our great fraternity. Now, you face your last challenge. Tonight won't be easy. You'll be tested continuously. Listen to what you're told. Speak only when told to speak. And if you make it to the morning, you will come out of these woods as a Delta Iota Kappa brother. Good luck."

Trevor turns and heads into the woods, Brady and Tim following behind him. As they disappear, Damian takes a step toward us, motioning to the ground.

"Start collecting sticks, wood, branches, whatever you can find that will burn. Tim will show you where to put it," he says. "Don't stop collecting until I tell you to."

If we had been able to wear a watch or have our phones, I may have a clue as to how long we've been collecting sticks, but it's been at least a couple of hours. The pile of debris we've collected is proof of that, as it's grown to be man-high and wide enough to fill a swimming pool. The four of us are coated in sweat from head to toe. We share angered glances as we pass back and forth from the woods to the pile just beside the circle of trees where we conducted our initiation on the first day. We've come to know this spot as the Sacred Circle—trees planted by the DIK-Rho founders back in '22.

As I toss my thousandth bundle of sticks onto the massive

pile, I notice Damian coming toward us through the quickly darkening woods.

"Pledges, let's fuckin' go! Circle up on me," he yells out.

We trot over, but as we reach him, he takes off running, waving us on. "Let's go! Follow me!"

After a half-mile or so of running, I hear the sound of flowing water. Damian cuts right and we follow behind him. Slowing, he works his way through a collection of thick bushes. The sound of water grows louder as we continue down a narrow path. As we reach an opening, a wide river is revealed, flowing powerfully. Brothers line the riverbank, and some of them stand atop a massive boulder just in front of us.

Trevor is one of the brothers on the boulder and he smiles as we approach. "Pledges, welcome to Trust Rock. Come on down and get acquainted," he says, sounding like a goddamn game show host.

We carefully trek down to the river's edge and climb up onto the rock one by one.

"Link up!" Damian yells, hoisting himself up on the rock after us.

We link up awkwardly on the uneven surface of the boulder, our line zig-zagging.

"Trust Rock," Trevor says, letting his words linger.

I barely hear him. I'm focused on the rushing water, something to take my mind off the pain in my knees and ankles.

"Generations of brothers have stood upon this rock, just as you are tonight, as pledges for the last day. You will either come out of this a DIK brother, your two months of pledging just a small part of your lifetime in our brotherhood, or you will have spent two months wasting your time. The choice is yours." Trevor's eyes trail to Damian and he gives him a little nod.

Damian walks toward us in a hurry, a finger jabbing at us. "Get on your fucking faces, pledges. Push-ups!"

Boy, does this feel fuckin' familiar.

We drop to the ground on our hands in the push-up position.

"On my count. Down. Up. One! Down. Up. Two!" Damian continues until we get to thirty, and then he yells for us to stand and link back up.

He shuffles toward the group of brothers on the boulder across from us and then Brady steps forward. He's staring me down, and I stare right back.

"Pledges," he says, his eyes still on me, an evil grin crossing his lips. "Get down to your fucking skivvies!"

We look around awkwardly at each other for a moment when Damian steps forward.

"Are you cocksuckers deaf? Get your fucking clothes off!" he yells, a snarl on his face.

We reluctantly do as we're told, stripping off our clothes, and Carter, Jeremy, and I crack up laughing as we spot Mac in his tighty-whities again.

"You didn't learn your lesson the last time?" I crack between laughs.

"Shut the fuck up!" Brady yells. "Link the fuck back up."

As we connect our arms again, Brady glares at me, his jaw clenching. I look back with relaxed features, a slight grin on my face.

"What the fuck are you grinning at?" he asks, his face just inches from my own.

I chuckle. "Just one more night, my friend. Enjoy it." I lean in a little, nearing his ear, and whisper, "And then I'm comin' for you. Just know that."

"Brady!" Trevor barks, taking a step forward. "Finish up."

Brady's smirk fades, and his eyes flit to the rock as he backs away.

Zane approaches us next. He clears his throat. "Ugh, just like jump up and down or something," he says, shrugging.

We comply.

"Okay, you can stop," he says, and then he returns to the group.

"What the holy fuck was that?" Tim grunts as he comes toward us.

"Shit's stupid," Zane mutters.

Tim waves him off, smiling wide as he approaches. "Hey, fellas!"

I fight the smile from my face as I look him over. He's wearing black combat boots like always, and a pair of cargo shorts, but only a woodland camouflage robe covering his upper body.

"Well, shit. Am I talking to myself here? I said, 'Hey, fellas!'"

"Hey, Tim," we respond together.

"How's Hell Night going for you?"

"Shitty as fuck," Mac mutters.

"Pretty much." Tim smiles. "Well, I'm gonna take it easy on you. Let's just see thirty jumping jacks, huh?"

As we unlink and start knocking out jumping jacks, my thoughts wander to these gentlemen and how homosexual this whole process has really been. I mean, they're making us jump up and down in our underwear for Chrissakes. There's more flopping going on than you get with one of those inflatable dancing dudes. And not that there's anything wrong with being gay, but when you consider how often these idiots throw around words like 'faggot,' you'd think the hypocrisy would be self-evident.

Apparently not.

Once we're finished, Tim says, "Alright. I'll let the other guys take over. Bye, fellas!"

"Bye, Tim."

He turns and makes his way back to the group as Sarge comes forward next. He's got a shit-eating grin on his face, especially for me.

Shaking his head, he says, "I'm sorry, man. I had to do it too, and I despised this shit just as much as you are right now. As with the Army, when you have to go through this kind of shit, once you get to be the one who dishes it out, well, you get a little payback."

I nod, smiling for the first time tonight. "I understand. Do your worst, buddy."

He grins, his eyes trailing over my pledge brothers. "Alright, gentlemen. Let's get wet. Hop in the river, go completely under, and then get back up here and link back up. And be fucking careful."

Mac lets out a heavy sigh, his shoulders dropping as we disconnect and make our way down the side of the rock and into the river. After getting soaked, we return to the top of the boulder and link back up.

Sarge nods, the smile still on his lips. "Feels good, though, doesn't it?"

"It actually does." I laugh.

"I got your back," he says, heading back to the group.

For two more hours, every single brother in the fraternity, starting with the officers, get their turn at us. We dress and undress countless times. We've done hundreds of push-ups, jumping jacks, squats, and sit-ups, which, against the jagged rock, absolutely kills a naked back.

Clothed now, we're led through the woods by Damian once again, and I'm completely drained. My shins burn as the old splints make their return, but I must keep up as all the brothers trail close behind. I don't know how much more I can take before I snap. My patience has whittled down to nothing.

As we make our way back toward the Sacred Circle, I can see a large bonfire roaring in a clearing, a short distance away from the pile of wood we put together.

Reaching the edge of the bonfire, Damian turns, motioning toward us. "Pledges, go collect some more firewood. I'll tell you when to stop."

I look at the massive pile of wood we collected earlier and scoff, shaking my head. As I set off into the woods, with every intention of lighting up a cigarette before I collect anymore fucking sticks, I think about grabbing one of their knives and going on a stabbing spree. I think of the headline: "Combat Veteran Kills Entire Fraternity, Self, in Woodland Massacre." I chuckle as I make it far enough away from the brothers to light up.

Pulling one out, I light it and take a slow puff, holding it in my lungs for a few glorious seconds, and then releasing it slowly.

Suddenly, the crackling of branches behind me startles me, and I turn to find Sarge coming toward me through the darkness. I let out a sigh of relief when I recognize him.

"Shit, thought you were one of those other fuckheads. Didn't feel like hearin' it."

"Nah, just me. How are you?" His brows are wrinkled with concern.

"Not good, man. I'm about to lose my shit, for real. That crap on the rock. I mean, for fuck's sake, it's only a fraternity."

He nods. "I know exactly how you feel, brother. Really. I was ready to fucking quit too. Had every desire to. But my pledge brothers kept me in it. I was their leader, as you are for *your* guys, and they needed me to stick around. Maybe this shit wasn't right for me. Maybe I would've been better off walking away that night. But my pledge brothers needed me. All this bullshit makes them feel a part of something. I didn't want to take that away from them. You have to do the same. You know that."

Frustrated, I reluctantly nod, knowing he's right. "How much more of this, Sarge?"

"I can't tell you. I'm sorry, Bish. As much as I want to, and as much as I feel for you, I think it's important to see this through the right way."

"I fuckin' hate you," I mutter, a slight smirk on my face.

"Nah, you love me. And you're stuck with me, so you got no choice."

I laugh.

"Stay out here for a bit," he says, motioning to my cigarette. "Have a few smokes. Relax. I'll cover for you."

"You sure?"

He nods. "Positive. Just come back over in a little bit."

"Thanks, man."

"Don't mention it. Just get your mind right out here. Shake it off. Then come back and finish this thing out right."

"Alright. Will do."

He flashes a quick wave, before turning and heading back off into the darkness.

I take another drag, leaning back against a tree, and let the smoke out with a heavy sigh.

For my pledge brothers, and only for them, I will see this through. But I'm going to need about ten cigarettes to settle my nerves first and to save me from a life in prison for the murder of every last motherfucker out here.

For two more hours we collected wood. In fact, I'm certain we've put enough wood together to build a fucking ark. I took fifteen minutes and four cigarettes to clear my head, to put my focus back on my pledge brothers, and to reconfigure my way of thinking. I went through shit in basic, during deployments, and while recovering, that blows this shit right out of the water. I searched for that warrior mentality that got me through the worst of my injury and eventually found it. For the remaining two hours, I collected wood with a smile on my face, Collective Soul hits playing on a loop in my head.

Damian whistles loudly, the kind where he uses his fingers and it sounds like a fire alarm. His voice calls through the dark, "Pledges, get your asses over here and line up!"

Slowly, the four of us work our way through the woods to the bonfire and line up in front of Damian. The brothers, all one hundred and seven of them, have made the area around the clearing look like a campground. They've all got chairs or stumps to sit on, dozens of coolers at their sides, the smell of reefer in the air, and music blaring from a truck parked near the Sacred Circle. Most of them are shitfaced. Seeing the beers in their hands and smelling the dope makes me ache for a little something to take the edge off. Just a beer will do.

Maybe a six-pack.

Probably a case.

"Get on your faces!" Damian barks, spittle flying from his lips.

We get in the push-up position and await further instruction.

"Seeing as you all half-assed your time on Trust Rock, we're going to have to go through each brother again. You'll do it until you get it right, and we'll go all night if we have to," Damian warns, standing right beside our heads.

"This is bullshit," Mac grumbles. "We did everything you guys asked of us. We didn't half-ass a goddamn thing!"

"Shut up!" Damian yells. "You speak when you're told to speak. Was that not clear earlier?"

"I just don't get the point of all this. We did everything you asked!" Mac repeats, exasperation in his tone.

Damian squats down, right next to Mac's face. Mac turns his head to look at him and Damian sneers. "Listen here, you ginger bitch. I will keep you in that goddamn position until the fucking morning comes if you don't shut your cocksucker."

"*Hey*," I bark, my brows furrowed, my heart racing. "You can do what you have to do without belittling him. That isn't right."

Damian turns to me, the sneer deepening.

"Now, why the fuck are you speaking, pledge?" Brady says, standing from his chair.

Trevor stands too. "Brady. Sit. Down."

I keep my eyes on Brady as he begrudgingly returns to a seated position, shooting me a death stare.

I smile and wink at him before looking at Damian again. "This can be accomplished without disrespecting my friend here. That's all I'm sayin'."

"It's okay," Mac mutters.

"No," I respond. "It's *not* okay"

Damian slowly stands, his eyes still on me, when he says, "Push-ups, pledges. On my count. Down. Up. One! Down. Up. Two! Down. Up. Three!"

———

KNOWING a few psychological tricks from my experience in basic, I thought having to redo every brothers' smoke session was a ploy. I figured after a few of them took their second turn, they'd make us gather more wood, or maybe we'd be told our night was done, that we were brothers. Wishful thinking, of course.

Each brother *did* in fact smoke us again, going through the same routine, except for when it came to getting wet, which was traded in for a rousing session of fireman's carries.

My body hasn't been tested like this in forever and I feel it in every single movement. I can hear it with every creak of my joints. On the final brother—Chunk, of all people—we're again in the push-up position, having just done twenty, when he orders us to drop completely to our stomachs and put the bags back over our heads. He has us stay that way for a few minutes as footsteps are the only thing we hear amongst nature's orchestra.

Out of the silence, Trevor says, "Stand up and take a brother's arm. We need to talk in private."

Standing, I feel an arm link with my own and I'm led away in slow steps.

"Hey, it's Sarge, man."

"Oh shit, what's up?" I say, as we continue onward.

"I'm really sorry about this, man. I just—I can't even believe it."

"Can't believe what?"

"Someone found out about you smo—oh shit, nevermind, you'll see in a second. I'm just ..." His voice shakes, the concern thick in his tone. "I'm just sorry, man."

"Pledges." Trevor's voice echoes. "We have some unfortunate business to discuss. It's come to my attention that Bishop snuck away for a few cigarettes a while ago, as reported by brother Chunk. Obviously, tobacco was specifically restricted, as your list clearly stated, so—guys, I'm sorry. When one fucks up, everyone suffers. You all will either have to drop the pledging process and have wasted the past two months of your life, or you restart the pledging process from day one. Those are your only two options." He hesitates before adding, "I'm sorry. I really am."

"*What?*" Mac gasps.

"I'm sorry, guys, but I'm fuckin' out. Fuck this stupid ass shit." I go to remove the sandbag, but Sarge tugs it back down.

"What about your pledge brothers, Bishop?" he asks in a concerned tone.

"I don't give a fuck," I spit, my voice sounds as if it's not my own, gritty and emotionless.

"I ain't stickin' around either, gents," Jeremy says. "Ain't no way I'm goin' through this horse shit for a second time. Y'all must be higher than hell. I'm fuckin' out of here." There's a hesitation, and then he says, "What the—" before his words are snuffed out.

"It's one choice or the other. You decide right now," Trevor says.

"I'm out," Mac says.

"Um, I don't know. Bishop?" Carter asks.

I scoff. "Out as Elton John, bro. Sorry."

"Then I'm out too," Carter says.

"Alright, sorry about that, guys," Trevor says, though his tone says anything but apologetic. "You can take off your sandbags and we'll get you back to the house."

I pull my sandbag off immediately and see every single brother in the fraternity standing behind Trevor, and they have smiles on their faces. After a moment of awkward silence as the four of us look over them with questioning glares, Trevor leads all the brothers in cheer.

He takes a step forward, a wide smile on his face and his hands clapping, as he says, "Gentlemen, welcome to the DIK family! You fucking made it!"

For a moment, I'm in shock. I can't process whether this is legitimate or just another game they're playing.

Sarge embraces me, whispering, "Congrats, Little Bro," in my ear. As the genuine smile remains positioned on his face, and the others continue their congratulations and applause. Without trickery, the shock morphs to enthusiasm and relief.

"Now, let's get you guys back to the house to party!" Trevor yells, waving his arm in the air to rally everyone. "First-year brothers, take care of the bonfire."

I turn to Sarge, brows scrunched in confusion. "What about all that wood?" I ask.

He chuckles. "It's for the end-of-year party."

I shake my head, scoffing. "Jesus Christ, we were fuckin' slave labor then?"

Sarge nods with a smile. "Sucks, doesn't it?"

"Like Jenna fuckin' Jameson in her prime."

TWENTY-EIGHT

A fter the short ride back to the DIK house, we're met with a spotless basement. On the bar top sits the book Zane presented at our initiation, with every brother's name written in it from the past seventy years. Next to the book, the skull and dagger lay, as does a stack of framed certificates.

"New brothers, link up for the last time, facing the bar," Trevor says, his tone light, a smile on his face.

It reminds me so much of basic training, yet again, when we were finishing up our last twenty-nine mile ruck march with ninety pounds on our backs. The drill sergeants lashed out at us, called us every despicable name in the book, threatened us with another twenty-nine miles. And then our boots crossed the finish line, the walkway toward our platoon area and barracks, and the drill sergeants angered scowls turned to wide smiles, excitement exuding from most of them. Obviously, a few remained coarse. It's just how they were. But most began congratulating us, calling us infantryman for the first time. The feeling of that complete juxtaposition in their demeanor made the finale that much sweeter. It took the pain away in a flash. It instantly made *all* those miserable weeks become just specks in the rearview.

My joints no longer ache; my muscles are no longer tired. I feel exhilaration as I link up with my brothers, Trevor and Damian standing before us. Even Damian has a smile on his face now. Zane grabs the book from the bar top, Brady grabs the skull, and Tim grabs the dagger, and they line up on the other side of Trevor.

"You guys have been one of our best pledge classes," Trevor says. "No shit. You've worked together quicker, and more effectively, than any pledge class I've ever seen, that's for sure. And that includes my own."

"Same here," Damian adds, nodding approvingly.

Trevor motions toward me and continues, "Obviously, Bishop, you played a huge part in that. We really thank you for being a part of this pledge class, and now a brother within this fraternity."

My eyes flit to Brady, who carries the usual scowl for me on his face.

Looking back toward Trevor, I shake my head, replying, "It's all about these guys next to me. A team is only as strong as its weakest link, and we didn't have a weak link among us. Everyone contributed. Everyone put forth a hundred percent. And outside of Mac ..." I chuckle. "They did it without complaint. Couldn't have asked for better men to go through this with."

"Hey!" Mac says, looking at me from down the line.

I turn to him and smile, shrugging.

"If the boot fits, fucker," Jeremy adds, laughing.

"Well ..." Trevor motions to the book in Zane's hands. "You all ready to become brothers of Delta Iota Kappa? Give me a fuck yeah!"

"Fuck yeah!" we respond, louder than we ever have before.

"Bishop. Are you ready to take the oath and become our newest brother?"

I grin, more excited than I ever thought I would be to see this moment. "I sure the fuck am."

Trevor nods. "Then come forward please and take a knee."

I do as he asks, and he grabs a small wooden stool with a quill pen and ink jar atop it, setting them in front of me. Damian then sets the book down on the stool and opens it up to about three quarters of the way in. Half of the page is full, and I see the last name signed is Chunk's.

"McKenzie 'Knuckles' Bishop, do you solemnly promise that you will be loyal to the Delta Iota Kappa fraternity and Rho Chapter, abiding by our rules, living by our principles, and promoting the DIK way of life, to discharge your obligations to the brotherhood faithfully, and to use all honorable means to contribute to the interests of our fraternity?"

"I promise."

"Do you understand our Declaration of Principles, the seriousness of their contents, and the legacy in which you are continuing?"

"I do."

"Frater Bishop, we welcome you as the newest brother in the Delta Iota Kappa fraternity as Scroll Number five-six-four-five. Please sign the scroll."

I take the quill, dabbing it a few times in the ink, and I sign my name on the scroll, just below Chunk's, next to slot number five-six-four-five. As I finish, all the brothers who have collected in the basement behind us cheer loudly.

Trevor puts out his hand with a smile, and I shake it, standing to my feet as I do.

"Welcome to the fraternity, Bishop!" he says, motioning toward the still cheering crowd behind my pledge brothers. "Go ahead and join your new brothers."

I turn, nodding toward my smiling pledge brothers as I pass them, and approach the group behind them. Sarge hands me a beer, high-fiving me with his other hand, and the others congratulate me as well.

"Brother Mac, are you ready to sign the scroll?"

"Fuck yeah, I'm ready," Mac responds in an excited tone as the volume in the basement lightens.

After Mac, Carter, and Jeremy take their own oaths and sign their names upon the scroll, Trevor opens the basement door and a flood of well-dressed women come down the stairs.

"Now, brothers new and old, let's fucking party!" Trevor yells.

As the four of us pledge brothers congratulate each other, I spot Damian and Tim approaching with two bottles in each of their hands.

"There's one more part of your Hell Night we forgot to mention," Damian says, cracking a mischievous smile.

Eyeing the bottle closer, I immediately recognize it as Mad Dog 20/20. My stomach churns as I think back to high school and all the Mad Dogs I stomached and then subsequently vomited back up.

Damian hands a bottle each to Jeremy and Mac, and Tim hands his to me and Carter. The other brothers, now intermixed with the newly arrived girls, form a circle around us.

"On my count, you gotta tip those back, boys, and chug the whole thing," Damian says, motioning to the bottles in our hands.

We eye them first, and then each other.

Mac groans.

Jeremy and I shrug.

"No belly-achin', boys. We got an audience," Jeremy says, opening up his bottle, and the rest of us follow suit.

"Alright, Fraters," Trevor yells out. "On three. One. Two.

Three!"

We throw them back and almost instantly every other brother in the basement begins shouting: "Born beside the river, raised by a bear. Sharp set of teeth and a thick coat of hair. Two brass balls and a thick steel rod, I'm a dirty motherfucker. I'm a DIK, by God!"

I'm halfway through and it feels like I've been drinking for hours. Mac has already stopped, spit up, and restarted twice.

The pause after their chant lasts the briefest of moments before they begin shouting again, the volume deafening.

"Rebel, Rebel, Rebel, ride or die tonight. DIKs don't play the 'play dead' game, we'd rather fucking fight. Trouble, Trouble, Trouble, come and see what's up. DIKs don't need no girls, 'cause we've got your moms to fuck."

Finishing the Mad Dog first, I let out an exasperated breath as the liquid churns in my gut. Watching the others, I can't help but laugh at Mac as he pussy lips the bottle and has only finished a quarter of it. Jeremy will be the next one finished as Carter's struggles almost as much as Mac.

The brothers begin chanting again, as quickly as they had finished the last one.

"What's that? Jock strap! Who the hell are we? DIKs by God, you should know a thing or three. One, we're the greatest, best there ever was. Better than your sister on that scene from Bang Bus. Two, we're the strongest, united all as one. Stronger than the bedsprings of your girlfriend's futon. Three, we're some scoundrels, dirty rotten pricks. We'd rather be the takers, Beta Chi can suck our dicks!"

Jeremy finishes, letting out a groan. Carter eventually finishes too, gasping, and looking over at Jeremy and me in disgust. He wipes an arm across his lips as the brothers continue chanting, Mac still struggling with his bottle, but getting close to finishing.

"Rat shit, bat shit, dirty rotten thieves. Beta Chi guys like to suck a dick or three!"

Mac finishes and immediately bends over, a hand to his knee, his breathing heavy. He shakes his head as the brothers continue their chant.

"Love us. Hate us. What are we to do? We're the DIKs of Crescent Falls. Who the hell are you?"

They finish the last line louder than any other before it, and it's deafening. Carter and Mac, both now somewhat recovered, look over all the brothers as they finish out their chant, enamored by the sight of it all. I imagine, like me, they want to learn the chants as soon as possible, so that next time they can join in.

"Fraters," Damian says with a smile. "Slam your bottles." He motions to the floor and takes a few steps back, as do those who encircle us.

We look at each other and shrug, taking a few steps back and slamming them into a hundred little pieces on the concrete floor.

Damian looks back. "First-year brothers, clean it up! Tim, start the music. Let's fucking celebrate!"

I'M NOT sure how many moonshine shots and beers I had before I realized Ember was in the basement. She now stands beside Holly, chatting away with some of the brothers, as I sit on the couch a short distance away. She periodically glances in my direction, and each time I catch her, she darts her eyes away.

I want to talk to her, but I'm unsure of what to say. And now there's Carleigh in the mix. God, how my feelings for her have grown. What started as simple infatuation has become complete desire. I can't help it. She fits everything I look for in a woman, from her beautiful heart to her incredible body, and the way her honest eyes gleam when she smiles. I likely have no real chance with her, but the idea of it energizes me.

I remember, too, a time when Ember had my heart racing, and looking at her now, in a short, skin-tight black skirt, and a purposely shredded Metallica t-shirt barely covering a sports bra, I'm wondering if she dressed this way for me—to make me yearn. With her breasts as perky as they are, the side boob the shirt creates is instantly dick hardening. She wears a backwards snapback that she *knows* I fucking love, and holy hell, is it hard for me to understand anything Jeremy and Mac are discussing next to me.

It's like I'm seeing her for the first time again. The warm rush of familiarity, and desire, and connection sweeps over me.

"You oughta just go talk to her, Bish," Jeremy says, slapping my arm.

I shake my head. Looking at him, I reply, "Dude, she probably wants nothin' to do with me. And I'm so fuckin' drunk, I don't know what the fuck I'd even say."

"Bishop." Jeremy looks at me intently. "She's been starin' back at you for like an hour and a half. Do you miss the girl or not?"

"Fuck yeah, I miss her. Beyond just bein' a sick-ass chick, she is one of the best fucks I've ever had, by far."

"Well, I wouldn't lead with that," Jeremy says, laughing. "But just tell her you'd like to see her again or somethin'. Shit, don't make me do it for you!"

"Fuck you. I would *kill* you." I laugh. Catching her wandering eyes again, I say, "Fuck it. I got this."

Standing up too quickly, I stagger a few steps before steadying myself, luckily without her seeing any of it. I didn't realize how quickly the alcohol had run through me. As I approach her, she glances at me and I smile. I motion my head behind me and mouth the words, "Can we talk?"

Her bottom lip slips between her teeth as her eyes trail to the group in front of her before they eventually fall back on me. She gives me a little nod.

"Front porch," I mouth and point toward the exit.

She nods again.

I smile, making my way to the stairs, heading up and outside to the porch, lighting a cigarette on the way.

Taking a much-needed puff, my heart races. My nerves go haywire. I worry about what I'll say, or that I'll say something wrong, or stupid. Even sober, I'd be tongue-tied with her, but as drunk as I am, I'm bound to fuck something up.

The opening front door brings my head shooting around. I take a deep breath, trying to calm my nerves. Ember comes through the doorway and smiles. She has a clutch in one hand and her flask in the other.

"It's really good to see you. I've missed you around here," I say, standing and giving her a hug as the door closes behind her.

As we separate, she passes me a tight smile, her eyes falling to the couch. She motions toward it, saying, "Wanna sit?"

"Sure," I respond, taking a puff of my smoke and plopping my ass down on the couch.

She sits a little more gracefully than I and crosses one leg over the other, taking a sip from her flask.

"How have you been?" I ask, feeling fully original.

"I've been good. Classes have been a bit of a bitch lately."

"Yeah, mine too. I'm seriously gonna be lucky to even be able to use these credits."

"That bad?"

I shrug. "With pledging, and now this counseling bullshit I have to do, school has taken a back seat. Can't bring myself to stay focused on it long enough to fully process anything."

"Counseling?"

"Yeah, from the fight."

Her eyes flit to her hands as she starts picking at her nails.

"Your friend actually really hooked me up. Well, his parents did. They agreed on a deal where I just have to do this seven-week substance abuse program and help a little with his medical bills. Saved me havin' to go to trial, and potentially, jail."

"Well, that's good. How has the counseling been?"

"Pretty brutal, actually." I chuckle. "I'm not the open-up type, really."

"You've always seemed pretty open to me."

"About certain things, yeah. But other things, like how I feel, that's a different story. It's like pullin' teeth for me."

"Do you have a nice counselor?"

I think to Carleigh and fight the smile that wants to spread across my face when she comes to mind.

A 'nice' counselor? How about the sexiest fuckin' counselor the VA's ever employed?

"Yeah, she's pretty awesome. Been doin' this a long time, so she knows her shit. I'm not so sure the process would be goin' as well as it has with anyone else."

"What do you mean?"

"Well, like I said" —I take a drag from my cig and continue, the smoke coming out with my words— "I'm not the most open of people when it comes to expressing my emotions. I need someone who knows their shit. To open me up. Luckily, she does." There's a brief silence between us when I ask, "How's your friend, by the way?"

"He's not, like, my *friend* friend. He's just kind of a friend of a friend. But he's doing better. You really messed him up, Bishop. He's lucky it wasn't much worse."

"I know," I mutter, hanging my head a little in shame.

"The way you got that night … it scared me. I'm sorry I just disappeared on you, but you were … yeah, you just scared me.

You got the same look my ex used to get before he'd put his hands on me. And then you did put your hands on me ..."

"I'm so, so sorry for that, Em. I really am. I've felt like absolute shit about it. I just—I lost myself for a second there. I blacked out. I was just so full of rage and just ... instinct. I have no recollection of either beatin' him as bad as I did, or pushin' you away. But you have to know, that isn't me. That's not who I am, or what I represent as a man. Men who hit women are reprehensible to me. I-I'm just ... God, I'm just so sorry. I hope you got all my texts, and I'm sorry for sendin' so many. I was just infuriated with myself and needed to apologize. I needed you to know I was truly sorry. I still do. I need you to know, Em."

"I believe you. I do. I just worry."

I can see her fighting back the tears by the way she clenches her jaw. A few tears escape anyway, a little mascara running along with them, and she hides her face.

Forcing a laugh, she says, "I'm sorry. I'm being such a pussy."

Tossing my cigarette into the ashtray, I put a hand on her shoulder. Reluctantly, she looks at me, tears welling in her eyes, thin black streaks running from her eyes to her chin, and an adorable little whimper escapes her trembling lips.

"Talk to me," I whisper. "*Please.*"

"I just really liked you, Bishop. *A lot.*" She hesitates, pointing toward my face. "I'm saying too much. I can see it in your expression," she says.

"No, no, no. If anything, you're not sayin' enough. I wanna know what's goin' on inside that head of yours."

She laughs, shaking her head with wide, suspicious eyes. "Highly doubtful. I believe you told me once, when we first started getting to know each other, that you have internal scarring ... a lot of it. Well, so do I. More than I could ever admit to myself or anyone else."

"Is that why you disappeared? Why you ignored me?"

"Absolutely. My high school boyfriend, the only guy I've ever really loved, near the end of our relationship, he got abusive, verbally, physically, emotionally ..." Her voice trails off as she takes a thick gulp. "... sexually. And for a while, I blamed myself. I thought maybe if I could've done something different. If only I could've fought harder."

"It wasn't you. It was him."

She puts a hand up, a tight smile on her face. "I know that now. That's what I had to learn. I had to figure it out on my own. That if I didn't have the strength to run, if I didn't have the strength to at least tell someone else who actually loved me, well, then maybe next time, I wouldn't survive."

"I'm sorry, Ember."

"I'm sorry too, Bishop. That's why I'm here. That's why I came to the party. I'm sorry I didn't give you a chance to explain yourself, maybe redeem yourself. I wish I could explain how I felt at the time, but when I pulled you off him—or at least tried to—the look you gave me before you pushed me away, it was the same look he gave me. It was a hungry look, like you wanted to see me in pain."

I shake my head, shame washing over me in anxiety tingling waves. "I really am ashamed of myself. I wish I remembered it. I wish I could defend my actions. But they're indefensible. I got no right to put my hands on you, and I'll forever regret that I did. You didn't deserve it. And I know I don't remember it, but I know me ... I know what I represent and who I am. I don't hit women. In that moment, I can only assume my mind was overwhelmed and concentrated on him, and anyone who got between us was just collateral damage."

As a look of offense creeps onto her face, I put a hand up in retreat. "I didn't mean it how it came out. I just mean, when I black out like that, I see no one but my target."

Her features relax. "That's dangerous."

I nod. "I know it is. And, honestly, regardless of what I had to drink that night, I've blacked out sober, too. It wasn't an alcohol thing. It was a predatory thing. A survival instinct. I felt challenged. So, I attacked with unrelenting aggression. It's not perfect. Nowhere near flawless, but it's kept my ass alive, and up on both feet. I've never been knocked out, thank God. Never been caught off-guard either. There's somethin' to be said for that."

"Well, I don't have that same aggression or ultra-vigilance, and I haven't found myself in any fights or attacks, outside of the one."

"This is a three-part response, all of which you will hate. You ready?"

She chuckles, nodding.

"One. You're lucky. All women, regardless of skin color, nationality, looks, size, location, et cetera, are at risk at all times."

She rears her head back, scoffing. "*What*? So, as a woman, I should have to always watch my back because I have a vagina? That's ludicrous."

I go to speak, but hesitate, grinning instead, as I realize the fine line I'm treading. "So, let me finish listin' my three parts first, and then I'll answer questions. Deal?"

I reach out my hand, and after a moment, she reluctantly takes it, shaking it before she crosses her arms. She tilts her head and arches an eyebrow.

"Men are fuckin' pigs," I continue. "I'd be comfortable in sayin' sixty-five percent of the men in this world are hedonistic, selfish, inhumane assholes. Of that sixty-five percent, I'd set the meter at ninety-seven percent of those sick fucks would rape a woman, if they knew for a fact they could get away with it.

"Now, you take one of these assholes and you throw alcohol or drugs in the mix ... maybe there's a young drunk woman wanderin' home alone at two in the morning, maybe a woman who parked her new Benz at the back of the lot during an afternoon shoppin' session so it didn't get banged up, only to give the man who had been stalkin' her for months an opportunity to pounce. Both of those things have really happened, by the way.

"Women aren't the weaker sex. I'm not sayin' that. Not even close. I'm pretty confident in sayin' y'all got us in the smarts department in spades. But when it comes to size and strength, there's no argument. It's biological. Are there exceptions? Of course. Just like with anything else. But, overall, a stronger man, with mental health issues, comin' across the 'right' opportunity, has all the potential in the world to strike. It's up to the woman to even the odds."

"And how do you suppose we go about doing that?"

"Easy. A handgun, proper training, and the awareness and experience to know when to use it."

She smirks, tilting her head with a look that says, "Boy, do I got a surprise for you." Pulling out her wallet, she digs in, searching a bit and takes out a card. She hands it to me, and I discover it's a concealed carry permit, her gorgeous mug in the bottom right corner.

The next thing she pulls out of her purse is a small pistol, chrome, with pink grip plates. "You mean, like this?" she asks, holding the gun up, trigger finger in proper position along the side of the barrel.

"Well, shit. Color me impressed."

"Uh-huh." She smirks, returning her card and handgun to her clutch and settling it in her lap.

"I'm glad to know you know what you're doin'. Not quite sure why I doubted you."

"I'm not either." She smiles, shrugging. "Maybe next time you won't."

She hesitates a moment, the only sounds between us those

of a passing car here and there and the occasional drunken shout. She looks over at me with her innocent eyes, a tight smile on her face, and she asks, "How about we try being friends? Kind of start over? I don't want you out of my life. I've missed you. But there's just so much I need to figure out about myself before I get involved with anyone. And in the short time I've spent with you, I know I could fall for you."

"I knew it too," I mutter.

"And I don't want to be hurt. My heart is just too bruised right now to handle any more pain. I decided shortly after that stuff happened with you guys, that I was going to take some time for myself. No dating. No sex. Just me, my thoughts, and occasionally my vibrator." She grins, shrugging, before she adds, "Or often as fuck. Whatever."

"I get that, totally." I give her a small smile and pat her hand.

"I should probably go get Holly and head home. We've got a big test on Monday to study for."

"No problem at all," I say, standing. She stands too and I add, "It was so great seein' you tonight and gettin' to talk to you a little bit."

"It was great talking to you too, Bishop," she says, hugging me. "Maybe we can have a study date in the library or something soon."

"Anytime. You got my number." I crack a smile as she waves, flashing a smile of her own, then turning on her heel and walking away. I find myself wanting to chase after her but fighting the urge. I want to give her the time and space she needs, because the truth is, I could love that girl. I knew it from our first real date. And that feels like the last thing in the world I need right now.

I smoke one more cigarette before heading back to the basement to make my rounds. My bed is calling, and a good drunken jack-off session is now in order.

TWENTY-NINE

"Well, you look far more rested than you did the last time we met," Carleigh says, eyeing me as I position myself in the seat across from her.

"Yeah, finally done with that pledging crap." I let out a sigh of relief. "Can't tell you how good it feels not to have to clean up after a bunch of kids anymore."

"And more time for your studies?" She gives her brows a little wriggle and I chuckle.

"Yeah, we'll see. More sleep doesn't make the classes any less boring, unfortunately."

"Do you like *any* of your classes?"

"Not a single one." I laugh, shaking my head. "It's all those bullshit classes everyone has to take but nobody needs. I can't be bothered."

She shrugs. "Some people do use them. And I think it's beneficial to get a well-rounded education."

I nod, replying, "For sure, but I don't need some bullshit college administrator to decide what's important for me to learn. I'm never gonna use algebra again, or literature, or any of that shit. It's a waste of time and taxpayer dollars. We've got the internet these days. Before that, encyclopedias and books. I'm a self-educator. I believe in satisfying every curiosity. And I've learned a hell of a lot more on my own than I ever have in any classroom."

"Well, you're smarter than many. I'm the same way. But what do you have, one more semester of these classes before you get to your major?"

"Yeah, but what major?" I grin.

"That's your job to figure out." She quirks an eyebrow, her chin against her balled fist, her elbow atop the desk. She's gotten so much more relaxed with me in this space, her demeanor night and day from our first visit, though the sarcasm and repartee are still as strong as ever.

I catch my eyes trailing her neck, down toward her button-down dress shirt, the buttons undone just enough to see the slightest bit of cleavage.

Fuck, Bishop. Control yourself, man.

"I saw that," she says, giving her head a slight shake. "Keep your head in the game, Bishop. We've got a job to do in here."

I point back toward the door. "And what about out there?"

She rolls her eyes. Ignoring me, she says, "So, have you thought anymore about your major? Maybe getting into BSU's theatre program?"

I shrug. "I don't know if Crescent Falls, Pennsylvania is where I would want to be gettin' an acting degree from."

"So, you've thought about transferring then? Where to?"

"Yeah, I've thought about it. More so since we've been goin' on and on about it," I say, smirking. "I guess you're right about me havin' an opportunity here, bein' retired and all, to chase a dream. I had someone else mention the same thing to me ..." My voice trails as my thoughts roam to Ember, and how badly I miss our conversations. It's rare to find someone you can get so comfortably deep with in conversation. "I definitely can't see myself doin' a nine to five, not ever, and if I ever did find myself there, I don't think I'd last very long."

"Wait, can we backtrack a little bit here?" she asks, leaning back in her chair and crossing her arms.

"Which part?"

"The part about me being right." She flashes me a wide smile.

"Oh, we've got a boaster here." I nod, arching an eyebrow. "I'll remember that for the next time I'm right."

"Which would be when? Have you been yet?" She smiles again, a glimmer in her eye that makes me think she might be starting to dig me a little.

"So, we've got jokes today, Doc?"

"Oh, McKenzie, just call me Dave Chappelle."

"If you ever call me that again, I will straight up walk my happy ass out of here and straight to jail," I say, narrowing my eyes at her but grinning too. "And did you really just reference Dave Chappelle? You like him?"

"Why do you look so shocked? Of course, I like him. I'm a living, breathing human being after all, and he's a dang genius."

"You got that right. We ought to order some Chinese food sometime and watch Clayton Bigsby and Tyrone Biggums."

She shakes her head, a concerned look taking up her features. "Stop it," she scolds.

"Stop what?" I ask, acting innocently with two hands to my chest.

"You know exactly what you're doing."

"Askin' a beautiful woman out on a date? Yeah, I do." I grin, unsure of where this is coming from, but enjoying watching her squirm in her seat.

"I am old enough to be your mother. Give me a break."

"What does age have to do with anything? It sure doesn't bother me."

She sits back in her chair, shaking her head, her face turning red as she seems to be fighting a smile.

"Well now, back to the matter at hand, i.e. your *counseling session*." The smile breaks free, her face fully flush now. She clears her throat. "Okay, Lord, you just love getting off track, don't you?"

"Nope. I just like gettin' to know you. Hence, the date request."

"Listen, even though I know you're just pulling my strings here, you can't talk like that. I'm your doctor. The VA would not approve in the slightest. Even in a joking manner."

"I am absolutely *not* pullin' your strings, nor do I have any intention of lettin' you get in trouble for anything. Just a harmless 'get to know each other' date."

"Bishop." She shakes her head again, her face reading exasperation. I know I'm pushing my luck. "You're ridiculous. I'm forty-seven, for God's sake."

I shrug. "And?"

"You're twenty-five."

"Gonna be twenty-six soon," I reply, smirking. "And?"

"*And*, I'm your doctor. Now, stop getting us off track. We're here to talk about you."

"And that's why I wanna go out sometime. So, I can start askin' *you* questions."

She takes a deep breath, busying herself with some papers on the desk, then asks, "Bishop, how has the drinking been this week? Have you cut back as we talked about at our last session?"

I don't respond right away, smirking as I lean back in the chair and cross one leg over the other, resting my hands in my lap.

"Not too bad. I won't lie, I got shitfaced Friday night. That was our initiation into the fraternity. Other than that, I spent most of this week recovering," I say, chuckling.

"How much less would you say you're drinking these days as compared to before?"

"Significantly less. Before the fight, I was drinkin' damn near every night. Now, maybe a couple times a week."

"And how do you feel?"

"I smoke a lot more cigarettes." I laugh. "But, other than that, I think I'm doin' okay. It was a little easier when I was so busy with the pledging stuff. Now that I have all this free time, and I'm actually a brother, it gets a little harder to fight."

"And what about after this, when you aren't being monitored? Do you think you'll return to your previous consumption level?"

I take a moment, my eyes to the ceiling, as I think over her question. I look back toward her and shake my head. "No, I really don't think I will. Weed ... yeah, I won't lie about that either. I'm gonna be smokin' again the moment I'm able to, but the alcohol, I don't think so. I never really craved it before, not like I think an alcoholic would. It was more of a boredom thing. I think I just need to find more hobbies. Find more ways to busy myself. And probably hang out at the frat house less."

"You should probably focus a little more on that schoolwork too."

"Well, now you're soundin' like a mother."

She shrugs. "Somebody has to do it. I don't know what your grades look like, but if what you've shared in our sessions is any indication, you certainly need to be prioritizing a little bit better."

"Oh God, Carleigh. You're turnin' me on here."

She shoots me a glare, tilting her head and lifting her brows in that "Watch it!" kind of way, and she points her pen at me. "You want to pass this program, Mr. Bishop?"

"I'd really like that, yeah." I smirk.

"Then behave yourself when you're in that chair."

A smile spreads across my face. I motion toward the door again, giving my brows a little dance. "And out there?"

I'm met with that death stare of hers, but her eyes read something different. In them, I can see intrigue brimming.

THIRTY

It was earlier this week when I got the call from Jensen, now a Staff Sergeant in charge of his own squad down in Fort Campbell, as he was quick to inform me. I don't blame him for being proud. I'm proud of him too, but he used to be my soldier. Now, he's moving up the ranks quickly and that should've been me. Shit, I would've had my own platoon by now.

He said he'd be in town this weekend visiting family in Pittsburgh and would love to see me. While I'm excited to see him as well, I'm nervous. I've managed to put the Army in my rearview for the most part these days, but I know seeing him again will rehash some of those old memories, and it's going to hurt just as much as it's going to make me feel the warmth of nostalgia.

I haven't seen Jensen since my hospital days, when gauze was wrapped around my head and pain medication was pumping through my veins. My right eye just days removed, leaving an empty socket, the remaining eye staring off in the distance, unfocused, my mind lost in the pain of my present state. In the world of the medicated half-living.

Jensen was always a good soldier, a friend even, but he disappeared just like the rest of them after I was wounded. He moved on with his life and forgot about his good ol' one-eyed Sergeant.

Leaving his dinner invitation unrequited for a few days, I knew I would eventually cave and text him, agreeing to a meet-up. As much as I resent those who I served with, who so easily seemed to turn their backs on me when shit hit the fan, I still have an innate desire to see them, to feel that camaraderie once again, to tell those old stories. I feel a need to escape my present, the counseling session with Carleigh the other day stirring up a lot of shit, bringing about feelings and emotions I've stuffed down for a long time. Feelings of inadequacy and disillusionment. And a frequent desire to snuff out any sort of feeling with whatever substance I can get my eager little mitts on.

Those same feelings and emotions I carry with me on the ride to Pittsburgh, plans to meet Jensen at his hotel bar awaiting me. It's not that seeing him will bring up some of that resentment. I can push that aside. I worry more about seeing him, hearing about his current life in the military, and feeling that empty, aching loss I feel when I think about being there again, fighting for something. Feeling worthy. The same feeling I get when I watch military movies now. I just can't stand when those 'what-ifs' bombard my every thought. It's a hollow, fruitless feeling.

When I enter the hotel restaurant, I spot Jensen sitting at a corner booth where he said he'd be, though he didn't warn me about his unnatural growth.

"Jesus, dude. Are you eatin' the steroids one spoonful at a time?" I ask with a laugh as I approach.

Jensen's eyes brighten as he spots me, and he stands, pulling me in for a hug. "Holy hell, man. Look at you. The man, the myth, the legend himself," he says as we release hands and take a seat in the booth across from each other.

My eyes are still on the biceps that threaten to shred his shirt sleeves with the slightest flex. I motion toward them. "Seriously, Jensen. Did they stop checkin' for 'roids, or did you find some shit that goes undetected? How much have you even fuckin' gained?"

He shakes his head, waving me off. "Twenty pounds. And it's all natural, baby. I've just been hitting the gym harder the past couple years. Cleaned up my eating."

"Fuck you!" I shake my head, waving him off as well.

"No lie. Gym built."

"'Needle in the ass' built."

He flips me off. "Shut up, tell me what you've been up to, shit stain! How's freedom?"

"Not as good as that fightin' life you're still livin'."

"Shit. With my own squad, it's like I'm a babysitter now. My fun is in the rearview, man. It's all counseling and training bullshit these days." He laughs.

"I'd still rather be leadin' soldiers."

"Oh, come on. Civilian life can't be that bad."

"Not terrible," I respond. "It's just different. I miss what we all had over there."

He nods as if he understands, but he doesn't. He won't until his time comes to move on.

"I can't imagine, man," he says, shaking his head. "I think a lot about you. You and Barker."

"How is he, by the way? I haven't heard anything from him in a long time."

Jensen frowns, his focus shifting to the tabletop. He shakes his head. "Not looking good, brother. He deleted his Facebook a couple months ago. He hadn't been using it anyway. I've sent a few texts. Nothing. Last I heard, he was still down in San

Antonio going through treatment. Just had a kid. I don't know. I think there's some issues with his baby momma going on."

"His leg still that bad?"

"I don't think it's the leg anymore. At least wasn't the last I saw him. I think they finally grew the femur back. The burns were why he was still in rehab. Again, we're talking a year since I've heard or seen a thing."

I shake my head, my lips tight. "I hate that I lost contact with him. Or that he did with me. Or that I didn't try harder when he was still talkin' to me. I don't know."

Jensen shrugs. "What can you do? You can't help those who don't want the help."

He downs his drink and signals for the waiter.

"How many you got down already?"

He chuckles. "I'm visiting family. How many do you think?"

We both order drinks, and the waiter retrieves Jensen's empty glasses, three already. As he departs, Jensen nods toward my head. "What's with the scar? That wasn't there before, was it?" he asks, and I mindlessly feel for it, forgetting it was even there.

"Don't even ask. Long story," I respond, waving him off and dropping my hand back to my side.

"The usual hooligan behavior you always find yourself in, I imagine?"

I shrug. "I don't find it. *It* finds me."

"You remember that podunk bar in Georgia?"

I nod, chuckling. "How could I forget?"

"Do you think that dude has any feeling left in his face?" Jensen asks with a laugh.

I shake my head. "Not if my foot had anything to say about it."

"I still can't believe you did that."

Shrugging, I say, "Sometimes I feel bad about it, but then I remember he was hittin' a woman. Takes any pity away pretty quickly."

"I think about that shit all the time," he says, grinning, as the waiter returns with our double Jameson on the rocks, a drink we've always enjoyed together, one of which he's already gotten quite acquainted with tonight. The waiter then takes our food order before departing again.

Jensen lifts his glass, waiting for me. When I meet mine to his, he says, "To kicking the shit out of some random wife beater in the middle of *Deliverance* country."

I nod. "To makin' sure that same mouth he used to talk shit met the *goddamn* ground."

Jensen laughs. "And his fucking teeth left in your wake." He shakes his head and throws the glass back. I do the same, letting the memory of that night run through me.

I had just gotten my stripes, and I was out celebrating with my guys. We had decided on a trip to Fort Benning, Georgia from Bragg to meet up with some Infantry buddies of ours and stopped in the middle of nowhere for beers along the way. After leaving the fine establishment, all it took was seeing some redneck punk with his hands around his lady's throat to set me off.

I was raised in a household of abuse; I haven't put up with any of it as an adult.

He didn't have much time to respond before I was on top of him, slugging him in the face with everything I had. It baffled me that she was trying to pull me off of him, trying to protect the man who, moments ago, was choking the life out of her. I paid her no mind though. I hit him a good twenty times until my friends pulled me off, the dude's face left a bloodied tattered mess. It was when he looked up, spitting blood toward his girl, and he said, 'You'll get yours later, bitch,' that I really lost it. I broke free from my friends' grip and soccer kicked him in the face, so hard I could feel his nose crumple against my shoelaces.

As my friends pulled me toward the waiting car, the dude's girlfriend hitting me with every fist and curse word she could muster, I realized brainwashing isn't reserved for the movies. It happens every day to the strongest of people. Love is funny that way. It can be the greatest thing in the world ... or the worst. The heart makes its own choices sometimes, and they're not always good ones.

"For real though, was that from a fight?" Jensen asks, breaking me from my daze.

"Yeah, somethin' like that."

"What's that even mean?"

I narrow my eyes at him. "It means you know exactly how I fuckin' got this." I chuckle. "Why do you have to be so nosey?"

"You ever gonna retire those fists?" he asks.

I shrug. "When the good Lord stops puttin' deserving faces within arm's reach."

"I don't think that'll ever happen," he grunts, taking a sip of his whiskey.

"If the present is any tell, the future looks full of blood-stained knuckles."

He chuckles. "How have you been otherwise, Rocky?"

"I'm a civilian. What more is there to say?"

"You could've stayed in, right?"

I lean forward. "As a fuckin' radio operator? Maybe a fuckin' 88 Mike, drivin' trucks over there? I mean, fuck, Jensen, I'm an infantryman. There's no changin' that. I don't wanna do anything else."

"It would've at least given you direction."

"How much have you had to drink? Because no way would you talk to me like this three years ago."

"Three years ago, you were my squad leader."

"And what am I now?"

"My former squad leader. And current friend. At least I like to think so."

"You are, but I've earned your respect too."

"I'm just trying to help, boss. That's it. No disrespect meant. Not ever."

I hesitate, jostling the ice in my glass, and then say, "Okay, sorry. I'm bein' unfair. I think I just need to get on your level."

"Good luck." He laughs. "I've been going since two." After a moment of hesitation, he adds, "Hey. Thanks a lot for congratulating me on getting pinned last month, by the way." He passes me a facetious wink.

I narrow my eyes at him. "Jensen, how the hell was I even to know?"

"Well, if you had social media like the rest of us ..."

"Oh, c'mon. Enough of the frat guys give me shit about not havin' one of those things. I don't care to know when you fuckers are goin' to the gym, or foldin' laundry, or whatever the hell else people feel the need to announce to the world. Besides, I think havin' one of those things would get me in trouble. I'd certainly offend someone on a daily basis. My thoughts and opinions are best left to internally."

He chuckles. "Happens just about every day."

"Yeah, see?"

He scrutinizes me with his eyes. "So, you're in a fraternity now, huh?"

"Yeah, what of it?"

He shrugs, a smug look on his face I don't much like. "Aren't you a bit old for that?"

"I'm not even the oldest one in the frat," I argue, though I have to stifle a laugh as I think of the two, maybe three, others who are older than me out of a hundred and seven.

"Still. What the hell, man."

"I don't like this new you," I half-joke as the waiter brings us fresh drinks, setting silverware down for us as well.

He wriggles his eyebrows. "You love me."

I shake my head. "You always were my worst soldier," I say, chuckling, and he looks offended.

"Too far, fucker! Too damn far! You know Wilson gets that honor."

I laugh, thinking about Private Wilson, who spent about six ridiculous months with us before he was chaptered out. At one point, his weapon was tied to his wrist with 550 cord, so he was forced to take it everywhere with him. That was about the third time he'd lost his weapon. His night vision goggles followed soon after.

"Hey, Wilson had promise." I grin. "I think he would've made a fine squad leader."

"I think you're losing your fucking mind, man. That fucker could barely tie his own shoes."

I scan his features. "Well, fuck, at least he could grow a decent beard." I motion toward the patchy strawberry blond beard wrapping his chin. "What's this shit on your face?"

He runs his hands through the face pubes. "Hey, we can't all grow that shit like you do. The dudes from fucking ZZ Top envy your shit, motherfucker."

I stroke my beard, which has thickened substantially over the past few weeks, nodding. "True. But dude, your face looks like a taint right now. Like an old man's taint. You need to remedy that."

"Hey Bishop, I don't tell you how to suck your boyfriend's cock, don't tell me how to handle my beard."

"*Face taint*. Not beard. Face taint."

"Fuck you," he responds, laughing, and takes a sip of his drink. "You seeing anybody now? I know last time we talked, you were with that one girl."

"Chelsea."

"Yeah, her. How's that going?"

"She broke up with me in December. I think she just didn't wanna buy me a Christmas present."

We chuckle.

"Smart girl," he says. "Can't say I haven't pulled that move a time or two." Shrugging, he adds, "So, you're just raking up the pussy down there in Crescent Falls, huh?"

I narrow my eyes and tilt my head. "C'mon. You know me better than that. That's never been my style."

"Well, you had to have gotten your dick wet at least. Even you must have needs."

I shake my head. "You're an idiot."

"No, I'm a man."

"A married one, at that. Even my spotty sex life must eclipse yours. Does she even know what your cock looks like anymore?"

"You bet your ass she does."

"Could she pick it out of a cock lineup?"

"A cock lineup?" He thinks on this for a moment. "Yeah, I think I'm alright. I've got a unique bend to mine."

"So, you can piss around corners?"

"Just about."

"No way she picks your dick out of a cock lineup. I bet you guys are at the strictly celebratory sex stage now, huh? Countin' down to the once a year birthday blowjob?"

He shakes his head, but his face tells me at least part of what I said is true. It cracks my shit up. "That's what I thought," I add.

"Tracy still sucks my dick every Saturday, thank you very much," he says proudly, crossing his arms.

"The fact that it's even scheduled ..." I laugh, giving my head a quick shake. "How y'all doin', by the way? She get over all that shit that happened after you got back?"

He shrugs, his focus shifting toward the crowded bar. "Could be better. Could be worse."

"Three years later." I shake my head. "That's why you keep your married dick out of strange vagina, my friend."

He scoffs. "It's not my fault she went through my phone."

"No, but I imagine you didn't trip and fall into that waitress's pussy either." I grin as he rolls his eyes.

"I was drunk," he argues, though I'm not sure if he's trying to convince me or himself more.

"Well, that should hold up in court. 'Listen, Judge, I know I killed that guy, skinned him, and wore him as a Halloween costume, but I was drunk. So ... maybe a pass this time?'"

He chuckles. "At least she didn't divorce me and take me for everything I'm worth."

"Nope. Just mandated blowjobs and solo family trips from here on out." I wink at him and click my teeth.

He lets out a labored breath and says, "I'm beginning to think she only wanted to catch me in something, so she didn't have to come with me to visit my family anymore."

"I remember the stories you once told," I say, laughing, as the waiter approaches with our food. "I'm not so sure I blame her."

"Thank you." I nod toward the waiter, raising my glass. "Can we get two more, please?"

ONCE EMPTY PLATES have been pushed aside and a few more drinks have made their way down our gullets, I can feel the drunken buzz in my limbs, a tingle between my ears. Jensen is a swaying mess, still coherent, but beaming in his drunken state.

"I'm so glad you came to see me, man," he announces,

drawing my attention from the quickly filling restaurant and bar area.

"Of course. Anytime you're around this way, definitely hit me up."

"Same with you and Fort Campbell. There isn't a whole hell of a lot to do there, but Tracy and I could think of a few things to get into. No fighting though." He points a finger at me. "I know how you get around cherry privates, and there is a shit-load of them there. There's not a bar in town that's not crawling with them."

"Shit. It isn't much different than college."

"Says the guy who decided to join a frat."

I chuckle, nodding. "You got me there. I don't know what the fuck I was supposed to do though."

"What about their student veteran organization?"

I shrug. "I emailed them. I didn't get a good vibe from the guy I talked to, some Coast Guard prick. I looked at their website, and ..." I hesitate, shrugging again. "Just looked like a bunch of fuckin' wannabes."

He laughs, taking a drink of his Jameson. "You crack my shit up, man," he says, his shaky eyes meeting mine.

"And why is that, Jensen?"

"Never giving much of anything a chance." He puts a hand up defensively, probably noticing the heavy scrunch in my brows. "And I mean that endearingly."

"How so? Do tell."

"Who am I to judge anybody? It's endearing because everyone has their own unique quirks and qualities. One of yours is being suspicious of everyone and everything."

"It seems to work for me. I have some good friends. Pretty good life. I take chances when those chances present decent outcomes."

"Good friends? Yeah, but how many are close?"

"Not many live near me."

"No, not proximity close. I mean, close to your heart."

"What kind of Lifetime shit are you sayin'?" I ask with a chuckle.

"I'm saying, how many of your friends do you keep up with? Share your life with? Get close to? When's the last time we talked before this week? And you were about to back out somehow, I know it. It's why you didn't confirm right away. You had to keep a foot out the door, just in case."

I let out a nervous laugh, my focus shifting away from him as I shake my head. "No. I wanted to. I just wasn't sure what I was gonna do this weekend. Was thinkin' about a lake trip."

He nods, his look borderline condescending. "Uh huh."

"Oh, fuck you, Jensen," I scold in a joking tone. "You better drop this high and mighty routine. Don't let me remind you about your first few months in the Army, you dumb shit."

He laughs. "What the fuck does my DUI have to do with anything?"

"It isn't the DUI I'm thinkin' of, but the tears shed after."

A shade of red takes over his face. He averts his eyes to the tabletop. "I was wasted, you asshole."

"'Sergeant, I don't wanna go back home. Please help me!'" I laugh, shaking my head at the memory of this man when he was just a boy, brand spanking new in the Army and drunker than can be at the MP station, bawling his eyes out. I continue, "Don't you even start poutin'! I've told you this before, you will get shit for that until the day they cover me in dirt."

As he handles his whiskey glass, a look of resignation takes up his features. "Even though you're a fucking dick for bringing that shit up again, I'll never forget that's when I looked at you and said, 'That's who I aspire to be when I'm an NCO. *That's* a leader.'"

My eyes fall to my glass, shoulders dropping slightly. I get the uneasy, sinking feeling I always get when someone compliments me. I've never taken them well. Lucky for me, Jensen fills the silence. "When you took me aside to talk to me ... you remember that?"

I nod, sipping some whiskey.

"You weren't even my squad leader then. And my own squad leader—Sergeant Isaac—you remember that asshat?"

I nod again, chuckling.

"He treated me like I just killed his children and fucked his wife in front of him. Like, fuck, dude, I know I messed up, but get the fuck out of my asshole about it. The Article 15 was bad enough. I didn't deserve his contempt."

I shrug. "At the end of the day, it's why you ended up in my squad. And I'm damn proud of your turnaround."

"It's because of you, and that day. You said to me, 'We all make mistakes. We all fuck up. This is not a wall, it's a speed bump.' You told me to pick my head up, to stop feeling sorry for myself, and to drive the fuck on."

"Nothin' special about those words, Jensen. But I'm glad they helped."

"They were special to me. It proved to me that I wasn't done yet, that it was just a hiccup."

"And look where you are now."

"I love you, Bishop. Man, really." He lifts his glass, hands shaking, his glossy eyes meeting mine. "And I mean that nohomo obviously," he adds.

I clink my glass against his. "You sound like a fuckin' millennial sayin' that 'no homo' shit. Can't we men just accept that we feel emotions too without thinking it automatically changes our sexual orientation? I mean, c'mon."

"Yeah, yeah. You know the infantry."

As I take a drink, I give him an agreeing nod.

"Holy shit," Jensen mutters, his glass still held in the air, his focus shifted toward the noisy bar behind me. "Brooo."

I look back to see what's caught his eye, but spot nothing out of the ordinary. There are certainly more people crowding around the bar now, and what started out as a quaint scene has quickly turned into more of a nightclub atmosphere.

Turning back toward him, I ask, "What?"

"You see those chicks? Fuck, I love cougars, man." His eyes are still glued on the bar, his mouth slack.

I turn back around reluctantly. "Aren't you married?" I ask, scanning the crowd for these 'cougars.'

"Doesn't mean I can't look," he says as I spot the pack, a couple of them with big fake tits, all of them in incredible shape; their nails are done, their hair is perfect, and their dresses are tight. Two of them wear leopard print.

I nod. "Yeah, pretty go—" My words are abruptly snuffed out when my eyes land on Carleigh in a figure-complementing maroon slip dress that works well with her dark black free flowing hair. I turn back toward Jensen and try and fight the look of surprise from my features, but to no avail.

He studies me. "What?" he asks, pointing a finger at me. "What did you see?"

"Nothin'. What are you talkin' about?"

"Your face. You look like you just saw a ghost."

I shake my head, pretending to not have a clue what he's talking about. "Nope. Just lookin' at the cougars." I take a sip of whiskey and then shake it in front of him. "Another drink?"

"You know someone over there, don't you?" he asks, though it comes out more like a statement.

I take another nervous drink before giving him a quick shake of my head. "Sure don't, buddy. I think you're just drunk."

He tilts his head. "Oh, I'm absolutely shit-canned, but I know how to read faces, and that face you just made was one of recognition. Now, tell me who you just saw before I go over there and ask them all if they know you."

"You wouldn't."

He would.

He shrugs. "I gave you another option."

I sigh, shaking my head as I feel resignation take hold. "My therapist is over there."

"Therapist?" His eyes shoot over my shoulder and toward the bar. "Which one?"

I wave a hand in front of his face. "Hey, fuckstick, it doesn't matter. Let's just get another drink."

"No, tell me, or I will go over there searching for her." He has wild eyes as he scans the bar area. "Is it one of the cougars? Tell me it's one of the cougars."

Ignoring his question, I say, "They'd probably end up tacklin' you, thinkin' you're some nut job." I laugh.

"Which one is it?" he asks, his eyes still on the bar. "Please tell me it's one of the cougars."

"Maroon dress. Black hair."

His eyes go wide, mouth slack. "Damn, bro! You tell *her* all your dirty little secrets?"

I put my fingers to his chin and force his eyes away from them and to me. "Can you stop fuckin' starin'? They're for real gonna think you're a nut job."

"Let's get them over here, bro."

I shake my head firmly. "*No*, we are not invitin' my fuckin' therapist to join us drinkin'."

"But Bishop, her friends are hot! And *her*, well fuck, how do you not just think about fucking her every session?"

I laugh, rolling my eyes and shaking my head, knowing full well I've spent plenty of time in that chair across from her, thinking about what it would be like to have my way with her, and to watch her have her way with me. It's an invasive thought I find myself fighting often. Jeans are a requirement for sessions now. I learned that the hard way my second session when my basketball shorts were little protection against the stiffy I was sporting by the time the session was over.

"You're out of your fuckin' mind, Jensen. Stop fuckin' lookin' over there. I'm serious."

"I have to go to the bathroom," he says, standing with a drunken grin on his face.

I put a hand up to stop him. "Jensen, *no!* Don't you dare talk to her."

He continues as if I've said nothing, so I grab his shirt sleeve and yank him back toward me. He almost trips over his own drunken feet.

"Hey!" he yelps. "You fucker." His eyes bounce around before they eventually find mine.

"You cannot say a word to her." I put a pointer in his face, my other hand still holding on to his sleeve. "Not a word, Jensen!" I fight the grin from forming on my lips as I look at his pathetically twisted face. It's as if he's battling a serious case of dysentery.

"I won't. I won't." He puts his hand up as he passes me a drunken smile and waves two fingers. "Scout's honor. I just have to poop."

"I swear, I will hurt you," I say, letting him go and returning to my seat. I narrow my eyes at him. That stupid grin tells me he hasn't listened to a goddamn word I've said as he shuffles his way toward the restroom. I watch to make sure he doesn't stray off course. He doesn't. And that he makes it to the bathroom in one piece. He does ... just barely.

It's been thirty minutes since Jensen left. Thirty-two minutes and sixteen seconds, if I'm being precise.

I've looked over my shoulder for him frequently, but never spotted him. I'm just hoping he's still in the bathroom shitting his brains out and hasn't pulled Carleigh somewhere without me noticing to tell her my life fucking story. He's so drunk, I wouldn't put it past him. After a few minutes, I switch sides of the booth so I can watch the front door, bar, and bathroom area better, without staring over my shoulder like a weirdo. Jensen is nowhere to be seen. I realize Carleigh has disappeared too at some point when my back was still turned.

I scan the bar area, my drink in hand and the ice quickly diluting the whiskey. I've paid the glass no mind, nor the phone in my pocket, which I could've used to text him had he not left his own at the table. Instead, when I do look at it, I see only time, and how much longer it's been since he's left.

Brief thoughts cross my mind that lead me to believe he may be simply passed out on the toilet, and that's the only thing keeping me seated and my mind from completely spiraling. Well, that, and the fact that I'd prefer not to look like a total creep searching for them if she's just using the restroom. If he *is* still on the shitter, and I happen to run into Carleigh now, as drunk as I am, I'm sure to say or do something offensive.

It's when I'm a second from exiting my booth, having grown weary from the waiting, that I'm stopped in my tracks, slack-jawed and nauseous.

Jensen walks in little zig-zags from the front door of the hotel, Carleigh on his arm and laughing at his antics. They're coming right for me, but their attention is on each other, so they don't see the panic in my features.

When she looks up and smiles as they near, I fight the surprise from my face, mouthing, "Sorry," as I nod toward Jensen. She shakes her head and waves me off as they approach.

Jensen spots me and smiles. "Bishop! Look who I found!" He puts his hands up as if he's presenting Carleigh to me. I force a chuckle, my insides burning, anxiety barging its ugly head in.

"Well, Jensen, appreciate you disappearin' for thirty minutes, first of all ..." I let my words linger as I stand, putting my hand out for Carleigh. "Carleigh, good to see you. I see you've met my *dear friend*, Jensen." I say the words with all the sarcasm I can muster as I shake her hand, my eyes shooting to Jensen, who has a wide, wasted smile on his face and a far-off gaze.

He hesitates for a moment as I let her hand go. His eyes find mine, and he says, "Did you see I got Carleigh for you?" while presenting her again like he's Vanna fucking White.

"Yes, Jensen. I just shook her hand actually ... about two seconds ago ... right in front of your face." I point to the space between Carleigh and me. "*Right here.*"

Jensen looks at my finger, then at me, and then at Carleigh, before he motions toward the booth. "Have a seat, Hun!"

She hesitates, looking at me as if she's awaiting my go-ahead.

I nod slightly, a tight smile on my face. I worry what he must have already told her.

He takes a seat beside her, his empty glass banging hard against the tabletop. Looking toward the glass, he chuckles and then shrugs. "Oops." Taking a drink from his drink-less glass, his eyes roam over to Carleigh. He motions toward her with his head. "You see I found Carleigh?" he asks, lowering the glass back to the table, luckily, without the bang this time.

"I'd prefer a night without more side eye from the tables next to us." I lift my brows, my focus on Carleigh. "You see what happens when men get married and have their first free night out in a year?"

She laughs. "I already know all about that," she says with a look of guilt.

"Hey!" Jensen barks, his brows scrunching together. He peers at me. "I went out just last month for your information. Might've even been three weeks ago."

"Wow, man. Slow down. I mean, you're like twenty-four, twenty-five? It's time you hang up your fun boots and start *really* applying yourself." I pass him an exaggerated thumbs up.

He laughs. "But still. Not once a year. Tracy lets me go out every couple weeks. And she doesn't even text me that much when I'm with the guys!" He holds up his phone, showing me his recent notifications.

"Jensen," I say between laughs. "Do you have any fuckin' clue how many times your woman has texted you?"

"Huh?" Jensen's lip curls back, his brows furrowing, his drunken eyes flitting to the ceiling. "Texted who?" His eyes fall back on me.

I bust out laughing, and Carleigh does too, as I motion toward his phone. "Check your notifications, my friend. I get the funny feelin' you're completely fucked."

He checks his phone, scans it, and it takes a moment, but before long, his jaw drops, his eyes going wide. It's then I know he sees all the text and call notifications waiting for him on his phone, her name stacked one atop the other. He races to unlock his phone and begins reading them, a frantic look in his eye.

I just smile, my eyes trailing from Jensen to Carleigh. "So, I have to give you an open apology for whatever he may have said or done in his time alone with you."

"I did nothing!" Jensen announces, his eyes still on the phone.

"He really didn't," she responds, waving me off with a smile. "He just talked a lot about you and the friendship you two share. It was endearing."

"I'll probably have to remind him of this particular experience tomorrow." I glare at Jensen. "I really wasn't trying to disturb your night."

She shakes her head. "My friends all just left anyway. I wasn't really ready to go, and then Jensen here asked me to smoke." She motions to him as he takes another fruitless drink. "I may have needed one after the night I had." She shrugs.

I shoot Jensen a scowl. "You fuckin' smoked and didn't come tell me? You know I smoke, and you know I haven't had one since I got here."

He just grins, his finger still working the cell phone screen.

"I could use another one," Carleigh says, shrugging.

"Yeah!" Jensen adds, putting a pointer finger in the air.

As I stand, I wave him off and shake my head. "No fuckin' way. You smoked without me, we're smokin' without you. You sit your happy ass right there, call your damn wife, and grab us more drinks."

He looks toward the drinks and then back up at us with a frown on his face. He crosses his arms and leans back into the cushion. "Fine!" he says, sighing heavily.

"Great," I say, a wide faux smile on my face as I put a hand out for her. She takes it, standing from the booth, and then follows me to the front door.

Once we're outside, I pull two cigarettes out, claiming our spot around the smoke pit. I hold one out for her.

"I hope Reds are okay," I say as she's about to take it.

She stops in her tracks, her hand inches away from the cigarette when she says, "Reds, huh?" She smacks her lips, her face scrunching with displeasure as she finally takes it from me and eyes it.

I pop the other between my lips and light it, taking a deep puff as I wait to light hers.

She still eyes the cigarette in her hand cautiously, finally slipping it in her mouth and waiting for the spark.

I light her cigarette, eyes on hers as the Zippo flame dances ... and then she's puffing as I pocket the lighter before a cough erupts. Then another, and another. She holds the smoking cigarette away from her as she vampire coughs with the other arm.

Taking pleasant puffs from my own cigarette, I smile through the smoke, setting a hand to her back and patting it lightly. "You okay?"

"Yeah," she says weakly, shaking her head. "It's been a while since I smoked last. I mean, before the one Jensen gave me."

"And before that?"

"Twelve years."

"Damn!"

"Yeah, it was hard quitting. I shouldn't even be smoking this one." She eyes the cigarette between her fingers again, studying it and the smoke that dances from its smoldering tip.

"Well, you get no more from me then. Ever. I can't be an accomplice."

She rolls her eyes, and it's then I notice the drunken glint to them. "Shut up. If I don't get one from you, I'll just bum one from my friend Allison. She still smokes. Even though they're Camels." She grimaces with disgust.

I chuckle, reminding her, "Your friends aren't here anymore, love."

She looks around for a second, turning and snapping her fingers when she says, "Oh yeah. Shit. Well, I'll get another one from your friend then."

"Fair enough. His girly cigarettes probably go down smoother anyhow."

As if proving her adequacy, she takes an extra-long puff and holds the smoke in her lungs for a moment. Her forehead dances, as if she's fighting off a coughing fit. She lets the smoke out of her mouth in little Os directed right toward my face.

"Talented," I say, nodding, as I track the little O's from creation to dissipation.

"I get it from my momma," she says, crossing her arms and pursing her lips like a fucking early nineties rapper.

"Do you really?"

She shakes her head, eyes wide as she takes another drag. Letting the smoke out, she says, "Lord, no. My mom never knew I smoked. She hated the stuff."

"You know what's crazy, Carleigh?" I ask, taking a pull from my cigarette as her beautiful eyes meet mine.

"What?"

"I've shared so much with you already and I still know so little about you."

She shrugs. "It's my job. And it's not about me. It's about you, Bishop."

"Is it wrong of me to want more than that ... more than just a doctor-patient relationship?"

The surprise in her features and lack of response sends a jolt of burning anxiety through me. I wouldn't have been so forward without the alcohol, and at this point, as her tongue is tied and mine serves as a placemat for my foot, I'm left to stutter my way through the silence.

"Ugh, I mean. Fuck." I give up when the words just won't come. Her eyes are on the concrete now. The embers of her cigarette are moments away from meeting the filter.

"It's okay." She waves me off, taking a long puff and killing the rest of her cigarette. As she lets out a smoky breath, her eyes trail to mine. She looks hesitant, nervous, as she bites her lip, dabbing the cigarette out in the ashtray.

"You're just so fuckin' gorgeous," I blurt, whiskey-produced words, with no other help needed. Taking a deep breath, I keep my eyes away from her, though I can see her staring at me through my peripheral. I can see the white of her teeth too, as her mouth hangs open.

"Bishop ..." Her voices cuts through the empty silence between us.

My cigarette is burnt out but still clutched between my fingers. "No, I get it. I'm really not trying to be inappropriate."

"I know. I know that," she says, setting a hand on my arm. "It is a huge compliment. It's just ... with our professional relationship, I think it's best to make smart decisions. Even drinking with you tonight was too far. I shouldn't have come over. I kept telling myself not to in my head, but your friend there, can be quite ... uh, convincing."

I nod, cracking up. "Which you can imagine was just really great for my early twenties."

She laughs. "I can only imagine." Out of nowhere, a look of seriousness crosses her features and she takes a deep, worried breath. "Listen, Bishop, I'm sorry you've seen me like this. You weren't supposed to."

"Please! If anything, it helps. It makes you feel a little more human."

She smiles. "Last time I checked, I wasn't an android."

"So, since I am considerably more drunk than you are, perhaps you can forgive me for the conversation I'm about to trigger, but ... is me bein' your patient the only thing keepin' you from talkin' to me about this further? Our 'professional relationship' as you put it."

She cocks her head, an eyebrow arched. "First off" —she puts a pointer in the air— "talking to you about what?"

I take a step forward, tilting my head slightly. "About how completely and ridiculously attracted to you I am."

A nervous laugh escapes her mouth and she puts up both

hands to halt it, to no avail. She shakes her head with a wrinkle in her brow. "You *definitely* can't talk like that."

"If you answer the question, I never will again."

She hesitates for a moment, tapping a pointer against her chin as she thinks, before she asks, "Wait, can you repeat the question?"

"If it weren't for me bein' your patient, would you let me kiss you right now?"

She takes a step back with a slight look of shock. Not an uncomfortable one, not as if she's trying to get away, but as if she's worried about how close she already is ... about what she might do.

"Bishop. We really can't talk like this. We still have so many sessions left." She finally notices the burnt-out filter between her fingers and tosses it into the ashtray, reminding me I have to do the same.

"I'm just speakin' hypothetically."

"Speaking realistically," she says, shrugging. "I could be your mother, Bishop. I'm an old lady. So, regardless of doctor-patient relations, there *are* other reasons nothing could ever happen between us."

I take a step forward, the alcohol running my game. I'm so reserved normally, but if you get an adequate amount of Jameson in me, I'm the smoothest motherfucker you've ever seen.

"You think your age bothers me? It doesn't. Does it bother you?"

She looks around nervously, biting her lip again as she searches for the words. "Bishop, you have to stop. It is such a mistake being here. I should have left the moment your friend approached me."

"What did he say to you, by the way? He was gone a long time."

She shakes her head. "I'm sorry, Bishop. He was drunk."

"Sorry for what?"

"He shared a lot with me. A whole lot. Some things I would've liked to have discovered on my own ... during our sessions. I tried to stop him, but he wouldn't. Not until I told him we should get back inside." She looks toward the front door. "Speaking of which, we should probably go back in. Your friend may be naked and dancing around in there by now."

"I wouldn't doubt it."

We laugh until the seriousness of our conversation comes back into view.

"So ... what did he tell you?"

"He told me he was here visiting family. That you guys served together." She smiles. "He has a lot of admiration and respect for you."

"He's a good kid. Did he say anything else?"

She bites her bottom lip, and she has no clue how her affinity for it drives me to realms of desire I'm not quite comfortable with.

"I can see it in your face. Just tell me."

She hesitates, her eyes flitting away from mine as she seems to search for the words. After a few long moments, she says, "He told me about the explosion."

I scoff, shaking my head. I pull my pack of cigarettes out and put another between my lips. After offering one up to Carleigh, and she declines, I pocket the pack and light the smoke, taking one nervous drag after another before finally asking, "What about it?"

"How much of it do you remember?"

"I have two different recollections. Now, what did he tell you?"

"What do you mean 'two different recollections'?"

I take a puff and shake my head as I scoff the smoke out. "Is this a therapy session, Doc?"

"I don't know, McKenzie." She puts her hands on her hips. "I thought honesty was your thing tonight. So, let's use that."

"I don't want to feel like every time I'm with you, it's clinical ... so you can study me."

"I'm your therapist. What other kind of situation would you expect between us?"

"Somethin' natural. A situation where we are both open and honest about this mutual attraction."

"Bishop, I—"

I put a hand up. "No, I know you're gonna say there's no attraction from your end, but I know, and you know, it'd be a lie."

She's about to say something but hesitates, taking a deep breath.

"Carleigh, I find you irresistible. Your age? What the hell does that mean when we're talkin' about real human connection? Hell, what does it mean when you don't even look it?"

"Bishop ..."

"Tell me now, Carleigh, that you haven't ever thought about kissin' me. Not once. Tell me you haven't thought about what it would be like, on a proper date, and not stuck in a tiny little office and in the confines of a doctor-patient relationship. Tell me now, and I will go say goodbye to my friend, I'll head home, and put on some *King of Queens*. And I'll drink a beer since I can't smoke a joint."

She laughs, shaking her head.

"And I'll continue wishin' I could watch it with you, and wonderin' what it would be like to ask you questions, to get to know *you*, to hear *your* truths. I think about that a lot."

She scoffs, but it's followed immediately by a dimple-inducing smile. Shaking her head, she says, "Bishop. You must stop. I'm your doctor."

"Answer my question though. If you weren't my doctor ..."

"Yes, I've thought about what it would be like to kiss you!" she says, letting out an exasperated breath.

I smile. "That's all I needed to hear." I take a step forward, and she takes a step back. I place a hand on her elbow and she bites her lip.

"Oh, Bishop," she mutters.

I kiss her before she can say another word, and much to my surprise, she kisses me back. Hard. Her lips dance with my own, the softness of them electrifying. Pulling her into me, I cradle her cheek with one hand, simultaneously backing her against the brick wall. I can hear people exiting the front door behind us, but I pay them no mind. I'm too preoccupied with this sexy fucking cougar in my arms and her perfect, delicate lips working so effortlessly with my own.

I pull back from her and she lets out a slow breath, her eyes still closed.

"Lord ..." she whispers.

"I've wanted that since the day I met you," I respond, shaking my head, lifting her chin with two fingers to bring her eyes to mine. She slowly draws her eyelids open, a look of contentment in her features.

"This is so, so bad," she says, though there's a smile on her face. "So bad."

I kiss her again, ignoring her words and concern, instead relishing in the feeling of complete desire that wraps me up like a blanket.

As our lips part, I say, "Can we go back in and get another drink? I think it's time I started gettin' to know you."

She looks worried. "Oh boy, I don't think I like the sound of that."

"Come on, Ms. Jacobs." I wrap an arm around her shoulders and lead her toward the door. "Let Doctor Bishop get a peek inside that head of yours."

My lips curl into a smile as she rolls her eyes.

As we make our way inside, I spot Jensen staggering toward us. He puts up a hand. "I didn't think you guys were coming back," he says, stopping just before us, a wide, drunken smile on his face.

"I'm not that much of a dick," I respond. "You wanna grab another drink?"

He shakes his head stiffly, putting his bottom lip out. "Not a fucking chance. I'm taking my happy ass to bed. The wife's pissed. I need to go give her a call." He points toward the elevators before his eyes fall on Carleigh. He puts his hand out and she takes it. He rests his other on top of hers. "My dear," he says, locking eyes with her, "it was so great talking with you tonight. Remember what I said." He winks and motions toward me without much stealth. "Treat my boy right."

She flashes a tight smile as he winks at her. "Okay, Robert. Thank you."

He lets go of her hand, smiling, as he turns his attention to me.

I glare as he puts his hand out for mine. Grabbing it, I bring him in and whisper, "I'm gonna fuckin' kill you," before letting him go.

He just laughs, waving me off before he turns on his heel and heads toward the elevators. "Text me if you want to crash here tonight, Bish," he says over his shoulder.

"Yeah, I probably will, buddy."

He waves a hand in the air as he stumbles toward the elevator bay.

I look toward Carleigh. "You know you're gonna have to tell me what the hell he told you about the explosion and why you asked me what I remember about it, right?" I say, narrowing my eyes at her.

She laughs, motioning toward the bar. "A drink first?"

I nod, and she leads me to the only open space at the cluttered bar.

She orders two shots of Fireball as my eyes analyze her features. She seems to hold something new she hadn't held when we last spoke. As she turns, catching me staring, she smiles self-consciously, shrugging as her eyes meet the floor.

"What?" she asks softly.

"I'm just really curious what y'all discussed," I respond, and wrinkles of concern take up her forehead.

"Why's it such a big deal?"

"I could ask you the same thing."

She looks me dead in the eye, and I smile.

"Because I haven't seen that little shit in years," I say. "He used to be *my* soldier, and I'm wonderin' what the hell he told the woman I'm interested in."

Her cheeks go red and her eyes fall to the shots the bartender sets down in front of us. "Bishop ..."

"What, Carleigh?"

"We can't."

"We should."

"Regardless ... we can't."

I blindly grab the shot, lifting it to my lips with my eyes still on hers. "What did he tell you, Carleigh?" I ask, and then down the whiskey.

"A lot about you as his squad leader. Like I said, he has a lot of respect for you. And ..." Her voice trails off, her eyes on the shot as she brings it to her lips and throws it back.

"And?"

"And, just, other stuff."

"Carleigh!"

"I can't believe you're trying to make me tell you what your incredibly drunk friend

talked to me about. Do you know how out of his mind he was?" She shrugs, a wary look in her eye. "I mean, really, Bishop, he was so messed up. What he said doesn't matter."

"It matters because you're my therapist, and what you hear about me from outside sources may affect the way you treat me. I deserve to know."

She grins, a hand meeting her mouth. "Funny how *now* I'm your therapist, but twenty minutes ago ..."

Got me there.

"I'm not gonna be mad at him. I just wanna know what you know, for no other reason than I won't sleep tonight if I don't. So, for fuck's sake, tell me."

She lets out a heavy sigh, before she says, "He told me about you carrying your guys out of there."

I take a deep breath, nodding, though I don't know why. Finally, I say, "He was the only motherfucker to escape relatively unscathed, though the shrapnel in his leg didn't make him too effective at helping to carry people." I force a laugh.

She nods, frowning in concern. "Yeah, I think he holds on to a lot of that still. He carries it with him."

I laugh. "You think that after talkin' to him for thirty minutes?"

Her face remains unchanged as she nods. "Yeah, I'm a therapist, after all."

"Well, I don't remember any of it." I shrug. "And it did no fuckin' good anyway."

She sets a hand on my shoulder. "God, Bishop, I don't want tonight to feel like a therapy session. I hadn't in a million years anticipated seeing you tonight, but I have to at least say this. You *must* stop punishing yourself for all of this. You did everything you could. *Everything.* You carried two of them out, for God's sake ... blinded in one eye with shrapnel in your face. I mean, Bishop, do you understand what that takes?"

"They didn't survive," I respond, my voice shaking, my heart pounding in my chest. I lean an elbow against the bar and drop my head in my palm, letting out a deep exhale.

She cups a hand around my elbow and leans in. "I'm sorry," she mutters. "I didn't mean to upset you."

I wave her off, forcing a tight smile. "I asked you. It's my fault." I hesitate for a moment before adding, "No, it's not my fault. It's that drunk bastard's fault." I point toward the elevator bay.

"I'm glad he told me though. Would you ever have?"

"Told you about the explosion?"

"No, I can read your files for that. I mean, what happened after it went off."

"I don't talk about it often. To me, it's fiction." I motion toward the incoming bartender. "Another drink?"

"Yeah, Grey Goose and tonic, wedge of lime, please," she orders.

"And I'll take a double Jameson on the rocks."

As he departs, she smiles, saying, "I definitely shouldn't be here drinking with you." She puts a hand to her forehead. "For the love of God, I'm your substance abuse counselor."

Her tone begins to worry me. "Hey, do you want me to stop drinkin'? I can. I'd choose hangin' out with you over alcohol any day."

She turns red, grinning. "No, have your drink. I won't make you choose. But I should be getting home here in a few minutes. I need to get some sleep, and I don't need one of my friends stumbling back in here, asking questions."

"Why not go somewhere else? Somewhere with dark corners made for kissing," I say, cocking my head.

She laughs, waving me off. "You stop. I really do need to get some sleep. And why do I get the feeling you have effectively derailed our earlier conversation?" She smirks.

"I've seen your diplomas. You're quite the brain. I had no doubt you'd catch me. Shall we continue?"

"Sure you don't mind?"

I nod my head as the waiter sets our drinks down in front of us. I throw some cash down and grab mine, shaking the ice around to properly chill the whiskey.

"So, if Jensen was the only one with recollection of what happened, he's the only one who can really paint the picture. It's not just a story, Bishop. It's fact. And you have the Silver Star to prove it." She takes a sip of her drink.

"He told you about that?"

"Yeah, but I saw it in your retirement paperwork too."

"Oh yeah."

"I know they don't just give that V for Valor away for nothing."

"I guess I just don't really credit myself for anything because I don't remember any of it. It wasn't a conscious decision to carry them out."

"I think that's what makes it even more special. You were running on instinct, and instinct alone. And your instinct said to carry your men to safety, no matter the cost."

"Instinct and a heavy dose of shock-induced adrenaline." I laugh, taking a drink.

"Well, yeah. Thank God for that, too. You pulled your brothers out, Bishop, and regardless of what happened next, they received proper honors, a proper burial, and closure for their families. Who knows what would've happened had you not gotten them out of there when you did."

I shrug, taking a nervous sip of the whiskey. I don't mean to shut down when the emotions start to overwhelm me, but in my current state of inebriation, it's that much harder to keep the pain from my features.

"Hey," she says, putting a hand on my cheek and smiling. The compassion in her eyes and the authenticity behind her smile warms me. "Don't you even think another second about it. Let's have some fun, huh? Wasn't it your turn to play doctor?"

I tilt my head, eyeing her with a grin. "I don't think that was supposed to turn me on as much as it did."

She scoffs, laughing as she bats a hand at my chest. "You are capital T, trouble, Sergeant Bishop. Just plain *trouble*." She throws her drink back and then eyes the glass. "And I think that was my cue." She takes down the rest of her drink and settles the glass on the bar top.

I place a hand on her elbow. "No, not yet! It's still so early. Playin' doctor, remember? I have so many questions still."

She chuckles. "When's the last time you checked the time? Maybe, we can grab dinner or something soon?"

"Before our next session?"

"I'll try! I promise." She looks around for a moment before kissing me. It makes my body rage with desire.

She separates from me, her eyes closed, a smile on her face. Opening her eyes slowly, she says, "It's been a fantastic night, Bishop."

"An unforgettable one." I give her one last peck before she makes her way to the door, leaving me with a racing heart, a hard dick, and a yearning for her unlike anything I ever remember feeling.

I head up to Jensen's room with a grin on my face as the night plays out in my head. I think about what it'll be like with her for the first time, cradling that thick ass with one hand, the other grasping her long braided ponytail like a rein, playing 'now you see me, now you don't' with my thick cock and her wet pussy. And then ... letting her take control.

THIRTY-ONE

"Wish I would've heard from you this week," I say, flashing a tight smile as I analyze the wrinkles in her forehead, the sadness in her eyes.

"Bishop ..." Carleigh lets out a heavy breath. Her eyes still stray from my own, as if she feels guilty of something. "I want to say so much, it's just ... it's hard." She bites her bottom lip, dropping her head into her hands. She lets out a groan.

"You're a therapist. Aren't you supposed to be good at this whole talkin' thing?"

I smirk.

She forces a smile, but the dread remains in her eyes. "What happened, Bishop, it shouldn't have. It was a mistake," she says in a hushed tone.

The words strike me in the chest like a brand, but I fight the disappointment from my face. "A mistake? What, gettin' to know each other?" I wave my hand around the room. "Not caught up in this goddamn white ass room?"

"Bishop ..."

"I just thought it was different. It seemed different." There's a little whine to my tone and it makes my skin crawl. I lean back in my chair to look a little more at ease, but the tension in my shoulders remains. "It felt different."

"I told you at the start of the night that I just couldn't do this. I'm your therapist. We have too many sessions left. And God, Bishop, I'm forty-seven years old. How old are you again?"

"You know the answer to that. So ..." I respond, my jaw clinching as the anxiety rolls over me like a storm, my face red hot.

"So, it's a big difference! And I'm your doctor," she repeats, as if that'll change the fact that I find this woman irresistible—even more so now that her brow is all furrowed and her face is flustered.

The tangled feelings of insecurity and desire confuse me. Overwhelm me. "You can't deny what we both felt that night in each other's arms, kissing. It was different. It was electric."

She looks nervous, her eyes continuously flitting toward the closed door. "Can we not talk about this here? We really should be doing therapy during this time."

"Where then? When?"

She breathes out a heavy sigh and nods her head toward the computer. "Is the number we have on file your cell phone?"

I nod.

"How about I call you tonight? After work ... say ... eight o'clock?"

"You're lyin'," I respond, putting both feet on the floor and leaning forward, studying her. She looks me in the eyes now, a new confidence in her stature.

"Well, you'll just have to wait and see, won't you?" she says, tilting her head down and pinching her brows. A smirk appears.

"I guess I will."

"How has your week been?" she asks, jumping right into it.

"I had an absolutely incredible Saturday night." I grin, and she shakes her head.

"*After* Saturday. Anymore drinking this week? I know you haven't been the past two days. Donna brought me the results."

"Nothing but a few beers on Sunday."

"And the trace amounts of marijuana in your urine?"

A spiky heat prickles up my neck. "I swear I didn't smoke!" I plead.

She puts a hand up to calm me. "No, you're fine. It was only trace amounts, which tells us it was secondhand, but you really need to watch that. You don't need to be around it. It'll just tempt you, and all the time we spend together over these seven weeks will go to waste, you'll face charges, and I will have failed you here."

"I don't think I'm as addicted to this stuff as people would like to think."

"If you had to quit everything right now, could you? Say you were sent to jail over this. Can you tell me sincerely that you wouldn't feel the effects of withdrawal?"

I take a deep breath, my eyes tracing the lines of the tile floor and my thoughts racing.

"No, I couldn't quit everything and not feel fucked up."

"That's okay. You aren't lesser of a man for admitting that. You're not weaker somehow. In fact, I think it makes you stronger."

"I gave up a lot when I left home at sixteen … I wasn't sure where I was gonna sleep for a good while. Barely graduated high school." I pause, catching myself as the words spill out. I hadn't thought about them, simply let them fall from my lips.

"But you did."

"Thank God for that." I chuckle, passing a quick glance toward the ceiling.

"What about after high school? What was it like?"

"Well, when I joined the Army, I gave up a lot, too. I gave up the freedom to piss, sleep, and eat when I wanted to. I gave up the ability to tell a grown-ass man screamin' in my face to back the fuck up. I gave up a lot when I decided to get out of the Army and pursue this whole new life. I've given up a lot in this life. But I've controlled my own destiny each step of the way. I had the final say. I chose to leave home because I knew it'd make me better to get away from them. I chose to join the Army because I knew it was my only way out of that shithole I call my hometown. I chose civilian life because I knew I got everything out of the Army that I possibly could. It was time to move on. I made these choices for my own betterment. I took control."

She nods. "You mention 'giving up' a lot. Is there some resentment for having to give up so much?"

"A lot of resentment all around, I guess. I wouldn't have had to give up so much if I had a better start to this life game. I do love the Army, and I loved serving, but I wonder sometimes what it would've been like to have lived a different life."

"We all do. Really. I think it's in our DNA to question our past. But it does us no good. You are where you are, and you've been through what you've been through, for a reason."

"See, and I know that to be true. But it doesn't change a damn thing. I still worry and wonder. Sometimes I think about what it would've been like to have missed that mission too. I think that's when my problems really started. It's when I lost all control."

She leans in, her brows wrinkled. "Lost control of what?"

"Of everything. After the RPG. Any semblance of control was ripped from my hands. And then, this alcohol thing ... it's just the path set forth from that day. My injury and addiction are two peas in the same fucked up pod."

"Bullshit." She scoffs.

"Which part?"

"You can tell me you drink because of the explosion. That, I buy. That, I can understand. But to say it's a path set out for you. To imply it can't be changed. It's bullshit."

"I never said it couldn't be changed."

"I said 'you implied it'." She smirks as her fingers twirl the pen. "The question is, how much control do you really have? Personally, I think you have far more than you give yourself credit for, but that means nothing. You have to know it too. And down the road when you're done with therapy, and this mess is behind you, will you have enough control to not let the alcohol control you?"

"That is the question of the day." I smile, but a determined look remains on her face.

"You have to be willing to fight, Bishop. You have to take back control. This is a disease. It's a sickness. And if you're not careful, it can swallow you whole."

"I know. I watched my own father's dance with the bottle. I promised myself I'd never get like that. But in the Army Infantry, you drink. It's a way of life."

"And what about after you were hurt, while you were rehabbing?"

I chuckle. "You don't even wanna know," I say, shaking my head.

"I certainly do."

"I was a mess."

"How so?"

"Well, first off, Walter Reed was a mess. No leadership. No accountability. I went to appointments and then nothin' ... no direction. No real support system. So, I spent a lot of time alone, oftentimes in pain. For a year it was like that ... maybe a little less. I knew no one, didn't drink a whole lot because I didn't wanna leave my barracks room, but I was slowly dying inside. I thought about suicide a lot. Not about doin' it. I told you, I've never thought much about that. I focused more on the aspect of me not bein' around anymore. What it would be like ... whether anyone would miss me."

I gulp, clearing my throat before continuing, "And other guys are droppin' like flies in their own barracks rooms around me, overdosed on their pain pills, most of 'em. A gunshot too, my first year. Guys couldn't handle the loneliness ... the quiet ... the battle. I handled it as best I could, stuffin' all that agony, anxiousness, and desperation deep down, where they could hide away for a while. And they did. I fell into habits. Comedy shows, usually sitcoms. Comedy and action movies. Drama, if I was feelin' weepy. They'd play on repeat, one show after another. One movie to the next, and it saved me. It really did. I fell in love all over again with all those movies that stole my heart when I was younger."

"And when did the alcohol come into play?"

I chuckle, the memory of the man I'd grow quite close to over a year's time washing over me. "Once I met my buddy Tim. He was a man's man, with a rough edge to him. Pretty boy looks with a country boy's swagger. The ladies fuckin' loved him, and after gettin' to know him during occupational therapy, I came to see why."

"He was injured as well?"

"Yeah, he lost his leg to a roadside bomb. One that killed the rest of his guys. He never showed a sign of despair over it, though. Never talked about it, really. And in turn, I didn't talk about the men I lost. We bonded over other shit. Baseball, girls, video games, and eventually, Jameson. I'd never really had it before him. But I admired and looked up to him. He was the man I wanted to become, even if he was only two years my senior. He was just so ... grounded. Level-headed. Always so aware of his actions, and the actions of others."

"Do you still keep in contact with him?"

I don't even feel the tear well in my eye, but I do feel it

cascade down my cheek. I'm quick to catch it with a shaky finger.

Her compassionate eyes study me. "What happened, Bishop?"

I take a deep breath, letting it out slow as my hands squeeze the hand rests. "He missed the fightin' too much. I tried to talk him out of it. Tried to get him to get out and go to college like me, but he was too set in his ways. Like me, the Army was the only thing he ever loved. Unlike me, a set of real legs isn't as imperative as two workin' eyes. He worked his ass off to get back in the fight, and before long, I was left alone again. It wasn't too long after that I met Chelsea."

"And your friend ... what's his name?"

"Sergeant Adrian Lang."

"Did you keep in touch with Sergeant Lang?"

"For a while. I called him every now and then, once he got to his new unit in Germany. From the sound of it, he was gettin' used to the workload with a prosthetic, and they were rampin' up for a deployment."

A knot tightens in my throat and my palms sweat; the tears punish my eye sockets, but I fight to hold them back.

"I didn't even find out until four months later." I draw in a quick breath. "From a fuckin' Myspace post. I couldn't—" I drop my head in my hands and let out a groan. "I just couldn't fuckin' believe I had to find out he was killed from some random fuck's Myspace post. I couldn't believe he made it out alive once, just to go back again and never return. I lost it. Fuckin' lost it. Deleted that Myspace shit, the Facebook I had started, any presence I had online. I closed myself off from everyone, and I drank. Poor Chelsea, she was there for the worst of it."

I smile, though the sadness engulfs me.

"You know ... as much as I want to hate her for how she ended things, as much as it hurt me to see her go, I don't blame her one damn bit. I hate who I was then. I don't much like myself now. There's a lot I'd change, but I'm proud to look back on who that man was and say, 'I don't even recognize him.'"

"That's *excellent*. We need to continue encouraging that progression. You've come so far on your own. Let me help you to get the rest of the way, will you?"

"I don't think I have a choice," I joke, but she narrows her eyes at me. My eyes drop to the floor in defeat. "I will let you help me. I want you to help me. I guess, maybe, I need you to."

"If you want to change, I mean, really want to change, the power is in your hands. With everything you have gone through, you've developed an unparalleled strength. We are going to use that strength to fight this addiction."

"Can we use a different word?"

She scrunches her brows. "Different word?"

"Yeah, a different word than addiction. It has such negative connotations."

"What would you like me to call it then, Bishop?"

"Hmmm ..." I tap a pointer against my chin before shrugging. "Maybe, like, The Thirst. Kind of sounds like a superhero. Or we could go with unmanageable vice?"

She stifles a laugh as she shakes her head at me. "This isn't funny. Addiction isn't funny."

"Alcohol enthusiast kind of is, though," I say, grinning like an idiot. "Has a nice ring to it too."

"You actually called," I say into my phone, sprawled across my bed with *Scrubs* on the tube. "I wasn't expecting that."

"Well, I said I would. And we do need to discuss this," Carleigh responds.

"We do. Over dinner, maybe?"

"Bishop!"

"What? It's just dinner, Carleigh."

She hesitates, taking a deep breath, before she says, "Bishop, I'm your doctor and you're my patient, and my job is to get you better, not to engage in inappropriate communications. *This* even is too much. I could get in a lot of trouble."

"The last thing in the world I'd wanna do is get you in trouble. I wouldn't tell a soul, whether we saw more of each other outside of the office or not."

"We just can't, Bishop. It's such a complicated situation. Yes, I have feelings for you, I think you're an incredible human being, but we must maintain professional bearing. There is no other option."

"And in three weeks, when I'm no longer your patient?"

"We can discuss things further then, okay? It's doctor-patient until that point."

"Yes, ma'am."

"I'm serious!" she says in a firm tone that's far more adorable than I'm sure she intended it to be.

"Okay, Carleigh. Doctor-patient relations *only* for the next three weeks, and then I sweep you off your feet."

She chuckles. "Yeah, okay, Romeo. We'll see. Have a good night."

"Wait! Carleigh, before you go ..."

"What?"

My lips curl into a grin. "What are you wearin'?"

She scoffs, chuckling a little when she repeats, "Goodnight, Bishop," and there's a click over the line.

I set my phone on the nightstand, a wide smile on my face as I think about three weeks from now, and the inevitability of our tryst.

THIRTY-TWO

I don't often spend Saturday evenings at home. In my adult life, it's only been done a handful of times, and each of those times was likely due to a bender the night before. I didn't really feel like fucking with anything tonight, much to my pledge brothers' disapproval. They tried to get me over to the house for the glow party social DIK's having in the basement, but it's all become the same old shit. I love hanging out with my guys, but I'm sick of that scene. Sicker of it with each day spent as an official brother.

As George Michael works the banana stand across the room from me, I'm in bed, sitting up, with blankets warming my legs, a cold beer in my hand. It's only my second of the night, and more for the taste of the hoppy IPA than any desire to get drunk.

Taking a swig, my attention is grabbed by a text alert on my phone. I glance over, and when I see the name, and then the time, my heart flutters. I grab my phone and quickly unlock it, pulling up Carleigh's text.

What are yko doibg

As I'm typing, another text comes through. *Oh my God. Text walking. What are you doing??*

I respond, *Hahaha I'm in bed. The better question is, what are YOU doing???* My eyes remain locked on the phone, like I'm awaiting the most important text of my life.

Is she really trying to hang out?

Finally, another text comes through. *Up for a drive? Bad night.*

In a hurry, I text back, *Absolutely! Where you at?*

Lucky's Comedy Club. Dark corners perfect for kissing...

I change into nicer clothes like a runway model on speed, and then throw some putty in my hair before collecting up my cigarettes, wallet, and keys, and heading out the door.

My excitement is palpable, so damn intense that I feel flush across my chest, my heart racing nearly as fast as my Jeep, cruising the narrow, ill-lit country roads. I shoot prayers up to the heavens for no cops to pull me over as I get ever closer to the outskirts of Pittsburgh where Carleigh awaits, her perfect lips like the hare at a dog track. I'm the greyhound, hungry and driven.

With the city skyline lighting the distance, I take the exit and navigate my way through a rundown area of town, tattered convenience stores and open-air laundromats included. A short distance later, I spot the large lit-up Lucky's sign, and pull the Jeep into the parking lot, scanning the dingy exterior with curious eyes.

Interesting choice.

After a quick hair check in the rearview, I hop out of the Jeep and head toward the front door. There are a few cars in the lot, but not as many as you'd expect for a place that serves alcohol on a Saturday night. Walking inside, I first notice how dark it is.

She wasn't kidding.

A balding middle-aged man is on the stage, a mic in hand, the spotlight on him. He talks about how much he hates those little stick figure car stickers. I nod my head in approval as I scan the room. There are maybe ten people seated at little round tables near the stage, and a few more at the bar near the front of the place. A few couples take up couches against the far wall, except the very last one, where Carleigh sits alone, her eyes on me and a smile on her face. She's got a drink in one hand as she passes me a little wave with the other.

I wave back as I approach, smiling wider than I probably should. "Hey, you," I say as she goes to stand, but wobbles and sits back down to steady herself.

She smiles, shaking her head as she stands completely now, leaning over the short table between us to hug me. She smells like a combination of Chanel and gin.

As we part and she sits back down, I joke, "You know, for a substance abuse counselor, you sure know how to knock 'em back," as I join her sitting.

She rolls her eyes, responding, "Shut up. It's been a hell of a day."

"What happened?"

"Want to get a drink first?" She points toward an approaching waitress. "Two drink minimum."

"For sure. Double Jameson on the rocks, please," I order, and the waitress nods and smiles before turning on her heel. I look back toward Carleigh just as she lets out an exasperated sigh.

"I just found out my husband got this other woman pregnant." She scoffs. "At fifty-freaking-two."

"*What?* I'm so sorry, Carleigh. How did you find out?"

"His mother. We're still very close. She called me today and told me she thought I should know."

"Are you guys gettin' a divorce?"

"We sure as hell are now. I'm meeting with my lawyer again tomorrow to start the paperwork. I wasn't sure before that, because, you know, twenty-one years is a long time. I invested a lot into this marriage. I was the good wife. I did the dishes. I cooked. I cleaned. I gave him a blow job anytime he wanted." She looks at me with sincerity in her features. "I'm not talking just birthday stuff. I'm talking whenever he wanted it. And then he just stopped wanting it." She takes a drink and then shakes her head. "I don't know when it happened, or how, or why, but slowly, over time, he started caring less and less, and stopped wanting me at the same frequency. And I tried everything. I mean, everything. I bought the cute little outfits, surprised him at work in his office at lunch in nothing but a trench coat. And do you know what he said? That jackass said, 'How could you do something like this? This is my job!' Like I had committed a damn crime or something."

I shake my head. "Fuckin' idiot."

"Right?! And come to find out, he was fucking—ugh, having sex with one of his girls in there the whole time. One that I know of. Who knows how many there have really been? He's probably had them all in there."

"Sounds like divorce has been a long time comin'."

"When you invest as much time and energy and love into a thing like I have with this marriage, it's just not the easiest thing to walk away from it all. I loved him so much. Heck, I still do. I can't lie to myself about that. But he has hurt me beyond how much I ever thought a person could."

"I'm really sorry you're goin' through this," I say as the waitress brings my drink. I take it from her and thank her and sip a little as Carleigh orders another.

"I'm sorry to give you this crab fest. I just needed someone to talk to, and all my friends got too drunk to be of any help. They're all these divorced cougars anyway, always out on the prowl." She shakes her head, her eyes read envy. "I don't think I could ever be like that."

"Don't be sorry about a damn thing. I'm actually pretty certain I've requested your honesty a few times already. I've been dying to pick your brain."

"Well, pick away. There's so much stuff going on up there, I could talk for days."

"Please, feel free to." I take another drink as her expression changes from that of frustration and anger to a slight look of seduction.

She bites her bottom lip before she says, "But we have some dark corner kissing to do too."

I shrug. "I'm yours for as long as you'll have me tonight, gorgeous."

She smiles, stroking her long black braid before she kisses me deep and passionately, her hot tongue an on switch for my hard-on. My dick stiffens as her hand meets my thigh, and it ticks to full form when she takes my bottom lip between her teeth, biting just to the point where pleasure meets pain, and I *fucking* love it.

As her lips leave mine, it takes me a moment to open my eyes. When I do, I see she still has hers closed, and she runs a slow tongue across her bottom lip. Her eyelids slowly creep open and she smiles.

"I kind of missed that," she says.

"I *definitely* missed that."

A loud shriek through the PA system draws my attention to the stage. The MC chuckles, giving the mic a few good taps before thanking the balding comedian for his act.

"Everybody now put your hands together for our favorite Saturday nighter, JD McGinnis, The Ragin' Redneck!" the MC says, and my mouth drops open.

"No fuckin' way," I mutter.

"What?" Carleigh asks.

Looking back toward her, surprise still written on my

features, I reply, "That's my fuckin' fraternity advisor. He's a fuckin' lunatic. I didn't know he did stand-up. Though I'm not the least bit surprised."

I look back toward the stage as JD takes the mic from the MC and gives him a pat on the back. He's wearing a pair of crocs with white socks, jean shorts, and a t-shirt with the sleeves cut off. There are two sides on the front of the shirt. On one side, there's the female silhouette from a bathroom sign. Above it reads 'My mom.' Just beside it is the silhouette of a stripper riding a pole and above that it reads 'Your mom.'

I chuckle, shaking my head. "This ought to be rich."

"How's it goin', folks?" JD says loudly into the mic.

The docile crowd's response is subpar.

"Well, hell, who shit in y'all's cornflakes this mornin'?" JD continues, pacing the stage back and forth slowly, purposefully. "Now, I don't know what's up y'all's ass, but I had a fist in mine last night. No lie. And I ain't talkin' the Korean girl's hands who does my pedicures neither. I'm talkin' Wilt Chamberlain's girthy mitt. I know what y'all are wonderin'. I can see it in yer damn faces. I'd judge me too if I were you, but hell, ya just don't know how good it feels 'til ya try it. I actually got in trouble a few weeks ago with the gastroenterologist's office. Yeah, bet ya didn't think I knew what that word was, did ya?" He cracks a grin. "So, I guess them doctors don't take too kindly to my repeated phone calls. And I kept tellin' him, it don't make no damn sense to me that they ain't got recreational colonoscopy options. I've offered 'em plenty of money. Like, 'ay, Doc. I want a camera up my ass. Let's fuckin' go!'" He shrugs. "But what do ya do?"

"I miss that," Carleigh says, grabbing my attention.

As JD continues in the background, I turn toward Carleigh. Arching a curious eyebrow, I ask, "Miss what?"

"Well, I mean, not the fisting and the colonoscopy stuff, but just, that kind of stuff in general." She blushes and her eyes flit to the drink held unsteadily in her hand.

"What stuff?"

"Ugh!" She scoffs, shaking her head. "You don't want to hear it. I'm just drunk."

"No, no, no! Tell me."

"Butt play, okay? I miss it. When my husband and I were first married, and the sex was still good, we did it all the time. It's a different sensation. Not better, just different." She shrugs. "I miss it," she repeats. "And I'm just drunk and horny."

I gulp, fighting back the heat that's now sweeping over my body, the desire intensified times a thousand, my dick now crammed against my denim uncomfortably.

"What?" she asks, looking away bashfully.

"That was just probably the sexiest thing you could've ever admitted," I say, shaking my head.

"Really?"

"Absolutely! You're right about it. It's not better. Certainly not worse. But different, and fuckin' incredible."

She bites her bottom lip, her cleavage getting redder as she cracks a mischievous smile. Her eyes slowly trail back to the stage.

"Thanks for what's goin' on in my pants right now, by the way," I say, chuckling as my eyes fall back on JD too.

Suddenly, she grabs my cock, and turns back toward me. As my eyes roam slowly from her hand to meet her eye line, my mouth gapes, and she says, "In due time." Her hand returns to her drink and I want to whine for her to put it back, but I chuckle instead, shaking my head.

"You are gonna be the death of me, woman."

"You have no clue, Bishop. No clue." She hesitates before she adds, "Soon though."

It's hard for me to concentrate on JD with Carleigh's last

words still lingering between my ears, thoughts of her unclothed, seeing that sexy thick body naked for the first time swirling about in my mind.

"Ya know what I mean?" JD's voice becomes clear again, but the thoughts of her remain. He continues, "There ain't no shame in pissin' yerself, is all I'm sayin'. I ain't proud of it, no. But I've learned to accept it. Ya learn the importance of vinyl mattresses, folks, real damn fast. I'm tellin' ya."

I crack up laughing, thinking about that stupid mattress in my apartment back in Crescent Falls, and every barracks room I've ever had.

"I served in the Army, ya know. And I was over in the desert durin' the first Gulf War." For the first time tonight (though it's gotten better since JD took the stage) the audience comes alive, clapping loudly. "Thank y'all," he continues. "I just drove trucks, but let me tell ya, when yer job is drivin' fuckin' trucks back and forth across the goddamn desert for long stretches at a time, a pissin' problem is 'bout the last damn thing ya need. By the time I ended the trip from Kuwait to Baghdad, I had two passengers worth a' piss bottles beside me. Had to be upwards of a hundred. I don't wanna say I threw a bottle or two toward some hajis and told 'em it was lemonade, but ..." He shrugs. "I ain't no liar. Now, I see yer judgin' faces, but ya gotta understand this—urine's gotten a bad rap over the years. It's sterile. It's environmentally conscious. And, well, I'll tell y'all the truth—it tastes pretty damn good."

I shake my head, laughing at his absurd ass, when Carleigh's hand returns to my dick, first catching me off guard, and then owning my full attention.

Looking at her, I warn, "You keep doin' that, and I'm gonna need to drag your ass to the bathroom. Or go take care of business myself."

Giving my crotch one last good grab, she removes her hand

and replies, "One, no you won't. If anyone is getting you off tonight, it's going to be me." She passes a seductive smirk, "Two, bathroom sex? If it weren't this nasty place, I'd be dragging you there myself." She smiles wide before she kisses me, cupping her hand against my face too. As our lips part, she says, "We need to get out of here soon, honestly, and while you can still drive."

"After him?" I point toward the stage, a wide smile on my face.

"He better hurry," she purrs, her hand returning to my cock and staying there this time as she faces JD once more.

***

It's not long after entering her apartment that she starts to kiss me, more than the pecks she dotted my neck with as I drove here. I make note, as the waves of pleasure roll over me, to ask her later why the fuck her husband ended up with the house.

Our walk into the apartment and toward her bedroom is uncoordinated as we cycle between making out and tearing off each other's clothing one piece at a time. By the time we make it all the way to here room down the hall, we're completely naked. To my utter delight, she flips on a dim light on her dresser, exposing her incredible body. I'm taken back by it; not surprised by her desire-inducing curves so much as I'm surprised by their effect on me. As I had already figured out from the hours spent in her office, she is shaped to the exact standard of my perfect woman. When it comes to a woman's body, though all of them are beautiful in their own right, I believe as they did during the 1600s—the Baroque period—where women had shape to them, curvaceous hips, a cock-raising ass, and gorgeous full tits.

She stands there in the dim light, her arms crossed in front of her, a nervous look in her eyes. "What?" She bites her bottom lip. "I have a few holiday pounds left over."

I take a few steps forward, cupping her elbows with my hands and pulling each arm away, exposing her breasts. I look her over, admiring her perfect quarter-sized nipples and the thin landing strip that leads to that sexy slit, jet black like the long hair she has braided and resting beside her right breast, framing its excellence.

"Carleigh, you have the sexiest body I've ever seen."

"Oh, shut up!" She scoffs, rolling her eyes and pushing me away, but I step closer to her, my naked body against hers, and I slide a hand to her full ass cheek, clutching it tightly.

She gasps, closing her eyes for a moment.

"I'm not even fuckin' kiddin'," I whisper, my lips to her ear. "I thought you were sexy clothed, but seein' you naked is like an out-of-body experience."

She scoffs again, leaning back and batting a hand against my chest. "Now, how many women have you said that to?"

"Zero." I grin. "I'm not your normal almost twenty-six-year-old. I don't just fuck around. I like connecting with another. I like experiencing someone fully. I like passion and seduction."

"Do you know how wet you're getting me?" she whispers breathlessly, her weight against me once more, her warmth radiating.

I pull my head back a little, and looking into her eyes with a grin, I reply, "I'd really love to find out."

"I'm yours for the taking, Bishop," she mutters, flashing me hungry eyes.

I push her back onto the bed, forcefully, and she falls with a gasp. She lands, and before she can do much more than look at me, I move my hands to her perfectly thick thighs, and I spread them, maintaining eye contact with her the whole time. I want her to know how many aching minutes I've spent in that seat across from her, dying to experience this right here.

She's already trembling, her legs like vibrators against the sides of my head as I lean down into her. Her moans deepen as my tongue trails circles around her bud, teasing her, making her squirm with desire. I suck in, my tongue lashing against her clit, and with each rapid stroke, her body tenses and relaxes in a cycle.

My cock is aching, so ready to be owned by her, to feel her for the first time ... and I hope to fucking God not the last.

Standing up straight, I command, "Turn over. I wanna see that perfect ass."

"Yessir," she replies, her bottom lip slipping between her teeth, her eyes just slits. She stands, turns around, and bends over so that her stomach is flat against the bed, her voluptuous ass perked up and waiting.

Taking a cheek into each hand, I shake my head, letting out a sigh. "Jesus, woman. You are ridiculously sexy. So fuckin' wet."

"You have no idea how turned on I am right now. I haven't come like that in—God, just fuck me. Please, fuck me. I need you in in me so bad."

"And I need you, but Lord, I'd have to be an animal not to do this first." Spreading her ass cheeks, I dive down toward her, my tongue out and connecting with her tight little asshole. She lets out a light squeal of both pleasure and surprise as I circle her hole with my tongue. Her subsequent whimpers send surges of pleasure through me, heart-racing pleasure like the kind I felt when I was a teenager just discovering the whole wide world of sex. She makes it all feel so brand new again.

Her whimpers build to desperate moans, and the sheen from her absurdly—and deliciously—wet pussy, makes my hunger for her impossible to ignore. Not that I'd want to. I stand up straight, my hands still spreading her ass cheeks apart, and I lead the tip of my dick to her pussy, which glistens from the cum and saliva I left behind. Slowly, I work my dick in, the warmth electrifying, the feeling rushing up and down each limb.

Working her pussy in slow thrusts, I wet a finger with my tongue and begin lightly circling her asshole with it. Her moans intensify, her breathing heavy. Her whimpers slay me. They will me to work a finger inside her asshole slowly as I thrust my hips harder. She gasps as I settle my entire finger inside her, and each time I pull my dick out of her and thrust back in, I come hither my finger in her asshole, working both holes simultaneously. I'm driven like a madman by her quickly escalating screams of pleasure. When she shouts my name, I can feel my dick pulsate inside her, ready to unleash the cum that's been building since the first day I sat across from her.

"Oh fuck, Bishop, I'm going to come again. Oh God. Oh God," she cries. "Oh my *God*!"

She drives her ass up into me, her arms sprawled out like she's being searched and hands clinching the bedspread as her whole body seizes.

"Put it in my ass, Bishop," she manages to say between labored breaths.

Slowly removing my finger and dick from her, I grin as she lets out a moan. Leaning down on top of her, I move my lips to her ear and whisper, "Are you sure?"

"Oh God, yes," she whispers. "Please fuck my tight little hole, Bishop. I need it so bad."

Kissing her neck first, I straighten and meet the tip of my cock with her asshole.

She gasps already and I've yet to do a thing.

I spit in my hand and wet my dick with it before entering her, one slow inch at a time.

"Oh fuck!" she cries, her head tilted to the side, and I can see her face is completely flush now.

I continue until I'm settled inside her, and she cries out in pleasure. Just the feel of her tight warm hole surrounding me, even with no motion, stirs the cum in my sack. Never have I felt an asshole so perfect in my life.

"Start slow, baby," she says, looking back at me. "And then *fuck me up*."

Her words send a signal directly to my balls, letting them know to get ready to fire. As I slowly work my cock in and out of her tight hole in smooth strokes, she drops her face into the mattress and lets out a satisfied moan, which is muffled by the bedspread. Leaning down into her, I reach a hand to her mouth for her to suck, while my teeth nibble her neck, all the while, my hips thrusting in coordinated movements meant to hit just the right spot.

Her breathing picks up right along with my pace, her whole body red now, her hands white-knuckled as they death grip the bedspread. Streaks of red across her back mark where my nails have been

"It's happening again. I'm almost there," she gasps. "Oh my God, I'm going to come again."

This time I'm going to come with her. The floodgates have opened, my resistance disposed of.

As she screams out in orgasmic pleasure for the third time tonight, I unleash a load of cum inside her as I slam down into her hot ass for the last time, settling against her with my dick still inside, the all-out buzz from orgasm transitioning to the usual post-coital numbness that my seizing muscles cause.

"*FUCK!*" I'm an animal, my humanity set aside as the orgasm floods me with an electrifying euphoria. I turn and collapse down beside her, my chest rising and falling with each ragged breath.

She turns over, kissing me on my stomach and chest, before she lays down on her back beside me, her head upon my chest as she lets out a pleasured sigh.

"Wow." She lets the word linger, a wide smile on her face, her eyes closed. "That was amazing!"

"You're tellin' me." I chuckle. "I've thought a lot about that this the past month. *A lot.* But never could I have predicted it would be *that* good!"

"I haven't felt anything like that in my entire life. *Ever.* Not even in the best days of my marriage." She looks at me and smiles, patting my chest. "I just may have to keep you around once our sessions are finished."

"I sure hope you do." I hesitate before asking, "No regrets?"

She shakes her head firmly. "Not a single one. That was everything I've wanted, everything I've thought about for so long. I want more. I want *so* much more."

"The night is young, beautiful." I smile, motioning toward the sliding glass door that leads to a small balcony. "But dear Lord, do I need a cigarette break. Care to join me?"

"Absolutely. I mean, I won't partake, but I'll keep you company."

"Yeah, that's what I meant." I smirk, standing from the bed slowly, my legs still wobbly as I start to get dressed. "I was hoping you weren't back on the habit at least."

"No. I nearly coughed up a lung after that night at the hotel." She stands too, taking a moment to steady herself, her eyes going wide. "Jesus. I can barely feel my legs."

I laugh.

"I'm serious," she says, laughing too as she grabs a satin nightgown from a hook on her bedroom door and throws it on. She then leads me out onto the balcony.

Lighting up a cigarette, I take a puff and eye her through the exhaled smoke. "Can I ask you somethin', now that we got that first round out of the way?"

"Sure."

"Why did you have to get an apartment? Why not him?"

She shrugs. "He has a lot more stuff at the house than I do. His home office. The home gym. It just made more sense for me to move out."

"How long have you been here?"

"About four months since we separated. Since I found out about everything."

"How did you find out? If you don't mind me askin'."

She puts a hand up. "It's okay. I don't mind." Smiling, she says, "You know, when we first got together, there weren't cell phones. You had personal ads to meet people, but I never knew anyone who used them. After we had been married for a little bit, and the internet started becoming a thing, I never in a million years suspected anything. Nor did I know enough about online dating, chatrooms, whatever, to think anything of it. So, I never paid it any mind until, one day, I did. I was looking on his computer for an old photo of mine for a family reunion and stumbled upon some nudes ... and not of me! Well, that got me snooping, and I found more than I ever bargained for. Years and years of infidelity."

"How long did you stay with him after you found out? The first time, I mean."

Her eyes fall to the balcony floor as a look of shame crosses her face. "Probably another five or six months, I suppose. Enough time to find out he wasn't going to stop. And now, with him knocking his secretary up ..." She lets out a heavy sigh, lifting her palms into the air. "What do I do?"

"Well ..." I take one last drag of my cigarette and then dab it out onto an ashtray on a side table. I exhale the smoke and continue, "He's missin' out. *Big time.*" Kissing her first, I then motion to the bedroom. "Round two?"

She grins. "Promise to give it to me like you did before? My ass needs more attention."

"Fuck, I can certainly comply. Happily." I smile, tapping her ass with my hand. "Now, hurry up and get in there."

She passes me a playful look, scurrying in as she the gown slips from her shoulders to the floor, that beautiful ass beckoning me again, willing me into the room after her.

I stop abruptly as she turns around, and say, "Wait a second ... what are you doin' with an ash tray out here?"

THIRTY-THREE

My phone rings, annoyingly waking me from my slumber. Rubbing my eyes first, I check the time on Carleigh's alarm clock: Two o'clock in the morning.

I grab the phone, spotting Sarge's name, and press answer.

"Hey, Sarge. What's goin' on, man?"

There's silence over the line.

"Sarge?"

I hear a sniffle and some rustling in the background. "Yeah," he mutters.

"What's wrong, man?"

There are more sniffles across the line. He clears his throat. "I just, it's ... I don't know how to say it." He breaks down crying.

"I'll come over, bro. Whatever it is, we'll work through it. Okay?"

He hesitates before muttering, "Okay."

I hang up and race to put on clothing. Carleigh stirs in her sleep next to me. I lean in toward her, kissing her forehead, and she wakes with a smile.

"Are you okay?" she asks in a raspy tone, her eyes just little slits.

"Yeah, something's goin' on with a friend. I need to go see how he's doin'."

She sits up, leaning on an elbow. "Who is it?"

"Sarge. My Big Brother in the fraternity. He's a military guy too. Former Army Ranger. Didn't tell me what's up, but he's not one to call for just anything."

"Oh okay. Drive safe, please."

"I will." I smile, kissing her lips and then her forehead again. "I'll text you when I get there. Keep my spot warm?"

She's on her side now, the blanket falling and exposing her beautiful breasts. Patting the spot next to her, she says, "It's all yours. We both are."

She winks, and my dick throbs in my pants at her words. I yearn to stay, to fuck her silly and then hold her all night, but I need to be there for Sarge, whatever it is he has going on, just as he's been there for me.

"Talk to you soon, gorgeous," I say, blowing her a kiss before I make my way out the door, down the steps, and out of her apartment, walking with a purpose and desire to make sure my buddy is okay, all while a raging fucking hard-on still pushes angrily against the denim.

After a short drive, I reach Sarge's apartment, and park the Jeep. Hopping out, I hurriedly walk to his front door and knock.

There's no answer.

I knock again.

Nothing.

Trying the door handle, I see it's unlocked, and I cautiously open the door.

"Hey Sarge, you in here, bro?" I call out into the darkness.

Nothing.

Taking a few steps inside, I see light pouring from a back

room down the hall, and I call out again, "Sarge, buddy, it's Bishop. I don't wanna get shot today, man. You in here?"

"Back here," his gravelly, tired voice responds.

I walk down the hall, toward the open bedroom door at the end. Peeking my head inside, I see Sarge seated on the edge of his bed, shirt off, and an empty bottle of vodka beside him. Another is smashed to bits on the carpeted floor, along with a few broken picture frames. Looking closer, I see all the pictures feature Sarge with the same man. I'm assuming it's Jonah.

"*Fuck*, what happened, bro?" I tiptoe past the scattered glass shards, making my way to the bed. Moving the vodka bottle over, I take a seat beside him and place a hand at the nape of his neck. He takes heavy, congested breaths, his eyes puffy and red, his cheeks glistening.

"There have been signs for a while now. That maybe he wasn't happy," Sarge responds, sniffling and wiping an arm across his face. "I guess I've noticed them and just didn't want to believe it."

"Did he break up with you?"

"Worse."

"Cheated on you?" I ask.

He nods. "Has been for some time now."

"Fuck, Sarge. I'm sorry, man. I know you two have been together a long time now. What a fuckin' twat."

"Five years. Five years wasted. And he was fucking around on me for two of them. God, how could I be so stupid?" He scoffs, dropping his head into his hands. A new wave of tears takes hold.

I give his neck a good squeeze. "Fuck him, man. If he's gonna fuck around on you, he's not worth your time or your tears."

"It doesn't matter anyway. He doesn't want me anymore. He said he fell in love with this Chaz guy."

"Fuckin' Chaz. Who the fuck names their kid Chaz?"

"I think it's short for Chester."

"Well, fuck me, that's even worse. *Chester*? When your name's so bad that the best alternative you can come up with is *Chaz*, well, you might as well just off yourself. After killin' your parents, of course, for givin' you such a stupid fuckin' name in the first place."

Sarge laughs, shaking his head. He snorts back through his congested nose and says, "It *is* a stupid fucking name."

"You wanna put bologna on his car?"

"What are you, twelve?" Sarge asks, a judgmental arch in his brow. He hesitates before adding, "You have to use cooked spaghetti. It works better."

We both laugh loudly.

His eyes scan the nearly destroyed room and he shakes his head. "*Fuck*, I really lost it. I'm sorry I called you, Bish. I just didn't know who else to turn to."

"Dude, don't even mention it. Anytime. Anything. Anywhere. You holler. Now ..." I stand, surveying the room. "Let's get this place cleaned up and plot out some good revenge, huh?" My lips curl up into an evil grin.

WITH THE ROOM reasonably clean now, and our plan in place, Sarge and I sit at the computer, working up the first part of the plan.

"So, do we wanna go all out here? What should I put?" I ask, looking over at him.

He grins, responding, "Let's make a few. We'll link one to his cell number and the rest to his emails. Click the personal ads, right there." Sarge points to the screen where Craigslist.org sits. I click the personal ads tab and a list comes up. He points to one that says, 'Casual Encounters' and he says, "Yeah, click that one. And click on the Male for Male section, then 'New Post.'"

I do as he says, and a post template pops up.

Sarge smiles. "Okay, put twenty-three-year-old twink looking for daddy to use and abuse my asshole. I like fisting and wet sports. Particularly interested in some Kentucky Klondike Bar action."

I stop typing and look over at him with furrowed brows. "What the fuck is that?"

He laughs out loud. "Freezing a shit and fucking someone with it."

I pretend to gag. "Is that a real thing?"

He shrugs. "It's a real term. Fuck knows if anyone actually does it. I wouldn't doubt it though. Had to come from somewhere."

"Holy shit. He's gonna get some real superstars hittin' him up. This is gonna be epic."

"Fuck yeah. That one's good. Post it and let's do another one."

I press the post button and then open a new one, awaiting directions.

"Alright, for this one put, DL Army guy, thirty-two, looking for CBT, FF, and scat play."

After typing what he's just said, I look at him, grinning. "It's like another fuckin' language. Translate, please. For those of us who aren't in the know."

"Fist fucking, cock and ball torture, and shit play."

I crack up laughing. "I like the DL Army guy addition. Should be quite popular."

"Oh, he'll have every queen from here to Pittsburgh contacting his ass." He motions to the screen. "Let's do another one and make his address a gloryhole meetup spot."

"Oh, my God, fuck yeah!"

He hesitates, a look of shame crossing his features. "Wait, are we really doing this?" Sarge asks, his hands on his hips. "It seems so immature."

I pause for a moment, looking toward the screen and then back to him. "Maybe just keep it up for an hour?" I ask, shrugging.

He grins. "Might as well make it two."

THIRTY-FOUR

I never did get ahold of Carleigh after leaving her house for Sarge's place. I assumed she fell asleep, being as late as it was and all, but she didn't message until Monday morning. I had messaged her three times by that point like a fucking amateur. She let me know she had a great time, was looking at her schedule for the week, and that she would find some time for us. She asked about Sarge too, and I told her he was okay, that I'd tell her more about it when I saw her next, and that I couldn't wait.

It's now Thursday, 10:59 in the morning, and I'm moments from arriving at her office having not seen her since our night together and having not heard another word from her since that Monday morning message. I fought the urge to message her again after my 'Good morning' text yesterday, and it was a close one. I haven't stopped thinking about her since the morning I left her house, my mind running through not only the hours we spent fucking in every way imaginable, but also running through our dates, and our sessions, the time I've spent with her, the admiration that has grown since we first met.

She looks up as I enter her office and passes me a tight smile, a little bit of nervousness in her features.

"Doc, how you been?" I ask, putting my hand out for her to shake as the door closes behind me.

Her eyes land on my hand and then trail up to meet mine. "What is that? And don't you call me 'Doc.' You know how I feel about it." She motions to the chair across from her. "Sit down," she says, cracking a smile.

I do as asked as she seems to read my facial features, her eyebrow curiously quirked. "So ... what's with the formalities?" she asks.

"I didn't think I was doin' anything out of the ordinary." I grin, and she shoots me a glare.

"How's your week been, Bishop?"

"Well ..." I shrug. "Pretty uneventful. I was really hopin' to hear from this lady I had a whole lot of fun with, but she never reached out."

She shoots me a pained expression. "I know! I'm really sorry! I actually meant to message you back last night, but figured we'd talk today. Things have been really crazy this week, with the lawyer and everything. And then my husband was served yesterday morning, and he was not happy one bit."

"What did he do?" I ask, leaning forward in my chair.

She waves me off. "Nothing crazy. He was just contacting me a lot. Contacting our friends. Just being a bit of a nuisance."

"I'm sorry to hear that." I hesitate, a little guilt taking hold, and then add, "I completely understand about this week, you know? Don't even worry about it. We have all the time in the world to make up for it. Last session is next week and then we're free and clear after that."

I wriggle my brows, and she smiles, but it's tight, forced. "I had so much fun with you last weekend. I really did. Thank you for letting me vent a little. And release a whole lot of stress."

"No, I should be the one thankin' you. I had an absolute blast, in every aspect of that night. And by the way ..." I lean in and whisper, "I'm dying to be inside you again."

Her face goes flush, her nervous eyes meeting the closed door before they fall back on me. "I've thought a lot about it," she says softly. "I may have had to use the memories a time or two for vibrator inspiration."

I scoff. "And you didn't call me? I would've gladly taken care of your needs."

"Oh, I already know you could've. Ugh, I hate that I'm going through all this stuff. I hate that you even saw me like that. I'm still your counselor, after all. Regardless of what may have transpired. I hate that the roles were reversed Saturday night."

"I don't. I'm so glad to get to know more about you. To see the real you, the you with problems just like the rest of us." I pass a quick chuckle before adding, "To be able to see you outside of here. It's just different, and so much better."

"It is, but in here is important too. We still have work to do."

"We have two sessions left, Carleigh. And I'm doin' really well. Not drinkin' too much. Haven't touched a lick of weed in almost two months. My grades are at least a little better. And I've been lookin' more into acting classes. I've been thinkin' more about it and might try and come up with a plan by the end of summer."

"Have you decided whether you'll stay or go?"

I give her a wide grin. "Well, I guess that kind of depends on how all this plays out, huh?"

She smiles back, brushing some hair behind an ear. "Always the sidetracker." She pokes her tongue out at me.

"Talk about gettin' sidetracked. You show me that tongue again, and we may have a whole other problem on our hands entirely." I waggle my brows and she smiles; her face flush once again.

"Oh my ... I can only imagine. Ugh, to be perfectly honest, do you know how often I've sat in here and thought about how nice it would be to get fucked on this desk?"

"God, I love when you say *fuck*. It sounds so much filthier comin' out of your mouth."

"I try my best to maintain a professional bearing, to keep things classy, to be the good girl, but God, Bishop ... I'm a filthy woman. I am. I've even used my vibrator here before. I keep one in my desk drawer ..." she says, an eyebrow arched. "It has a remote."

"Carleigh, I need you to take your vibrator out of that drawer, put it in your pussy, and give me the remote."

Her eyes trail to the door and she bites her bottom lip. "Bishop, I can't. It'll just make me want to fuck, and we can't fuck here. As much as I've thought about it, and as hot as it would be, what if we were to get caught? I'd lose everything."

"Is there a lock on that door?"

She nods.

"Then we won't get caught. And that fear of gettin' caught you got, that's what makes it so fuckin' hot." I look at her with intent. "Now, Carleigh. Take that vibrator out of that desk, put it in that hot fuckin' pussy of yours, and hand me the remote."

She hesitates before she opens the center desk drawer and pulls out a pink egg. Her hand disappears into her lap, and I can tell by the look on her face when she puts it inside. Her needy eyes flit up to me, her hand retrieving a small remote from the drawer, and she hands it over.

I take it from her before she can change her mind, turning it on, stirring her in her chair. I watch her for a moment, her skin turning red, her eyes closing and jaw clenching, before I turn it up a little.

"Ooooh," she gasps, smiling wide as her eyes open. She

grabs her breasts with both hands and starts working them, any reluctance she felt before now giving way completely to desire.

"Now, Carleigh. Tell me what's been botherin' you," I say, my face straight, my tone doctorly.

She giggles, her hands running from her tits, down her stomach, and then back up.

"I'm having come problems, Doctor." She pouts.

"You're havin' trouble coming?"

She moans, closing her eyes for a moment, before they open back up, and she says, "No, Dr. Bishop ... I come just fine." She smirks, her eyes closing. "That's the problem. I crave it. And I need a good thick cock to feed the craving."

I tilt my head as her eyes open. "I'm glad you chose me, Carleigh. I do believe I can help you. I've developed a very specific routine for sufferers like you. It has been ninety-nine-point-nine percent effective."

She breaks character for a moment, though the pleasure from the vibrator is still made apparent by her trembling body, and she asks, "What about the remaining point one percent?"

I smirk.

I hadn't even thought of it. I don't even know where I pulled that percentage from.

Shrugging, I reply, "She had sexual anhedonia."

She bursts out in laughter, but just as she does, I turn the vibrator all the way up and her laugh becomes a yelp. She slams her mouth shut with both hands, her wide eyes flitting to the door.

I'm grinning like an idiot. "Carleigh, are you open to the treatment I have to offer?"

She gasps, lowering her hands, as her bottom lip trembles. She nods.

"Good. The proper initiation to my program requires oral copulation. Are you prepared for that?"

I turn the vibrator back down to low, and she eases her tension a little, nodding with a pouted lip. I scoot my chair back with both feet and stand, unbuttoning my jeans and dropping my fly. I motion for her to stand as I sit back down, removing my shoes and pants and tossing them aside.

"Now, Carleigh, this is very important. Are you listenin'?"

As she slowly saunters toward me, she nods again, an innocence in her features now as she continues playing the role that intensifies my desire for her.

"You must swallow the cock. If the tip doesn't touch your throat, and there's no gagging, well, then it's all for nothin' and we'll have to restart. Do you understand?"

"Yessir," she whispers.

"Now, get on your knees."

She does as she's told, kneeling at my feet, eyeing my cock as she reaches for it.

I grab her incoming hand, smirking when I say, "Now, now, Carleigh. If we're ever to cure you of your come hunger, you must learn patience."

"Yes, Doctor."

I wrap my fingers around my pulsating shaft and lift it up, exposing my sack. Pointing to them, I say, "You must start with the balls. I want your face buried in them."

"Mmmm." She dives toward my midsection, her lips connecting with my balls, the hot saliva tightening my sack immediately.

"Yeah, Carleigh, just like that ... so fuckin' good."

She looks up at me with seductive eyes, pulling back long enough to say, "I feel better already, Doctor. What a miracle cure you've discovered!" She grins, her mouth connecting with my balls again. She swirls a soft tongue around the entirety of my sack before she takes one of my balls into her mouth, sucking on it like a dick, and my God, does it get the pre-cum going. It's leaking out of my cock now so bad that some of it drips down onto her forehead. I wipe it up with my finger and hold it close to her mouth.

She licks it clean when I say, "I think we're ready for the next stage. How do you feel, Ms. Jacobs?"

She grins, replying, "Oh, Doctor, so much better already, but I'm afraid my desire to come is still there." She shrugs.

"That's okay. Remember, this is a process. Now, get your throat acquainted with the tip of my cock, sweetheart. It's only gonna hurt a little."

She grins before running her tongue from my balls, slowly up my shaft, and then swirling it around my cockhead. She spits on the tip, before she uses her hand to polish it.

"Good girl. Now make him disappear."

She opens her mouth wide, her eyes locked on mine, and swallows every last inch. With her top lip resting against my pubic bone, she holds her hungry stare. Abruptly, her throat begins pushing against the head of my dick.

It's the look on her face that threatens to do me in. It's just about the hottest thing I've ever seen.

I moan as she works my cock in and out of her mouth, her hot tongue cradling the underside. "That's it. You're doin' so well, Ms. Jacobs. *Too* well, in fact."

She pulls my dick out of her mouth, keeping it grasped in her hand as a line of spittle still connects us. She pouts.

"Am I in trouble, sir?"

"No, no. You've done quite well with the treatment already." I put two fingers to her chin, looking down at her as she is right now, on her knees, obedient, submissive; it turns me on like no other. "There's just one more step, and I worry it might be too much for you. I want you to be comfortable with our work together here. It's important for your recovery."

She nods, keeping the innocent look on her face, and feigns concern. "I'm willing to do *anything* to feel better."

"Good." I pass her a devilish smirk. "*Very* good. I'll need you to strip down. Keep that egg inside you. And assume the position over the desk. Bein' inside that beautiful ass of yours again is the most vital part of my program."

"Oh, Doctor..." she says, standing and beginning to unbutton her blouse. "How did you know that's *exactly* what I need? It did wonders for me the last time." She winks, tossing her blouse to the floor, and removing her heels and dress pants next.

As she strips out of her bra and panties, left bare naked and beautiful standing before me, I motion toward the desk.

"Assume the position, Ms. Jacobs. And in order for this to work, I'm sorry to say, we will need to turn up that assistive device inside you." As she makes her way around the desk and bends over on top of it, I turn the vibrator up. She squirms, letting out a quiet gasp. Tossing the remote to the ground with her clothes, I stand and remove my shirt, all the while admiring her with insatiable desire. Making my way toward her, seeing her bent over her desk as I had always fantasized about while sitting in this office, is one of those experiences you just have to savor.

I've always liked to take my time, from foreplay to orgasm and back around again, with the fervor such an experience should always be shown.

And as I stand over her, watching her writhe atop the desk as the vibrator gets her off for the umpteenth time, I'm overcome with a swell of a combination of desire, dominance, and satisfaction that disrupts my every sensation.

Eyeing her hole, as sexy as it is, and the egg peeking out from between her pussy lips, moves me to taste her again.

Spreading her ass cheeks, I run a tongue from clit to asshole and back, collecting every drop of cum she's made already.

"You taste so good, Carleigh."

"Thank you, Doctor."

"That's such a pretty little hole you have. Is she ready for the finale?"

She shoots her eyes back at me, arching an eyebrow. "Bishop, if you don't fuck my ass like it's the last time ever, I will sit you in that chair and make it happen myself."

"Tsk, tsk, tsk, Carleigh. That's not a part of my program. We will have to get that treatment in another time though. *Soon, too.*"

"Mmm, then you better give me that cock right now. I *need* to feel you come inside me again. You don't want to disappoint me, now do you?"

"That's the last thing I intend on doing, my dear. I won't stop until you're completely satisfied," I say, leaning down and spitting on her ass. I then spit in my hand and stroke my cock a few times, before I work my head in.

"Yes! That's what I need. That right there," she says, her hands hooking the edge of the desk so hard they've turned ghost white.

"Mmm, you like it rough, don't you?"

"You have no clue. Fuck me hard, Doctor," she demands, and I willingly oblige, building up speed and force to a point where I feel like I may hurt her.

"Is that okay, Carleigh?"

She gasps, holding her hands to her mouth to keep herself quiet. "Oh God, yes," she mutters into her palms, her eyes beginning to roll. "Just like that."

Picking up the pace, I can feel the orgasm building, the vibration from the egg inside her pussy quickening the process.

"You ready for my cum, Carleigh?"

"Fuck yes, Bishop. Give it to me."

I groan as the sensation builds, no longer centralized in my balls, but overtaking my entire midsection. My cock stirs inside her, preparing to blow, when I take one last thrust, orgasm burgeoning, and hold my dick inside her.

"Oh ... my ... fuck!" I gasp, nearly losing it as the cum pours out of me and into her.

I pull out slowly, a shudder overtaking my buddy as a sting reverberates from my sensitive cockhead. Letting out a heavy breath, I then pepper a trail of kisses down her back.

"Christ, you are incredible, woman. I swear to God, I've never felt anything like being inside you. Not ever."

She stands up, smiling as she removes the vibrator with a faint yelp, and then she wipes an arm across her brow.

"I cannot believe we just did that." Her eyes go wide as they trail to the door. "I hope nobody heard us."

As I retrieve her clothes from the floor and hand them over, I say, "I think we're good. There isn't another office close by. I'll tell you what, though ... there were a few times I thought I was gonna lose my shit." I smile, grabbing my own clothes, and starting to put them on as she does the same.

"You're telling me," she says, buttoning up her blouse and repositioning her pants. She unbraids her ruffled sex hair and combs her fingers through it a few times. Glancing at the clock, she says, "It looks like our session is just about over."

"I think that may have been our best one yet."

"And so against the rules..." Her words linger in the air as she sets a hand to either cheek, a look of guilt overtaking her features. "I can't even believe I just did that."

I approach her, setting a hand to her elbow as lines of concern cross my forehead. "Please don't regret this. I'd hate it if you did."

She drops her hands and smiles, though it seems to be more

for my benefit. "No regrets, Bishop. I just need to make sense of what's going on with me right now. This... this is out of the ordinary for me. *Way* out of the ordinary. Like, I must've lost my freaking mind."

"That sure sounds like regret to me, Carleigh."

She shakes her head. "No. I promise. No regrets."

"I hope not. And I hope I get to see you again. Soon."

"I'm going to be busy tomorrow, but what about Saturday? I think that would work."

Setting a hand to her hip and pulling her close, I say, "If it involves you, I'll *always* makes shit work. You just let me know. I know you've got a lot goin' on."

"Saturday, I promise." She smiles. "Now, get out of here. I have another patient coming soon."

"You won't be havin' the same kind of session with them, now will you?" I wink at her.

She rolls her eyes. "Get out of here, Bishop." Hugging me, she pecks me on the lips, and then the cheek, before giving me a little push. She turns and makes her way back around the desk.

"Definitely going to have to clean this up," she says, her eyes scanning the cluttered desktop.

I wink at her and smile. "Until our next session, Ms. Jacobs."

"Goodbye, Bishop," she responds, smiling back at me.

I turn on my heel and head for the door. Reaching it, my hand on the handle, I turn back slowly, mouth agape. "Oh, my fuck, we forgot to lock it!" I say with wide eyes.

A hand meets her mouth, her own eyes widening, before a nervous laugh escapes her lips. "I can't even deal right now. We are so dang lucky, you know that?"

"No kiddin'. I didn't go through six weeks of counseling just to end up in court at the end of it anyhow." I laugh. "Next time we'll remember to lock it, huh?"

"Next time, I'll remember not to tell you about my twisted fantasies." She sticks out her tongue.

"No, no, dear. That's not right. You have to tell me every last one, so I can make each one a reality."

As she finishes re-braiding her hair, a smile on her face, she says, "Bye, Bishop. I'll text you soon."

I blow her a kiss and open the door, striding out into the hall. As I make my way through the hospital to the parking garage, I walk with the boastful cockiness of a man who holds a dirty little secret.

THIRTY-FIVE

There aren't many times in my life when a woman I've only known a short time, and only fucked twice, has possessed my thoughts so incessantly. Yet, again, Carleigh has disappeared on me without explanation. A text I sent her last night, telling her how incredible she felt and how much I loved being inside her, went unanswered, as did the one I sent at around eleven today, when I asked her about our plans for the evening. It's Saturday, after all, and she sounded as excited as I was for it. It's now ten p.m., and I am *fuming*. Fuming not only because I've been ghosted for no apparent reason for the second time, but also because I'm so damn bothered by it in the first place.

I've tried shaking it. I've been watching sitcoms all day, had a six-pack of Sweetwater 420, and ate nearly an entire pizza (not to mention the pint of Ben & Jerry's I fucked up afterward), and still, the persistent thoughts of what I could have done wrong run through my head like an endless, confusing slideshow.

Did I not fuck her right?

She certainly seemed to enjoy our time together, both in and outside of the "bedroom."

Was it something I said?

I've run every word I've uttered through my head. I've been nothing but polite, respectful, and honest with her from the get-go, when the circumstances dictated it. And I fucked her like a porn star when the clothes came off.

Is she afraid of her feelings? Could that be it?

I pull up our text exchange and type, *Hey, not sure what's going on, but I think you might be afraid. Afraid of what you're feeling. Afraid of my intentions. I want you to know, I feel it too. I've felt it since the day I laid eyes on you. Something was different. Something was powerful. I feel pulled to you. Connected to you. I hope that's not saying too much. I was just really excited about seeing you tonight. I'm excited to see more of you, period. Hope you're well. I'd at least like to hear from you.*

After pressing send, my heart races. I read over the message a thousand times, scrutinizing every single *fucking* word.

I am so fucking stupid.

I head to the kitchen for another beer, anything to quell the anxiety that binds my insides. I open the refrigerator and grab blindly for a bottle, my eyes on the phone when it abruptly lights up and the text alert chimes. Slamming the fridge door shut, I scurry to the counter and snatch the phone.

Bishop, my heart is breaking right now. Literally, BREAKING. I've written and deleted about a thousand messages to you today. I just didn't know how to tell you this. I hate, hate, HATE having to write it, because I do have feelings for you, but what has occurred between us shouldn't have. It was inappropriate of me. It should have never happened. It was a mistake. This isn't your fault. None of it is and I really need you to know that. This is all on me.

I frown, worried and confused. I respond, *WHAT is on*

you? And what is happening here? I thought we had a good time. I thought we were on the same page.

The wait is excruciating, regardless of how short it is, as the slew of text messages from Carleigh stream in, one after another, indicating she's written me a short novella—of excuses, no doubt.

We did have a good time. A great time. But it's a time that shouldn't have ever happened. I'm beaten up over this, I really am, Bishop, but my husband and I are going to try to work things out. I know you'll never understand this, but it's not something someone who hasn't been through it could ever really understand, just like with me and your service. And you know, I can never thank you enough for that. For everything. I can't see you again, Bishop. I just can't. I told Ronnie about us anyway. I had to. And he doesn't think it's a good idea we finish out the sessions. You've passed the program, obviously, and all you'll have to do is come in at your usual time next week to take your last breathalyzer and urinalysis. Bishop, again, I'm so incredibly sorry this all happened. I can be so dang stupid sometimes. You've done so very well these past couple months. Be proud of yourself, and please keep it up. Good luck to you. And thank you for all the life you brought back into me since we met. You're a special soul. Please, PLEASE, don't message back. Ronnie is upset about this whole thing and I really want things to work between us this time. I need them to. I'm sorry, Bishop.

I can only laugh, a painful laugh appropriate when shit really hits the fan. The slightly crazed laugh of a man left completely fucking blindsided.

As I open the beer bottle that's sat idly in my hand, I run responses through my head, certain that at some point tonight, I will have a goddamn novel worth of shit to send her.

THIRTY-SIX

I n the past twenty-four hours, I have finished off a case of beer, eaten excessive amounts of fast food, and smoked nearly two packs of cigarettes. What I haven't done is left the house, except to restock the aforementioned brew and cigs, and I surely haven't responded to Carleigh.

I'm fucking proud of that.

I don't really care to see anyone right now, and with finals coming up in two weeks, I should be studying anyway (as if I'll manage to get a lick of that done.)

I'm on my way to slumber town now, at ten o'clock at night, which has become quite the norm for me since pledging ended. With all the beer I've consumed, sleep seems like the only good idea. The boob tube is on, and I'm wrapped up in my blankets like a burrito when my phone suddenly rings, startling me. Letting out an annoyed sigh, I reach over and grab the cell, seeing Sarge's name flash on the screen.

Answering, I ask, "Sarge, is everything okay?"

I hear loud commotion coming from his end but nothing distinguishable.

After a few moments, Sarge's voice comes over the line. "Is

everything okay?" He scoffs. "Have you not seen the news?" There's a subtle drunken slur to his words.

"News? What news?"

I can barely hear him over the chaos in the background.

Somebody laughs.

Someone else chants U.S.A.

"Bro, how am I the first one to be telling you this? Bin Laden is *fucking dead,* man!" he shouts into the phone. "*We fucking got him.*"

It takes me a moment to make sense of what he's just said. I can hardly believe my ears.

"What did you just say?"

"Seal Team Six got Bin Laden's ass in Pakistan earlier today. They just released the information to the press. He's fucking dead, man!"

"I can't even believe this. I feel like you're fuckin' with me here."

"Check the news, man! But do that while you're getting your ass to the DIK house."

"The DIK house? What the hell are you even doin' there?"

"Bro, everyone is here! *Everyone.* You'll know what I mean when you get here. Take a cab, you won't be able to park anywhere close to the house."

"Huh? Why not?"

"Trust me, bro. You'll see what I mean when you get here."

"Okay, Sarge."

"You coming?!"

"Yeah. Just let me get dressed and grab a cab, and I'll be right over."

"See you soon! Get ready to get your 'shine on! Tonight is for celebrating, my friend."

"Oh Lord."

I hang up the phone and lumber out of bed, pulling up the

news and verifying that Bin Laden was, in fact, killed earlier today in a raid in Pakistan.

Well, Halle-fuckin'-lujah!

Once dressed, and in the cab, I make the short trip to campus. It doesn't take long to see what Sarge meant. As the cabbie pulls toward the quad, I see thousands upon thousands of students covering every square inch of both the Commons and frat row that runs just beside it.

"Looks like I gotta let you off here, buddy. They got the road completely blocked off. I wonder what's going on."

I throw him a twenty and open my door. Before exiting, I say, "You don't know? Bin Laden was killed."

His mouth goes slack, his eyes wide. "You're shittin' me."

I shake my head. "No, sir. Not shittin' you one bit."

He laughs, shaking his head slowly, a look of awe painted on his features. "Well, I'll be damned. You be safe out there, huh?"

"You too. Have a good one." I exit the cab and start walking toward the crowd. There's a buzz of electric energy and excitement that sweeps over the entire area. A roar of conversation, laughter, and cheering permeates from the *massive* crowd, overwhelmed only by music blaring from a few different frat houses. I would estimate there are nearly five thousand students every which way. Pushing my way through the congested crowd, up the street to the DIK house, I can't believe the chaos that surrounds me. Kids are hanging off porch railings and pissing in every available crevice, standing on cars that were unfortunately parked on frat row at the absolute worst time. Alcohol is being downed like it's the end of the fucking world. The smell of weed hangs around me like I'm kicking it with Snoop's people.

I have entered Sodom and Gomorrah.

Finally spotting the DIK house through the raucous crowd, I see Sarge standing on the front porch with a number of other brothers around him in clusters, all drinking and laughing. As I approach, Sarge notices me and throws his hands into the air.

"Bishop! What up, bro! Get your ass up here and kill some of this moonshine with me." He holds up a mason jar and the fact that the 'shine is clear scares the living daylights out of me.

Making my way to the porch, I slap hands with a few brothers before meeting Sarge by the couch. He takes me in for a bro hug; the giddiness he's exuding is infectious.

"We fucking did it, man!" he says, separating from me and handing over the jar. "We got that sonofabitch."

Taking the mason jar from him, I ask rhetorically, "You had a bit to drink tonight, bud?"

He laughs. "Just wait until you try that shit. I brought the good stuff for tonight's festivities."

I eye the jar, my throat going dry. I take a thick swallow. "I got a feelin' I'm gonna hate you after this."

"You're gonna *love* me. More than you already do, I mean."

I open the jar and hesitate before I take a big gulp.

"Whoa!" Sarge's eyes go wide, and it takes but a second to realize why.

It feels like I just poured hot fucking lava down my throat. It doesn't stop when it hits my stomach either; instead, it leaves a trail of fire from my lips to my gut.

"Oh, my fuckin' God!" I gag, spitting a few times to try and rid my taste buds of the flavor, but to no avail. "That was the most toxic shit I've ever tasted." Spinning the lid on the jar first, I hand the nausea-inducing concoction back over with a quick shake of my head. "Here, take your fuckin' poison."

He grabs it, chuckling as he opens it back up and takes a drink of his own with not so much as a grimace.

Pulling out a cigarette and lighting it up, I take a heavy drag to coat my mouth and give me something to taste other than toxic moonshine. Letting the smoke out, I ask, "You see my pledge brothers around this shit show?"

"Yeah, they just went downstairs to get another drink. They should be right back."

As Miley Cyrus's "Party in the U.S.A." takes over the speakers on the DIK porch, I hear my name being called out from behind me. Turning, I see my pledge brothers approaching, all of them looking like they've had quite a few drinks themselves.

"Good to see you, dude!" Mac yells, slapping hands with me. He adds, "Congratulations, man! What a day!" as I then greet Jeremy and Carter.

"When did you guys get here?" I ask.

"A few hours ago. I sent you a text, but I figured your ass was passed out," Jeremy says. "Wasn't expectin' to see you."

"Well, I wasn't planning on doin' shit, but with this goin' on, are you kiddin' me? I wouldn't miss it. That motherfucker's day has been comin' for a long time. Did they say what they're gonna do with the body, by the way? It'd be fun to string his ass up right at Ground Zero so people can throw rocks at him, or something. Survivors first. Then New Yorkers. Then everyone else. It could be a fuckin' tourist attraction."

They all laugh, and Sarge shakes his head. "There won't be any body. No burial. The Navy 'buried his body at sea.'" He throws up air quotes.

"Wait, I don't get it. What's with the air quotes?" Mac asks. "You don't think he's really dead?"

Sarge shakes his head. "Nope."

"What the hell were you so excited about on the phone then?" I ask.

"Well, because I think they really got him. I just don't think he's dead. How the fuck are they just going to give Public Enemy Number One a burial at sea? I bet the Seals were ordered to take out every target, *except* Bin Laden. Probably told them to take out his kneecaps or something. The CIA probably has that motherfucker in some basement in Uzbekistan, pulling out his fingernails and castrating him with a blowtorch. Why do you think I'm so damn happy? Death would be too easy for that motherfucker. He's going to die slowly. No doubt about that."

"No way!" Mac says. "You really think that?"

Sarge shrugs. "I wouldn't put a thing past our government. Not a goddamn thing."

"Well, fuck," Mac mutters.

"Dead or not, what the hell is this shit?" I motion toward the massive crowd covering all signs of road or grass or parking lot as far as the eye can see.

"Just wait," Carter says with a grin, taking a sip of his beer.

"What do you mean?"

"This kind of shit happens here all the time," he responds. "Big football or basketball wins. Big losses, too. There was one time they rioted over the changing of the mascot name—from Braves to Pilgrims—after enough complaints. The school hates the rioting. They always try to prevent it, but it never works," Carter says, his gaze set on the mess of people. He points up the road. "You see the cop cars up there?"

My vision shifts to the top of frat row where two cop cars sit, their occupants standing rigid near the open doors as they scan the crowd. "Yeah."

"Well, eventually, this shit is going to get out of hand. People are going to start fucking shit up. Breaking shit. Probably burning shit. And those cops are going to come and shut all of this down. Or at least try to. I don't know about this one. This is the craziest I've ever seen it."

"Burnin' shit?" I ask.

"Oh yeah." Sarge nods, a grin on his face. "Big time. It's been going on here since the sixties. They'll either start a dumpster fire, or they'll grab one of the cum couches from a frat house and light that fucker up."

Scrunching my brows, I say, "No way"

"Yes way."

"That's fuckin' ridiculous. What's the point to all that?"

"What's ever the point?" Sarge shrugs. "They're drunk kids. Fucking shit up is in their DNA."

As I'm about to respond, I spot a kid on top of an SUV on the road below, waving an American flag around in the air. He drops it onto the road and seems to have no intention of picking it up as people begin to trample it.

I can't believe my eyes.

Do these kids even have any clue what they're celebrating?

I motion to the stereo system. "Sarge, turn that down real quick for me?"

"You got it."

As he heads to the stereo and turns it down, I lean over the railing and yell at the top of my lungs, "Hey, you! With the green hat!"

The kid looks up, as do some of those around him.

I point to the flag on the ground and bark, "Get that fuckin' flag off the ground!"

He shoos me away, going back to dancing and whooping atop the SUV.

"Motherfucker!" I growl. "It wasn't a request. Friends of mine have fuckin' died for that flag. Now, pick it *the fuck* up!"

He shoots his eyes up toward me, a scowl on his face. "Fuck your friends, and *fuck* your flag," he says, turning away from me again, but leaving me with his middle finger.

"Oh, fuck no!" The anger boils within me. Heat trails up my back as I ball my hands into tight fists. Starting my way across the porch, I feel a hand grab me and yank me back. I stumble a bit, turning to see Sarge is the one holding on to me.

"Let me take care of this one, bro," he says. "You don't need any more trouble your way."

I nod, and he makes his way to the parking lot, through the crowd, and down to the road where the SUV is parked. Leaning over the railing to watch, I see Sarge make his way to the flag first, pushing people out of the way to get to it. He squats, picks it up, and tucks it into the crook of his elbow. The kid still dances atop the car without spotting Sarge's movement.

Sarge eyes the kid for a moment, shaking his head before he lifts his other hand up high, wraps his fingers around one of the kid's ankles, and yanks him off the SUV. The kid comes crashing down onto the road like a sack of bricks, the air forced out of him when he hits.

Sarge casually strolls back to the porch, walks right up to the stereo, and turns the volume back up. Bruce Springsteen's "Born in the U.S.A." plays now.

I laugh as he approaches me as if nothing's happened. He holds out the flag. "Help me fold it?"

"You got it." I smile. "Thanks, bro. That was fuckin' awesome."

As we fold the flag up the proper way, Sarge replies, "Maybe that'll teach him to disrespect the colors."

"Yo, he's still unconscious," Mac gleefully chirps, his hands straddling the porch railing as he takes in the scene below. "You may have done a little more than teach him a lesson. I think you knocked the stupid out of him. Might have even killed him," Mac says over his shoulder with a chuckle.

Sarge sets the folded flag on the couch, and then waves Mac off, replying, "He'll be alright. Should've fucking listened."

"Shouldn't have been on top of that vehicle anyway. If that were my ride, I would've kicked his ass myself," Mac says, and we all laugh. *"What?"*

"The day you beat somebody's ass is the day I cut off my dick," Jeremy jokes.

"Fuck you. I can fight," Mac says, offended. "It isn't about the size of the dog in the fight. It's ab—"

"Oh, shut up. A skinny motherfucker like you probably made that shit up after gettin' his ass kicked." Jeremy lifts Mac's arm in the air and inspects it, but Mac yanks it away.

"You keep running that mouth and you'll see," Mac says, a cocky look crossing his face.

Jeremy laughs, nodding his head slowly. "Yeah, Killer. I ain't gonna hold my breath."

Mac punches Jeremy's arm, but he doesn't react. Instead, his eyes trail slowly from Mac, down to his own arm, and then back up, before he busts out laughing.

"Your hand okay, Small Fry?".

"I hate you." Mac takes a seat on the couch and crosses his legs.

"Oh, cheer up, Mac. You know Jeremy only fucks with you so much because he knows it gets to you," I say, smirking.

Mac shakes his head. "It's 'cause he's an asshole."

"Do I need to have you two kiss and make up?" I ask, laughing.

"Yeah, I like the sound of that," Jeremy responds, making kissy faces. "Mac, you wanna little piece of this country ass?"

Mac glares at Jeremy. "Not even if you were the last ass on earth."

Sarge cocks an eyebrow, his focus shifting from Mac to Jeremy. "They ever stop bickering?" he asks, grinning as he motions toward them.

"Rarely. They're like fuckin' toddlers."

An abrupt commotion from down the street pulls our attention. Four guys whoop loudly as they carry a beaten-up couch from the Sig Ep house, hundreds of others cheering them on in a crowd that encircles them.

"Here we go," Sarge mutters. "Fucking idiots. They're going to ruin the celebration for everyone."

The four Sig Ep kids drop the couch in the middle of the street as another kid douses it with the contents of a gas can.

"They're way too fuckin' close," I say, shaking my head. "Dumb fucks are gonna blow themselves to kingdom come."

"Ah shit," Mac says from behind me. "Piggies are starting to suspect something too. They're looking down there."

A random from the crowd that surrounds the couch tosses his cigarette onto the gas-soaked fabric, just as the other idiot walks away with the gas can, and the couch goes up in a matter of seconds, flames dancing into the sky. The crowd backs up a bit as the intensity of the fire grows.

The cop cars flip on their reds and blues, drawing my attention, and they slowly work their way down frat row, which may have even more people than when I first arrived, if that's possible. As the cops creep down the road at a snail's pace, waiting for kids to move out of their way, sirens blaring into the night sky, I move my attention back to the fire, which has grown even taller. Some of the kids who surround it have begun throwing boxes, wood, and anything else they can find atop the ever-growing flames.

A few of them have started their assault on some unsuspecting road signs, pulling them down until their parallel to the ground before moving on to the next one. Others have begun mingling around the front door of the Commons, and I worry the anarchy will spill into there before long.

A firetruck makes its arrival known with blaring sirens as it sandwiches the crowd with the cops from the opposite side, though they can't get to the fire from their side either, as the crowd around it has grown far too dense. They blare their horn, but either people don't give a shit, or they're too drunk to even realize they're in the way. A few scatter like bugs, but nowhere near enough for expedited arrival. From the looks of it, the couch will be nothing but metal wire and ash by the time the firetruck arrives.

I look at Sarge, disgust in my features. He shakes his head at the chaos below and takes a sip of his moonshine.

"This is fuckin' absurd, dude. Absolutely absurd. Do they even know what we're celebrating here today?" I ask. "I mean, do they really get it?"

"I highly doubt they've given it much thought," Sarge responds. "The kids these days, man. It's not like it was when we were younger. They've changed. I blame social media."

"I don't think you're too far off there, my friend."

He adds, "There's no discipline anymore. No respect. They're selfish, bored, and lazy. What do you do with that?"

Mac slaps the back of his hand against Carter's bicep. "Didn't you say this couch burning stuff started in the sixties?"

Carter chuckles. "It sure did."

Mac's eyes trail to Sarge and me. "Listen to you old fucks. Kids haven't changed. *You* have."

I nod my head with a grin. "You may be right on the money with that one, Mac. I think maybe I am gettin' too old for this kind of shit." Turning back toward the burning couch, which has died down in intensity a little, I can only shake my head, overwhelmed with the feeling that I just don't belong here. I'm not so sure I ever really did. All the things I enjoyed about this life when I got here annoy the piss out of me now. All the things that made sense to me then are now so discombobulated. So pointless.

"Guys ..." I say, my eyes still on the fire, my back to them. "I don't think I'm gonna stay here any longer."

"Heading home already?" Sarge asks.

"No, I don't mean tonight, though I think it *is* about time I head back." I turn back toward them fully, motioning toward the fire burning behind me. "I've seen enough of this shit." I pause for a moment before continuing, "What I meant was, I don't think I'm gonna stay here in Crescent Falls after the semester's over. I've been thinking a lot about it these past few weeks and I just think it's what's best for me. I think, maybe, I've overstayed my welcome around here."

"What the fuck are you sayin'? Overstayed your welcome through whose eyes?" Jeremy asks, wrinkles of concern in his forehead just like the others around him.

"My own eyes. Guys, listen, I only made it this far because of you. Y'all are my brothers for life. I don't take that lightly, nor will I ever. I just don't feel like I fit in here anymore. I can feel myself regressing, not movin' forward as I should be at this stage in my life. I hate my fuckin' classes. And, honestly, I'm startin' to hate this frat," I say in a softer tone, so I can save myself any potential headaches due to prying ears. Only Sarge shows any bit of understanding. If I had to guess, he's probably thought about leaving this place a time or two himself. If it weren't for Jonah, he probably would have already. Maybe, now that Jonah's proven to be a complete asshole, Sarge can meet me out in LA after he finishes schooling. I imagine plastic surgery in California can be quite lucrative.

"You can't leave, bro!" Carter pleads, shaking his head, his face twisted in confusion and hurt. "That's not how this works. Pledge bros have to stick together."

"And we will," I respond. "Trust me, the shit we've been through, it's forged our bond. Nothin' breaks that."

"Where the hell are you even gonna go?" Jeremy asks, his features relaxed for the most part but an uneasy tension in his tone.

"I'm goin' out to LA. Decided I'm gonna try my hand at acting."

"No shit? That's fantastic!" Sarge smiles wide, his brows relaxing. Of all these guys, he's the only one I've spoken in detail with about my desire to act. He knows it's not born of some need for fame or notoriety but driven by a genuine passion for losing myself in a well-written character, and the fulfillment gained from truly owning a room from atop the stage. Passing an approving nod, Sarge adds, "*Really* great to hear, Bishop. Seriously. Why not go for it? You'll never know what could be until you do put yourself out there."

"Sarge, shut up, you ain't helpin' here," Jeremy says, jabbing a pointer at him. He glances over at me. "You can't go, man. You're our leader. What the hell are we supposed to do without you?"

The concern in his features now, opposite of the borderline apathy he showed initially, tugs at the heart strings a little.

"As heartwarming as that is to hear, Jeremy, and I mean it, it really is ... not even your pretty ass could keep me here. I'm ready to move forward. Progress. Grow. Y'all just need to come out to Cali and visit sometime soon."

Carter scoffs. "Alright, you're totally bullshitting us," he says. "You have to be."

"I'm not, man. I'm really not." I look back out toward where the fire once blazed, now just smoldering ash and metal, and see the cop cars have finally arrived at the scene, the fire truck too. The crowd now pelts the dismounted police and firefighters with trash and bottles from the hills and porches that overlook the scene, and there are so many individuals throwing things, and so many within the vicinity, that officers have no chance of catching anyone in the act.

Turning back, I pass my pledge brothers a look of resolve. "This place just isn't for me, guys. It never really felt right. But you got to know, nothin' changes between us except location. That's it. Our friendship" —I motion to the five of them— "that'll never change. You guys are my brothers. Besides, we've got two weeks left to kick it and talk more about all this shit. Plenty of time to make some plans."

"This is just crazy. I was not expecting this tonight," Carter mutters, his gaze fixed on the distance, seemingly struck by the realization that I'm not bullshitting him here.

I take a step toward him and put a hand on his shoulder. Looking him in the eyes, I say, "Bro, nothin' changes. I promise you that. Everything will work out just fine. Alright?"

He reluctantly nods. "Yeah, yeah. I know. This just sucks big time. I don't—I," He keeps his eyes away from mine, hesitating for a moment, and then he continues, "I don't know what to think here. Or what to say."

I give his shoulder a tight squeeze, and then I lean in, reiterating. "All is good, brother. All is good. Seriously, don't worry about a thing." Dropping my hand to my side, I scan the rest of my pledge brothers. "I need to get some sleep though, guys, I'm drained, but y'all still wanna meet here tomorrow for a date at Club Library like we talked about?"

"Sounds good," Mac responds. "Not too early though. I'm gonna be shitfaced tonight."

"We said eleven, right?" Carter asks.

I nod. "Yeah, if that works for y'all."

"Still early, but I can manage," Jeremy says, winking.

Carter and Mac nod. "Same."

"Am I allowed at this shindig?" Sarge asks. "I've got some finals of my own to study for."

Looking at Sarge, an eyebrow quirked, I rhetorically ask, "What do you think, fucker?"

"Alright, well, then I'll be there, or here, or whatever."

My eyes fall to the half empty moonshine bottle in his hand and I smile. "Yeah, we'll see, Sarge. We'll see."

"You certainly will see when I'm standing on this front porch at eleven waiting on your lazy ass," Sarge says, passing me a sly smile.

"Uh huh." My tone drips with sarcasm. I pass them a quick two finger salute and then turn, crossing the porch toward the parking lot. Once I squeeze my way down the congested road, I make it about halfway to the smoldering couch frame when I hear Carter calling out my name from behind me. Turning back, I see him running to catch up.

"What's up, man?" I ask as he slows to a stop.

"I want to come with you," he blurts, and then bends over, resting his hands on his knees as he catches his breath.

"Huh? Come with me where?"

He straightens. "To LA. I got nothing here, Bish. I got no real family left. My dad gave his life to the bottle and died right along with the rest of my family in that accident."

"Carter..."

"Don't 'Carter' me, bro. This is what I want. It's what I need. I can't stay here either. No way."

"What about school?"

"I'm a freshman. The few credits I do have will transfer over. What's the difference between going to school here and going somewhere out there anyway?" He hesitates. "I don't want to invite myself or anything. If you want to go alone, I totally understand. I just ... I don't know ... when you were talking back there, I could relate to everything you were saying. I don't fit in here either. And honestly, Bish, you're like a big brother to me. I don't connect with a whole lot of people and, you know, I get it if you don't want me to, or whatever. I'm just—"

I put my hand up to silence him. "Bro ... do you really wanna come? One-hundred percent? No doubts?"

"Yes! One-hundred and *fifty* percent. Zero doubts," he responds assuredly.

I smile, patting him on the shoulder. "May 20th then. Last day of classes. Have your bags packed and ready to go. We'll have a long drive ahead of us."

His eyes go wide, his mouth gapes. "*Are you fucking serious?* You really don't mind?"

"You think I wanna move all the way across the country by myself? Fuck no, man. Welcome aboard!"

He hugs me, his excitement feels almost tangible. "Dude, this is going to be the best shit ever! I can't wait!"

"Glad to have you joining me, man. Seriously. Talk more about it in the morning?"

He nods, the smile still wide on his face. "Sounds good!"

We slap hands, and then he turns on his heel and walks away with a new pep in his step.

I smile, appreciating the fact that I not only feel fully content in my decision to leave this place, thanks to a painful assist from Carleigh, but that I'll have a partner in crime along for the journey now too.

THIRTY-SEVEN

I wake the next morning with a new sense of clarity, a belief that I'm doing the right thing, and a buzzing excitement for the end of the month, the semester, and my time here at Buchanan State.

It's a beautiful morning as the swell of spring has arrived. It's night and day compared to when I first rode into town nearly six months ago, frost coating the ground and a nasty chill in the air. Now with summer knocking at the door, and the rolling hills, and the mountains beyond them, vibrant and alive with vegetation, Crescent Falls is one of the most beautiful places I've ever seen.

Cruising down the road with my top and doors stripped from the Jeep and left back home, or what will be home for only the next two weeks, I make my way to the frat house to meet up with the guys. We're a week away from finals and in much need of some time at the library. If I'm to transfer any of this semester's credits, I need to kick ass on all of my finals.

As I pull up to the frat house, I spot Jeremy and Carter waiting on the porch for me. They pass a wave as I put the jeep in park, and climb out, lighting up a cigarette in the process.

Taking a long puff on my cigarette as I scale the porch stairs, I approach them and put out a fist.

"What's up, bro?" Carter says, bumping knuckles with me, Jeremy following suit.

"Not too much. How y'all feelin'?" I ask.

"I feel like I got run over by a fuckin' train, man." Jeremy chuckles, shaking his head in shame. "Way too much goddamn beer last night."

"I feel fine," Carter says, shrugging. "I went home early. Those two assholes were goners by the time I left though." He looks at Jeremy with a grin. "I don't even know how your ass made it home."

Chuckling, Jeremy says, "A kindly cab driver and the wherewithal to get the fuck out of here before my world really started spinnin'."

"Mac didn't go home with you?" I ask.

Jeremy shakes his head. "Nah, I left before he did. He was smokin' weed and drinkin' with some of the other brothers when I finally called it quits. Didn't wanna come with."

"I bet that motherfucker is face down on the cum couch right now." I laugh, heading toward the parking lot and motioning for them to follow.

"I surely wouldn't doubt it," Jeremy says from behind me. I reach the side door and open it, turning back toward him with a scrutinizing stare when he adds, "He and that couch have grown quite close this semester."

I chuckle, letting Jeremy hold the door while I walk into the basement. Trotting down the handful of stairs, I quip, "Jeremy, you've spent just as much time getting up close and personal with that couch as Mac has. You've got no room to talk," and then I scan the room in its entirety with a lip reared back. The entire basement is trashed, red solo cups and empty beer bottles strewn about the ground, pong tables, and couches, and all three trashcans overflow with empty beer boxes and crumpled beer cans, cashed liquor bottles, and fast food waste. There are a couple brothers passed out on the couch, their faces adorned with Sharpie graffiti, but there's no sign of Mac.

"Looks like he's bailed already." I glance around the room once more, and then say, "Carter, maybe give him a call really quick before we head out. "See if he can meet us at the library if he's even awake."

"Gotcha," Carter responds, digging in his pocket and pulling his phone out as I start walking toward the steps, my eyes still trailing the messy room for any sign of Mac's translucent flesh or ginger red hair.

I'm about to go up the stairs when I hear Mac's "Get Low" ringtone play from behind the bar. I look back, brows furrowed in confusion as I see Carter with the phone to his ear, his own eyes narrowed on the cluttered bar top.

"Left his phone here, maybe?" I speculate, walking toward the bar. "Or maybe he—" Reaching the other side, I stop in my tracks, frozen in horror.

Jeremy and Carter approach from behind.

"What's wrong, Bi—" Jeremy stops just behind me, his shoe digging into my heel, and I hear him suck in a whooshing breath before he yells, "Mac!"

Mac lies sprawled across the concrete floor, a mess of empty beer cans scattered around him. His face has a sickening blue tint to it, which is hidden only by his patchy beard and the countless profanities and cartoonish phalluses scrawled in Sharpie where his beard is not. His eyes are open but vacant, his sclerae yellowed. As I drop to a knee next to his rigid body, and set a hand atop his own, I find he's cold to the touch, the rest of his body that same awful blue. Putting two fingers to his neck, I feel a pulse but it's faint, fleeting. Fear rips through me, as does a surge of adrenaline, when I look back, and with desperation in my tone, I yell, "Carter, call 911!"

THIRTY-EIGHT

I feel beat up.
   Worn out.
   Emotionally *drained*.
   It's been two days since Mac's heart beat for the last time in the University of Pittsburgh Presbyterian emergency room. We watched as his parents wept when doctors delivered the terrible news, no more than a couple hours after they arrived on the soonest flight they could get out of Boston. We consoled them as they fell to their knees, wrapped in each other's trembling arms and breaking out into a fit of retched sobs, their cries filled with a sorrow and pain not even I am familiar with. I've lost friends —*best* friends—but to lose a child, a child so young at that, is something I hope to never face personally. To see Mr. and Mrs. McDonald as their only son took his last gasping breath is to know the apex of heartbreak and pain.

   We cursed the motherfuckers who left him there to die, who drew dicks on his fucking face as the alcohol began to kill him, vowing to Mac's parents that we would find out who did it, though we knew in our hearts—at least I knew—that it was improbable.

No one fessed up to drawing on his face or leaving him passed out behind the bar. Those who saw him late that night said he didn't look any drunker than normal when they left, and the others who stayed the night in the basement could've been victims themselves they were so intoxicated. They were of absolutely no use.

I was initially worried that Sarge's moonshine was a contributing factor in Mac's death, but he was quick to ease my concerns, promising he has never, and would never, give his moonshine to anyone underage, and I believe him.

With Crescent Falls just a week and some change from fading to nothing in my rearview, LA on the horizon, and with the fraternity's complete lack of empathy or responsibility in regard to Mac's death, I have severed all ties with the organization. My fraternity certificate has been shredded, and with a little help from a credit card and Zane's shitty room lock, my name has been Sharpie'ed out of the fraternity scroll completely. The act of writing in the scroll with anything but the sacred quill is strictly forbidden, which makes it that much sweeter.

I don't care anymore. They are as dead to me as they left Mac. The majority of them might as well be six feet under too as far as I'm concerned.

I've said my goodbyes to the few brothers I did like within Delta Iota Kappa and I promised to email my new California number to them when I get it. The rest of them can fuck right off, and I let them know just as much the last time I was at the house a few days ago. I went in yelling like a mad man, the overwhelming sadness within me externalized in the only way that made sense ... anger. I cursed the younger brothers who played no real part, shaming them for being a part of such a worthless unbrotherly organization. I stormed Trevor's room and said a few choice words, something along the lines of 'Karma is a bitch, my friend, and yours is comin' soon ... by my hand or the Lord himself.' Damian received much the same, and though he puffed up, and threw around a few choice four-letter words, I didn't spend enough time on his floor for any altercation. As soon as the words left my lips, I was walking away, headed toward the stairs for Brady's room. It wasn't words I had for him though. No, I had a special treat for him. The lucky little bastard has no idea how close he really was to an ass kicking had he not left the house when he did.

Despite my languishing sorrow over Mac's death, and the anger I use to mask it, the bond with those brothers I have met and fallen in love with has strengthened tenfold from the loss. The three of us remaining recognized that in order to keep Mac's spirit alive, we have to keep the friendship between us alive too. Jeremy, in his grief, pledged to join Carter and me in California. Breaking down in tears last night, he told us he could no longer stay in Crescent Falls and be a part of the fraternity with Mac's death hanging overhead. Nor could he stay behind as the two of us left. He had talked to his parents, he said, and after much argument, they finally relented so long as he maintained his grades once he transferred. I don't know if he's for real, or if his new plan to join us is just a product of his own heartbreak, but the idea of it excites me—what little bit of excitement I can currently muster.

I'm left with a nagging sadness that has just about crippled me this week as I drag myself through my finals, most of which I'm sure I've failed. It's hard to really care about much after losing him. It's hard to see the significance of some stupid test when I'm reminded yet again that a life can be snuffed out so quickly, so unfairly, without a moment's notice. There are no goodbyes. No last words. There is only silence.

If it weren't for my last breathalyzer and drug test today, and a session I most certainly intend on having with Dr. Jacobs, whether she likes it or not, I would still be in bed, mourning the loss of someone who not only grew to be a dear friend, but someone I began to see as a little brother.

And I can't help but blame myself. If I had stayed that night, swallowed my anger and hung out with my guys, things may have been different.

Once I get to the clinic and meet with the nurse, we knock out my last urinalysis and breathalyzer, my eyes remaining locked on Carleigh's closed office door down the hall. For the briefest of moments, our last encounter behind that very door crosses my brain, and I can almost see her there, bent over the desk, her body writhing, but I'm quick to force the thoughts away.

Instead, I let all the things I've been dying to say take hold; the things I've thought about for weeks now. I'm hurt, and confused, and I have questions that need answered. Things that need to be said. I don't know if she was at one point genuine and just got scared, or if this was all just a big game, but she fucked me up good, and she owes me an explanation. I won't leave this hospital without one.

Once the nurse finishes up, she turns to me, and says, "That'll be it, Mr. Bishop! Dr. Jacobs said she already let you know the last session is more of a formality, and is not needed, so you are free to be on your way."

"Actually, I was hopin' to speak with Dr. Jacobs." I point down the hall. "Is she in her office?"

"Yes sir, but she asked not to be disturbed. She's very busy today."

I wave the nurse off, making my way toward Dr. Jacob's office despite the nurse's request. I can hear her clogs click-clacking against the tile floor behind me.

"I'm sorry, Mr. Bishop. She was very adamant about no one bothering her."

Reaching the office door, I turn back, my hand on the door handle, and I say, "Oh, it's alright. This'll only take a minute."

She goes to say something else, but I ignore her, opening the door, and barging into the office, catching Carleigh off-guard. She lets out a little yelp as she stirs in her chair, surprised, a hand meeting her heart as she takes a steadying breath.

"Mr. Bishop!" the nurse scolds, grabbing my shirt sleeve.

Once the shock wears off of Carleigh's face, she puts a hand up and waves the nurse off. "It's okay, Donna. He's fine. Can you shut the door on your way out? Thank you."

The nurse passes a confused look between me and Carleigh, and then she shuffles out, shutting the door behind her.

"Session is in, Doc. We need to chat," I say, plopping down in my usual chair across from her.

"Bishop, I'm really—"

"Really busy, yeah, the nurse mentioned that. I'm really sorry to be such a pill, but I figured one more session was in order. Just a few minutes. What do you say?" My tone is purposefully patronizing.

"Bishop ..."

"One of my good friends died on Sunday. Big celebration for Bin Laden's death, and all that."

She looks at me with remorseful eyes. "I'm really sorry to hear that, Bishop. Who was it?"

"One of my pledge brothers. Alcohol poisoning. Kind of ironic, don't you think?" I don't give her any time to answer. "But listen, I don't want your pity. Just your ears. And, in a minute or so, a goddamn explanation I think any decent human being is owed. Sound good?"

She lifts her hands up. "Do I really have a choice?"

"Not a chance in hell. This is *my* time. I deserve it. So yeah, I lost a friend on Sunday, the day after you decided to throw all your bullshit on me. I don't have to be a rocket scientist to figure out I was given one last good fuckin' on Thursday, taken out to the goddamn pasture like Ol' fuckin' Yeller. Don't even waste your breath denying it. There's no changing my mind. I did appreciate one last good nut before you discarded me, though ... But to be fucked over for him, of all people. I mean, fuck, Carleigh, some of the shit you told me about him. Really?!"

"It's complicated."

"It's really not. You fucked around with me while you were feelin' things out with your piece of shit husband, figuring out what you wanted to do. That's cool. But did you have to get so involved? Did it ever have to go past that first kiss? Did the kiss even have to happen? Why pull me into this mess? You're supposed to be the fuckin' professional here."

Her head drops, a shameful look crossing her features. "I know," she mutters. "I'm sorry. I just, I couldn't help myself with you, Bishop. And the alcohol—"

"Yes, the alcohol. Let's blame that." I slow clap. "Really great substance abuse counselor behavior, Carleigh."

She glares at me. "I will *not* sit here and be ridiculed by you."

"Just tell me what happened then. Tell me when. Tell me what I did wrong and why that *fuck* got chosen over me."

"It wasn't like that, Bishop," she says, her features softening a little, a wrinkle of concern replacing the furrow in her brow. "It's not like that at all. You didn't do anything wrong. Nothing! That message you sent me Saturday night ... I bawled when I read it. You are an incredible man, Bishop. I meant every word I said to you, all of it, but I love my husband. I will *always* love my husband. And I have to do our relationship the justice it deserves. I've put this much time in, so much of myself into this relationship. If he is making a clear and valiant effort to get better, I have to take that into consideration."

I put my hand up. "Wait, wait, wait. So, what exactly

changed in the past week? What about the baby? Gonna play *Brady Bunch*?"

She rolls her eyes and shakes her head. "That's absurd. They decided not to keep the child. He said when I served him with divorce papers, his whole world crumbled, that he gained clarity. He came back to me and told me about the abortion, told me how he cut all times, how much he wanted and needed to get help. And I believe him. He's given me every password to every account. He's started getting counseling. He's really trying."

I smirk. "Must have been a *very* busy and trying week for him, what with the whole personality transplant and all."

"I've answered all your questions, Bishop. And it's really painful seeing you and being talked down to by you right now. Can we end this, please?"

I nod, glaring at her with my lips pinched together. "Yeah, I think I've heard enough of the bullshit and fairytales for one day." Standing from the chair, I hesitate for a moment before I look her in the eyes and smile. "You know, Doc, all the talking you do in here. All the Dr. Phil bullshit that's come out of your mouth over the last, what, twenty years sittin' in that chair, all the advice you've dished out ..." I take a few steps toward the door, opening it and letting my words linger in the air.

I look back toward her once more, my hand on the door handle, my head held high. "You'd think, just maybe in all that time, you would've picked up some of your own advice. May have helped you in the future when this bullshit fairytale marriage of yours is sure to self-destruct. Shitty people don't change, Carleigh. Take care of yourself, huh?" And with that, I shut the door, walking away from her office with a wide, toothy grin as the weary nurse glares at me from her station.

THIRTY-NINE

With Carter and my shit all packed up in the Jeep, and while we wait for Jeremy to finish up with his last exam, I head to the Commons to meet Ember for a quick bite. I begged her to meet me for a good week through texts, to see me before I leave, to give us a chance to clear the air, but she was busy with her own finals and hadn't any time until now.

As I stroll through the open Commons' doors, I spot Ember near the back of the dining area, a table to herself and a tray of food sitting in front of her.

"Hey Em," I call out as I approach her with a smile. She stands and gives me a hug but seems apprehensive about it. As we take a seat, I add, "You look really good, by the way. It's been too long, you know?"

"It has." She nods in agreement. "The whole 'trying to be friends' thing went out the window fast, huh?"

"I know. I'm really sorry. That's why I wanted to meet you. I didn't want to move away, maybe never see you again, and not be able to at least apologize, face to face."

She smiles. "I'm just giving you shit. I've been super busy

with these stupid finals, studying, and then a bunch of sorority crap, so I definitely haven't been living up to my end of the bargain either."

"In my defense, I did text asking to see you a few times. I remember getting shot down an equal number." I grin and pass her a wink.

"Well, we're here now."

"That we are."

She motions her head toward the food court as she pops a ketchup-dipped fry into her mouth. She blocks her mouth with her hands and asks, "You eating?"

"Eh, not too hungry."

"Weren't we supposed to meet for lunch?" She chuckles, shaking her head.

"Honestly, I didn't care what the hell we did. I just needed to see you before I left."

A smile tugs at her lips, her eyes soften, her shoulders relax. "When are you heading out again? Today, right?"

"Yeah, right after Jeremy finishes his final."

"He's going with you?"

"Yeah, both him and Carter are."

"Wow, that'll be so nice having some friends with you. Are you excited?"

"Crazy excited!"

She dips a fry in the ketchup, but holds it steady for a moment as she eyes me, and says, "So, I take it I'll be seeing you on TV real soon?"

I laugh and shake my head. "Yeah, I don't think so. I'll be lucky if I get a herpes commercial my first year in LA. It's a battlefield."

"I've got nothing but faith in you." She smiles, and her words bring a smile to my face as well.

"I've missed you, you know that? I've had so much I've

wanted to say. So many thoughts running through my head sense that night."

"Well, you're here now. Spill it."

I shrug. "I just wish sometimes that things could've been different. That I wouldn't have fucked that kid up. That we could have seen whatever it was between us through. Because it was something, wasn't it? Did you feel it too?"

"Of course, I did, Bishop. And it *was* something ... something special."

"But then I also think maybe that was just life's way of wakin' my cruise controlling ass up. It's been a crazy five months. Five months of highs and lows, and everything in between, and I think I needed that time to try and figure some things out. I've met some incredible friends ..." My voice trails off, my mind caught in the memory of Mac, and the familiar ache roots in my chest.

"I'm sorry, Bishop. I heard about Mac. I wanted to message you. I really did. I just didn't know what to say, and the past couple weeks have just been so busy. I guess I just forgot."

"You actually did message me. A few nights after it happened."

She scrunches her brows. "Did I?"

Chuckling, I respond, "Yeah, you really don't remember?"

She shrugs. "I assume that's what four hours of sleep, twenty hours of studying, and a hundred shots of espresso a day for two weeks will get you. I can't even be bothered to change out of my fucking PJs." She motions her hands toward the oversized hoodie and yoga pants she wears, as if she's showing them off.

"Well, I appreciate you reaching out, regardless of whether you actually remember it or not." I stick my tongue out at her, smiling. "And I can't tell you how thankful I am you saved some time for me today, because honestly, out of everything that's happened this semester—the good, the bad, the ugly—it's gettin' to know you that tops the list. After everything, it's you and our time together that means the most to me. You have no idea how much meeting you made all the bullshit I went through worth it. I can't imagine having to leave here without saying that."

"You trying to make me blush?" She smiles from behind her hands.

"I mean it. You are somethin' else, woman. You are so unique and centered, and so incredibly smart. I know, no matter where you go from here" —I point toward the textbook opened up in front of her— "no matter how you do on your American Lit final or any of the other ones for that matter, you're gonna go far, and you're gonna age beautifully, both inside and out. Whatever man is lucky enough to end up with you ... well, fuck him," I say, grinning.

She laughs, shaking her head and rolling her eyes. "You're such a schmooze today."

"I mean, I can pull back a little. You need me to insult you? Even things out."

Taking a sip of her soda, she shoots me a glare, and after swallowing, she says, "That depends. Do you value your life?" Her face remains straight, no sign of breaking.

"I do, in fact. And I've seen you in action. So, no, thank you. I'll stick with the compliments."

She smiles and says, "You'd actually be pretty proud of me."

"Oh yeah? More so than I already am?"

She nods. "I think so ... in a week, I'm heading to Europe. London first, and I'm just going to wander by train all over the place from there for a month, maybe two. Who knows? The one-way flight there is already booked."

"Wow! Congratulations, Em! That's such big news! I'm proud of you, you know? You're gonna have the time of your life."

"Thanks." She smiles sweetly. "I'm crazy excited about it. It took a little bartering with the parents, but when I informed them of just how much money I have the potential of making through vlogging, they caved."

"You're gonna crush it!"

"Thanks, Bishop. So are you! I really can't wait to see you be everything I always knew you could be. You have this good aura around you. You're inspiring, charming and intelligent. You're going to make it in no time at all. I just know it."

I laugh, brushing her comment off. "Yeah, well, I won't be holdin' my breath, but I appreciate the vote of confidence."

"I know you'll make it. And I'm always right, so...."

"Shoot, how did I forget that?"

"The typical senility that comes with someone your age?" She laughs out loud, poking a tongue out at me once she's finished.

"And you must've forgotten that age old saying, 'Mind your elders.'"

"I haven't forgotten, Old Man. I simply like breaking the rules."

Letting out a laugh, I eye my watch and sigh. My smile fades. "Well, fuck..."

"Gotta go?"

"Unfortunately. Jeremy should be done with his final by now, and we're trying to make it to St. Louis at some point tonight."

"Damn! Yeah, that's a lot of driving. Well, you have fun on your adventure, and don't be a stranger, okay?"

"You better not be either. You have to tell me all about your European trip this summer. And when you get back, maybe come out to Cali for a little bit for a visit?"

"Really?"

"Sure, why not?"

"Well, I'd love to, even though I'm not so sure you'd be able to handle more than a few days with me around. I can be quite the handful."

"I wouldn't bet on that," I reply, smiling. "And I'm a handful myself. We'll cancel each other out." I stand, pushing my chair in. "Keep in touch between now and then, you hear? I mean it. I'm gonna be gettin' a new number once I settle in LA, but I'll make sure you get it," I say, taking a few steps toward her.

She stands and says, "I will. You better keep in touch too. You don't have a very good track record." She cracks a smile as I rest a hand against her hip, pulling her in.

Wrapping my arms around her, I say, "I can appreciate the doubt. Happy to prove you wrong, Ember. I hope I get to soon."

As I'm about to let her go, she tightens her grip on me, squeezing her arms as she rests her head on my shoulder. She takes a deep breath and exhales unsteadily. I've missed the feel of her body enveloped by my thick arms, the smell of her perfume lingering around us. Something about her calms me, helps me to feel at peace, if only for a moment.

I'm hit with a tremendous jolt of pain, centered in my chest, as I leave her in my wake. I look back and see she's still standing, her hands resting in front of her, a sadness in her eyes. I force a tight smile and pass her a wave, my heart made to feel heavier as she blows me a kiss.

Turning, I take a deep breath, and I will myself to stay positive, to not let the 'what ifs' scare me into paralysis, and to embrace the unknown that lies before me.

Once outside, the sight of Jeremy and Sarge standing beside the Jeep with Carter takes away a little of the sting I feel leaving Ember behind. I pass a slight smile when Sarge spots my approach.

"Sarge, what's up, buddy?" I ask, greeting him with a hug. "I wasn't sure if you were gonna make it."

He shakes his head. "No way I'd miss seeing you guys off. I've got a summer course to finish up here until mid-July, and after that, I'm right behind you. I'll definitely be taking you up on that offer to come visit. I'll need a vacation when it's all said and done."

"Always welcome, my friend. July-ish ought to be perfect. We should have the new apartment all set up by then."

"Great. Well, I won't keep you guys. I know you've got a lot of driving to do today." He takes me in for another hug, tighter this time, and he draws in a heavy breath as he does. He lets it out slow, and then, as we separate, he says, "Man, I just, uh, got to say what an honor it's been, you know, getting to know you." His voice cracks, his eyes glistening. He shakes his head and groans. "Fuck, I hate this sappy shit. Just know, it's an honor to call you my brother."

"Honor's all mine, Sarge." I can feel the lump in my throat, beckoning the tears, but I fight them off, swallowing hard against the pain. "Thanks for everything this semester. I really don't know if I would've made it through this bullshit without you."

He shrugs. "Happy to help, man. Save me a chair and a margarita by the pool, motherfucker. July, we are doing some damage." Smiling, he waves to Carter, who has already claimed shotgun. "Hey, take care, Carter."

"You too, Sarge. Try to stay out of trouble and off NSAs radar."

"That's a hard thing to do when you make your own explosives, my friend," Sarge responds matter-of-factly and then laughs as he approaches Jeremy and hugs him.

Hopping into the front seat, I snap my fingers in front of the rearview.

"Let's go, Jeremy. Christ, as it is, it'll be two in the damn morning by the time we get to St. Louis, thanks to you."

"I had a test, you dick," he complains, approaching the back door, opening it, and hopping inside. "And I still had to pack."

I turn back, narrowing my eyes at him. "Whose fault is that?"

"I'm gonna say ... Carter's?" Jeremy says as he settles in his seat and shuts the car door. He smacks the back of his hand against Carter's arm.

"Oh, fuck you, Jeremy. I'm not your daddy," Carter responds.

"As far as you know," Jeremy says, grinning.

Sarge whistles loudly from behind the Jeep, drawing our attention. He removes the backpack from his shoulders, opens it, and digs inside. He pulls out a jar of moonshine and stuffs it between all of our bags in the rear section of my Jeep.

"So, you'll think of me your first drunk night in California," he says with a grin. Motioning toward Carter and Jeremy, he adds, "Watch it with the kiddos. It's the potent stuff."

"Will do, Sarge. Thanks, bro!" I throw up the Shaka as I put the Jeep in park and start to pull away. I watch Sarge shoulder his backpack through the rearview, he waves, and then he disappears into the Commons just as we reach the top of frat row, the DIK house to our immediate right. The front of the house is void of activity except for one shirtless brother. He throws trash off the porch onto the front lawn where more trash sits—lamps, a few old game systems and TVs, splintered bed frames, stained mattresses, and all other things one would expect to find in the dumpster of a frat house or dormitory at the end of the semester, not necessarily on the lawn. I imagine now that they don't have pledges to clean up after them, keeping any sort of cleanliness standard goes out the fucking window.

As I slow the Jeep, and pull to the side of the road, I can see Carter through my peripheral, a curious look on his face. Once the Jeep stops, and I shift it into park, Jeremy leans in between the front seats and stares at me until I face him.

When I eventually do, he asks, "Uh, what's goin' on, Bishop? You forget somethin'?"

"In fact, I did. Y'all wait here, okay? I'll be right back."

"What are you doing?" Carter asks.

I exit the Jeep, shutting the door behind me and not answering him right away. After a moment, I say, "Unfinished business. Just keep her runnin'. I'll be back in a second."

As I make way quickly toward the porch, Carter calls out, "Hey, Bishop, come back here, man. What the hell are you doing?"

I wave him off without turning around, as I stride across the porch to the front door.

"Go after him," I hear Carter say to Jeremy.

I abruptly turn on my heel, and then I lean my hands against the porch railing, peering down at them. "Don't you fuckin' dare!" I warn. "Keep your asses in the Jeep. I'll be right back." I then continue into the house.

Once inside, I march down the hall to the third door on the right, Brady's door, and I bang a balled-up fist against it. A few of the brothers who were cleaning out their rooms are now watching with intrigue. I ignore them, knocking hard once more before it finally swings open. Brady, at first, sneers at me, and then, upon recognition, a look of confusion crosses his face.

"What the f—"

"This is for that Theta Nu girl you tried to rape," I say, interrupting him first with my words, and then I immediately follow them up with a swift one-two punch combination. My right fist connects with his temple, staggering him a little at the very moment my left fist smashes into his nose. The force of the second blow knocks him back, and he trips over a half-packed suitcase, and crashes to the ground.

Blood drips from his nose, which now juts to the side a good twenty degrees, as he tries to get himself back up on his feet. He groans, swaying on two wobbly arms. He turns his head toward me, his eyes on mine, but they're distant, empty.

"I told you I'd get you, motherfucker. And if you ever even think of hurting another woman, and I find out about it, I'll kill you." I pause, taking a step forward, and then I yell, "Hey, I'm talkin' to you, dumbass. You hear me?"

Brady spits a thick blood clot to the ground, and then he uses the bed frame to pull himself up straight. He steadies himself as best he can against it, and then faces me. A new look of anger creeps onto his face, but he's still not stable enough to retaliate.

Pointing a finger at him, I continue, "I will fuckin' strap you up by your balls and slit your fuckin' throat like an animal." I take another step forward, putting my finger into his chest. "Try me. Just try me," I grunt, and then I promptly turn, walking past the gawking brothers who now stand in the doorway, and picking up the pace until I'm down the hall, out the door, and off the porch. Jeremy's door is open as if he was about to get out, but he freezes when he spots me hurriedly striding toward the driver's side.

"What the fuck did you do?" Jeremy asks, complete confusion on his face as he shuts his door.

Just as the front door of the frat house opens, and a few brothers pop their heads out looking for me, I put the Jeep into drive and tear out of the spot with an ear-piercing screech.

Going fifty in a twenty-five, I guide the Jeep down sorority row, right across Main street, toward the back roads.

Jeremy clasps a hand against my shoulder, and he says, "Yo, *Speed Racer*, start talkin'! Why the fuck are you drivin' so fast and why do your knuckles look freshly used?"

"Huh?" Carter snatches my right hand from the shifter and

inspects it for a moment, before his wide eyes trail to mine. "Brady?"

I nod, smirking.

"You idiot!" Carter scolds. "Why would you do that? You just got out of trouble."

Shrugging, I respond, "It needed to be done."

"What if he calls the piggies?" Jeremy asks.

"I don't think he will."

"But what if he does?"

"We take back roads to Ohio. We'll be good after that."

"You sure about that?" Carter asks, an eyebrow quirked.

"No, but I'm damn sure hittin' him felt real fuckin' good! Better than I even imagined." My lips turn up into an evil grin.

Jeremy laughs. "I can't say you're the smartest guy I know, but goddamn do you got some brass balls on ya." He settles back into his seat, laughing again, as Carter shakes his head in disapproval beside me.

I glance toward him and shrug, choosing to say nothing, and instead, letting the sound of the warm air as it rushes passed us, and the twang of the six string as a country song plays on the radio, take over.

As the summer sun's rays tease my exposed skin, I find myself filled with an unbelievable amount of hope.

Hope for the future. Hope for myself. Hope for my friends.

I find myself hoping for a life no longer controlled by my past and, for the first time in probably forever, it's right there within reach, just waiting to be grabbed, held tightly, and ran with like I've never run before. Toward my dreams, and life, and love, with two of the best friends a guy could ask for, and with one watching over us from above.

Carleigh (cmjacobs@pittvamc.org)
  M. Bishop (bishoparmy@mymail.com)
  7/25/11 12:29AM EST

Subject: I'm so so sorry...
  Bishop,
  What do I even say here? I'm an asshole. The biggest asshole.
I've spent days trying to figure out how I was going to word this,
what I was going to say. I've tried you through text a few times,
with no response, and I'm assuming there's a reason for that. Yet,
here I am, hoping that it's because you got a new number. And
hoping, maybe, you're wanting to hear from me too.
  I can only imagine the anger you hold for me is still alive and
well. I'd hate me too. I can't explain what happened any other
way than ... I freaked out. I was falling for you, Bishop. Every
dang day you spent in that chair, I fell a little more for you. There
aren't many like you in this world. Not many at all. And I'm
sorry that things ended the way they did. I made a mistake with
my ex (yes, he is actually an ex now. I really did it!) and I let
myself get freaked out by my feelings for you. It's not easy for me
to really even think about, and trust me, I do think about it all the
time. I always worry that I may have hurt you. I ALWAYS
wonder how you're doing out there in sunny California. So very
proud of you for making the move, and though I know it doesn't
mean much to you, it comes from a very genuine place.
  I hope to hear from you. I'm dying to hear from you, to talk to
you (maybe a phone call sometime?), to prove to you how sorry I
am. How completely, embarrassingly, emphatically sorry I am for
how I treated you.
  I hope one day you can find it in yourself to forgive me. I'll be
here waiting. I'll always be here waiting.

With all my heart,
Carleigh

EPILOGUE

Five Months in LA

"So, when's your lady gettin' here? Or when do I gotta put a shirt on, I should say." Jeremy laughs, sitting on the couch in our apartment living room, the apartment we've had for the last three and a half months, and much nicer than the shithole we called home for the first couple months.

"I have no clue, man. I told y'all that this morning. Two p.m., she gets in, but God knows what traffic will be like."

Jeremy glances as the clock on the wall, and says, "Yeah, so I got time."

I narrow my eyes at him, a finger pointed in his direction. "I'm tellin' you, fuckstick. If you still don't have a shirt on when she gets here, I'm deleting some *Entourage* from the DVR again."

Jeremy pauses the game, and turns toward me slowly, glaring. "You wouldn't dare."

"Shit, I'll fuckin' delete Glee too."

"Hey now," Carter pipes up from across the room. "Don't punish me too, man." He chuckles.

Carter continues cooking up a storm in the kitchen, and Jeremy mashes buttons on an Xbox remote, *Madden* on the TV, as his six-pack remains on full display.

"Why you so worried anyway, Bish? You scared she might see what ol' Jeremy's workin' with and come sniffin' around?"

I scoff. "Please, you wouldn't know what to do with her even if, by some miracle straight from the Lord himself, you had the chance. She's not the docile type like you're used to workin' with."

"Jealousy is really ugly on you, man," he says with complete sincerity, before he flashes me his pearly whites.

"One-fifty, shirt goes on, fucker," I warn, heading back to my room to continue prepping for her arrival.

The thing is I *am* jealous of that fucker's abs. He does nothing to earn them, no regulated diet or strenuous exercise, but they're chiseled like the Statue of David himself, and shit, who wants to look at that all day? My abs are much more defined than they've been in a long time, thanks to a new training regimen and a strict diet, but they'll never look like Jeremy's. I swear the guy must ingest tapeworms or something. No other way to explain it

Me? Well, over the past four months, I've maintained a diet that consists of chicken breast, rabbit food, and more chicken breast, and after a few miserable months of carb withdrawal and chicken breast overdose, my body really started to respond. I'd like to take all the credit for my new training regimen, and the diet that's borderline torture but effective as fuck, but who am I kidding? I have about as much self-control as Tony Montana with a rail of coke in front of him and a rolled up hundred already placed in his nostril. No, my agent of four months, Baker Richmond of Richmond, Scott, and Taylor, is the man behind my lifestyle change. My buddy Jude got me hooked up with him when we first arrived, as Baker is his agent for stand-up gigs, and after an inspired meeting, he agreed to take me on too. Baker is even working with JD now, who I suggested to him after catching his act, and feeling he could be something special with a little guidance ... okay, *a lot* of guidance. Still, the mouthy redneck's not so bad once you get used to him. He sure is good for a laugh when you're feeling down. No quarters required. Just hand him a beer and watch him go.

Considering Baker's gotten me three guest appearance gigs already—*CSI*, *Law & Order*, and a small bit on *Breaking Bad* that I will forever grovel at his feet for getting me—I'll do whatever the guy asks of me. *CSI* even just signed me on for a three-episode run. And who doesn't like to play a bad guy?

Besides the gym regimen Baker's got me on, he also put me in acting classes with renowned acting coach Lisa Powers, which, in its own right, gives the gym schedule a run for its money in terms of the commitment and exertion required. She's hard, but she's good, and she's absolutely the ying to Baker's yang when it comes to the amount of work I've found so soon.

"Jesus, guys!" Carter whines, crossing the room from the kitchen to the living room. "You're sitting right there, Jeremy, and you can't even fix this shit. You know I hate it when it's like this," he continues, as he reaches the photo of Mac on the wall beside the TV, our shrine to him, of sorts. A little bag of his ashes, which his parents graciously gifted us after the funeral, kept in a Crown Royal bag (the one in which he used to keep his joints), is nailed to the wooden frame. We talk to the photo and ashes too often for any of us to comfortably admit, and it's our thing—no, our *duty*—to give him knuckles every morning. We never miss a day, and if one of us forgets, the others are there to remind.

The photo of our brother is a favorite of ours. In it, Mac is higher than hell and wearing a tie-dyed Bob Marley t-shirt which swallows his tiny frame. His arm is wrapped around

Samantha, his Latina girlfriend, who plants a kiss on his cheek. Though we never knew much about her before Mac's death, we've grown quite close to Samantha since. Her devotion and love for Mac has never wavered. The three of us communicate with her often, and she is very close with his parents. It's nice to know that he was truly loved, all the way to the end, not just by his friends and family, but by her as well. And that he'll always be.

Carter straightens the frame, takes a step back to eye it, adjusts it once more, and eyes it a moment longer, before he finally nods his head, satisfied.

"You know, most of the time, I fuck it up myself," Jeremy says with a chuckle. "Just 'cause I know Mac would get a kick out of seein' your panties all up in a wad."

Carter shoots him a glare as he makes his way back to the kitchen. He's been cooking a ton lately, and currently has lamb shanks braising in the oven, which fills the apartment with a wonderful aroma. He's been going back and forth lately on whether to attend culinary school or just return to his normal studies. Having eaten his food for five months now, I have every bit of confidence in him finding success in that field. His paella is to *die* for. I just want to see him happy and I'm not sure if he really is. I worry about him often.

Motioning toward Jeremy, I bark, "Hey, shirt!"

Jeremy lets out a heavy sigh. "Fine! He hops up, heading to his room for a brief moment, and comes back in the middle of throwing a tank on. Six-pack properly stowed now, he plops back down on the couch. I notice his eyes flit nervously from the TV to the door as if he's expecting someone. He's been doing it since I got home from the gym an hour ago.

"Jeremy, why do you keep lookin' at the door like that?" I ask.

"I'm not," he says, his eyes on the screen now.

"Yes, you are. I just caught you for, like, the fourth time. You expecting someone?"

"Bishop," he says, looking me in the eyes. "I don't want your girl. Get it out of your freakin' skull." He laughs. "Though, don't make me try and steal her from you, because I certainly could."

"You fuckin' wish, Jeremy," I respond. "I doubt you even know how to work that poor bastard in your gym shorts." I put my hands to my mouth and feign shock. "Oh, no, it's a micropenis, isn't it? You poor thing..."

Jeremy shrugs. "Wouldn't you like to know."

"Not particularly," I joke, chuckling for a moment, until a knock at the door startles me. I pull my phone out and look at the time.

Only two. No update from the woman.

I turn, about to answer the door, when Jeremy races past me, nearly running into the door as his socks slide on the tiled floor in the entryway. He steadies himself, his back against the door and both hands up defensively.

"So, I don't want y'all havin' a stroke here, alright?"

"Huh?"

Another knock echoes throughout the apartment, and Carter leaves the kitchen—spatula in hand—looking as intrigued as I am. "A stroke about what?" he asks.

Jeremy opens the door, and I'm floored when I see who stands on the other side.

But not nearly as floored as I am when I see Jeremy wrapping his arms around none other than Sarge, and then they kiss passionately.

Carter and I stare, our jaws meeting the fucking floor. Our eyes seem to bulge out like some cartoon creation, as the two of them continue kissing, their hands roaming each other's bodies, not inappropriately, or even sexually, but with a fervor reserved for two lovers when long distance is no more. The need to touch every inch of them just to ensure that they're real, and that the wait is truly over.

They eventually separate, staring each other in the eyes for a moment, and they exchange broad happy smiles.

Jeremy whispers to Sarge, "It's so damn good to see your face. I've missed it," and then he runs the back of his hand along Sarge's cheek, over his deep-set dimples.

"Uhhh, can you maybe fill us in here, Jeremy? Because my brain is about to have a complete fucking meltdown right now," Carter says, his eyes wide and face slack.

I nod in agreement, the shock snuffing out any words.

They both laugh, looking at each other first, before Jeremy takes Sarge's hand into his and says, "So, I've been talkin' to Blake for a while now. About as long as the three of us have been friends. And we recently, um" —he looks over at Sarge and smiles wide, but there's a slight nervousness showing too— "decided to give the whole relationship thing a chance."

"Jeremy was there for me a lot when I was going through my shit with Jonah. And honestly, I kind of fell for him then. Didn't let him get away from me after that." Sarge grins, the way he looks at Jeremy so obviously sincere.

"Okay, sweet, but I think we're maybe missin' some of the story here, guys. Jeremy, you're gay?" I question, my mind running back over all of our experiences together. There are a few things that I could maybe question in hindsight, but nothing that I'd consider to be a red flag.

"Yes, I am," Jeremy replies coolly.

Looking over at Carter, I ask, "Did you have any idea?"

He shakes his head slowly, his bottom jaw still hanging.

I flit my eyes back to Jeremy and ask, "Since when?"

"Since forever." He chuckles. "It's not cancer, man. And it ain't the easiest thing to talk about. I grew up in the country. You learn to stuff those attractions and feelings down real deep, where nobody can find 'em. Not even yourself sometimes. I've just now started to kind of accept who I am." He smiles, squeezing Sarge's hand. "Thanks to Blake."

"Holy fuck," Carter mutters, making an explosion gesture with his hand beside his head, adding the sound effect with his mouth. "Brain dead. Done. Over. Kaput."

"And why are we just now findin' out? And why like this?" I ask, and I immediately pick up on my unintended defensiveness, as if he owed me the truth about his sexuality. I add, "Don't get me wrong, I'm glad you feel comfortable enough with us to just be yourself, that's all I could ever want, but, holy shit, there has to be a better way."

Jeremy laughs, shrugging. "Well, when Blake and I were discussin' him comin' here, that's when you and the lady started really talkin' again. Since y'all were gettin' hot and heavy on Skype, and talkin' relationship and plannin' a trip and all that happy shit, I figured Blake and me could piggyback off of that."

"Why?"

"Well, it's kind of a two-part answer," Jeremy responds, right when my phone's text alert goes off.

My Baby: Just landed!! I'm so excited to see you!

O*H, my God, it's here! It's finally here! Hurry up, woman! I need youuuuuu,* I text back, and pocket my phone, a wide smile on my face.

"She make it in?" Carter asks.

"Yeah, just landed. Hopefully, it won't be too much longer now." My focus returns to Sarge and Jeremy as they remain motionless in the entryway. "Wait, so, Jeremy, what does my girlfriend visiting have to do with you comin' out to us? I don't see the correlation."

"Well, see," he says, sighing. "It's kind of like this. We figured you'd be so busy spendin' time with your girl and havin' wild monkey sex, that we would have plenty of time for our own fun. For fuck's sake, we ain't even gotten to go all the way yet, unlike y'all—and then we also figured with y'all bein' so busy, we wouldn't be bombarded with questions, which, neither one of us really wants to answer at this time."

I point toward Carter and say, "Yeah, but Carter's still here every day, and without a romantic prospect in sight, and I'm sure he's loaded up with enough questions to last you the whole trip." I chuckle, but Carter doesn't seem to hear me. He remains frozen, staring blankly at the two of them with the spatula white-knuckled in his hand.

"Shit, you see that look on his face? I'm pretty sure we broke him." Sarge laughs.

"Anyway, like I said ..." Jeremy pulls Sarge closer to him, looking him in the eyes. "We got a few months of action to make up for and we don't have a whole lot of time. So ..." His eyes trail to his room and then back to me. "We're gonna go ahead and go do that."

Jeremy grabs Sarge's hand and pulls him toward his bedroom. Sarge shrugs, waving goodbye with his free hand, a devilish smile taking up his face. It may be the quietest I've ever seen Sarge.

"Wh-wha-what th-th-the ..." Carter stammers.

"I know, buddy. I know," I say to Carter, my eyes flitting back to the two of them as they reach the bedroom. "This isn't over, fuckers!" I call out. "You owe me a dinner while you're here at least, Sarge. You're treat."

Jeremy's bedroom door slams shut. I'm left without response.

I look over at Carter, who remains slack-jawed and in shock.

"Carter!" I yell, and his head turns slowly toward me, a dumbfounded look on his face. "The lamb shank, bro ... I think it's fuckin' burnin'!"

THE WAIT for her to arrive is excruciating. I've checked an LA traffic website about a million times, and I've been pacing the living room for at least a half hour now. Meanwhile, Carter sits on the couch, resting his feet as the lamb shank sits in the oven, ready and waiting, and thankfully not burned. I haven't decided yet if I'll take credit for his work or not (just kidding ... probably).

Carter just mumbles, shaking his head periodically, as he still tries to make sense of the faint sounds of coitus currently seeping through the cracks in the door to Jeremy's room.

Suddenly, there's a knock at the front door. My heart leaps into my throat. I rush to my feet. The excitement is so overwhelming my hands tremble.

Swinging the door open, I see her on the other side, a Louis Vuitton suitcase at her high-heeled feet, and that gorgeous smile on her face as energizing as the last day I spent admiring it.

"Baby!" she yelps, dropping her purse to the ground and jumping into my arms. She wraps her arms around me, and then her legs, and I carry her a few steps into the apartment, eventually ending up with her back against the wall beside the door with a thud. I kiss her passionately, savoring the taste of her cherry lips. Video chat and phone calls are one thing, but there is nothing like seeing her in the flesh, and remembering, to the fullest extent, why I made this woman mine. Why she is my best friend. My partner in crime. My queen.

As our lips part, a wide smile spreads across my face. "Do you have any clue how much I've thought about this day?" I ask.

"You and me both, Bishop. You and me both."

I turn back to Carter, who has his eyes on us, and he finally looks to be gaining composure. "Hey Carter, look who it is!"

He waves, a tight smile on his face. "Hey Ember," he mutters. "It's, uh, it's good to see you again."

"You too, Carter," she responds, tilting her head. She turns toward me and asks, "Is he alright? Looks like he's seen a ghost." She looks around the apartment with curious eyes. "And what's that noise? It sounds like—"

"Um, yeah, that's kind of a long story," I respond, chuckling, and shaking my head at the nice little plot twist that was laid upon Carter and me this afternoon. "I'll tell you all about it in a little bit. First, should we ..." I motion my head toward the bedroom, waggling my brows.

Ember nods, her lips turning up into a wicked grin. "Yeah. We have some business to attend to, don't we?"

"Yes, my dear. Some very *very* dirty business," I respond, setting her down, and grabbing her bags.

Carter scoffs, shaking his head, and then dropping it in his hands. "I'm like the fifth wheel now. How did this happen?"

Shutting the door, I grab Em's hand and lead her toward my room across the hall from Jeremy's. We pass Carter, seated on the couch, and I say, "Love ya, buddy," in a sing song tone before we scurry into the room.

Just before I close the door, Carter yells, "Don't forget about the food I slaved over, asshole!"

His exasperated sigh is met by the thud of the slamming door.

AFTERWORD

I'm banking on the fact that y'all aren't those people who read the afterward first. Just a warning if you are, there will be a few spoilers below.

I've decided to write an afterward for the first time because this book has consumed me over the past four months. I have fallen in love with the storyline, and every one of my characters (including *loving* to hate Brady!). Of all my novels, I am most proud of this one. Why? Because we are in a new era now. We exist in a world where people care less about each other, where selfishness is rampant, moral lines are crossed, and broken cycles are created.

Our college fraternal climate is *fucked!* Our college climate in general is fucked. I can't even count the number of times I've read news stories about sexual assault on college campuses and teens losing their lives to excessive hazing. It's wrong, and it's going to require each and every one of us to change that climate. If we continue to turn a blind eye, nothing will ever change. College should be a fun, exciting time, not traumatizing. I know some of *Bishop* was hard to read, but I felt it necessary to remind everyone that the words frat, hazing death, and sexual assault are generally synonymous with each other at this point. Either people change their ways, fraternities actually follow the Principles they so love to harp on about and punish those who take part in such disgusting behavior, or there will come a time when the whole fucking system will need to be torn down. It's up to the rest of us to make sure that happens if the time comes.

This story is also about friendship. In writing this novel, I reflected on all the friendships that I've made over the years, from basic training to now. So many incredible people have helped guide me to this place of peace I now find myself in. I hope (as I do with most of my novels) that true friendship and the meaning of loyalty are your biggest takeaways from *Bishop*. Yes, I hope it makes you laugh, maybe cry, and I definitely hope it gets you hot, but more than anything else, I want you to finish *Bishop*, call up your best friend, and tell them how much they mean to you. Relationships end. Divorces happen. Lovers cheat. Friends, *true friends,* stick around for a lifetime, and no matter distance, nor time, that bond is worth strengthening, those friendships worth nurturing. I know they've saved my life a time or two.

Thank you so much for reading this book, for loving these characters, and for allowing me to write these stories for you! You, my dear readers, are my heart and soul. Thank you for being in my life and welcoming me into yours!

ACKNOWLEDGMENTS

What can I say? *Bishop* is only in your hands today because of so many incredible people.

First off, to my **Military Brothers and Sisters**, this book is for you. We are a special breed. We have accomplished great things, seen terrible things, experienced the highest of highs and lowest of lows, and we've done so for complete strangers, and for a government that wasn't always there when we got back. I want you all to know that I'm here, that I understand your plight, and I won't stop writing about, speaking about, and fighting for, our nation's veterans, and the struggles that come with transition back to civilian life. Keep fighting, battles!

Harvey... You were there when I was at my lowest point. No friends. No future. No hope. You took me under your wing and showed me there was life after injury. You never let me make excuses for myself, but you *always* treated me with compassion, understanding, and respect. I genuinely love you, buddy, not only because of what you've done for me, but for all the other lives you've changed as well. Much love, buddy!

Tim... We don't talk anymore, and I hate that, but that doesn't mean I'll forget all that our friendship gave me when we were going through the shit at Walter Reed. You were a brother to me, someone I looked up to, and respected, and *needed* during one of my darkest times. I love seeing you and your awesome little family getting along, and I know in my heart of hearts that the day will come where we chill again, and it'll be like a day hasn't passed. I look forward to that!

Cara... It's been one hell of a ride. I can now see all of our hard work starting to pay off. It really feels like we're hitting our stride. I say 'our' because this is absolutely a team effort. They may be my words, but your support, organizational, and administrative excellence, and story input has played a vital role in bringing us here. Thank you for being a friend! Love ya, lady!

Britto, Brad, Zane, and Pops... I don't have much family, but I got y'all, and that's more than enough. I love you guys so much. Britto and Brad, I can't even tell you what a blessing that child is. I can't tell you how full my heart has become since he's entered my life. Thank you for creating the most beautiful baby boy in the world. I can't wait to be the fun uncle who gets him into 80's movies and rock music! Zane, you beautiful, happy, handsome little child... don't you dare read this book before you're eighteen! Hahaha

To my wonderful **Readers**, thank you for giving me the chance to tell my stories. I love you all endlessly!

Finally, **the Lord**... I have questioned you often, unfortunately, cursed you a time or two, and wondered when your plan was going to start making sense, but you've never left me, and I know you never will. Through all the darkness in this world, you have shown me, time and time again, that every step is a necessary one; every roadblock, of vital importance, every heartbreak, a strengthening of the soul. I am at your mercy, Lord. And I am so incredibly thankful for the blessings you've given me.

ABOUT THE AUTHOR

BT Urruela is a US Army combat wounded amputee and Purple Heart recipient, turned contemporary author who has written both independent and traditionally published novels. He is the Co-founder and Brand Ambassador for VETSports, a 501(c)3 non-profit organization, a romance cover model, philanthropist, and motivational speaker. He currently resides in Tampa, Florida with his dogs, Kiko and Scout.